Antonia Barclay

and Her

Scottish

Claymore

Antonia Barclay

and Her

Scottish

Claymore

A
REBELLIOUS
ROMANTIC
COMEDY

JANE CARTER BARRETT

RIVER GROVE
BOOKS

Published by River Grove Books
Austin, TX
www.rivergrovebooks.com

Distributed by River Grove Books

Design and composition by Greenleaf Book Group
Cover design by Greenleaf Book Group
Cover image: ©Shutterstock/lineartestpilot; ©Shutterstock/MaryMo

Cataloging-in-Publication data is available.

Print ISBN: 978-1-63299-038-9

eBook ISBN: 978-1-63299-036-5

First Edition

To Scotland,
her gripping history, and her tenacious countrywomen.

And infinite thanks to my intrepid aunt, Alice Carter Steinbach,
whose indomitable spirit lives on in every turning page of this novel.

CONTENTS

OUR PACT

Dear Readers,

Let's have some irreverent fun and romp around the Scottish countryside with handsome bad guys, even handsomer good guys, and beautiful
badass heroines who set goals and meet their objectives with bold action
and unwavering determination.

And while we're romping, let's also make a pact: anachronisms,
prochronisms, and all forms of social, political, and fashion correctness
shall be cheerfully overlooked in favor of frolic and adventure.

Time to play!

With prodigious affection and gratitude,
Jane

Chapter 1

THE FRATERNAL PLAGUE

Scotland 1586

I t is a fact understood only by those females similarly afflicted, that the bad influence exerted by multiple brothers upon an only sister proves as timeless as the wind and as pernicious as the plague. And while those brothers harbor fairly fond feelings for their sister, they unanimously agree that she'll never truly be one of them, given the unfortunate nature of her forty-sixth chromosome.

Nineteen-year-old Antonía Barclay was a female so afflicted, and on a sun-kissed summer morning, she rode her horse across the softly rolling hills of Southern Scotland. With her dark hair streaming behind her, she galloped at a speed that would have given her father severe chest pains and her mother good cause to visit the wine cellar a wee bit earlier in the day than usual, had they known. She had slipped out of Barclay Castle at sunrise, unobserved, knowing full well that if her brothers found out, they would go straight to their parents with the incriminating information. The more Antonía thought about her brothers, and the fact that her morning ride could not be enjoyed without fear of repercussion, the more frustrated she became, and the faster she rode.

In fact, her frustration grew to such enormous proportions she felt like she would spontaneously combust if she didn't release her feelings. Pulling her russet gelding to a stop, she began cursing descriptively and at length. Nearby birds darted away and her horse snorted, shifting his feet. While Antonía acknowledged that cursing fluently was not an attribute of which to be proud, it provided a cathartic release, making it possible to survive three overbearing brothers.

She threw her left leg over the saddle and slid to the ground. Clad in what her mother would surely consider scandalous—a pair of her twin brother Oliver's trousers, as well as one of his shirts and jackets—she paced back and forth until she gradually calmed down enough to think in a balanced manner.

While Antonía had to admit that her brothers proved somewhat instructive in certain areas of her life, such as teaching her to swim, shoot, and ride, they'd also proven somewhat destructive in certain other areas. Cussing like a pirate, suppressing all emotion, and thinking like a man could hardly be considered constructive activities. On the other hand, by the time she'd reached her teens, she could outshoot one of them, outswim two of them, and outride all of them. She was starting to feel better about things until she remembered her present age group. She was almost out of her teens and faced with the age of treachery, also known as the age of marriageability.

Antonía knew she was in for it. Her brothers' changes in attitudes had become more marked over the course of the past few months. They were yanking the reins in on her hard; gone was the glorious unbridled freedom of youth. Even her youngest brother, who was her twin and held only a negligible age advantage of two minutes, now wielded his seniority over her as if it were his God-given right to control every aspect of Antonía's life. Her elder brothers were no different.

Although she had let them know, in no uncertain terms, that she would have none of it, they did as they pleased. However, quite unfairly, she was no longer allowed to do as *she* pleased. Her mother and father also insisted she become more "ladylike," with an eye toward snagging a duke or an earl in marriage.

Antonía dropped to the ground with a groan. Her horse walked over and nuzzled her neck. "If only my legs had not grown," she confided. For when she had scarcely turned fourteen, she had begun to grow. And grow. And grow.

No one had been able to understand *why* she was growing so tall. To her humiliation, she was the talk of the Scottish aristocracy and even the servants of Barclay Castle. The memory of the gossipers whispering behind her back still had the power to rile her.

"Good Lord, it doesn't make any sense at all!"

"Why, her perfectly petite mother barely reaches her daughter's shoulders!"

"Are not daughters supposed to be similar in size to their mothers?"

"No Barclay female has ever reached that lass's towering height!"

"Indeed, what do they feed that lass?"

Despite all protestations, by her nineteenth birthday Antonía Barclay was nearly six feet tall, raven-haired, blue-eyed, and high of cheekbone. But of all her extraordinary physical blessings, her brothers claimed it was her full, luxurious mouth that posed the biggest concern, as well as the most serious health risk for her would-be suitors, who happened to be their friends.

The boisterous, callow bunch would arrive at Barclay Castle under the guise of seeing the three brothers and then try to outdo one another in wooing Antonía. She attempted to be polite, but soon tired of the awkward bowing and fawning and overly descriptive compliments. After fifteen minutes or so, she would excuse herself and escape to her bedchamber, leaving the men below to debate the issue of what gave Miss Barclay's mouth its ineffable quality.

Antonía knew full well the content of her potential suitors' remarks. After every such episode, her brothers felt duty-bound to divulge the information in excruciating detail. However, only last week, her brothers had suddenly and without explanation announced a moratorium on their friends' visits to Barclay Castle. Apparently after much discussion, they had agreed that their cohorts were not worthy of even thinking about their sister. Hence, it was decreed that from that point forward, the Barclay brothers would meet their friends on neutral territory only—pubs, taverns, inns, and the like—but under no circumstances would they be invited or welcome at Barclay Castle.

Lord and Lady Barclay thought this an excellent idea, as did Antonía, but her brothers' interference still annoyed her to no end, so she kept her own counsel.

If her brothers or parents had been privy to her thoughts, they would have realized that not one of their friends had the slightest chance of capturing her attention, much less her passion. As far as she was concerned, her brothers' friends were inane, insipid, and uninspiring. She wanted none of it and none of them. She wanted a real man.

Accordingly, she regarded all prospective suitors to date as null and void. What she sought was something entirely different, something yet to be offered, yet to be advertised, though she was hardly desperate over the situation. Without conceit, she knew she was beautiful, highly intelligent, and, as such, confident that her expectations would someday be met. She would wait patiently for what she wanted, for what she needed, for what she would someday have.

In the meantime, she resolved to treat her bothersome brothers with a certain degree of calm detachment and an equal degree of benign neglect. Consequently, she ignored them as much as possible.

Antonía's horse whinnied, bringing her back to the rising sun and the fact that she was indeed going to be late for breakfast, and thus would be caught by both her brothers and her parents. She rose from the ground, brushed off her borrowed clothes, and mounted her horse in a long-practiced and graceful manner. Another talent her bumbling brothers could never hope to emulate. Putting heels to her horse's sides, she galloped back home to battle.

By the time she reached Barclay Castle, the sun had risen halfway above the distant hills. The Barclays did not breakfast early, and Antonía knew there was a chance she could slip in through the kitchen and up to her room undetected. She passed through the busy hub of cookery, and after giving the servants a conspiratorial smile, entered the hallway of the main house and stopped to consider her plan.

There was one vulnerable area through which she had to pass, and that was the hallway leading from the kitchen, past the dining room doors, to the stairway. The double doors were almost closed, with one left slightly ajar. She heard the sound of male voices as she crept past the doors, but the unmistakable boom of her father's voice stopped her in her tracks.

"Well? What do the three of you have to say for yourselves?"

Innately nosy, she had to know what was happening. Knowledge was power. She peered through the small opening. Her father stood at the end of the long dining table, his face red, glaring down at her three brothers. On one side was Matthew, the tallest of the three, and without doubt the handsomest, though all were considered by Antonía's friends to be quite attractive.

Beside him sat Will, the eldest brother and the shortest of the three. Though the two older brothers both had medium brown hair and hazel eyes, Will had the look of a scholar with his slightly thinner face, slightly larger nose, and slighter build, while Matthew had the classic looks of a Greek god and the shoulders to prove it.

Across the table from Will sat Oliver. Antonía narrowed her eyes at her twin. Where Antonía's hair was dark, her twin's was blond; where her nose was small, his was Roman; and where his lips were thin, hers were lush and full—according to her brothers' friends. Fraternal twins, Will called them, and Antonía was perfectly happy not resembling the brother who most thought it his job to run her life.

All three looked paralyzed with fear, and as Lord Barclay continued to glare at them, Antonía decided to make her escape upstairs. She took a step back, but her father's next words brought her to a halt.

"Dammit to hell, lads!" her father roared at his three sons. "One of you must know where your sister is!"

While Antonía thought her father an extremely generous and considerate man, "quiet" and "mellow" were two adjectives that could never be affixed to him. No one ever had to wonder what was on his mind, because the master of Barclay Castle enjoyed sharing his many thoughts with anyone willing to listen, and most especially with those he perceived as *less* than willing.

Antonía put one hand over her mouth to stifle a laugh as she watched her three less-than-willing brothers being forced to hear what was on Lord Barclay's mind on an otherwise fine summer day.

"It's not yet nine in the morning," he was saying, "and you've already lost your sister—who just so happens to be my *only* daughter. Your mother needs to speak with her, and there'll be hell to pay if we don't locate Antonía immediately!"

He slammed one hand down on the table and the three brothers jumped. Looks of anxiety passed between the unlucky listeners, because no one tangled with Lady Barclay and lived to tell the tale. Antonía almost felt sorry for the four of them. Despite her mother's compact size, the mistress of the castle was indeed a force to be reckoned with.

Lord Barclay fixed his gaze upon each of the brothers, stopping at last at Oliver. "You look ill," he said with little sympathy.

From her vantage point, Antonía shook her head. More likely her brother was still half-inebriated from the previous evening.

"I have a headache the size of Loch Lomond," Oliver grumbled.

"Perhaps if you were not drinking until dawn your head would not pound and you would know where your sister is." Lord Barclay resumed his pacing. "Good God, man, you're her twin! Can't you *sense* where she is? I thought twins did that!"

Oliver shrugged. "Does anyone ever know where Antonía is?"

"Don't be an imbecile," his eldest brother, Will, replied. "Of course we know where Antonía is *sometimes*."

"Like when she's sitting across from us at the dinner table," added Matthew, nodding.

"I *meant* unless she *wants* us to know where she is," Oliver said. "She barely—"

"One of you must know something!" Lord Barclay thundered, interrupting the exchange. "If you lads don't come up with something plausible, or at least plausibly deniable, within the next five seconds"—he scowled directly at Oliver—"each one of you shall be stripped of all privileges for a month. Now *where* is my darling daughter?"

Things were getting serious now, and Antonía moved closer to the opening, not wanting to miss anything. "Stripped of all privileges" constituted no pubs, no cards, and most serious of all, no lasses.

Matthew cleared his throat. "Sir, Antonía must be out riding. She often rises early and rides the hills before breakfast."

His father gave him a sharp, piercing look. "Matthew, is that where she is or is that a guess proffered in desperation?"

Matthew sighed. "It's more in the category of a very desperate prayer, sir."

"Enough!" Lord Barclay shouted, and Antonía decided that indeed, she had had quite enough as well. Drawing open the doors, she entered the room.

As every eye turned to her, Antonía stood in the doorway, looking from brother to brother before casting a shining smile in her father's direction. She moved to the heavily laden sideboard, helping herself to oatcakes, kippers, eggs, and butter. Sitting beside her father, she proceeded to eat her meal with complete indifference as her brothers gradually simmered down from full boil to a rolling boil.

Smiling in an indulgent manner, Lord Barclay spoke to Antonía in a gentle and loving tone. "And where have you been this morning, my darling daughter?"

All three brothers choked on their porridge in unison as Antonía implemented her strategy.

"I rode over to Deerfield, around the pond, and then back home again. I hope you didn't worry." She gave her father a feigned look of utmost concern.

"On the contrary, my dear," he said. "I'm ecstatic to learn that one of my children hasn't lolled about all morning recovering from excessive revelry." Lord Barclay leveled a cold glare of disapproval on his disheveled and dissipated sons.

Now realizing her brothers were in deep water with their father, Antonía became highly motivated to ensure that they drowned in it.

"Yes, indeed, Father, the sunrise was gorgeous this morning, all pastel skies and white clouds. I believe the Greeks refer to it as a primrose dawn." Glancing round at her three ailing brothers, Antonía happily observed that she was infuriating the lot of them. "You must all come with me one morning," she declared. "That is, *if* you are capable of rising that early."

"F-Father!" Oliver spluttered. "Do you really think it's a good idea for Antonía to be riding through the countryside in that . . . that . . . that god-awful outfit? She looks like a common stable boy!"

Antonía kept her eyes lowered, trying to appear demure and to keep herself from laughing. She was, after all, wearing Oliver's clothes. Unfortunately her choice of riding clothes had been under scrutiny for some time. But fortunately, Lord Barclay had always believed his darling daughter could do no wrong, and Antonía had so far prevailed, keeping Lord Barclay tied around each and every one of her delicate fingers. To attempt to untie even one knot would result in great humiliation to the person stupid enough to attempt the untying. Thus, when Lord Barclay responded to Oliver, Antonía hid a satisfied smile behind her napkin.

"Would you rather your sister break her neck by riding sidesaddle in one of those voluminous dresses in style nowadays? Those contraptions are deathtraps to a rider of Antonía's caliber. Indeed, my darling daughter shows common sense by wearing pants and riding like a man."

"I daresay other girls seem to manage it," Oliver said in a sullen voice. "Take Claire, for instance."

"Claire MacMillan?" Lord Barclay scoffed. "Antonía's best friend? She hates to ride horses and you know it. She can hardly bear to paint a horse in one of her portraits, and we all know what a damn fine artist she is, too. But getting back to the point, it's carriages all the way for our dainty Claire." He paused for a second, glanced at Matthew, and then chuckled. "Why she'd sooner marry one of you fools than ride a horse."

Lord Barclay winked at Antonía and she smiled back, but inwardly sighed. If only her brothers *would* marry! Then perhaps they would be too busy with their own lives to interfere in hers any longer!

"So, gentlemen," Lord Barclay said, his piercing gaze sweeping over the three, "will there be any further objections raised regarding my darling daughter's riding habits?"

"As a matter of fact, I do have another objection," Oliver said.

That's right, Antonía thought, as she buttered a scone from the basket on the table. *Dig your grave a little deeper, Oliver.*

"Do you mind telling your darling daughter to take a bath after riding and before coming to breakfast? She smells like the inside of a barn." He waved one hand in front of his face, squinching up his nose in disgust.

"Indeed, we could discuss the retentive powers of the olfactory," Will said, eager, no doubt, to gain his father's attention.

Antonía rolled her eyes. "I'd rather smell like the inside of a barn than the inside of a distillery." She put all the disdain she felt for her brothers in her tone. "You three reek to high heaven this morning. Alcohol is emanating from every pore of your collective bodies. Why don't you gentlemen give your livers, as well as my lungs, a break every third day or so?"

"Antonía, darling, must you be so anatomically graphic at this hour of the day?" a feminine voice chastised.

Antonía turned to see her mother gliding into the dining room. Lady Cassandra Barclay was petite with catlike, slightly upturned green eyes and golden blonde hair. She ran her household with gentle efficiency, and her family with an iron hand.

"I beg your pardon, Mother, but your sons are repugnant."

"Here, here, don't blame me!" wailed Will. "I've hardly been able to get a word in edgewise."

"Thank heavens for small miracles," replied Oliver, sparking a spate of derogatory words amongst the brothers, while Antonía assumed an air of calm detachment. If she tried very hard to appear poised and ladylike, perhaps her mother wouldn't notice her riding clothes.

Taking her place at the breakfast table, Lady Barclay appeared duly impressed by the verbal pandemonium. "My dear Lord Barclay," she said, one corner of her mouth moving upward in amusement, "I see you have this hullabaloo well under control."

Antonía raised her brows as she saw her mother surreptitiously squeeze Lord Barclay's upper thigh under the table. She rolled her eyes again. Her father made no pretense of his unrelenting desire for his wife, which Antonía found altogether nauseating.

He leaned toward his wife, his voice low, but not so low that Antonía couldn't hear him. "Well, I did have matters well under control . . . that is, until you placed that very delicate hand of yours in that very delicate area of mine. Consequently, it will now prove necessary for you to perform damage control directly after breakfast, m'lady."

"Perhaps we should discuss it now?" she asked, rising again from her chair.

Antonía stifled a groan as the two sidled out of the dining hall and left her at the mercy of her brothers.

"What were you thinking, Ant-face?" Oliver demanded, using his own special nickname for her.

"I was thinking I wanted to take a ride," she said, folding her napkin carefully and placing it back on the table.

"You do take a risk when you ride alone," Matthew said, her middle brother milder in tone than her twin. "It's not a good idea."

"Indeed," Will interjected, "most accidents happen either in the home or on horseback. 'Tis a well-known fact."

"Just as it is a well-known fact that no decent man would ever make an offer of marriage to a woman who does a reckless thing like riding alone in the middle of the night dressed as a man!" Oliver glared across the table at her, and Antonía could no longer suppress her anger.

"It was not in the middle of the night," she said, returning his glare, "and I wonder who taught me to dress—and ride, I might add—like a man?" She pretended to ponder the question, tapping her chin. "Oh, yes, I remember now"—she slammed both hands down on the table—"it was my brothers!"

"That was when we were children," Oliver retorted.

"You're grown now, Antonía," Will said. "You cannot behave as you did as a child."

"And why not?" she demanded. "I don't see the three of you curtailing your own activities!"

The three exchanged confused glances, and then Will spoke up. "But we are men, Antonía."

She leaned back in her chair and folded her arms over her chest. "And your point is?"

Matthew, the most even-tempered of the three, sighed. "You know our point. It was one thing for you to run wild with us as children, but now you must think of your future. No gentleman will marry you if you continue to act so rebelliously." He ran one hand through his thick hair. "Really, Antonía, you are torturing us with your behavior, for it is we who are sworn to protect your name, and you make it exceedingly difficult!"

"I torture *you*?" Antonía stood, hands on her slim hips, furious at the three stooges blinking up at her. She pointed at Will first. "Wasn't it you, dear brother, who held me captive in the library three days a week for hours at a time, making me read the torturous Middle English works of Chaucer, Dante, Boccaccio, and Petrarch?"

He looked at her in confusion. "Father said I could."

Antonía had to clench her fists to keep from throwing a scone at him. Yes, the most disturbing notion of all was that her beloved father, Lord Barclay, had actually sanctioned his daughter's literary torture. The feminine mind should never be neglected! No daughter of his would have mush for brains! And his darling daughter agreed, but Will had deliberately chosen the most boring subjects, delighting in keeping her cooped up in the dark library and teaching her the most boring writings in all of history.

"And you—" She turned to Matthew, who seemed to shrink down in his chair a bit. "You know what you did!"

Matthew, though a lad of few words and modest reserve, had nevertheless felt it his duty to contribute to his sister's "education" when she was a child. Thus, when she was twelve, he had taken her to an unfamiliar glen well beyond the Barclay Castle borders, and abandoned her there as the sun descended behind the softly rolling hills of Southern Scotland.

"In retrospect, I feel slightly guilty about that incident," Matthew conceded. "But in my defense, I was trying to teach you self-reliance. Father did it to the three of us. I thought it important."

"I came home covered from head to toe in mud and thistles," she said, her voice low, her eyes narrowed.

"And I combed them out of your hair, remember?" Matthew said, looking perplexed.

She turned to the last one, the worst of all—her twin. "And you—do you remember when you carved a dart blower, complete with tiny but deceptively sharp darts, and proceeded to chase me around the castle, blowing darts into my leg? I still recall extracting one from my ankle with a pair of forceps."

"I was teaching you how to think on your feet," Oliver said, and then stood, glowering at his sister. "I did the same to Matthew and Will. And you made me beg and plead with you not to tell our parents, remember?"

Antonía waved one hand in dismissal. "I never intended to tell our parents about any of your torturous games, because, frankly, I can take care of myself. But now I see that I'm nothing more to the three of you than an inferior female whose honor you must protect in order to sell me to the highest bidder."

Will and Matthew rose then too and the three began talking all at once, but Antonía was done with them. She turned to leave, just as her mother and father came back into the dining hall, Lady Barclay tucking stray bits of hair back into her elaborate coiffure.

Lady Barclay arched a pretty eyebrow at her husband and then turned toward her children, her smile disappearing. "Before you leave, I'd like to speak to you about your slovenly habits. Of course, this offense does not apply to you, Antonía darling." She reached over and patted her daughter's hand. "Your bedchamber is always in meticulous order. Your brothers' rooms, on the other hand, are a midden!"

Antonía could not resist throwing her brothers a smile of triumph.

"As you are well aware, the servants will be cleaning the bedchambers later today and since I'd be far too ashamed to subject them to your pigsties, I took the liberty of tidying your rooms earlier this morning."

"With all due respect, Mum," chimed in Will, "when it's all said and done, who cares what our bedchambers look like?"

His mother's green eyes radiated with something other than maternal warmth.

"Because," she said, "I've noticed that when it's *all said and done*, everything is *said* and nothing is *done!*"

The three brothers exchanged worried glances, and Antonía almost laughed out loud. No doubt they were all trying to remember if they'd left behind any incriminating evidence—dirty socks under the bed, glasses by the bed, lasses in the bed. Oliver spoke up, his irritation evident.

"Really, Mother," he said, "what is the point of hiring servants if you're going to do all the work for them? Aren't servants supposed to serve you and not the other way around? Why pay people to clean the castle if you're going to run about and clean it first? It's simply not logical!"

"It's logical if you're female," interjected Lord Barclay.

Antonía's eyes widened and she lifted her water goblet to her lips. "Uh oh," she murmured into the glass.

Lady Barclay turned and settled a set of scalding green eyes on her husband. "Lord Barclay," she enunciated slowly, "I fail to appreciate the patronizing ring of your last remark. You'd be well advised to tread very carefully from here on out."

She turned to her sons. "And as for the three of you—from this day forward, you shall maintain your bedchambers in a neat and orderly fashion. And if you fail to heed my warning, you will answer to your father—and me."

"That's right, lads!" Lord Barclay thundered. "You'll answer to *me* if there's so much as a single sock on the floor of your bedchambers. Now, your mother and I have matters to attend to in the wine cellar, so we'll be on our way." He stood and offered his wife his hand.

Antonía held her breath. So far she had escaped her mother's steely gaze. Although Lady Barclay had given up her battle against her daughter's penchant for wearing her brother's clothing while riding, she could still give Antonía *the look*.

"Not so fast, Henry," Lady Barclay said, and Antonía closed her eyes. When her mother used her husband's Christian name, it boded well for no one. And the lady's next words sealed Antonía's fate. "I haven't had a chance to speak to our daughter about *you know what*."

"Damn," he said, "I forgot."

Damn indeed, Antonía thought. Her mother's "you know what" phraseology never augured fine things for her future, and she knew she was doomed to yet another mother-daughter tête-à-tête. And while her father was under his daughter's bewitching spell, her mother was, unfortunately, wholly immune to it.

"Sit down, Antonía."

Antonía did as she was told, watching her brothers and father waste no time in fleeing the room. Though her mother looked harmless enough, sipping her tea with her little finger crooked, Antonía was not fooled. She knew her mother was about to lower the boom.

Using her usual term of endearment for her daughter and speaking it as if it were her middle name, she began, "Antonía darling, I have purposely neglected to tell you this for some time, because I know how much you dread social occasions."

Antonía almost groaned aloud. Although her mother was aware of her daughter's distaste for all such events, Antonía was also aware that Lady Barclay simply could not understand it. Cassandra Barclay was an innately social creature with an enormous capacity for attending parties, balls, dinners, salons, musical nights, and any and all events involving all the "right" people.

"As you are aware," she went on, "your father and I have allowed you to avoid at least three balls over the course of the past several months. As you'll recall, you pled illness on the first occasion, injury on the second, and on the third, you were simply absent when it was time to leave. Tomorrow night, however, shall be a different story altogether. There is a ball, and you shall attend." Her gaze swept over her daughter. "In *ladies'* clothing," she added.

Antonía blinked, trying her hardest to appear sincere. "Tomorrow night? Oh dear, Mother, I'm afraid I cannot. I have an—an—embroidery lesson!"

"Embroidery!" Her mother scoffed. "You have never so much as picked up a needle in your life!"

Antonía gave her a complacent smile. "Which is why I need lessons, Mother dear."

With a snort of disdain and a hard, no-nonsense expression, Lady Barclay looked her daughter square in the eye and lowered the boom completely. "You, Antonía Margaret Caroline Barclay, are going to the ball! If I have to shackle you to my wrist until tomorrow night, I shall. If I have to lock you up in your bedroom until tomorrow night, I shall. If I have to send you to Will's all-day literary meeting tomorrow—and I warn you, the topic is Chaucer—*I shall.*"

Chaucer! The thought of being trapped with her brother at such an event would almost be worse than the ball.

"No! No!" cried Antonía. "Anything but Will's literary torture chamber. I'll go to the ball, I promise. Just please, please don't feed me to that pack of intellectual blowhards."

"Not only will you go to the ball, young lady, but you will like it. Or, at the very least, you'll act as though you do. And should you fail to exude anything less than abandoned enthusiasm, you'll be spending the rest of the summer quarantined in the library with Will and his idol, Geoffrey. In fact, I can personally guarantee that you'll glimpse neither the light of day nor the saddle of a horse for the remainder of the summer."

The thought of not being able to ride for so long scared Antonía straight into submission. Her mother was a small but very scary lady. Seeing she had no other choice, Antonía gave in graciously.

"Very well, Mother. I promise I'll be as good as gold at the ball. I'll dance every dance. I'll talk to all of your friends. I'll have Claire select my ball gown. I'll smile at all of your sons' insipid friends. You have my word of honor that I'll party from sundown to sunup . . . nonstop."

Lady Barclay's eyes widened in alarm. "Antonía darling"—Antonía breathed a sigh of relief at her mother's endearment—"while I thoroughly applaud and endorse your spirit of cooperation, I would never encourage you to *smile* at your brothers' *friends*."

Antonía did her best not to look too self-satisfied at the success of her words. Her mother's worst fear was that she would marry one of her brothers' boorish friends. Mother and daughter both understood that if Antonía flashed a ghost of a smile in the general direction of a group of young men, there would be a stampede. A flicker of hope darted into her heart. Surely her mother wouldn't want her to attend if her brothers' friends were present.

"Now promise me, Antonía darling, that you will happily attend the ball but you will *not* make overtures, of any kind, to your brothers' friends."

Antonía slumped in defeat. "Yes, I promise, on both counts, Mother, I truly do," she vowed.

"Splendid!" Lady Barclay said. "Now my friends will actually believe I have a daughter." Then her voice softened. "I purposefully did not mention the ball until now, in order to spare you from as much anticipatory anxiety as possible." She lifted her teacup and took a sip.

Antonía sighed. Her mother was always analyzing her simply because she was not socially extroverted.

"This also means," Lady Barclay said, setting the cup down, "that I swore everyone to silence—in particular, Claire. So do not be angry with your best friend for not telling you about her parents' ball. As you know, I can be very persuasive."

"Claire! The ball is at Claire's and she didn't tell me?" Claire couldn't keep a secret to save her life, and had certainly never kept one from her best friend. Antonía narrowed her eyes. "God's nightgown, what did you hang over Claire's head to keep her quiet?"

"You certainly have little regard for my powers of persuasion," remarked her mother with a rueful smile and shake of the head. "But if you must know, I threatened to tell her parents about her clandestine meetings with Matthew. Those two have been tiptoeing around for nearly a twelvemonth. Why they don't just go ahead and announce their engagement is beyond me."

"While you may doubt my regard for your powers of persuasion, my regard for your powers of perception is unequivocal and of the highest order," Antonía admitted. Up until now, she hadn't an inkling that her mother knew about the attachment between her brother and best friend.

"It should be," her mother said, and her smile widened. "However, let's not digress. Claire will be here soon with a selection of ball gowns for you. Knowing your aversion to shopping, we spared you the chore by doing it ourselves. And no offense, Antonía darling, but Claire possesses a much better sense of style than you do."

"None taken, Mum, I couldn't agree with you more. And, frankly, I couldn't care less about what I wear to this stu-stu-" She began to stutter, realizing she was in imminent danger of spending the summer in the library. "Stu-stupendous party," she finished. "I mean, of course Claire will pick out the perfect ball gown, and only my sparkling personality will outshine it at this ridic—" Biting her tongue, she stopped herself again. This was going to be harder than she'd thought.

Lady Barclay fixed her steely green eyes upon her daughter. "Watch yourself, Antonía darling," she warned, "or you'll be set adrift in the library before you can say *The Canterbury Tales!*"

Backtracking quickly, Antonía tried to redeem herself. "I was going to say this 'ridiculously wonderful' ball, Mother . . . really I was."

"Mmm," Lady Barclay mused, rising from her chair. "I'm going to trust you just one more time, but you're skating on very thin ice. One slip, young lady, and you know what's in store for you."

Antonía watched her mother leave, straight-backed and confident that her daughter would obey her. *Yes, indeed,* thought Antonía, narrowing her eyes, *but poor little Claire doesn't know what's in store for her!*

Chapter 2

THE VEXATIOUS MISS BARCLAY

After her mother's merciful departure, Antonía flew out of the room and up the stairs to her bedroom. After shutting the door with definite closure, she paced the floor, muttering to herself.

"A pox upon these stupid balls! God's teeth, why do people hold these ludicrous affairs anyway? And why do they feel compelled to subject me to them? All those people stuffed into one room. All the commotion. All the noise. All the humanity. I can't breathe, just thinking about it."

She mentally thrashed and flailed over her predicament until she heard a knock at the door. In no mood to talk to anyone, she spoke before thinking, and in a distinctly unladylike manner.

"Who the hell is it now?" she exclaimed, and then clapped one hand to her mouth, her heart pounding as the door opened. To her relief, her best friend Claire breezed through the door, followed by Antonía's personal maid, lugging several frocks.

"Lucky for you, dear Antonía, that I was not your mother." Stunningly attired in a size 00 Yves Saint Laurent forerunner, accompanied by a Stella McCartney cross-body bag prototype, she directed the maid to place the bundle of dresses onto the bed and then dismissed her before turning to Antonía. "And what has you so agitated on this fine summer morning?"

"As if you don't know," Antonía said, glaring at her friend. "And what makes you think I am agitated?"

Claire burst out laughing. "My first hint was the friendly greeting spiced with your favorite expletives."

"Not all my favorites, actually," she grumbled, still miffed at Claire's nondisclosure of the ball. "I save the first three for special occasions."

"I stand corrected," Claire said. "However, please be advised that you should never save anything for a special occasion, because life's moments are a precious and finite commodity."

"In that case, in deference to the fathomless depths of your platitudinous wisdom, I will use all of my favorite expletives right here and now!" And so she did, expelling a stream of well-chosen invectives in the specific direction of the impending Deerfield ball.

When she completed her litany, she opened her eyes and saw Claire gazing at her, calm and collected.

"Do you feel better now?" Claire asked, looking unruffled and altogether too complacent. "Really, Antonía," she said, moving to the white brocade chaise lounge across the room, "you're getting yourself all in a twirl over nothing." She sat down, spreading the skirt of her pale green gown around her. "It's only a ball, for goodness' sake. We're not forcing you to eat English food or swim the English Channel or socialize with Englishmen."

Claire glanced away and Antonía wondered what information her friend was hiding this time. Transparency seemed to be an issue. Turning back toward her, Claire hurried on.

"We'll drink a few drinks, dance a few dances, and then retire to a cozy corner where we can verbally abuse everyone in sight. Flaying our friends for their fashion foibles is always such a special treat." Sighing in satisfaction, Claire leaned toward Antonía. "Now that I've put the party in proper perspective, doesn't it sound fun?"

"No," Antonía said bluntly. "And what would possess you to sit in a cozy corner with me when you could be canoodling in that very spot with Matthew?"

Claire's deep brown eyes widened and she rose abruptly. "I have no idea what you mean," she said, and began arranging the garments on the bed in an agitated manner.

Antonía smiled at her friend's obvious discomfort, said nothing, and said it well. She took Claire's seat and observed her. Although clearly distracted, every square inch of Claire MacMillan bespoke comforting warmth.

Claire was not classically beautiful, but her features were delicate and nymph-like. She possessed a high degree of poise and self-confidence, as well as warm, cinnamon-colored hair; warm, almond-shaped brown eyes; and warm, golden skin. In fact, Claire was reminiscent of a comforting piece of warm cinnamon toast on a chilly Scottish morning—of which there were plenty. It was a wonder that only one of Antonía's brothers had fallen in love with her.

Antonía watched as Claire kept rearranging the gowns on the bed, clearly in a state of high flutter. The longer she fussed with the dresses, the redder her face grew, until Antonía couldn't bear it any longer.

"Claire!" she said. "Are you suffering from apoplexy, or what?"

Claire jumped, startled, one hand to her chest. "If I weren't, I certainly am now."

Antonía rose from the chair, walked to the bed, and flopped down beside the dresses. "Sorry, I thought a bit of shock treatment was in order."

Claire lifted her chin. "I assure you I am physically well. However, I *am* suffering from emotional distress of the acutest kind—not that you seem to care. Although your brother has asked me several times to consent to courtship, I've refused him on every occasion because . . ." She stared down at her hands, looking uneasy.

"Because what?" Antonía prompted.

"Well, I've refused Matthew because"—she jerked her head up, hurt reflected in her brown eyes—"you know what they say: even a *reformed* rake makes a bad husband, and your brother *does* have a reputation. Plus, he's been seen with another woman at the last three balls."

"That's impossible," Antonía said, dismissing her friend's words. "Matthew loves you."

"How would you know?" Claire demanded. "*You* haven't attended a ball for the last six months! You're always feigning typhus or smallpox or some other terrible disease. You've proven no help whatsoever."

Fully aware that her list of irritating foibles tallied in the double digits, Antonía jumped up from the bed to wrap her arms around her friend, leaning her head against Claire's. "Sorry again, dear Claire. But why didn't you tell me sooner?"

The girl took a deep breath and released it slowly before speaking. "For your information, discussing this particular issue with the sister of the man I love proves to be very difficult."

"Actually, you make a valid point," said Antonía, trying to think of a way to help. She took her friend by the hand and pulled her across the room to the small chaise lounge again. Antonía sat and tugged Claire down beside her. "Let's start from the beginning. I'm going to ask you a series of questions and I want you to respond honestly."

"Agreed," said Claire honestly.

"Tell me, did you observe Matthew with the *same* woman on each occasion?"

"Yes, he was with the same woman each time, which I'm not sure makes it better or worse, although I suppose we can't accuse him of being fickle-hearted, however—"

"Just answer the question without providing analysis," Antonía interrupted. "Now, let's try again. Did Matthew observe *you* at these gruesome affairs called balls?"

Sharing Lady Barclay's fondness for society in all its ugly shapes and sizes, Claire objected, "Look, Antonía, if I can't analyze, you can't editorialize."

"Fair enough," said Antonía. "I'll withdraw the adjective and rephrase the question. Did Matthew know you were present at these events?"

"No, I avoided him like the plague."

"Which is a very good thing to avoid in this day and age—the plague, I mean, not my brother. Now, please describe the woman in question."

"She's about my height, but far more generous in girth, and she sports an unusual . . . growth upon her nose."

Antonía tapped one finger against her chin as she mused over Claire's story. "In other words, our mystery woman is short, fat, and has a wart on her nose?"

"Yes," Claire said, her face falling. "And he prefers her to me."

Antonía laughed so hard she almost fell off the chaise lounge, while her friend glared at her, obviously annoyed.

"Indeed, Antonía, I'm delighted my heartache provides you with such easy amusement."

"No, no, I'm sorry," said Antonía, wiping tears of mirth from her cheeks. "I know the identity of the woman in question. She's my cousin, Kyrie Muir, from Strathpeffer, and my father regularly browbeats my brothers into dancing with her. Poor Matthew. While you were busy condemning him, he was being, for all intents and purposes, stretched on the rack."

Claire's mouth fell open and relief swept over her features, then terror followed. She raised one hand to her mouth. "Good Lord, what have I done?" She stood and walked back and forth, wringing her hands.

"Nothing that can't be fixed by ripping off your bodice and throwing yourself in Matthew's specific direction," advised Antonía, stretching out on the chaise lounge and crossing her feet at the ankles. "You know how men are."

Claire blinked and looked at her friend, one corner of her mouth quirking up. "So you're saying the redress is to undress!"

"Precisely!" Antonía agreed. "And I commend you on your shrewd summation."

"You are a terrible influence on me, Antonía Barclay, but I do thank you for your help. I will speak to Matthew tonight." She headed for the dresses, new life in her voice. "Now," she announced, "it's time for me to handle your case—quid pro quo and all that." She picked up a dress of burnt orange velvet and hauled the heavy thing up to her shoulders.

"And who was the moron that declared Latin a dead language?" Antonía said, impressed by Claire's grasp of the ancient Roman language. "And, by the way," she added in irritation, "I don't have a case. God's bones, Claire, that dress is hideous."

"My dear Antonía," her friend said, "you may look perfect on the outside, but you are far from perfect on the inside. For the last several months, you have avoided any affair remotely social in nature by pleading imminent death or riding away on your horse and hiding. And, by the by, this dress is perfectly lovely."

"It's a debacle. And I haven't been hiding. I've just been biding."

"Biding what, pray tell?" asked Claire. She discarded the burnt orange monstrosity to one side and then chose another gown from the bed.

Antonía breathed a sigh of relief. The new gown was a deep burgundy, which was dazzling, though she would not, of course, own up to it.

"Biding my time, of course," Antonía said, stretching her arms over her head. "I'm waiting for *your* brother to grow up so I can marry him. It's only fair, since you insist on snaring one of mine."

"You're impossible, do you know that?" Claire said with a laugh. "My brother is eight years younger than you. You'll be a shrunken old prune by the time he reaches adulthood."

Antonía sat bolt upright on the chaise and swung her feet to the floor. "Careful, Claire. We are both nineteen, and thus you're condemning yourself to a state of decrepitude at the ripe old age of six and twenty. Matthew will be none too pleased to discover your old raisin rump sleeping beside him within the mere span of seven years."

Claire laughed at the image, then her smile faded and she glanced away. Antonía stood and walked over to her friend.

"What is it?" she asked. "When you won't meet my eyes, I know that something is afoot."

"Well . . ." Claire cleared her throat, fidgeting with the buttons on the dress she held. "Speaking of love lives . . ." She took a deep breath and then spoke rapidly. "We have an extremely handsome guest staying at Deerfield, and I know you'll find him exceedingly handsome too. His name is Mr. Claymore and he's nine and twenty, very tall, and has intensely blue eyes just like yours." She took a breath and Antonía started to interrupt, but Claire plunged on. "He's from Inverness and has made an enormous fortune making swords or lances or lancets or something like that, and rumor has it he's richer than the king and I would have designs on him myself but, as you know, I've already surrendered my heart to your brother"—another deep breath—"so why don't you stop behaving like a reclusive hermit and actually try being nice to a man for once in your life because you know I'm really beginning to worry about you and I highly recommend Mr. Claymore because—"

"*Claire*," Antonía said, hands on her hips as she stared down at her friend. Claire was clutching a terribly ugly yellow dress to her chest and practically panting from the exertion of her run-on sentences. "Although

I greatly appreciate your concern, need I remind you that your last two recommendations proved abysmal failures?"

Claire shrugged and tossed the yellow gown aside. "Well, sorry, Antonía, but how was I to know that one of them preferred shot glasses over lasses, and the other preferred lads over lasses?"

Antonía picked the horrid yellow dress up and pretended to admire it.

"Don't even think about it, it's not even designer," Claire warned.

Ignoring Claire's advice, she held the gruesome garment up against herself and, looking in the mirror, replied, "The one who preferred lads over lasses was rather sweet and might have had possibilities, but for the fact that he was smitten with Oliver. The other one, however, was a total disaster. Dear God, the boy was a hopeless drunk. He guzzled so much whiskey he nearly depleted Scotland's annual grain supply in one night."

"Oliver?" Claire frowned. "And why Oliver? Why wasn't he smitten with Matthew?"

"For once I followed protocol. I didn't ask and he didn't tell."

Claire continued her analysis. "Matthew is ever so much handsomer than Oliver and has a lovely disposition, while Oliver—"

"Oh, absolutely," Antonía said. "Shall I introduce Matthew to him at the ball?"

Their gazes locked and then Claire's eyes widened, her mouth fell open, and she collapsed onto the bed in a fit of laughter, gasping between spasms.

"Laughing hysterically is a truly sorry method of expressing remorse," Antonía said, trying to look stern. Then she fell upon the bed as well and the two laughed until an abrupt knock on the door made Antonía sit up.

"It might be my mother!" she whispered. "You're supposed to be the respectable one! Get up, get up!"

Catching her breath, Claire managed to sit up and smooth down her dress.

Antonía called out pleasantly, "Whomever it may be—beggar, churl, rogue, or ruffian—you are, hereby, cordially invited into my chamber," which set Claire off again into gales of laughter.

But when Matthew Barclay walked into the room, her friend grew immediately silent and shrank back into the voluminous dresses, while Antonía rose to greet her brother.

"Matthew?" she said, peering at the man as if she didn't recognize him. "Is it you, visiting my chambers? How very odd."

Matthew's handsome face turned a slightly deeper hue. "I heard a great amount of laughter as I passed by your room, dear sister. Just how many magic mushrooms did you sample down at the bourn this morning?"

"Not enough to make you disappear, unfortunately, but it beats licking toads."

Matthew laughed and, on the verge of making himself comfortable on her bed, stopped short when he discovered it occupied.

Turning instant gentleman, he apologized profusely. "Miss MacMillan, I'm so sorry, I didn't realize you were here."

Claire hastened to cross the room to his side. "I'm so glad to see you, Matthew. You are just in time to help me convince Antonía not to wear this despicable yellow dress!"

Antonía's personality contained equal shares of romanticism and pragmatism, and so she was impressed by her friend's decisive gesture, as well as her brother's reaction. Swiftly but gently, he took possession of Claire's hand and lifted her fingers to his lips.

"Indeed," he said, "I care not if she goes stark naked, if I can but have a moment of your time, Miss MacMillan."

Claire blushed prettily, and Matthew guided her toward the door.

"Matthew," Antonía called after him, "was there a reason you came to my room other than to abduct my best friend?"

"Yes, right," he said distractedly. "I came to tell you that Mother wants you to choose *two* dresses from that heap, not just one."

"Why do I need two dresses for one ball?"

"You'll need another one for tonight."

Antonía cast a watchful eye upon her brother, waiting for the other shoe to drop, which it did, loud and clear, with his next words.

"We're hosting a dinner party for the MacMillans and their houseguests here at Barclay Castle tonight."

Antonía stifled a groan. "Wonderful."

Claire, the traitor, appeared to be savoring a taste of Heaven with

Matthew's arm encircling her slender waist but turned at the door and narrowed her eyes.

"And, dear Antonía, one final bit of fashion advice. If I see you in that yellow dress tonight—you *will* be sorry!"

Antonía did not see her love-stricken best friend for the rest of the afternoon, but as dusk fell upon the Scottish borders, she hurried up the stairway leading to the south turret of the castle. She had promised to visit her former nanny, Minnie Munro.

Reaching the hallway, she was surprised to see Matthew bounding up the stairs toward her. With his face still flushed with passion he announced to his sister, "I suppose I should say thank you."

"Thank me for what?" Antonía asked. Although she knew the answer to her own question, she nonetheless wanted her brother to verbalize his gratitude more specifically—but he wasn't falling for it.

He cocked his handsome head and gave her a smug look. "I *should* say thank you, which means I won't, if you continue to plead ignorance, which I know is hardly a stretch for you."

Realizing she wouldn't get any more out of her brother in the way of appreciation, Antonía conceded. "Very well. You're welcome. Just remember, now you owe me." But as she turned to resume her journey down the hall, Matthew blocked her way, his voice more somber than normal, especially considering the recent upturn in his love life.

"Antonía, stop and listen to me. Claire was adamant that I warn you about one of the guests who'll be at the dinner party tonight. His name is Rex Throckmorton, and according to Claire, he's very aggressive, very arrogant—obviously very English—and he wants to meet you in the worst possible way."

"Why would he want to meet me?" she asked, bewildered by her brother's tone as well as his words.

He cleared his throat and looked away from her. "I honestly don't know whether you realize this or not, and I certainly don't intend to fuel your humble vanity, but you're not exactly ugly." His gaze darted back to her, and one corner of his mouth twitched nervously. "Over the course of the last few years, you've earned quite a reputation as a great beauty in this part of the world."

"Matthew, if you could be a wee bit more nebulous, it might help clear things up for me."

Her brother shook his head at her sarcastic remark, but Antonía's level of frustration was increasing in direct proportion to her level of confusion so she dropped the sarcasm, hoping to coerce her brother into making sense.

"I'm sorry," she said. "That was rude. I'm listening."

"Rex Throckmorton heard about your reputation as the most beautiful woman in Scotland. He intends to play William the Bastard and make a conquest during dinner tonight."

"Well, it sounds like he's got the 'bastard' part down pat," Antonía said.

"I wouldn't be quite so flippant if I were you."

"Oh," she sighed. "So I'm his conquest?"

Matthew nodded. "But there is some good news. Rex's father, Sir Basil Throckmorton, evidently knows his son is an idiot, and he's in the habit of running interference."

"Two rotten Englishmen instead of one—now there *is* a piece of good news," she said. She waved one hand dismissively. "I am quite capable of handling a couple of Englishmen."

"Stop it, Antonía!" he snapped. "Claire is really worried about you."

Her own temper flared. "What a farrago of nonsense. Do you really think Rex the Conqueror is going to lunge across the dinner table and drag me out of the castle with my family and friends looking on?"

"No, because you'll be sitting between me and Claire, and we plan to keep a sharp eye on you."

"I think not," Antonía said, lifting her chin. "I appreciate your concern, but I shall not sit between you and Claire. No doubt you two will be playing footsie under the table all through dinner. With that seating arrangement, I'm more likely to get wounded by friendly fire than hostile Englishmen."

Matthew folded his arms over his chest and Antonía did the same.

She'd be damned if two pompous Englishmen were going to come into her home and terrorize her.

"First of all, have you told Father?"

"Father will likely give you to Sir Basil if he asks. The man has agreed to fund some of our parents' newest business ventures."

"Oh really?" Antonía replied, arching a skeptical brow. Her father doted on her, and Matthew knew it. He was just trying to scare her. "Let's meet the problem head-on. Tell Mum to seat me between the Throck-mortons. But if it makes Claire feel better, you and she can provide secu-rity by sitting directly *across* from me."

"Your female logic defies all that's logical, but have it your way. I've warned you and if you choose to be stupidly stubborn, then let it be on your head!" He spun on his heel and headed down the stairs.

Resuming her trip down the hallway, Antonía stewed over the situa-tion. How dare her brother attempt to exert control over her! She could take care of herself. Yes, indeed, she'd already formulated a plan to rid herself of those two vile Englishmen: she'd simply bore them to death. She would be so dull, so lifeless, and so vapid that both father and son would be yawning over their soup. Matthew and Claire would then real-ize how ridiculous they'd been to worry about her.

But as Antonía raised her hand to knock on Minnie's door, she started to question the wisdom of her plan. After all, Matthew had said it was her beauty that the Englishmen were so fixated upon, her "crown" of being the most beautiful woman in Scotland. Perhaps boring them to death wouldn't matter one whit.

"Antonía, ducky, is that you I hear dawdling outside my door?" a croaky voice called from behind the door.

"'Tis I," Antonía answered, slipping into the Scottish vernacular as she often did when vexed.

"Well, don't be talking to me through a piece of auld wood, ducky!" the voice commanded. "March your long legs in here and let's have a good old-fashioned chin-wag."

Antonía opened the door and entered the room. It was small and rather dark, as there was only one tiny window. Facing that window, Min-nie sat in her bed, propped up by several pillows that looked as though their cases could have benefited from a wash. The bed was a four-poster affair, with a mountain of well-worn comforters atop it, also in need of laundering. Antonía made a mental note to send the maids in after her visit. A single lit candlestick sat on a small table next to the bed, along with a hard-backed chair.

"How are you, dear Minnie?" Antonía asked, seating herself in the chair beside the woman's bed. She wrinkled her nose at the smell of several distinctive odors.

"If you overlook the consumption and a few other little things, I'm as fit as a flea," the vice-riddled, tough-as-nails octogenarian replied. "And praise be to Heaven for tobacco and whiskey. They'll restore me to full bloom in no time."

Accordingly, she downed a shot of the drink and then began striking a flint against the tinderbox she held. After a few seconds, a flame appeared and the old woman pulled a small pipe out of the top of her nightgown. She lit the contraption and put it to her lips.

"Yes, indeed," Antonía remarked dryly, "it's a fact generally accepted that smoking and drinking are two of the best remedies for consumption. Smoking, in particular, is highly regarded for its wide therapeutic window." She adored Minnie, but her justification for her bad habits never failed to confound.

"Now, don't get sassy with me, ducky!" Minnie said. "You know how we old folk enjoy our afflictions and their attendant therapies. So until someone shows me scientifical evidence proving tobacco is harmful to my health, I'll just puff merrily along, thank you very much." Whereupon Minnie blew several perfectly shaped smoke rings up toward the ceiling. "Besides, I'm too old to die young so I may as well abuse myself happily while I circle the drain."

Antonía laughed. Although her brothers had seen fit to take it upon themselves to "educate" her, none of them, including Will, had taught her nearly as much as Minnie. She kept up with all things scientific and had encouraged her young ward's natural curiosity.

"Now, seriously, ducky, why don't you join me and quaff down a shot or two of fine Scottish whiskey? Your spirits appear to be flagging this evening, and it *is* a scientifical fact that a wee bit of whiskey is divine medicine." Minnie filled two shot glasses with the amber-hued liquor.

"No whiskey for me, Minnie, but I appreciate the thought," Antonía said. She turned and walked over to the tiny window and watched the moon rise slowly above the softly rolling hills of Southern Scotland.

"Still a wee bit of a teetotaler, are you, lass?" remarked the hard-drinking old woman, quaffing down both shots. "You're missing out on one of life's finest pleasures. It's excellent stuff, my girl." Her words dissolved into a hacking cough, which lasted for a good two minutes.

"Now tell your old nanny what ails you," she croaked when she could breathe again. "Your spirits are definitely down in the dumps tonight, ducky."

Antonía sighed. "Nothing exotic, Minnie, just the usual dread of socializing. There's a party here tonight, followed by one at the MacMillans tomorrow night."

"Ducky, you must confront your fear head-on."

"It's not a fear. I just hate socializing."

Minnie continued, "How are you going to find yourself a handsome young laddie to marry if you don't make yourself available?" Cough, hack, cough.

"You're trifling with me, aren't you, Minnie? My brothers are friends with every available laddie in Southern Scotland, and let me be the first to assure you they're all just like my brothers: dissolute, dissipated ne'er-do-wells. I can't be bothered with any of them, or for that matter, with any of these never-ending social obligations that keep raising their ugly heads every time I turn around." She folded her arms across her chest and lifted her chin. Even Minnie seemed to be against her.

The nanny laughed and then broke out into yet another coughing fit. "I enjoy your spirited commentary," she said, once she found her breath again. "It's a welcome change from sitting here listening to my symptoms." Her "therapeutic" pipe had died out, and she lit it again.

"Ducky, you do make me laugh. And while I'm aware that you're acquainted with most of the available laddies in the area, I'll never agree that they're *all* dissolute, dissipated ne'er-do-wells. Certainly a few of them are nothing to write home about, but most are fine young men."

"Very well," Antonía said, feeling miffed. "Then perhaps it will make you happy to hear that I am having dinner with two Englishmen tonight. One quite eligible, although revolting and odious."

"Whoa, ducky! I told you to confront your fear, not sacrifice your life over it!" Minnie cried, and then began choking on her pipe or her whiskey or her sputum or the news or, most probably, a combination of all four. Slowly recovering from her attack, she managed to whisper, "How did this come to pass?"

Whereupon Antonía related her saga of woe to her concerned audience who listened intently and seemed to become increasingly alarmed as the tale unraveled. When she finished her tale, Minnie was in a state of high agitation.

"Listen to me, precious," she said, her wrinkled old face intense and remarkably sober. "Those two Englishmen—do you happen to know their names?"

"Sir Basil Throckmorton and his son, Rex," replied Antonía. "Have you ever heard of them?"

"No," Minnie said, blinking rapidly.

Antonía was suspicious. Her nanny always blinked rapidly when she was lying.

"Minnie . . ."

"It's never a good idea to get too cozy with the English," she muttered. "You'd be wise to stay as far away from them as possible, my precious ducky." Visibly shaking now, the nanny began hacking again, even worse than before.

Antonía pounded the woman on the back as she coughed and hacked. Why was Minnie so upset about the Throckmortons? It must be important if she would lie about it. When the woman finally settled down, Antonía pulled her around to face her.

"Minnie, I want the truth. What do you know about the Throckmortons? If you love me, then tell me!"

The old woman shook her head and wiped spittle from her face with the back of her hand. "Jesus, Mary, and Joseph," she said, shaking her head. "I can't believe that old devil has resurfaced after all these years." She reached out suddenly and grabbed Antonía's arm. "You must stay away from him, ducky. Sir Basil Throckmorton is cunning and ruthless, a dangerous enemy, and if he were to discover—" She broke off, coughing again.

Sir Basil Throckmorton? But Claire had been worried about *Rex*—was the father as bad as the son? Well, he was an Englishman, so that was bad enough.

"Minnie, can I get you anything?" Antonía asked in concern, as the coughing attack showed no signs of abating. "Some honey? A cup of water perhaps?"

Minnie looked at her with horrified eyes. "Water?" Her coughing stopped and she shook her head vehemently. "No—no thanks, ducky. After I smoke my pipe and have another drink, I'll be right as rain."

She cackled a bit at this and then quickly sobered and leaned toward Antonía. "Mind what I say—stay away from the Throckmortons," she said. "Sir Basil and his son are not to be trusted."

Antonía shrugged, unwilling to let her ailing nanny know how much these warnings were beginning to weigh on her nerves. "I'm not afraid of any Englishman."

"Hmmm." The old woman patted Antonía's arm and then lay back upon her pillow. "In this case, ducky, you should be." She took another puff on her pipe. "Now, my precious, go get ready for the party."

Antonía stood, but still clasped her nanny's hand. "Minnie, I don't like leaving you when you're so ill."

"Well, look on the bright side," the woman said, and then laughed. "I won't be contracting leprosy anytime soon!"

Antonía frowned in confusion. "I beg your pardon?"

"It is a scientifical fact that if you have consumption, you will never get leprosy."

Antonía blinked. "Where did you read that?"

Minnie waved a hand toward the door. "Never mind, ducky. Just stay away from those Englishmen!"

Now thoroughly confused, Antonía gave her nanny a hug and left, not realizing until she was on her way down the second flight of stairs that she'd forgotten to find out what Minnie feared Sir Basil Throckmorton might discover.

What *she* discovered—back in her bedchamber—was that she was running extremely late. The thought of her mother's threats, combined with her lethal glare, lent speed to Antonía's preparations as she stripped off her clothes and began to rifle through the gowns on her bed.

Freely admitting her fashion sense was limited, she decided to follow Claire's ultimatum about the yellow dress, though it was tempting to wear the miasma just to thwart her friend's advice. Too risky, she concluded, recalling her mother's dagger-like eyes. One dress eliminated. That left about ten more.

For one fleeting, murderous second, Antonía felt an urge to strangle her best friend for abandoning her before the dress decision had been settled. But knowing crime never paid, she made the pragmatic decision to wear any dress that fit. And, since there seemed to be a dearth of dresses for Scottish women nearly six feet tall, she soon made a molehill out of a mountain.

She chose a blue dress, vaguely familiar to her, and once that decision had been made, Antonía rang for her maid. Through much physical exertion, the woman managed to get her dressed in just under an hour. At last properly attired, her hair pulled back, up and off her face, Antonía dismissed the maid and prepared for the ordeal ahead.

How she dreaded walking out of her room! But she knew that she must, or she would risk her mother's wrath. She took several deep breaths and, without thinking about it further, she wrenched the door open and hurried into the hallway, letting it slam behind her. She was rushing, trying desperately not to trip on her long skirts, when all at once a young man of gigantic, ungainly proportions stepped in front of her.

"Excuse me," she said, realizing he must be one of the guests, "may I please pass?" But instead of stepping aside, the man took a step closer, forcing Antonía to take a step back. Before she realized it, he had backed her against the wall of the hallway, his hulking form too close for comfort—or hygiene.

"You must be the legendary Antonía Barclay," he said, his breath a cross between dung, whiskey, and fermented garbage. "You're even prettier than I expected. I'm Rex Throckmorton."

Antonía stared at him, struck speechless. So this was the man Matthew had warned her about. He was tall, bald, and fat, with a doughy face and a nose like a potato. His eyes were dark, beady, and lascivious. Her heart pounded against her chest as he smiled, revealing mangled, yellow teeth.

"Well?" he demanded. "Are you deaf and dumb, woman? Or do you earn your keep by just standing about looking beautiful?" She gasped as, without warning, he pressed himself against her.

She tried to push him away, but it was like trying to move a megalith. "I was just momentarily astonished," she replied with frigid civility, "to discover the circus had come to town." Antonía looked up at the huge man and arched one brow. "You *are* one of the clowns, correct?"

"So the legend is as feisty as she is beautiful," he said, leering down into her cleavage.

Repulsed by every single thing about him, but in particular his putrid smell, Antonía gritted her teeth and began to feel panicky.

"Do you enjoy bullying women," she said, struggling to keep her voice cold and steady, "or is this your idea of chatting us up?"

To her surprise, he stepped back. "I was actually looking for the dining hall. Your brother told me it was located in the north turret, but evidently I've been misinformed, my love."

The dining hall was on the opposite side of the castle, and mischievous as her brothers were, they would never send a suitor—or even a guest—to her room.

Antonía glared at the buffoon. "Allow me to inform you that you're in the wrong turret, on the wrong floor, and in the wrong hall. And God knows, I can only wish you were in the wrong castle!" She moved as if to go and then turned back, chin held high. "And do not, under any circumstance, call me 'your love'!"

Antonía pivoted to storm away, only to cry out as the Englishman grabbed her roughly around the waist and pulled her to him. She realized, and with a healthy degree of dismay, that she was most definitely in big trouble. Rex Throckmorton was powerful, mean, inebriated, and worst of all, he wasn't afraid to put his grimy hands all over her.

"Release the lady!" a deep, unfamiliar masculine voice cried. "Or by God, I will skewer you and present you at Lord Barclay's table, along with the reason for your skewering!"

Throckmorton released her and Antonía stumbled backward, right into the arms of her rescuer. His hands went around her waist and she jerked her head up, wondering if things were about to go from bad to worse.

But warm blue eyes stared down into hers. "The name is Claymore," he said. "Breck Claymore."

Chapter 3

DINNER, DISEASE, AND A DATE

S *he swept through his soul like a gale force wind.* Breck Claymore gazed down at the woman in his arms, an extraordinary sight to behold. Cheekbones that defied gravity . . . lips that defied logic . . . grace and beauty that defied description. "Pretty" didn't even begin to describe her, although "staggeringly beautiful" was a fairly good start. She was so breathtaking he had to force himself to take a breath.

Claymore had resisted quite a few beautiful women over the course of his nine and twenty years, but in the crucible of one moment he had fallen, and fallen hard. Never before had he seen a woman who had come even remotely close to matching Miss Barclay's physical splendor. She was something different altogether—bar none.

Much to his credit, he sensed there was a great deal more to the lady than her incomparable exterior. When that oaf, Rex Throckmorton, had blocked her way, the fire in her eyes had sent a burst of admiration through Claymore. Here was a woman who knew her own mind and wasn't afraid to show it—something rare, in his experience, with a lady of her background.

"I believe you can release me now, Mr. Claymore," she said, her voice faint, her lips so close to his that for a moment, he almost did the unthinkable. Then he realized the compromising position in which they stood—as well as the fact that Rex Throckmorton must be dealt with, posthaste.

He took a step back and let his hands fall away from her waist. "I beg your pardon," he said, bowing slightly, trying his best to keep his hearty

Scottish burr subdued. "Are you all right, m'lady?" He glanced around, looking for Throckmorton. "Where is that bastard?"

The lady turned around in a whirl. Claymore drew in a sharp breath. If Miss Barclay's incandescent beauty and independent fire had forced him to the edge of the proverbial cliff of love, it was the swing of her slender hips that now made him desperate to leap from the safety of bachelorhood and free-fall into the abyss of husbandhood.

"Gone, thank God! Though I will be forced to dine with the—what did you call him?" She smiled up at him, and Claymore thought his heart would break from the joy of it. Yet there was a tension around her sweet lips, no doubt left over from her encounter with Throckmorton.

"A bastard," he said softly. "Not a polite word to say in front of a lady. Forgive me?"

He watched as her gaze roamed over him, pausing at his kilt—his best one made from the finest wool in Inverness in a subdued plaid of blue and gray. He had worn his new linen shirt and a gray velvet jacket for the occasion. He was a rich man, but he feared his well-worn knee-high boots revealed his lack of polish. But the beautiful Antonía put his fears to rest with her next words.

"You're a Highlander," she said with what sounded like delight. "I don't know as I've ever met one before."

"Aye, we are a rare breed in the softly rolling hills of Southern Scotland," he said, daring to wink.

She laughed, and he was relieved to see the last of the tension leave her face. Then he frowned, recalling her words. "Throckmorton is invited to supper? Are you sure that's a good idea?"

"Blame my parents," she said, gloom settling over her features.

Claymore made up his mind. "I will speak to your father immediately," he said. "He must know the disrespect with which you were treated by that bas—" He cleared his throat and she gave him a mischievous smile. "That ill-natured miscreant," he amended.

"Thank you." She laid one hand on his arm and Claymore had to fight the urge to take her in his arms and kiss her senseless. "But I think it would place my father in an awkward position, since Rex's father, Sir Basil Throckmorton, is a powerful man."

"Antonía, you're late, as usual!" Someone shouted from behind them. Claymore turned to see a young man striding down the long hallway toward them.

"My brother, Oliver," Antonía said with a sigh. "I'm late for supper."

"I am a wretched rogue for detaining you." He took her hand, and holding it in both of his, he saw the sparkle in her eyes.

"Well, my wretched rogue, are you dining with us tonight?" she asked.

Was it his imagination or did she sound a little breathless? "I will indeed, Miss Barclay. Dare I hope to sit beside you as we dine?"

She lowered her incredibly long lashes and then swept them upward again. "Time will tell," she said.

A tease. He was more in love than ever.

He turned and gave a half bow toward her brother, as he came to an abrupt stop. Time enough for introductions later, he thought. He needed a moment to pull himself together before facing the dazzling beauty at the dinner table.

After bidding Mr. Claymore a reluctant farewell, Antonía allowed Oliver to hurry her down the hallway to the large dining hall reserved for the sumptuous dinner parties her mother loved to throw. *If only I had something to throw at Rex Throckmorton,* Antonía thought as the brief interlude with the handsome Highlander faded and the memory of Throckmorton's near assault came to mind.

Oliver ushered her in through the large double doors, opened to allow the servants room to bring in each of the twelve courses planned for the evening, and then he promptly deserted her. She glanced around for Mr. Claymore, but he was nowhere to be seen. However, she did spot her brother Matthew hurdling over several pieces of expensive objets d'art in his ardent desire to claim his seat beside Claire. She felt the usual tremors in her stomach as every eye turned to her, and then relaxed a wee bit after seeing that most of the guests were her parents' usual party suspects.

But Antonía's brief respite ended at the sight of Rex Throckmorton signaling her with both beefy hands to come and sit beside him. She slowed her pace and considered her options. She could plead plague and leave, she could insist on a new seating chart and sit with her parents, or she could put on her big girl breeches and take her self-inflicted seat between the two Englishmen. Taking the high road, she accepted her doom and walked toward Rex Throckmorton.

Arriving at her disagreeable destination, she graciously accepted Sir Basil Throckmorton's charming salutation and allowed him to kiss her hand. Antonía was more than a little surprised to find him a handsome, elegant man, certainly past his bloom, but nevertheless seriously attractive. His dark hair had silver at the temples, giving him a distinguished air, and his dark eyes were intelligent and bespoke a quick wit.

As she compared the two Throckmorton men, Antonía could only shake her head at the random and capricious workings of the human gene pool. Indeed, it seemed that Mother Nature had gone to great lengths to manufacture a father so handsome and a son so loathsome.

Apparently it had been decided between the two men that Rex would help Antonía be seated. She kept a fair distance from him as he pulled out her chair and she reluctantly took her seat. With all the fine motor skills of a yoke of oxen, he then shoved her chair toward the table so forcefully that he damn near knocked the wind out of her. After safely regaining her breath, Antonía shot him a baleful look before turning her attention to the elder Throckmorton who began the conversation with a fount of compliments.

"Miss Barclay," he said in a low, deep voice, "I know we've only just met, but I must tell you that your astonishing beauty defies all words ethereal." Flashing a phenomenally charismatic smile, he then added with open admiration, "And your gown graces your figure with heavenly perfection. When you entered the room, you floated, rather than walked."

At that moment, however, Antonía saw Mr. Claymore make a late entrance. He paused to speak with her parents at the other end of the table, no doubt apologizing for his appalling tardiness. He was a bit of a rogue after all, though a polite one, and she found herself smiling at the thought.

He glanced up as if he'd heard her speak, and their eyes met, his blue gaze reminding her of their moment clasped together in the hallway. Sir

Basil cleared his throat and she realized she hadn't responded to his lavish compliments.

"Why, Sir Basil," she said, turning to him with a brilliant smile, "if you insist upon showering me with hyperbolic praise, I shall be forced to invent a flaw just to persuade you of my mortality."

The elegant Englishman returned her broad smile. "You would have to invent one, my dear, because none exists. And what a beautiful dress," Sir Basil went on, "but it's nothing in comparison to your beauty."

Antonía slid a quick glance toward the other guests and found Mr. Claymore seated across from her and two seats down. He sat with his arms crossed over his chest, a wary glint in his eyes as he watched her.

"Indeed, Miss Barclay," he continued, "I find your intelligence as comely as your face. Have you ever read Chaucer?"

Antonía fought the urge to roll her eyes. "Yes, of course," she said, "my very favorite author."

"He is mine, as well," Sir Basil said, beaming down at her. "Ah, *The Canterbury Tales*."

She was saved from replying and from throwing a plate at her brother Will, seated a few chairs away, as servants began filing into the room carrying large platters of food. The aroma silenced even the doltish Rex.

Antonía inwardly rejoiced that supper had come at last. Perhaps the Englishmen's mouths would be kept too full to allow additional conversation. To her dismay, Rex not only filled his mouth, but also continued to talk, displaying his masticated food with each syllable.

"Miss Barclay," Rex said, "I'm dumbfounded that you aren't wearing a ruff."

"You have the 'dumb' part right," she muttered under her breath.

"You aren't exactly a woman of fashion, are you?" He swallowed and lifted one huge hand to gesture toward the other guests.

Provoked by his words, Antonía glanced around the table. Except for Mr. Claymore in his Scottish Highland regalia, she was indeed the only one at the table not sporting the huge accordion collar she loathed and despised. Belatedly, however, she realized that without the ruff, her dress was left with a dip to her neckline. When she turned back to Rex, he was practically drooling into her décolleté and she recoiled in disgust.

"Though I have to say, I prefer you without the ruff after all." Rex gave her breasts one more thorough going-over before he picked up a turkey leg and bit into it like a ravenous dog.

A quick glance across the table told Antonía that Mr. Claymore was growing a trifle heated under his velvet jacket as he watched the exchange with a pronounced frown. She arched one eyebrow in his direction and lifted her chin. God forbid that he think she was one of those women who looked for a man to rescue her every time she turned around. His frown dissolved into an approving smile, as if he knew the intent of her fearless pose. Then he glanced at Rex and his smile disappeared.

Sir Basil spoke up, distracting Antonía from Mr. Claymore and proving himself adept at diplomacy by changing the subject from fashion to the less controversial one of politics.

"By the way," he said, "at the behest of Queen Elizabeth, my son and I are meeting with your King James tomorrow to discuss his mother's unfortunate situation."

Raising a single eyebrow, Antonía remarked with feigned civility, "Sir, you possess a remarkable gift for euphemism as well as for delayed reaction. I believe *our* king's mother has been *your* queen's prisoner for well over eighteen years."

In his usual charmless manner, Rex chimed in, "*Your* Queen Mary was a damn fool to step foot inside England! And we Englishmen do not suffer fools gladly!"

Tilting her head to one side, Antonía replied, "That being the case, you must find it exceedingly difficult to live with yourself, Mr. Throckmorton."

Sir Basil chuckled. "You don't think too much of my son, do you, Miss Barclay?"

Antonía gave him the slightest sliver of a smile. "Your remarkable gifts are once more shining through, Sir Basil. To be honest, I don't think of your son at all, but if I were masochistic enough to give him a moment's thought, I'd most assuredly despise him with a profound depth of feeling."

"You are indeed captivating," Sir Basil murmured. "Not only do you possess astounding beauty, but I am enchanted by the sharpness of your mind. You are so unlike the cloying, solicitous women who beg for my attention, as well as my affection. You speak your mind"—his dark eyes quickened and he took her hand between his—"and in doing so, what a brilliant mind is spoken."

"Miss Barclay, were you born in Scotland?" Rex blurted, sending little pieces of meat into the air.

Antonía threw him a bone-chilling glare. "Yes," she said, biting off the word.

"How very odd," he replied. "Judging from your frosty disposition, I supposed you a native of Iceland!"

A spate of laughter erupted from the vicinity of Antonía's brothers. Lord and Lady Barclay cast piercingly reproachful eyes upon their three sons who quickly refilled their wine glasses, wisely turning from further fraternal frivolity.

Sir Basil gave his son a stern look before turning back to Antonía. "Miss Barclay," he said, "your father told me that you are an accomplished harpist. At what age did you begin your study?"

Antonía gave a faint deprecating laugh. "Sir Basil, I am my father's only daughter, so naturally he embellishes upon my accomplishments. But to answer your question, I was five years old when my mother began my instruction."

Rex began counting on his fingers, mumbling to himself loudly, then announced, "So, if you're nineteen now, then you've been playing the harp for nearly ten years."

Antonía couldn't resist the temptation to expel a little more venom his way. "Mr. Throckmorton, have you checked in with the Scottish Order of Mensa yet? I'm quite certain they're awaiting your call with bated breath." She gritted her teeth. War was brewing.

Sir Basil threw his head back and laughed. Apparently he enjoyed hearing his son insulted. "Do you practice your instrument daily, Miss Barclay?" he asked.

"Yes," she said, growing weary now of the subject, the father, the son, and the supper.

"You must be very proficient at *plucking* by now, Miss Barclay," Rex chimed in. "I've always said that all the ladies enjoy a good *plucking*." He leered at her and she rolled her eyes. "And that being the case," Rex went on, "why don't you teach me to play and we can *pluck* together." He slapped his leg and howled in delight, bringing everyone's attention to their end of the table.

"Rex!" Sir Basil hissed, his long-suffering patience apparently at an end. "I forbid—"

But Antonía cut him off by standing, disgusted but hardly daunted by Rex's innuendos. "Mr. Throckmorton," she declared loudly, "I wouldn't *pluck* with you if you were the last man left on God's good green earth."

Silver forks dropped, wine goblets teeter-tottered, and succulent Scottish salmon—caught that very morn in the meandering River Tweed—was gagged upon as Antonía's icy reply brought conversation and eating to a standstill. War was preordained.

"Miss Barclay," Rex said, rising to tower over her, "extraordinary *assets* such as yours should never be allowed to turn frigid from want of use. And by lucky chance, my love, I'm available to thaw you out and warm you up." He pulled her into his arms.

Lord Barclay stood up. Mr. Claymore stood up. All three of Antonía's brothers stood up.

"How dare you speak to my daughter in such a contemptible manner!" Lord Barclay bellowed.

"This is an outrage!" Oliver cried.

"You arrogant ogre!" Will shouted.

"It's—indecent!" Matthew managed, after Claire stuck her elbow in his side.

"By God," Lord Barclay blustered, "I don't care if there are multiple witnesses to the killing, I will tear him apart, limb from limb!"

"Release her," Mr. Claymore said, but his steely-eyed gaze said much more as Rex obeyed the order by letting her go.

War had officially been declared.

But Antonía did not want war with the Throckmortons. Too late she remembered Minnie's cautionary tale. If her nanny was afraid of these men, Antonía should do her utmost to prevent what appeared to be impending bloodshed.

Rex was turning all sorts of interesting shades of rage, when suddenly Claire stood up.

"Mr. Throckmorton," she said, "you look rather flushed. I fear you are suffering from an extremely high fever of an idiopathic nature." She glanced at Antonía and widened her eyes. Antonía gave an imperceptible nod.

"A fever!" barked Rex. "I've never felt better in my life! I don't have a fever!"

Whereupon Antonía slapped her hand on Rex's Neanderthal forehead and offered a second opinion.

"Gracious, Mr. Throckmorton, although you most certainly have a fever, it is *not* idiopathic in origin, but rather a pathognomonic sign of a very serious illness."

"Serious?" he said, a bit of meat falling from his wide-open mouth.

Shaking her head as if to indicate the hopelessness of his case, she announced somberly, "There is no doubt in my mind. You are suffering from a raging case of hoof-and-mouth disease unquestionably contracted by sticking your foot in your mouth on a nonstop basis. To obviate the risk of contagion to public health, Miss MacMillan and I shall meticulously fumigate the affected areas once you've departed Scotland. You must return to England at once and take to your sickbed. Strolling about in the Scottish night air may very well result in your doom!"

"Doom?" he echoed, releasing her as he stumbled backward and clapped his own hand to his head. "Fadda?"

With a sigh, Sir Basil rose. He bowed to Lord and Lady Barclay and the brothers. "My apologies for my son's . . . illness," he said. His gaze flickered to Mr. Claymore, and Antonía felt her heart begin to pound. "And as for you, Claymore," he inclined his head, "I have a feeling we shall meet again."

Taking his son by the arm, Sir Basil half-led, half-pushed him out of the dining hall as he protested all the way. "I need a poultice!" Rex cried. "I need a spoonful of honey! I need a potion!"

As his voice faded down the hallway, Antonía sank down into her chair, aghast at the thought of what she might have unleashed upon her family—and Mr. Claymore.

Before the silent room could react, Lady Barclay stood. "We shall now adjourn to the music room." She turned to her daughter. "Antonía, I believe you were going to favor us with some music tonight." She smiled at her guests. "After all, chamber music doth soothe the savage beast."

Under any other set of circumstances, Antonía would have balked most vehemently, but all things being equal, her mother's suggestion offered a way out of this most awkward of situations. Accordingly, Antonía complied dutifully and without objection.

The guests filed out of the dining hall and into the music room, where they found chairs waiting for them, along with sweetmeats and more wine. Antonía took her place at her harp. Perhaps her mother was right, for as soon as she began to play, the savage beast within her began to feel calmer; and when Mr. Claymore walked in and took a seat at the very front, she closed her eyes and felt very calm indeed.

Breck Claymore felt a sincere satisfaction in knowing he had been right. There was a great deal more to Miss Barclay than just her incomparable beauty. When she spoke, when she gestured, when she made any slight movement at all, it was executed with an effortless grace and an innate stateliness known only to the highest of the highborn. If he hadn't known her *not* to be royalty, he would have surely presupposed it. Her regal bearing, her majestic manner, and her commanding presence were undeniable and patently evident, as was her musical talent now being displayed.

Consequently, he had been deeply disappointed when once inside the dining hall, Miss Barclay had taken her seat between the Throckmortons. However, he had held himself in check as he was seated too far from her to engage in conversation, or simply bask in her radiance, as he desired. Now he consoled himself with the knowledge that the Throckmortons had left Barclay Castle, and he was still here. In fact, he wasn't going anywhere until Miss Barclay agreed to marry him. But first things first—he needed a plan.

As he watched her play the harp, once again proving her innate gracefulness, he planned his strategy to optimize his goal of winning Miss Barclay. First, he had to tackle the problem of securing Lord Barclay's permission to court his only daughter, and next, there was the even more unsettling problem of Miss Barclay herself.

Undoubtedly, the vast majority of unattached men in the country could be found queued up outside Barclay Castle on any given evening. But not completely unaware of his considerable assets, Mr. Claymore quickly dismissed the competition and instead, with regret, left Antonía's concert and sought out her father to ask for a private audience.

Lord Barclay was more than welcoming and led him into his library. There, after half an hour of drinking wine and listening to the verbose laird, Mr. Claymore began to grow impatient. He was determined to obtain his consent to woo Antonía—that is, as soon as her father decided to stop sharing his many thoughts on a wide array of subjects.

"Indeed, Mr. Claymore, a man must be tough and hardy to live in the border country of Southern Scotland!" opined the generously opinionated Lord Barclay. "For centuries now, we've been holding down the fort for the entire country. Our querulous English neighbors keep us Lowlanders quite busy. Highlanders don't know how lucky they are to be living up in the hills, far away from the cantankerous English. Such a fractious lot!"

"Indeed," Claymore said, smiling to himself.

"Down here in the south—now that's another story altogether. We're exposed! Out in the open! So close to the English border we can practically spit across it! But I tell you, Mr. Claymore, we're tough as leather and hard as nails because of it. Indeed, the border country is no place for the fainthearted." Lord Barclay cast a keen eye upon him. "From the looks of you, Mr. Claymore, I'd say you could hold down several forts all by yourself. Please tell me about yourself—from where do you hail? What occupies your days?"

"I am from Inverness, my lord," Claymore replied, eager to share his accomplishments before popping the question of courting Antonía. "My family has been in the silversmith trade for centuries, and we've recently diversified into manufacturing and marketing two-handed swords with double-edged blades."

"Of course, of course," commented Lord Barclay. "The famous claymore sword! I've heard the Highlanders have grown quite attached to it. And come to think of it, so have a few unlucky Englishmen!" Lord Barclay chuckled at his pun, and Claymore joined in out of politeness. Then the older man sobered. "You're to be highly commended, my friend. Your sword is a beautiful and highly effective weapon. I've heard it bruited about that you and your four brothers are the only master craftsmen in the country who manufacture this type of weapon. Is it true?"

Anxious to ask his courtship question, Claymore fell into his normal burr. "Aye, my brothers and I are in business together and 'tis our design." He reached into the sporran hanging from his waist and took out a card he'd recently had a calligrapher design. It read:

> The Claymore Brothers
> Creators of The Claymore™
>
> Two-handed, double-edged silver blades sword
> Ideal for show or for an actual uprising
>
> Inverness, Scotland

Lord Barclay took the card from him, his eyes lighting up as he read the words. "A man with a job! A gainfully employed young man! A businessman, an artisan, and an entrepreneur all in one! What a concept! I love it. Indeed, my three sons need to take a few chapters from your book, Mr. Claymore. I believe a young man must have some type of meaningful occupation to capture his time and attention, do you not agree?"

But Claymore's patience was at an end. As the sound of his beautiful Antonía playing her harp drifted into the library, he was determined to get right to the heart of the matter, which, of course, was the matter of his heart. He turned to his convivial host and tried to be his most charming.

"Lord Barclay, forgive me for veering from the subject, but I have a request to make of you."

"Indeed? Well met, my friend, well met." Lord Barclay gestured with one hand. "What is it, good fellow?"

Mr. Claymore took a deep breath. "By your own estimation, I am a successful man, though not one of title. However, I am loyal and ambitious and would like to ask you and Lady Barclay to grant me the privilege and honor of courting your exquisitely beautiful daughter."

"Indeed, Mr. Claymore, you are a s-s-straight sh-shooter, aren't you?" stuttered Lord Barclay, clearly caught off guard by his guest's forthright approach to securing courtship privileges.

"Yes, sir," Claymore said. "I see no point in wasting time when I know exactly what I want, and the bottom line is I want to court your daughter." But remaining fully aware that what he wanted was in very high demand, he added, "After taking careful inventory, I can attest to the fact that the supply of young ladies of your daughter's extraordinary caliber proves extremely scarce. In fact, she's the one and only, and I have every intention of cornering the market."

"You're right, Mr. Claymore," Lord Barclay said. "When my daughter came of age, she attracted so many suitors that it created quite a stir here at the castle; however, while they were, on the whole, fine young men, not one amongst them possessed the strength of character necessary to match hers. Perhaps in a few years' time, with age and maturity, one of them will develop into that *one* worthy suitor. But as it stands presently, they prove far too weak of mind for a woman of my daughter's vitality."

"And so she has given up on marriage?" Claymore asked, trying to get a read on Miss Barclay's frame of mind. Surely she was not contemplating the life of a spinster, or—heaven help him—a nun!

Lord Barclay shrugged. "Antonía has her family, her horse, her harp, her best friend, and her books to keep her occupied. She requires no additional holds on happiness. However, she keeps her own counsel, so I'm never quite sure what she's thinking." After an audible sigh, he concluded, "Antonía is different from other young women, and I'm not saying this solely because she's my daughter."

"I believe you, Lord Barclay. I've never seen a more beautiful woman in my entire life." Claymore wanted to say more—wanted to confess that in one fell swoop he had been bewitched, beguiled, and bedazzled, not only by Miss Barclay's powerful beauty, but also by her equally powerful intellect. But the laird continued, his brows puckered above his ample nose.

"My daughter is beautiful, and so much more, but I think it only fair to warn you that she does have her foibles."

"Foibles?" Claymore frowned. As far as he was concerned, Miss Barclay was perfect.

Lord Barclay nodded. "Yes, my daughter is exceedingly strong willed. She thinks for herself and knows her own mind. She hates any type of social function, such as tonight's dinner party and tomorrow night's ball. She detests being told what to do, when to do it, or how to do it. She rarely expresses emotion." He paused, smiled, and then added, "But when she does, she does it very colorfully, indeed."

Lord Barclay's smile soon faded as he spoke again in a very earnest tone. "And lastly and most importantly, I must inform you that Antonía possesses a mysterious, indefinable quality that sets her apart from the rest of our family. I've yet to put my finger on it." He shook his head. "After nineteen years, I still cannot identify exactly what it is that makes her so different or what caused it. What I can tell you is that I feel certain she is destined for something of great consequence—something only a man of strong will and great love will be able to weather in their lives together."

"Aye," Claymore agreed. He had no doubt that Miss Barclay's destiny included greatness, and no doubt that his own strong will and great love were up to the task of weathering whatever came their way.

Lord Barclay rubbed his chin pensively and then peered into the other man's eyes.

"Now that you've been fully informed, do you still desire to court my daughter?"

"Yes, Lord Barclay," Claymore replied, "I still very much desire your daughter."

Lord Barclay raised one brow and his mouth relaxed into a smile. Claymore's face grew warm as he realized he'd omitted a very important infinitive from his eager response. He started to apologize, when the older man laughed and clapped him on the back.

"I admire a man of honesty and determination," he said, "as well as one who says exactly what he means and means exactly what he says."

"I am grateful for your kindness, m'lord," Claymore said. "And thank you for your understanding."

"And because of that," Lord Barclay went on, "and your other fine qualities such as your business acumen and the fact that Lady Barclay has given her approval"—he lifted one hand to his mouth in an aside—"not an easy thing to obtain, my boy—I hereby grant you our consent to court our daughter, contingent, of course, upon *her consent*. But please let me reiterate that Antonía can be . . ." He hesitated a moment as if searching for the right words and then finished "A great deal of work."

"Lord Barclay," Claymore said, unable to keep the excitement from his voice, "I am a man who thoroughly enjoys hard work."

Lord Barclay laughed. "In that case, I'm confident you'll be a happily challenged man because you most definitely have your work cut out for you." He again clasped the young man's muscular shoulder and added, "The only other sentiments I can offer are: good luck and caveat emptor."

Claymore grinned, but the twinkle in the laird's eyes suddenly struck him as a bit disconcerting. "My lord, your daughter cannot be that difficult to manage, can she? Are you certain you're not embellishing just a bit?"

Failing to laugh this go-round, Lord Barclay looked Mr. Claymore straight in the eye and said in a serious tone, "Let's get down to brass tacks, my good fellow. My daughter is exceptionally beautiful and, like most women of her station, she smells good and feels soft. *However*, she marches to the beat of a different set of bagpipes."

Claymore looked skeptical. "I cannot imagine Miss Barclay marching. And certainly not to bagpipes."

"Perhaps it is time for you to meet my daughter so you can form your own opinion. And, in any event, we may be rushing our fences. I don't intend to be cruel, but it wouldn't surprise me one iota if Antonía turns you down flat. My daughter has left a long trail of broken hearts in her wake."

But Mr. Claymore was not in the least haunted by the ghosts of the many men she'd sent packing. "My lord, I have no intention of lengthening the trail. I owe you a debt of gratitude for granting your consent."

In response, Lord Barclay massaged his chin meditatively, quaffed down his wine, and then stated soberly, "While I admire your optimism, Mr. Claymore, please remember that if Antonía does not grant you *her* consent, it's the end of the matter. Although both Lady Barclay and I extend our warmest approbations to you, we would never force a suitor upon our daughter."

"Yes, I completely understand and respect your position regarding your daughter. I will honor it without question," pledged Claymore. "Now, if I may take my leave—" He glanced over his shoulder toward the sound of harp music and the gorgeous object of his desire, still playing in the other room.

"Allow me to introduce you," Lord Barclay said, and added with a wry smile, "Who knows, it might be your lucky day."

Claymore followed him to the ballroom, impatient to set his eyes upon the woman who had so unexpectedly infiltrated his heart. Even if Miss Barclay were as strong willed as her father claimed, it mattered not. He was smitten beyond smitten. Nothing could deter him from winning her over.

Chapter 4

THE PHYSICALLY MAGNIFICENT
MR. CLAYMORE

Lord Barclay placed a gentle hand upon Antonía's shoulder. "Antonía darling," he entreated, "be my favorite daughter and allow me to introduce Mr. Claymore of Inverness, creator of fine swords."

With her head lowered in concentration, Antonía smiled; her father had no knowledge that she was already acquainted with Mr. Claymore. She continued to play but responded in a teasing voice.

"Lord Barclay, I thank you for your favor, but as far as I know, you don't have any other daughter in the world except for me. *However, if you do . . .*" She paused to execute a glissando and then concluded with a sly gleam in her eye, "Lady Barclay will no doubt darken your daylights."

Lord Barclay roared with such loud amusement that all eyes turned toward the source of the merriment and then landed upon Antonía, and after a moment shifted to Claymore standing by her side. There was a clamoring of talk and she sighed as she heard the observations of the crowd. She despised being the center of attention, but her father most assuredly relished it.

"Did I not warn you, Mr. Claymore," Lord Barclay said, after regaining his breath, "my daughter may play the harp in a heavenly manner, but she's certainly no angel!" He shook his finger at his daughter. "You should consider yourself very fortunate your mother wasn't standing beside me when you made that impertinent remark, young lady!"

"And you even more so, Father dear," replied his daughter who, having completed her piece, pushed back from the harp to greet Claymore.

As she rose from her seat, he offered his hand in assistance. In accordance with her normal attitude of contrariness toward all young men, Antonía had every intention of rejecting the proffered aid. However, he *had* helped her with Rex Throckmorton. And though she had thought him quite handsome and gallant, she knew her father—and her mother—no doubt had decided she should marry this man—this stranger. Well, she would have none of it. She would be polite and nothing more. Then she looked up and her eyes met Mr. Claymore's.

In a matter of seconds, she became so completely and overwhelmingly absorbed by the sight of him that she accepted his hand in a state of confused awe. Overcome by a combination of joy and disbelief, she felt her world turn over. A hundred other men had been unable to reach her, but with one look, with one gesture, he'd succeeded where the rest had failed. He had reached across the chasm, pulling her toward him, bridging the gap and locking them together.

She felt the completeness. She felt their oneness. Slowly rising to her full height, she remained in a state of flustered silence as Mr. Claymore smiled down at her. At last, a man she could look up to.

"Miss Barclay," he said with a slight bow, "I am honored to make your acquaintance at last. I have waited all evening to meet you." He gave her a conspiratorial wink, teasing her with the memory of being held in his arms.

Antonía's frantic brain scrambled for words, anything, some kind of phrase, even a simple platitude would do, but nothing would formulate—not even a monosyllabic response, much less a full, complete sentence.

This was an unmitigated disaster. Here was the man she wanted, the man she needed, the one and only man to whom she'd joyously and gratefully relinquish her maidenhood, but tragically, she was incapable of uttering a single word of the King's English. Or the Queen's English. Or English of any variety, royal or not. In fact, she was incapable of uttering a single, solitary peep.

In spite of the fact that Antonía's mouth failed to work properly, her eyes were in perfect operating order. Their gazes still locked, she instantly recognized the color of her eyes in his—how had she missed that before?

But there was much more to the windows of his soul than their hue. Indeed, they radiated kindness, warmth, sincerity, and twinkled with life. All signs indicated that Claire *had* gotten it right this time. The luck of the third attempt had proven the charm.

It was equally apparent that Mr. Claymore was much more than simply a handsome face and a hot body. His every mannerism bespoke openness, honesty, and integrity. In fact, within the space of a single epiphanous moment, Antonía perceived with perfect clarity that Mr. Claymore was the epitome of all the good things a woman might seek in a man.

So seldom is quiet dignity superadded to magnificent male musculature.

Lord Barclay cleared his throat. Antonía glanced at her fidgeting father and saw he had misconstrued her silence for abject disapproval. No doubt he was convinced she was about to hand this honorable young man his walking papers—as she had done to so many men before him.

But her father needn't have worried, because rejecting Mr. Claymore was the last thing on her mind. The man of her dreams leaned toward her to speak, when all at once Antonía saw Oliver and Matthew approaching in haste. Flatly refusing to sacrifice a single second of her time with Mr. Claymore to her brothers, or for that matter, to anyone, she swallowed her pride and prejudice and ordered her vocal cords to work.

"Mr. Claymore, would you please take a walk in the gardens with me?" she asked in a low voice, her cheeks flushed with her temerity.

Mr. Claymore's mouth curved into an even broader smile, and he lifted her hand to his lips before replying, "I was just about to suggest such a thing. I have been sitting far too long tonight." Without further ceremony, he turned and guided Antonía out of the dining room and into the moonlit gardens.

Antonía glanced back over her shoulder and saw the disgruntled looks on her brothers' faces. She could read the two of them like a book: No sister of theirs was going to amble about the castle grounds with a man *they* barely knew! She scowled at the duo, but she needn't have bothered. Lady Barclay positioned all one hundred and two pounds of her petite figure in front of her sons, hands on hips, and with complete and utter effectiveness, foiled their plan.

Antonía breathed a sigh of relief as she and Mr. Claymore walked through the huge double doors leading into the moonlit gardens of Barclay Castle. Although sheer desperation had fully restored Antonía's lingual powers, she remained quiet and reserved as Mr. Claymore led her through hedges of lush shrubbery and down rows of fragrant lavender. He paused to look up at the brilliant moon, and in a deep and increasingly familiar voice broke the silence.

"Miss Barclay, may I ask you a question?"

"Certainly, Mr. Claymore."

The moonlight touched his eyes and they sparkled in the darkness. "Were you riding near Deerfield early this morning?"

Miss Barclay frowned. This was the last thing she expected her new suitor to ask. "Yes," she said.

"And were you dressed in attire befitting a stable boy?"

"Yes, I'm afraid so, Mr. Claymore," she admitted, feeling her cheeks grow hot. Apparently Oliver's criticism had been right on the mark.

"And were you riding at a relatively high rate of speed, Miss Barclay?"

Really, was this what had been on his mind as he gazed at her so lovingly only moments before? She sighed and turned slightly away from him. "Relative to?" she asked, unable to keep the irritation from her voice.

"Relative to a sane person, Miss Barclay."

Now realizing the man was toying with her, she turned back to him. "Mr. Claymore, do you intend to be like my brothers and berate me for my riding apparel as well as my brisk pace?"

The humor left his face. He took her gently by the shoulders and bent his head to hers, his lips brushing her ear. "Miss Barclay, I promise you, my feelings for you are as far from brotherly as they could possibly be."

His gaze caressed her with such deep and open passion that for a moment she feared she might faint and end up face down in the aromatic herbs. Tenderly brushing her hair back from her face, Mr. Claymore confessed, "I'm extremely relieved to learn that the rider I saw this morning was *you*, Miss Barclay."

Recovering her breath, she asked in almost a whisper, "And why is that, sir?"

He grinned down at her. "Because I'd be seriously worried if I found myself falling in love with a stable boy."

She gasped and immediately felt as if she had taken a breath of the cool air at sunrise on one of her morning rides. Had she heard the magnificent Mr. Claymore correctly? Perhaps the omega-3 fatty acids from the salmon buffet had created this delightful sensation? Perhaps it was the brain-pleasing endorphins generated from strolling in the gardens? Perhaps it was the heady scent of pheromones emanating from this unbelievably handsome man? Or perhaps this overpowering, dizzying sense of well-being was caused by a confluence of all three factors? Whatever the reason, a heavenly blend of bliss now hummed happily through Miss Barclay's system.

Mr. Claymore searched her eyes with care and asked, "Miss Barclay, are you feeling unwell?"

Giving him a smile that he would later learn meant very good things for him indeed, she answered, "On the contrary, Mr. Claymore, I feel exceedingly well."

"Are you certain I haven't frightened you with my bold intentions?"

"Sir, you do many things to me, but frightening me is categorically *not* one of them."

Mr. Claymore took both her hands in his and gazed down at them, hesitating, looking as though he was trying to work up the nerve to say—or ask—something.

At last, he lifted his eyes to hers again. "Miss Barclay, may I ask you another question?"

"You may, Mr. Claymore," she replied, inclining her head.

But interruption was so very inevitable and so very predictable. Antonía turned at the sound of her twin brother's thundering command, "I say, Antonía, don't move a muscle! We need a word with you and Claymore." A brother's vociferous and unwelcome intrusion invariably proves to be a buzzkill to an otherwise exceedingly romantic interlude. Mr. Claymore, in particular, was very unappreciative, and reluctantly released her hands.

Claire stood between Matthew and Oliver, wearing an extremely apologetic expression upon her pretty face. "I told them it was of no consequence," she said, giving Oliver a look of irritation and a slightly less perturbed one to Matthew. "I'm so sorry to interrupt, but my parents are leaving soon. They need a good night's sleep to prepare for the ball at Deerfield tomorrow night."

"That's right," barked Oliver. "And since Mr. Claymore came to dinner with the MacMillans, he must leave with them as well."

Ignoring her brother, Mr. Claymore smiled at Claire. "Thank you, Miss MacMillan. Please tell your parents I will join them in just a few minutes. I will not keep them waiting."

Antonía watched gratefully as her best friend took her brothers by the arms and steered them back inside.

"I'm so sorry for the interruption, Mr. Claymore," she said. "You were about to ask me a question?"

He smiled. "Aye, m'lady," he said with a little bow. "Will you—would you—meet me at Deerfield Pond early tomorrow morning?"

She had never wanted anything more in her life. But an unchaperoned tryst? Her brothers would be fit to be tied if they found out. All the more reason to say yes.

Arching one brow, she smiled. "Wild horses couldn't stop me, Mr. Claymore." There was a noise at the double doors. Glancing over, Antonía saw all three of her brothers now, staring out at the spot where she and Claymore stood. Realizing tomorrow awaited, she was willing to give up the fight for the night. She smiled and bowed her head slightly. "It's late. I must say good night."

He once again embraced her hands, straightened, and moved closer, clasping her fingers as if they were precious gold. As Antonía looked up at him, his blue eyes blazed with a flame that went right through her.

"To be perfectly honest, Miss Barclay," he said, "the only good nights I'll ever have are the ones spent with you wrapped in my arms." With one hand he caressed the high slant of her cheek and whispered tenderly, "Sweet dreams, my darling Miss Barclay. The morning sun cannot possibly rise early enough for me." He took a step back and let her hands slip from his. Before she could gather her wits to return his sentiments, he was gone.

Looking out over the lush landscape of the MacMillans' Deerfield estate, Sir Basil's mind percolated with thoughts of power and lust, and his lust for power synchronized perfectly with his lust for Antonía Barclay. Basil Throckmorton had learned long ago that setting goals and obtaining them, no matter the cost, was the most effective method of achieving power. And if his carnal desires just happened to mesh with his high ambitions, so much the better, he thought, throwing his cape around his shoulders in one fluid motion.

The sun was streaming across the balcony where he stood, but a strong north wind made the morning air brisk. A swiftly moving figure came into his line of vision, catching his attention at once. Placing his teacup on the ledge of the balcony, Sir Basil focused his black eyes intently on the figure riding away from the estate. He recognized the rider almost immediately as one of the other houseguests—Breck Claymore.

Now what business could a lazy Highlander possibly have at this early hour of the day? Surely it was not a proper time of day for Claymore to peddle his wares. Those types of people never did, and never would, have a sense of propriety. He continued to observe his subject, who'd stopped his horse not far from the large pond located on the northeast side of the estate. With the summer sun rising steadily, Throckmorton was forced to turn his head away, and as he did, the answer struck him.

Claymore's business was Miss Barclay. Evidently he'd arranged to meet her for a morning rendezvous. Resuming his surveillance, Throckmorton fixed a sharp eye on the Highlander while contemplating the luscious Miss Barclay. Assembling his observations of her from the previous evening, Sir Basil then sorted and processed them through his highly analytical mind.

Antonía Barclay was extraordinarily beautiful, highly intelligent, and vivacious. However, there was also an air about her that defied description. The young woman's lofty stature, natural elegance, and acerbic wit were matched by only one other woman he'd ever known in his forty-nine years on earth.

True to his alchemistic training, Throckmorton challenged every assumption that he knew about Miss Barclay. With a vigilant eye still cast on the Highlander, he ran through his list of assumptions and compared them to the empirical data. In a matter of seconds, he arrived at the only possible explanation. And the only possible explanation meant that a major assumption about the exquisite Antonía Barclay was completely and totally false. What was thought to be fact was, in truth, fiction.

Sir Basil's mouth twisted into a nefarious smile. Not only would his lust for Miss Barclay mesh with his lust for power, it would catapult him to the most powerful position in England and arguably the world. But he wouldn't go off half-cocked. With his cool clinician's eye, he would continue to observe and evaluate for a certain period of time—and then, tapping into his inherent risk-taking nature—he would ultimately mastermind the greatest political coup the world had ever known. To hell with that pock-faced bitch of a queen! He would take down the English monarchy once and for all!

A loud rap on the door interrupted his hubristic machinations. Throckmorton didn't bother responding. His son rarely asked for permission.

True enough, Rex Throckmorton came barreling into the bedroom and, spotting something out the window, charged past his father to the balcony before returning to his father to report old news.

"Claymore's down near the pond."

"Thank you, Rex," replied his father coolly. "I have my eye on him, or should I say, I had my eye on him. If you'd be so kind as to take a step to your left."

Rex was outraged. "If I did that, I'd fall off the balcony!"

If only, thought his father. But realizing he needed his blunder-headed son for his dirty work, he explained and pointed in the correct direction, "I meant take a step to your other left. You're blocking my view of Claymore."

"Oh, yeah." After moving out of the way, Rex demanded, "Well? What are we going to do about him?"

"Nothing for the time being. The man hasn't done anything."

"Are you kidding?" bellowed his son.

"Rex, when have you ever known me to jest?"

"But you saw them together last night! Claymore was all over her!"

Weaving the web, Throckmorton asked, "And who does 'her' refer to?"

"ANTONÍA BARCLAY!"

"Thank you, Rex, but I'm not deaf."

"But I think you must be blind! Can't you see that he wants her?" Frustrated, Rex rubbed his bald head. "I swear to God, I'm going to kill that stupid Highlander. He's after her, and I want her!"

"And why do you want her, Rex?" asked Sir Basil calmly.

"Why the hell do you think I want her?" raged Rex.

"Now, Rex, what have I told you about answering a question with a question?"

"WELL, SHITE! Isn't that what you just did?" Rex's typically milk toast–colored face was now a vibrant shade of fuchsia.

"Only in the pursuit of bettering your verbal skills." But having had his fun, he decided not to antagonize his volatile son further. "Compose yourself, Rex, and then, as concisely as possible, expound on your intentions regarding Miss Barclay."

"I want to bed her, of course!"

"I suppose I asked for that," mumbled Sir Basil under his breath. And then looking into his son's face as closely as possible without getting sick, he remarked, "Miss Barclay would make any man a good wife. Have you ever considered getting married, Rex?"

"You mean I should ask Antonía to marry me?"

"No, of course not," Throckmorton said. And then in a sterner voice, he reminded his son, "We're English. We don't *ask*! We *take* what we want!"

Rex's blubbery lips curled upward. "You don't have to tell me twice. I'm on my way." He then turned a hefty shoulder toward his father.

But Sir Basil stiff-armed him. "Not yet. We need to gather more intelligence and then formulate a plan before we take her. Patience is a virtue."

"Since when have you become religious? Have you gone mad?" demanded Rex.

"In a manner of speaking, but I assure you there's a method to my madness." And then stepping closer to the edge of the balcony, he sighted another figure in the distance, riding toward the Highlander.

It was none other than the beauteous Miss Barclay.

From Breck Claymore's perspective, it took the sun *forever* to rise over the softly rolling hills of Southern Scotland. He had never slept less or felt better for it. In fact, he had never looked forward to a new day with such unbridled enthusiasm.

Unable to wait any longer, he had left for Deerfield long before dawn, and had sat astride his horse for what seemed like hours, trying to keep his impatience under control. When the sun finally did make an appearance, it did it in style, beckoning the day with a soft array of pastel colors and a light flutter of westerly winds. And that's when he spotted Miss Barclay rounding the pond on the back of a russet gelding. He set heels to his horse and rode to meet her.

"Well, if it isn't my favorite stable boy out for an early morning ride," he said, pulling up beside her, absorbing the heavenly sight.

Miss Barclay said nothing, only gazed at the panorama of the sunrise behind him.

Confused by her quietude, Mr. Claymore tried again. "You look astonishingly well this morning. In fact, Miss Barclay, I've never seen anyone look more *well*."

She winced.

"Miss Barclay, are you wincing in disappointment at my facetiously poor grammar?"

"Not at all, sir," she said, smiling. "I would never wince in disappointment at the sound of your voice, no matter how terrible your grammar might be."

Claymore moved his horse as close to hers as possible and placed his hand gently over hers. "I would sooner die than ever disappoint you, my darling Miss Barclay." He then searched her eyes, hoping the longing he'd seen there the night before had not been simply his own desire reflected back at him. Her lips parted and she breathed in a sharp breath of air, swaying slightly in the saddle. Alarmed, Claymore settled a steadying hand around her waist.

"It's all right," she said, her other hand covering his. "Sometimes your eyes—" she broke off and looked down at their clasped hands.

"Aye?" he offered softly, nudging his horse closer to hers.

She smiled up at him, but fell silent again.

Claymore felt his heart soar at her words, and, glancing back at the Deerfield estate, made a suggestion he hoped would not send her galloping away. "Shall we ride to the other side of the pond? It would be a bit more . . . private. I never had the chance to ask my question last night."

"Oh, I thought the question was if I would meet you here this morning." She slid him a knowing look under lowered lashes. "Was there another question?"

"Aye," he said, fighting the urge to kiss her senseless. "One more."

She threw her beautiful head back and laughed, then arched one brow and threw down the gauntlet. "Very well then, I'll race you there—that is, if you're game."

Minutes later they reached their destination, with Antonía in the lead. She pulled up on the reins as her horse thundered to a stop, with Mr. Claymore beside her, only seconds behind.

"I suppose you're going to say you let me win?" she asked, mischief in her eyes.

"Not at all, Miss Barclay, but I must confess to being blinded by the early morning sun as well as by your equally blinding beauty."

She looked upward, biting her lower lip as if trying to decide his fate. "Blindness," she said at last, "whatever the cause, is a legitimate excuse, sir, so I will, very magnanimously, call our little race a tie."

"You are too good and too generous to me, Miss Barclay," he remarked, all the while longing to hold her in his arms and kiss her with all the passion he felt for her. But committed to honoring his self-imposed rule—no consent, no kiss—Mr. Claymore suppressed, and quite admirably, his insatiable desire to reach over and do the deed.

"Mr. Claymore," she said, her voice hushed, "I have yet to demonstrate to you the full range of both my goodness and my generosity. Given the right set of circumstances, I could be very accommodating."

This time it was Claymore who almost toppled off his horse. Steam began to rise from the pond's glistening surface as the Scottish sun rose above the hills. Had he heard her correctly? More importantly, had he interpreted her meaning correctly? Was this glorious summer day heating up extraordinarily quickly or was it just his imagination?

But no, it was neither the weather nor his imagination. Every square inch of him felt the intensity of Miss Barclay's scorching heat, but despite his desire, the honorable Mr. Claymore beat down his passion and instead addressed the very necessary, but highly unpleasant, subject of the Throckmortons.

He had spent half the night dreaming of Antonía's lips on his, and the other half worrying about the altercation he'd interrupted in the hallway between Rex Throckmorton and the woman he loved. Claymore had been too smitten by the thought of courting Antonía to dwell upon the unpleasant event, but now he knew he must speak of it. Claymore hated to mention the topic at all, but the Throckmortons were extremely treacherous Englishmen.

Claymore threw his right leg over the saddle and slid to the ground, then moved to help Antonía from her horse. She stood within his arms once again, and he yearned to touch his lips to hers. But not yet. He took a step back and thought he saw disappointment in her eyes.

"Miss Barclay, before I ask my question from last night, I must ask another first."

She lifted her chin and he saw the playful spark in her gaze. "Are all Highlanders so inquisitive, Mr. Claymore?"

He despised having to break the mood, but he had no choice. "It's about Rex Throckmorton." Antonía widened her eyes. "Is there *more* to the story?" he asked gently. "I assumed when I walked up to you in the hallway before dinner last night that Throckmorton had just arrived. But now I'm wondering if I was wrong." She looked away from him, and Claymore's heart began to pound. "Antonía," he said, "did Rex Throckmorton hurt you in any way?"

"No," she replied, with a shake of her head. "You arrived just in time, Mr. Claymore. I promise you."

"You mean, you think he would have harmed you?"

Claymore saw her jaw tighten and he was suddenly filled with a furious need to kill Rex Throckmorton.

Then she laughed, tossing her dark head as if she hadn't a care in the world. "Who can say what an Englishman might or might not do, Mr. Claymore?" She turned back to him, an impish smile on her face. "*Must* we ruin our morning by discussing Englishmen? Isn't it enough that I had to endure sitting between two of them at dinner last night?"

She laughed again, but then her beautiful smile fell as she began to shake, and she looked up at him, dismayed.

"Antonía . . ." he said, moving to take her in his arms.

"You must think I'm a hopeless neurotic," she whispered against his linen shirt. "I wouldn't blame you if you left and headed back to the Highlands, just to get away from me!"

Claymore stroked her hair and felt her relax against him. "Everything's all right now, my darling Miss Barclay. I'm here and I'll *never* let anyone frighten or hurt you ever again. I will always take care of you." Her trembling gradually abated and they held one another.

But not surprisingly, with their story set against the backdrop of sixteenth-century Scotland, peace and harmony never lasted for long. In the distance, two riders could be heard, and then seen, thundering toward them at a speedy clip. Glancing over his shoulder to identify the interlopers, Claymore was forced to release his tight hold on Miss Barclay. He took a few steps toward the riders to get a better look and shook his head in disbelief. "Speak of the devils," he said under his breath.

But when he turned back to warn his darling Miss Barclay, she was gone. More specifically, she had mounted her horse, jumped the burn, and was galloping full speed back toward Barclay Castle.

Claymore mounted his own horse and rode hell-bent for leather to intercept the Throckmortons.

Entering the castle as unobtrusively as possible, hoping to avoid any and all questioning by any and all caring parents and annoying brothers, Antonía had *almost* made safe passage to the foot of the staircase when she was caught by her mother, who had been reading her brothers the riot act in the morning sitting room.

"Antonía darling, we're in the sitting room. Come join us, please," she called out.

Knowing she had no choice other than to obey her maternal authority, Antonía inwardly uttered her favorite curse word while outwardly accepting the inevitable. "Good morning, Mother," she said pleasantly, though yearning to take refuge in the privacy of her bedchamber.

"Good day to you, my darling daughter," replied Lady Barclay. "Please allow me a moment to dispense with your brothers before we have a nice chat." She continued her diatribe as Antonía reluctantly entered the room.

"How many times," Lady Barclay said to the three grown men seated on the elegant sofa across from her, "do I have to tell you boys that there will be no strange noises during or after meals, no sweaty, dirty clothes on the floor, no use of colorful language, no weapons at the dinner table, no drinking in excess, and positively no womanizing under my roof!"

Antonía hid a smile behind her hand as her brothers twitched and rolled their eyes and generally acted like the children her mother was scolding.

"*And,*" she said as their faces continued to twist and pucker, "may I say that if you keep crossing your eyes in such an unbecoming manner and making such contorted grimaces, your faces are likely to stick that way, and I daresay it'll serve you right. In any event, you are all fortunate that your father is occupied with Mr. MacMillan this morning, or he'd add his two pence as well. Now, go clean your chambers and leave me with your sister."

The fraternal threesome pretty much fell all over each other in their mad rush to exit the room. Lady Barclay, who remained as poised and serene as if she'd never borne three rowdy sons, poured two cups of piping hot tea and handed one to her daughter. Antonía sat down on the deserted divan, suddenly aware of her dusty "stable boy" clothing and took a nervous sip from her cup.

"How is our Mr. Claymore this morning, darling?"

How in the world had her mother known about their rendezvous? Antonía wondered, but not wishing a discussion, much less a lengthy one, she responded with a blunt, "Fine."

"Did you grant him your consent?"

"Consent to what?" Antonía asked, frowning in confusion.

"Oh dear, I've spoken out of turn," said Lady Barclay. "I hadn't intended to jump the gun, but now that the cat is out of the bag—" She sighed and took a drink of her tea, as Antonía's suspicions deepened.

"Mother, what have you done?"

"I?" She gave a deprecating little laugh. "I have done nothing, my dear Antonía. It was all your father's doing."

"Father?" The thought of what her father might have done made Antonía's head spin. The man was extremely generous, but a bit eccentric. "Mother, what has my father done? Tell me!"

"Goodness, don't get yourself in a twirl. It's wonderful news, actually. Last night, Mr. Claymore asked your father for our consent to court you. Since both your father and I regard him with the utmost respect and esteem, we granted our consent, *but only* if you grant yours as well. Your father and I would never insist you accept a man you don't want."

Relief flooded through Antonía. She took another sip of her tea as the implications of her mother's announcement sank into her soul.

Her mother frowned. "Antonía darling, aren't you excited? The most desirable bachelor in all of Scotland seeks your hand and yet you remain apparently unmoved, untouched by the news." She shook her head, looking quite resigned to her daughter's stoicism. Antonía continued to contemplate her cup of tea, but hearing her mother sigh, she finally spoke, if only to relieve her misery.

"Mother," she said, expressionless, "of course I am delighted that Mr. Claymore asked yours and father's consent. However, he has not asked *mine*. Don't you find that rather odd? Perhaps he's changed his mind." She covered her mouth to suppress a sudden, overpowering yawn.

Good heavens, thought Lady Barclay, stirring her tea. *I can squeeze more emotion out of my tea bag than out of my own daughter. Where does the girl keep her heart? In an iron vault? I ask her about Mr. Claymore and what does she do? She says only that he's fine and questions his intentions! Indeed, I'd have to be blind not to see that he's the finest young specimen of manhood I've ever seen. I afford her the perfect opportunity to gush about his physical magnificence, his open and amiable disposition, his good humor, his wit, his intelligence, his relaxed and disarming manner, his exorbitant wealth, his artistic talent, his business acumen, and most significantly, his obvious and ardent love for her, and what does she do? She yawns in response!*

"Mother . . ."

Has the girl no depth of feeling? No passion? No heart? Is she not the least bit excited that Mr. Claymore wishes to court her? If I were in her shoes, I'd be swinging from the chandeliers with joy!

Antonía rose and crossed to her mother's side, resting one hand upon her shoulder. "So often is martyrdom superadded to motherhood," she said in a doleful tone.

Lady Barclay sighed. "Indeed."

"When and if he asks, I shall consider his request," she said. "However," she gestured to her clothes, "I must bathe before my brothers find reason to complain of my hygiene again."

"Oh, Mr. Claymore will ask. There is no doubt about that," Lady Barclay told her, sounding disgruntled. "Your response is the only thing I'm worried about."

Antonía had had enough. She moved away from her mother and walked toward the door, but Lady Barclay wasn't quite finished with her.

"Before you barricade yourself in your bedroom, Antonía," she said, "please visit Minnie. I don't know the reason, but she wishes very much to speak with you."

Chapter 5

A MUNRO,
A CORBETT,
AND A GRAHAM

"Of course, Mother," she said and, with a polite smile, walked slowly out of the room until she reached the stairs. She then ran with unladylike fervor up to her room to the bath awaiting her. She had told her maid the night before to have a tub filled with water in the morning at eleven o'clock.

Just in case her mother changed her mind and called her back for further lambasting, Antonía flung off her riding clothes, jumped into the tub, and was bathed, toweled, and dressed in clothing more suitable for a lady in a matter of about forty minutes. She certainly didn't want to smell like the inside of a barn, and she entertained the distinct possibility that her brothers were more right than wrong on that particular issue. Seldom though they were, it was very annoying when her brothers were right. She braided her hair until her maid could attend to it, gathered her deliveries for Minnie, and walked the long hallway to the south turret.

Although the bath and fresh clothing had initially reinvigorated her, the feeling didn't last long, for no sooner had Antonía stepped into Minnie's warm, cozy room than she felt the sharp claws of fatigue scrape the spirit right out of her.

"Ducky, good to see you at long last. Where've you been all morning?" asked the old nanny, sitting and knitting beside the window.

"Out riding," she replied, suppressing a yawn.

"Aye, and I see you've brought me some therapeutic tobacco," observed Minnie. "I'm dying for a puff! But what are you holding in your other hand, ducky?"

"It's King James's report on the health risks and immorality of smoking tobacco."

"Is that so? Well, in that case, I'll just have to eat it instead, won't I?" After a hearty laugh followed by a consumptive cough, she added, "Toss the bag over to me, ducky."

Antonía handed over the contraband and flipped through the report as Minnie tamped a goodly amount of tobacco into her pipe and lit it.

"According to the king," Antonía said, "not all of the causes of consumption are known. Several environmental factors have been implicated, but evidence of a causative role exists only for *tobacco use.*" She looked up, awaiting her nanny's response.

Merrily dragging on her pipe, Minnie completely ignored her.

"You *did* ask me for scientific proof, remember?" Antonía prodded.

"Aye, but from what institute of higher education did our moral-minded mini-monarch receive his medical degree?"

"Good point," agreed Antonía, chucking the king's report into the dying fire. She collapsed in a chair next to her nanny. "Minnie, how many people do you know who are polydactyl? More precisely, people who have six fingers?"

The old woman eyed her suspiciously. "Is this a riddle, ducky, or are you trying to drive me deeper into senile dementia?"

"Neither, but if you're knitting a glove, you have one too many fingers going on there."

"Oh, dammit to hell!" Minnie cried. "Why do I torture myself with this absurd hobby? I've been trying to knit for over thirty years and I still can't get the knack of it!" The old nanny shook her head in disgust and, after taking another long drag on her pipe, threw her handiwork—needles and all—into the busy fireplace.

Antonía ducked to avoid dying young. "Being impaled by knitting needles is not how I envisioned my future."

Minnie laughed. "Aye, ducky, you always bolster my spirits!" She lit her dying pipe again and inhaled deeply and gratefully. "Being old is a crashing bore. Enliven my world! Tell me all about your Mr. Claymore."

Antonía groaned. "My mother told you, didn't she? I just left her a few minutes ago so I should've known."

"My word, you're a tough one, ducky! Let me guess—your good mother made yet another valiant attempt at a mother-daughter chat, and you promptly shot her down like a flock of low-flying geese."

Antonía nodded her head. "Why does she even bother, Minnie?"

"Aye, a very good question, and I have a very good answer. Your mother will never stop trying because she loves you with all her heart."

She sighed. "I know she does. And I love her."

"Well then, ducky, though the two of you have very different temperaments, can't you show your good mother a wee bit of compassion and throw her a crumb every so often?"

Antonía considered her suggestion for a moment and then shook her head. "I know I sound hard-hearted, Minnie, but here's the situation: If I did as you suggest, she'd only want more and it would never be enough. Eventually Mum would transform me into one of those women who sits around talking about their feelings, their fortunes, their social rank, their connections, and, God forbid, their clothes."

Minnie cackled. "Aye, ducky, that doesn't sound like your cup of tea at all."

Antonía tossed her old nanny a grin. "That's right—and do you know why?"

"I'll bite. Why?"

She reached over and gave the old woman's hand a squeeze. "Because I want to be just like *you* when I grow up—smoking a pipe, drinking whiskey, knitting misshapen gloves, and giving terrible advice."

"Aye, lass, then you do, indeed, aspire to greatness!"

They shared a good laugh until all at once Minnie grew sober. "Ducky, I need to be a wee bittie serious for a moment."

Antonía muffled a yawn and forced her heavy eyes wide open. "Then you must speak quickly, for I am dead on my feet."

Pipe in hand, Minnie sat back in her chair. "When I nipped down to the party last night, your father informed me that you and Mr. Claymore had already retired to the gardens. He also told me that the Throckmortons had left rather abruptly."

Another yawn. Goodness, but she was tired this morning! "The father's not bad," Antonía said, "but the son's a complete louse—he accosted me in the hall and insulted me over supper."

"That blaggart!" Minnie shouted. "Now listen, ducky—"

A sharp rap at the door interrupted Minnie, followed by the entrance of Antonía's brother Will looking all aflutter, or as aflutter as a man could look.

"I say, sister dear," said Will, without as much as a glance in her direction, "where did you put the king's antismoking report I loaned you?"

"It's in the fireplace, dear mannerless brother," Antonía said.

"In the fireplace!" he cried. "I have a conference with the king the day after tomorrow and I must return it. It's his only copy!"

"Sorry, Will, I didn't know, but it should be sitting right on top of the peat if you want to look." He rushed over to the smoking fire and grabbed the poker from the hearth.

Minnie laughed. "The king owes your sister an enormous debt of gratitude," she said. "Chucking that piece of rubbish into the fire was the only way to turn it into hot property!"

"I will pretend I did not hear you say such a thing, Minnie," Will said, still poking amidst the peat. All at once he dropped to his knees. "Eureka!" he cried. "Here it is, in its entirety! It's somewhat singed but otherwise intact." His attention shifted from the parchment in his hand and back to the fireplace. "But wait—what else do we have here?"

He used the poker and lifted something from the smoking peat. Two somethings. "Look at this! Gloves with six fingers apiece. Good heavens, what luck! This is the perfect pair of gloves for the king. He'll be overjoyed to receive them."

Antonía frowned at her brother. "Whatever in the world are you talking about?"

"Didn't you know?"

Antonía looked at Minnie and they both shrugged. Will took the gloves from the poker and shook them in their direction, dirt and ashes flying toward the women.

"Oddly enough, the king has six fingers on each hand," he explained.

"The six-fingered man," Minnie's voice was hushed. "Where have I heard that before?"

"I'm sure I don't know," Antonía said. Leave it to her nanny to make some great mystery out of something so simple. She looked around for something to distract her with and her gaze fell upon a bowl on the bedside table. "Anybody want a peanut?" Minnie greedily took the bowl as Antonía turned to her brother. "Isn't it quite bizarre for someone— anyone—to have six fingers? Let alone the king?"

It was Will's turn to shrug. "You know how royalty is."

The nanny and sister paused to exchange glances, and after a brief sweep of the second hand, the light finally dawned. Inbreeding.

Will clasped the precious paper and gloves to his chest, bowed to the two women, and let himself out.

"Now that he's gone," Antonía said, rising from the chair and crossing to the fire, "what is bothering you?" She turned to face the nanny, and Minnie's hand stilled in the bowl of peanuts. "I know you're fretting about something, so why don't you save us both a lot of time and trouble and tell me what's on your mind."

Minnie gave her a startled look and grabbed the glass of whiskey at her side, tossing the liquid back like water, almost as if she were fortifying herself for some great endeavor.

"Very well. I must ask you a very serious question." She paused and then rushed on, her voice sounding shaky, something quite unusual for the tough old bird. "Did you wear your hair up or down last night, ducky?"

Antonía blinked. That was not at all the question she had expected. She'd assumed Minnie's nosy nature would cause her to ask something personal about Mr. Claymore, such as, had he yet kissed her? Now, bewildered by the irrelevance of the query, she answered, her brows knit together. "I wore my hair up. Why?"

Minnie was shaking her head. "Are you planning to wear your hair in an updo again tonight?"

Deciding her old confidant had slipped even further into senility, Antonía tried to remain patient. "No, Minnie, I'm going to wear my hair down. I don't want the Throckmortons gawking over my birthmark again."

The old woman's mouth dropped open. "They saw it then?" Without waiting for an answer, she hurried on. "Antonía," she demanded, with uncharacteristic terseness, "where is your mother?"

"Minnie, whatever is wrong with you?"

"Where is your mother, ducky?"

"She and Father are already at Deerfield helping Claire's parents prepare for the ball. Why?"

"I would rather consult your mother first," Minnie said, rising from her chair and straightening her backbone, "however there is no time and I have no choice. There is no one but a tubercular, chain-smoking, whiskey-loving old nanny to tell you the truth, and tell you I must!"

She began pacing around the room, her shakiness having turned to strength somehow as she muttered to herself. "Damn! And no tobacco to help me through it. I shouldn't have puffed it all away in one sitting! Now I have no alternative but to inhale a depressingly clean breath of air and get on with my story."

"Minnie!" Antonía folded her arms across her chest. "Either tell me or don't. I have a great deal to do before tonight."

The nanny hurried to her side. "Ducky, you must listen to me well and do not interrupt until I'm finished," Minnie said in such a sepulchral tone that Antonía was certain she was about to be told she was being sent away to a nunnery. But, dutifully complying with her wishes, Antonía sat down on the hearth and listened closely while the old woman unraveled her strange tale, continuing to pace.

"There's no time to cushion the blow with sentimental slop," she began, "so I'm just going to spit it out directly, as is my way. You are *not* the biological daughter of Lord and Lady Barclay. Your true biological mother is the imprisoned Mary, Queen of Scots, and your true biological father is the late Lord Bothwell."

Antonía jumped to her feet, her eyes growing wide in horror. "What? Minnie, you have gone mad from too much tobacco and whiskey!"

Minnie shook her head. "If only 'twere true," she said with a sigh and then straightened her shoulders, facing Antonía. "You were born on a small island a bit north of here called Lochleven. It was a time of great political upheaval and social unrest. Your mother's reign was quickly coming to a tragic end, and she was duped into seeking the support of her English cousin, Queen Elizabeth.

"As the annals of these tumultuous times will someday report, Queen Elizabeth showed her cousinly support by imprisoning your mother in a succession of English prisons. She still resides in one to this day. Your father, James Hepburn, Fourth Earl of Bothwell, suffered a far more horrendous fate. Thrown into a Danish prison, he was tied to a post half his height and slowly tortured to death. He died some eight years ago."

Antonía felt suddenly faint and sat back down on the hearth. Why would Minnie tell her such a tale? Apparently encouraged by her silence, the old nanny plowed ahead with her narrative. To her credit, there was pain in the bleary old eyes and it was obvious that this was not a story she had been eager to share.

"Fully realizing her reign was doomed, the queen feared for the life of her unborn child—you, Antonía. So she sought the help of her dearest friend—Lady Barclay. Ducky, they had been friends for many years prior to the queen's imprisonment. Although no explicit statements were made, Lady Barclay, who was also expecting a child, offered to help Queen Mary protect her newborn in all ways possible."

Minnie's shoulders sagged then, and she paused as if gathering her strength. When she spoke again, her voice was somber.

"The fact that you and Oliver were born within mere hours of each other was a manifestation of divine intervention. Two hours after you were born, Queen Mary instructed me to take you to Lady Barclay."

"You?"

She nodded. "Aye. Before I was your nanny, I was your mother Mary's." Tears welled up in Minnie's eyes, putting Antonía's last doubts to rest. The girl stood and crossed to her, putting her arm around Minnie's bony shoulders as the old woman continued. "When I arrived at Barclay Castle, Oliver had been born only a few hours prior to your birth. According to the attending midwife, Lady Barclay had endured an excruciatingly painful labor and fallen unconscious soon after Oliver was delivered." She stopped talking, twisting her hands together, eyes fixed on the floor.

Antonía gazed down at the old woman who had cared for her for so many years and then led her over to her chair, pulling her down as she sat in the chair beside her. "Go on," she urged softly.

Minnie stared straight ahead, her hands on the arms of the chair, fingers clutching the ends. "Ducky, I fibbed atrociously to Lady Barclay's midwife, Mrs. Graham. I told her Lord Barclay had hired me to assist her. And fortunately, since men prove so reliably absent during times of labor and childbirth, Lord Barclay was not present to contradict my story." She shrugged. "In any event, I was trying to figure out a way to explain a second baby to the midwife, when divine intervention struck again. An urgent message arrived for Mrs. Graham stating that her own daughter had gone into labor and she was desperately needed at home. After assuring Mrs. Graham I was expertly qualified in the field of midwifery and neonatal care, I urged her to go to her daughter at once."

Minnie stopped talking again, looking very pale.

"And then?"

"And then, ducky, here's the part I hesitate to call divine intervention because it's more a matter of perspective, but label it as you will. In her haste to reach her daughter, Mrs. Graham tripped on the top step, fell headlong down the staircase, and rather conveniently broke her neck. She died on impact."

Antonía sucked in a sharp breath at the unexpected revelation. "Minnie, you didn't . . ." Her voice trailed off.

"What? No! Goodness, how could you think such a thing? I'm telling you the God's honest truth!"

"I apologize," Antonía said, feeling guilty for suspecting her nanny of violating the sixth commandment.

"After interviewing the entire household staff," Minnie went on, "I discovered that no one else besides the midwife had attended the delivery. Naturally, I wasn't going to look a gift horse in the mouth, and so I informed Lord Barclay and the servants that Lady Barclay had delivered twins: one very vociferous son and one very beautiful and much-wanted daughter. During the ensuing nineteen years, not one single solitary soul has ever been the wiser."

The full impact of Minnie's story hit Antonía like a knight on horseback, and she turned to her nanny with a circumspect eye.

"Ducky, don't look at me like that! I may have downed several shots within the past hour, but there's certainly nothing wrong with my memory. And as much as I'd love to present you with objective medical proof to substantiate my claim, I'm hindered by certain historical limitations."

So seldom is scientific savvy superadded to a quondam nanny, thought Antonía, but still . . . "Minnie, how am I supposed to believe this?"

"If you review the facts, ducky, circumstantial as they may be, you'll be forced to acknowledge the truth regarding your heritage. She held up one finger. "One, you are nearly six feet tall like your mother, Queen Mary. Two, you are raven-haired and blue-eyed like your father, the Earl of Bothwell."

"My *father* Lord Barclay also has blue eyes," Antonía interrupted.

Minnie ignored her and held up a third finger. "Three, you ride a horse in the exact same manner as your mother the queen—with terrifying velocity and reckless abandon. Four, you exhibit the regal attitude and rather rebellious temperament of a Royal Stuart."

"Perhaps I'm just a snob or a wee bit of a bitch," she suggested.

Minnie smiled and then hesitated. "Nay, ducky, for here's the conclusive piece of evidence. Number five—you and Queen Mary share the indisputable mark of a Stuart woman. You both have a crown-shaped birthmark located on the nape of your neck. It's a royal fact that beginning with Margaret Bruce and running down through the royal lines to you, all Royal Stuart women possess this extraordinary birthmark."

Antonía's mouth dropped open and she snapped it quickly shut. "Oh, come now! This is absurd!" Perhaps Minnie had finally snapped. Poor old thing. The asylum loomed heavily in her future.

The old woman nodded. "'Twould seem so. Very, very few people outside the immediate Stuart family know about the mark—or its significance. It's a great misfortune that Basil Throckmorton ranks amongst the very, very few."

"I've got to think all this through," Antonía said. She got up and paced back and forth in front of the fireplace.

Minnie sucked on her empty pipe for a moment, and then with a sigh, looked up. "I'm sorry, ducky, but you told me yourself that the Throckmortons gawked at your mark last night, so it's apparent they know exactly who you are! Trust me, my precious, they'll make every effort to destroy you, just like they have your mother."

"Why was Throckmorton so intent on destroying Queen Mary?"

"To make a long story short, he had been in love with your mother, as well as her power, for years. After her second husband—your brother's father—was killed under highly suspicious circumstances, Sir Basil proposed marriage to your mother, but she refused him. Sometime later, the queen married your father, the Earl of Bothwell, and soon thereafter became pregnant with you. Basil Throckmorton never forgave your mother for rejecting him, thereby scuppering his plans for power and position. Years later, he persuaded your mother to seek her cousin's help, all the while plotting with Queen Elizabeth to have Mary taken straight to an English prison as soon as she touched one Catholic toe to English soil."

"Where she remains to this day," said Antonía, nodding thoughtfully.

"Aye. Now, ducky, listen to me well. As Mary's child, you are in line to be heir to the Scottish throne. Now that Throckmorton knows—" She broke off and shook her head.

"Heir?" Antonía whispered. "If what you say is true and I am truly the daughter of Mary Stuart, then King James of Scotland is my brother."

"Lord o' mercy, yes! That moralizing, Bible-thumping, antismoking wee King of Scotland is your half brother. But don't fret." The nanny rose and crossed to her side, patting the girl's hand. "For all intents and purposes, the Barclay family is still your family, and they will always love and protect you—as will your great big handsome Mr. Claymore. Now *there's* a man who would never allow disaster to visit your doorstep."

Antonía waved her words away, her mind focused on the reality that had just imploded her life. "And so my mother—Lady Barclay, that is— still doesn't know?"

"Aye, ducky. After Lady Barclay regained consciousness, I introduced myself as a midwife sent by her friend, Queen Mary, to assist her in childbirth. I also told her that I would answer any questions regarding the birth of her twins. I was fully prepared to tell Lady Barclay the truth about you, but she didn't ask for a single detail. Your good mother said that no matter what the circumstances, she had been doubly blessed. She never questioned her gift and we never spoke of it again."

"And what do my father and brothers know?"

"Not one damn thing," replied the old woman. "They know nothing about the meaning behind your birthmark and nothing of your true identity. But don't you see, ducky, even once we tell them, it won't matter, because they love you. You know that as well as I. Listen now, we can talk more later about this, but as for now, you must go to the ball and act as if nothing has happened."

"God's nightgown!" cried Antonía. "You cannot be serious." She began to pace again. "My parents have no idea that I am in danger—which means they are in danger! And yet if I tell them, then I am no longer their daughter."

"You don't have to tell them," Minnie said. "Truly, 'tis up to you."

Antonía hovered between wanting to cry and wanting to throw something. How could this be? How could she have gone her entire life not knowing the truth?

"Why didn't you tell me before now?" she demanded, her fists clenched at her side. "Why, Minnie?"

Minnie scurried back to her chair and fished in her pocket, her eyes downcast. "Where's my flask?" she muttered.

"Here." Antonía grabbed the bottle of whiskey from the mantle and brought it to the old woman. "Drink. Perhaps it'll give you the strength to answer my question."

Minnie looked up, took the bottle from her, and chugged down a tidy portion. She wiped the back of her sleeve across her mouth and then nodded. "Aye. Maybe I should have told you sooner, but I knew 'twould put your life at risk. The enemies of Mary would try to use you as leverage."

"And yet, according to you, that's exactly what is happening now."

"Aye, ducky, aye."

"And what of Mr. Claymore?"

"What of Mr. Claymore?"

Antonía grabbed the bottle from her nanny and took a quick swig. The liquor burned down her throat. She coughed several times and then took a deep breath.

"Mr. Claymore must be told," Antonía said. "But he believes he's marrying the daughter of Lord and Lady Barclay, not the daughter of a deposed queen and her dead third husband!"

Minnie frowned. "Well, there is that. But never fear, ducky, for your Mr. Claymore is the one man who will always be there to love and protect you—no matter what your name."

"And now you make me sound like some pathetic, broken-wing case! I don't need protection from Mr. Claymore or from anyone else for that matter. And by the way, I greatly resent the implication that I cannot take care of myself." The memory of Mr. Claymore's fierce protectiveness when Rex Throckmorton had cornered her in the hallway darted through her mind, but she pushed it away.

"Well, there's little doubt of that," Minnie conceded, "however—"

"As the only sister of three brothers—" Antonía stopped speaking, realizing her brothers were not her brothers at all. She felt a strange mixture of sadness and glee as she continued. "My brothers taught me to ride and shoot and swim and yes, even partake of fisticuffs on rare occasion." Antonía frowned and returned to the subject at hand. "I understand why Basil Throckmorton would want to keep Mary from the throne, but what does that have to do with me?"

"*Revenge!*" Minnie hissed in a deep, hoarse voice and then fell into a fit of coughing. Antonía rolled her eyes and pounded the old nanny on the back. "The Throckmortons are akin to putrid, decaying pond scum. More soiled souls have never inhabited this world. If you don't take care, they'll destroy you and your family!"

Antonía raised one brow. "I'm still not certain what all this ancient court intrigue has to do with me."

Minnie shrugged. "I'll wager he planned to get Lord Barclay to agree to a marriage between you and his son. When your mother, Mary, heard of it, he knew it would break her heart and also—"

Antonía interrupted, staring straight ahead. "And then Sir Basil would be in line to the throne of Scotland . . . sort of." She narrowed her eyes. It was starting to make a wee bit of sense. And having understood the Throckmortons' goal, she now began to plot her strategy.

"Now, ducky, I don't know what you're scheming, but I'm telling you to stop it at once!" Minnie scolded in her sternest nanny voice.

"Exactly where is Queen Mary being held now?"

"I know of only one person who holds the answer, ducky," the old nanny replied cautiously, "but I'm *not* telling you because I don't like that strange glint in your eye."

"If you don't tell me, I won't go to the ball tonight."

"Fine by me, ducky, but I'm still not telling you!"

"Then I'll show the king's antismoking report to Lady Barclay," replied the very determined ducky. "After reading that little piece of damning evidence, my good mother will cut off your supply so fast you'll be sniffing the air for even the slightest whiff of tobacco."

"You wouldn't dare!"

"I would and I will if you don't cough up that name right now," threatened Antonía, driving a very hard bargain indeed. She continued to coerce, "Let's have it, Minnie. I still have to dress for the ball."

Minnie hesitated.

Antonía pressed even harder, "Minnie, if you don't give me the name right this minute, you can kiss your therapeutic tobacco *and* whiskey good-bye." She folded her arms across her chest and glared at the nanny.

Realizing she was stuck between a rock and an addiction, Minnie relented with a sigh. "I'll tell you only if you promise to attend the Mac-Millans' ball tonight and act as if nothing is wrong. As I said earlier, we'll sort out this mess in the morning."

"Fine, I promise to leave for Deerfield as soon as I dress. Now hurry and give me the name."

"Gus Corbett," coughed up the vanquished Minnie.

"Your brother-in-law?" asked Antonía in surprise.

"One and the same."

"Yes, it makes sense," mused Antonía, "considering Gus Corbett is the caretaker of Lochleven Castle." After putting the next piece of the puzzle in place, she stated more than asked, "Gus helped you bring me here the day I was born, didn't he?"

"Aye, ducky, you're a shrewd one, but I refuse to say another word."

"No need," she said. "You've already said enough to support your addiction."

She walked over to a bag sitting beside Minnie's bedroom door, reached inside, and took out more tobacco in a small pouch. She tossed it to her.

"Now, tell me exactly how to find Lochleven Castle, and don't you dare lie to me, Minnie, or that will be the last batch you ever smoke."

The old nanny told her how to reach her birthplace, and Antonía was relieved to hear the directions were relatively simple ones. After having Minnie repeat them several times, she headed out the bedroom door. She had promised to go to the ball and so she would, but only because the throng of guests would provide the distraction she needed to embark on her quest.

Chapter 6

NO TIME FOR PRETTY PROSE

Breck Claymore waited outside the entryway to Barclay Castle, leaning against the carriage Antonía's brother Will had brought round for his sister's journey to Deerfield. Thankfully, he'd been able to convince the young scholar to allow him to escort the beautiful Antonía to the ball. After all, her father had given his consent for him to court her. As soon as they were both inside the carriage, he intended to use the privacy to gain her consent as well.

The sun was making its way down to the horizon, painting the sky with deep purple and pink just as the great door to Barclay Castle opened and Antonía walked out. Claymore stepped away from the carriage, struck once again by the celestial nature of Miss Barclay's lavish blessings. Wearing a flowing white dress delicately embroidered in gold, Antonía's countenance reminded him of the goddess Aphrodite, perfect, yet powerful in her beauty.

Her dark hair fell in beachy waves down her back, while her blue eyes gazed back at him for a long moment. Lost in his spellbound wonder, the awestruck suitor felt his heart pound as his goddess showed signs of mortality by giving him a shy smile, her cheeks flushed with color.

He walked toward her, knowing his eyes gave away the awe with which he viewed her. But he couldn't help it. The woman was an absolute smoke show, in the best sense of the term. Taking her hand, he bowed, planted a gentle kiss on the back of it, and then turned it over and kissed her palm.

"Good evening, Miss Barclay," he said, drawing close to her, keeping her hand in his.

She lowered her gaze. "Mr. Claymore," she said, "I owe you a sincere apology for deserting you this morning on our ride, but please know I was not running from you." She looked at him intently and added, "I would never run away from *you*." She paused. "At least not without a very good reason."

"Did you think I'd let those ruffians assault you again, dear Miss Barclay?" he said as he led her down the steps. A footman opened the door, but it was Claymore who helped her into the enclosed waiting carriage. He wondered about the large bag she carried with her, but felt it was a little early in their relationship to challenge her proclivity for heavy baggage.

"Of course not, Mr. Claymore, and I thank you very much for understanding," Antonía answered as she took her seat and arranged the skirt of her gown, her eyes still downcast.

"I gave chase," he said, sitting next to her. At his statement, her head came up and, seeing the fire in her blue eyes, he had to fight back the urge to take her fully in his arms and kiss her slowly. But no, he would not. He would not kiss her until she granted her consent. He considered himself a man of infinite honor and impeccable integrity and as such, was bound and determined not to kiss Antonía until she had bestowed her full and unconditional consent to courtship upon him.

"And did you catch them?"

"Alas, Miss Barclay, I did not." Claymore hated admitting his failure. "However, I can promise that they'll never bother you again. They're officially persona non grata at Deerfield and at Barclay Castle. I had a word with both Claire's father and your own this morning after I returned."

"Speaking about being official," she said, "I never officially thanked you for rescuing me in the hallway and dealing with Rex."

"Aye," he said, "you did, by walking in the gardens with me last night and meeting me at the pond this morning." He cleared his throat. "Do you recall the unasked question I've been attempting to pose?" She nodded. "May I ask it now, Miss Barclay?"

Antonía leaned back in the carriage and gave him an inquisitive smile. "I'm all yours, Mr. Claymore."

Not yet, he thought. *But soon*. "Excellent answer, Miss Barclay, because it's the precise, and may I add, correct response that I wish to flow from your lips once I ask my question." Claymore took her hand in his. "I've obtained your parents' consent to court you, but it was granted solely dependent upon you giving yours." Recalling the many men she had mercilessly left by the wayside, Mr. Claymore hesitated in a rare moment of self-doubt before posing the all-important query.

"Miss Barclay, will you grant me *your* consent to be courted?"

Much to Claymore's relief, he discovered his momentary misgivings were entirely unfounded as Miss Barclay provided the precise and correct answer once again.

"I'm all yours, Mr. Claymore," she said, leaning against him and smiling up at him.

Finally, it was done! He had her consent and now quite naturally he wanted her kiss. Placing his hands gently on either side of her face, he leaned forward, and very nearly pressed his lips upon hers, but a sharp knock on the carriage door sounded. Will Barclay then wrenched it open, stuck his head inside, and produced yet another frustrating instance of brother buzzkill.

"I say, Claymore, are you taking my sister to the ball or not?" He gave them both a suspicious look. "What's going on here?"

"We were just about to leave," the frustrated suitor said, trying to remain polite.

"I'm glad you haven't left," he said. "It seems my brothers thought I was going with Antonía and left me behind." He started to haul himself into the carriage when Claymore, thinking quickly, stopped him.

"Of course," he said, forcing a smile. "But first, could you do me a favor and fetch my cloak? I left it on the settee in the foyer."

Will frowned but ducked back out. "Yes, but then we must hurry."

"Good idea!" Antonía said with an amused smile. "Hurry now, Will!"

As soon as the door closed behind her brother, Mr. Claymore reached up and knocked twice on the roof of the carriage. "Let's be off!" he cried.

With a jerk, the carriage moved forward, spilling Antonía into his lap. His arm went around her, and the two laughed as the horses broke into a fast trot, leaving Barclay Castle and her brother behind.

"Oh dear," Antonía said, "I do hope Will doesn't thrash you for this impolite abandonment."

Claymore gazed down at her radiant face. "Would you rather we turned back, dear Miss Barclay?"

"Better not. We'd be quite late to the ball and my mother would kill me!" She paused and, becoming more serious, prompted, "Mr. Claymore?"

"Yes, Miss Barclay?"

"Since we are now officially courting, does this mean you will dance every dance at the ball with me tonight?"

He nodded, feeling mesmerized by her nearness. "Aye, you're all mine from here on in," he whispered, "and every dance belongs to me."

Antonía slanted her head in contemplation. "Mr. Claymore, you don't strike me as a man who likes to dance. Admit it, you hate to dance. I feel it in my bones, so please don't bother to deny the fact."

Claymore thought for a split second before replying, aware his heart was smeared all over his sleeve. "Miss Barclay, I will dance every jig, reel, and gavotte if it gives me cause to hold you in my arms and adorn you with kisses every step of the way." He lifted one hand to caress the high contour of her cheekbone, while continuing to pour out his unveiled passion. "In fact, my darling, you can plan on dancing from dusk until dawn because I have no intention of ever letting you go."

Accordingly, she placed her hand lightly on his. "That was the precise and correct answer, and if we ever get ten consecutive minutes to ourselves, you shall be duly rewarded for it."

Claymore glanced around the carriage. "If I am not mistaken, my dear Miss Barclay, we are currently alone."

Antonía's left eyebrow shot upward. "Alone? And what about that frightful driver atop the carriage? Surely you wouldn't risk my reputation by implementing amorous advances upon me in such a public place? And so early in our courtship, too—how long have we been officially courting? Two whole minutes?" She shook her head in mock disgust. "This does not bode well for our future. Perhaps I should rescind my consent immediately. You would then be free to gallivant with women of lesser morals."

His answer was as swift as it was impassioned. "Miss Barclay, did I not tell you? Your consent, once granted, became irrevocable. There will be no rescinding on your part and no gallivanting on mine . . . *ever.*"

Claymore straightened away from her and groaned, remembering, too late, an errand he had already agreed to run. "My dear Miss Barclay, I must tell you something."

The brow arched again. "Sounds ominous."

"Beginning tomorrow morning, I will be gone for several days, perhaps a week. Your father has commissioned a set of swords, and I must travel to Edinburgh for engraving tools, as I left mine back in Inverness."

"Let me guess," Antonía said, "my father has ordered swords with his name engraved all over them."

"Exactly. In fact, I've noticed very few inanimate objects within his vicinity that do *not* bear his trademark. Apparently your father has quite a proclivity for decorating with his name."

"It's actually more on the order of a mania. But despite my father's affliction, he's a very kind and understanding man." Mr. Claymore nodded. "So it's really too bad I will have to beat him senseless for taking you away from me!"

Mr. Claymore laughed. "I adore your attitude, Miss Barclay, but I promise to return as soon as possible."

"Will you miss me?" she asked, glancing out the window of the carriage.

He leaned closer and whispered against the soft skin just below her ear. "Like you wouldn't believe, my darling." Then he lifted his hand to her chin, turning her face back to his. Without another word, he brushed his lips over hers, barely touching them, and smiled as he heard her indrawn breath.

"Oh!" she said. "Was that a kiss?"

He sighed in contentment. "Just the promise of a kiss. Believe me, darling, when it is, you won't need to ask, much less be able to form the question." He paused to touch her satiny hair and then added with deep-seated regret, "I truly deplore leaving you tomorrow."

She smiled the smile that foretold all things wonderful and replied with a hushed, "Haste ye back, my Mr. Claymore."

The fact that this was the first time Miss Barclay had used a possessive pronoun in combination with his surname was not at all lost on Mr. Claymore. He leaned closer again and said in a low voice, "Miss Barclay, you are making it extraordinarily hard for me to take my leave tomorrow, and were it not for my gentleman-like manners, I very much doubt I'd leave at all. But until I return . . ."

Claymore reached into his pocket and took out a black velvet box. He handed it to Antonía and her face lit with pleasure. She wasted no time opening the box and then exclaimed as she lifted out a long silver chain. Hanging from the chain was a miniature Scottish claymore sword.

"It's so beautiful!" Antonía slipped it over her head and pressed her hand against the pendant.

"Not as beautiful as you, dear Miss Barclay," he said.

Her blue eyes darkened, and leaning nearer, she brushed her lips against his. "Thank you, my Mr. Claymore. I will never take it off."

As the evening progressed, Antonía was amazed to find that for the first time in her life, she was having a wonderful time at a social event. True to his word, Mr. Claymore danced every dance with her; and with each song, she fell more in love with him. Which was a bit frustrating, since she was about to disappear from his life for an indeterminate amount of time.

She owed him an explanation, that much was certain; but if she told him the truth, what would be the outcome? She could only see two results: either he would break their courtship contract and she would lose him forever; or more likely, given his heroic nature, he would insist on joining her in her quest to find her mother—and put himself in danger.

That would never do. At present she was walking on the MacMillans' veranda, waiting for Mr. Claymore to bring her refreshments; but the longer she waited, the more she knew that this was the time to take action, before he returned. Ever prepared, she reached into her reticule and removed a folded piece of parchment.

"I'm sorry to have deserted you earlier," came the familiar voice of her friend Claire.

With a sigh, she tucked the note back into her reticule and turned to greet her friend. Sailing onto the veranda exquisitely attired in a size 00

Hubert de Givenchy precursor, accompanied by a Christian Dior Elizabethan choker necklace archetype, Claire MacMillan was the epitome of a sixteenth-century fashionista.

"I meant to help you dress before the ball, but Matthew and I—" She stopped, blushing.

Antonía inwardly groaned. "Claire, not another word! Please remember you're talking to me and he's my brother. Details concerning you and my brother—romantic, sordid, or otherwise—will no longer be tolerated. Just because I've facilitated your love life doesn't mean I'm obligated to listen to the ramifications of my achievement."

"Understood, but I think it only fair to inform you that you could learn something from my experience, because if you ever condescend to love a man . . ."

"Stop right there," threatened Antonía, covering her ears in what she knew was a highly juvenile fashion. "One more word out of your suspiciously swollen lips and I swear to God I'll throw myself off this veranda."

Claire crossed the stone patio and looked over the short wall surrounding the veranda. "It's only a three-foot drop. I daresay you might break a fingernail but nothing vital. Now about Matthew and me—well—"

"Claire!"

Her friend laughed. "Only kidding. I just wanted to apologize for not coming to help you dress earlier." She walked slowly around Antonía, her astute eye examining the white gown with its golden embroidery.

Claire took her sweet time assembling her critique, but finally said, "Quite nice." She then leaned forward to peer at Antonía's necklace. "A sword? A sword necklace?"

"Yes, Claire, it was a gift from Mr. Claymore, and speaking of Mr. Claymore . . ." She pulled her friend over to the stone wall. "Claire, I need your help."

Claire sighed. "What else is new?"

"This is important." Antonía rummaged in her reticule again and pulled out the note. "I need you to give this to Mr. Claymore."

"Where is that magnificent figure of a man? I still can't get over how he defended you at the supper table last night."

"Yes, and it wasn't the first time," Antonía said, and then bit her tongue, wishing she could withdraw the words.

"What?" Claire leaned in, clearly delighted. "Whatever do you mean?"

Antonía knew she shouldn't explain, but Claire was her best friend, and so she related the unfortunate encounter with Rex Throckmorton in the corridor outside her bedroom.

Claire was outraged. In fact, after hearing Antonía's account of the man's exceedingly unattractive display of barbarianism, she grasped her friend by the shoulders and demanded, "Tell me the truth, did he hurt you in *any* way?"

"Except for the disgusting gob of spit he left on the side of my face when he was trying to kiss me, no, Rex didn't hurt me—thanks to Mr. Claymore."

"You're in love!" Claire cried.

"What?" Antonía's face grew hot. "Don't be ridiculous."

Claire nodded in satisfaction. "You're in love with Mr. Claymore. Now, go on—did Rex get any further than the gross kiss?"

Antonía shivered. Deep down she knew that it would have been much worse than a simple, though disgusting, kiss. "I could have stopped him myself, of course," she said, brushing away the incident with the toss of her hand. "But it was nice to have Mr. Claymore at my side defending me."

Claire exhaled an audible sigh of relief. "Thank God he was there!" she said. "Because if that horrible man had hurt you, I'd kill him." She then raised her arms toward the heavens and vowed, "If he'd hurt one single hair on your head, I would've choked him to death with my small but extremely efficient hands!"

Laughing at the image, Antonía remarked, "In that case, you'll have to stand in queue behind Mr. Claymore."

"Really?" Claire said questioningly.

Antonía sighed, and then smiled. "You win. Mr. Claymore and I are officially courting."

In a rare outburst containing the official use of an official curse word, Claire responded, "I'm damn happy to hear it! But I have a good mind to tell my father and yours about what Rex did to you in the hallway!"

"No, Claire," implored Antonía, "please promise me you won't say a word to your father or anyone else about it. The Throckmortons are gone, and no real harm was done. I don't want this little episode getting blown out of proportion."

Claire paused, then shrugged. "I promise, but only because those dastardly Englishmen left! I hope and pray they're on their way back to England and never come back."

"Speaking of leaving . . ." Antonía pulled Claire a little farther from the doorway leading into the mansion. "I must go."

"Go!" Claire's carefully coiffed hair, brown as cinnamon toast, almost took a tumble as she jerked her head toward Antonía. "You can't leave! The ball has scarcely begun!"

"I've been here for four hours, Claire!"

Her friend grabbed her arm and Antonía squeaked at the vise-like grip of her petite friend. "Antonía, we will be serving the late supper any minute now. You can't leave!"

"I must, and I need you to give this note to Mr. Claymore." She handed the folded note to Claire.

The girl stared down at it, a perturbed look on her face. "What does it say? And where are you going?"

"I can't tell you, but I'm sure once my brothers and Mr. Claymore realize I'm gone, they'll figure it out and tell you."

"Why can't *you* tell me?" Claire demanded.

Antonía hesitated. Claire was the closest thing to a sister that she had, but she knew better than anyone that her dear friend could not keep a secret to save her life. And if she knew what Antonía was about to do, friend or no friend, she would sound the alarm because, well, because she *was* her friend.

"I'm sorry, Claire, I'll explain when I get back. Please trust me." She turned to go and was struck in the back by a small whirlwind as her friend threw her arms around her.

"Oh dear, please be careful," she begged, squeezing her around the middle so tightly Antonía thought she might faint. "And please do send word to me. Please?"

Antonía turned and hugged her back. "I promise, sweet Claire. Now please, give the note to Mr. Claymore! I must fly!"

She released her friend and, true to her word, flew across the veranda and down the steps leading into the garden. She had managed to sneak in her garment bag from the carriage and had stowed it beneath a settee in a little-used small parlor. To Antonía's surprise and relief, no one had questioned her about it, not even Mr. Claymore.

Now slipping past the butler at the door, Antonía retrieved her bag and fled back the way she had come, only to run smack into her brother Will.

"Antonía!" he stumbled backward from the impact. "What in the world? Where are you going? And what do you have in that gargantuan sack? Dead sheep?"

"Precisely," she said, nodding. "Mrs. MacMillan was worried she'd run low on haggis so I offered to bring some extra ingredients."

Will frowned and then laughed without humor. "Very funny." He shook his head. "I smell trouble, and you are, undoubtedly, at the root of it."

Antonía was at her wit's end. Mr. Claymore was likely already on the veranda and Claire in the process of giving him the note. She had to leave! She decided to pretend she was highly insulted. "Such vicious slander! Such monstrous calumny!" she cried as she turned to go. "Shame on you for besmirching my stellar reputation in such a despicable manner!"

"It's impossible to besmirch a fact, dear sister. You're trouble and that's a historically proven fact. But mercifully for me, you are not my problem tonight. If you were I think I'd shoot myself."

"Now you know how I feel every time you stick me with some idiotic Chaucer poem," she retorted.

"Yes, dear sister, but intellectual torture is exceedingly edifying, and therefore for your next assignment, you shall read and annotate the king's upcoming manuscript."

Antonía stared at him. So often is an overbearing manner superadded to ostentatious erudition. "Since when have you become best friends with the king?"

"Since he learned that I was a scholarly academic," he said, and then added in a condescending manner, "King James has asked me to help translate the Bible into English so that all of you plebian-types can read it. I start work Monday."

"Father must be ecstatic, but won't a job cut into your debauchery time?"

"I'll work around it," replied Will. "Now, back to the question of the bag—"

"Will!" Antonía cried in a hushed voice. "Quick! Look over there, by the door. Isn't that Sophie McGill?"

He spun around. "Where?"

She pointed toward the Deerfield entrance. "Claire's cousin from Aberdeen! You remember—the lovely little blonde lass who listened to your every pedantic word last Christmas?" Craning her neck, Antonía added, "Oh dear, you just missed her! She went inside." His reaction was just what she hoped for.

"I must catch her!" He started forward, then turned back and glowered at his sister. "No shenanigans tonight, Antonía. You will stay out of trouble, won't you?"

"Of course," she said, lying easily.

"Jolly good," he said, then he turned straight around and hesitated. She gave him a little wave of the hand and he finally headed up the stairs.

"Thank God!" she whispered, watching her brother leave in pursuit of Sophie McGill, who could, *theoretically*, be attending the ball.

Antonía then put her plan into action.

Mr. Claymore searched the ballroom for Antonía after returning to the veranda and finding it empty. He saw Will bow over Miss McGill's hand and then stride across the room toward the table of refreshments. Will's two brothers were already there, swilling down ale and sweetmeats as they welcomed the eldest brother into the fold, slamming him on the back as only brothers can, and casting amused glances across the room at the girl left waiting for him.

Perhaps the fraternal trio knew where their sister might be, or perhaps Claire would be the better informant. For surely if no one else knew, Antonía's best friend would, and since Matthew Barclay was her escort that night . . . Claymore crossed the room to join the three brothers and found he, too, was welcomed like a member of the family.

"Well met, well met," Oliver said, pounding Claymore on the shoulder. "Here is the man who shall free us from all of our cares and woes!"

Claymore laughed. "Shall I?" he asked.

"Indeed," Matthew chimed in, "as long as you intend to honor your commitment to our sister. Word is she has consented to your courtship!"

Claymore smiled then and nodded. "Aye, she has."

"Gadzooks, good fellow," Will said, lifting a glass of ale in toast. "That calls for a drink in your honor."

Claymore glanced toward Miss McGill, patiently waiting across the room. "Don't you have a wee lass in need of a drink, Mr. Barclay?"

"Call me Will," he said with a short bow. "And call these two Oliver and Matthew. We understand that soon you will be our brother." There was more pounding of Claymore's back as he accepted the mug of ale.

"A toast," cried Oliver, lifting his glass, "to the bravest man in all of Scotland!"

The two other brothers agreed, and the glasses and mugs clanked together before the men drank deeply.

"I am honored by your tribute," Claymore said, amused at the youths' boisterous approval of his courtship, "but why do you say I am the bravest man in Scotland?"

Oliver wiped foam from his lips and laughed. His brothers joined him, the frolics continuing until Mr. Claymore tired of it.

"I'll accept your answer anytime today, gentlemen," he said mildly.

"It'll take the bravest man in the country to court—and marry—our sister!" declared Oliver.

"And why is that?" Claymore said, putting down his mug and crossing his arms.

"Antonía is a handful!" Matthew said with a laugh. "She will lead you a merry life!"

Claymore relaxed. These were just the ramblings of typical brothers, pretending to be happy to pawn their sister off on some gullible fool, when in reality, they knew how much they would miss her. There was no other explanation, for most assuredly, Antonía must be the most perfect sister in the world, as she was the most perfect woman as far as he was concerned.

"I look forward to a merry life, my lads!" Claymore said, and lifted his mug to the three. After drinking more ale, he wiped his mouth and got to the point. "Speaking of your lovely sister, have any of you seen her? I left her on the veranda, and when I came back, she was gone."

The brothers exchanged glances again, but this time Claymore saw wariness between them.

"How long ago was this?" Will asked.

"Half an hour ago. Your father wanted to talk a bit so it slowed me down." The brothers nodded their understanding. Their father was quite the talker. Mr. Claymore continued, "I supposed she and Claire might be somewhere together, arranging hair and that sort of thing after all the dancing." He raised one brow as he noticed Will looking away furtively. "Have you seen her, Will?"

"Actually, I did see her." He began to fill his plate, keeping his eyes downcast.

"And?" Claymore sighed. Really these lads were a trial. Antonía must have the patience of a saint.

"She was outside, near the front of the mansion," Will said, finally glancing up. He looked guilty. Claymore narrowed his eyes, a wave of uneasiness sweeping over him.

"And what was she doing in front of the mansion?"

He shrugged. "She was carrying an enormous bag. Said the MacMillans needed extra haggis supplies." He shook his head. "Who knows what she meant? Antonía is prone to extravagant hyperbole."

"And which way was she headed when you left her?" Claymore asked, a prickling of unease in his veins.

"I—I—see here—I was not her babysitter tonight!" Will's voice rose and several heads, including Lord Barclay's, turned in his direction.

Mr. Claymore was a man of neither impulse nor hot-headedness, but where Antonía was concerned, his feelings were strong. He turned his attention to her middle brother.

Matthew scanned the ballroom for signs of their sister and then grumbled, "Whoever knows where Antonía is? She's so much trouble it's unbelievable."

"Believe it," replied Oliver.

"Well, I must go back to attend to my guest and seek higher ground until such time as the smoke clears," Will said, taking a step toward the lovely Miss McGill. Claymore clamped one hand down on his shoulder.

"I think not," he said in a friendly manner. "You were the last one to see Antonía, so tell me every detail before you leave."

"Fine, fine," capitulated Will. He again recounted his brief encounter with his missing sister.

"Was Miss Barclay behaving in an unusual or peculiar manner?" Claymore asked.

All three brothers shared tacit looks of puzzlement. "Who the hell knows?" Oliver interjected. "As far as we're concerned, she always behaves in an unusual and peculiar manner."

"She *was* acting rather twitchy," Will admitted, "and like I said, she was carrying a colossal bag with her. After her haggis answer, I didn't inquire further because I assumed her bag was filled with female paraphernalia of some sort. And as we all know, it's never a good idea to ask a female too many questions."

All four men agreed, then Oliver's eyes widened as he nodded in the direction of a big man striding across the ballroom. "The party may be over."

"One or all of us may be getting the William Wallace treatment soon," commented Will, his tone ominous.

Lord Barclay invaded the small group with force and bluster. After unloading a cathartic stream of choice curse words in the specific direction of his sons, he roared, "She's gone, isn't she? Ditched another ball! How many times must I repeat myself—apparently until I'm blue in the face. Where is my daughter?"

Whereupon Will, Oliver, and Matthew all took a step back and in unison pointed at Claymore.

"God Almighty!" exploded Lord Barclay. "Don't blame Mr. Claymore! The man has only known our Antonía for twenty-four hours!"

"Darling," said Lady Barclay, gliding up to place a comforting hand on her husband's forearm. She then glanced around the room and gave a wave of her hand toward Claire MacMillan. At first, the young woman acted as if she didn't see Lady Barclay signaling her. Instead, she looked up at the ceiling, down at the floor, anywhere except in the direction of Antonía's family.

"Excuse me," Claymore said, brows knit and head down as he crossed the room in four long strides. Taking Claire gently by the hand, he brought her back to the group. "Miss MacMillan," he said firmly, "do you know where Antonía is?"

Claire, teetering on a sky-high pair of size 6 Jimmy Choo forerunners, saw no choice other than to hem and haw.

"Antonía?" she asked, looking like a bright-eyed squirrel as she turned to Claymore and batted her eyelashes. "Wasn't she with you, Mr. Claymore?"

"Aye, she was, out on the veranda. I came in for drinks and when I returned she was nowhere to be found."

"You were out on the veranda with her, were you not, Claire?" Lady Barclay asked.

"Me?" she giggled nervously. "Oh no, I wasn't on the veranda."

All five looked at her as Lady Barclay fixed her with steely eyes. "I saw you on the veranda with my daughter while Mr. Claymore was gone." She reached out and gripped the girl by the arm. "Claire, she could be in danger."

Claire went completely still. Finally, she said, "Oh, God."

"Well?" Claymore asked, prompting her.

"W-well . . ." Claire stuttered and then without warning threw herself into Mr. Claymore's arms. "F-forgive me, Mr. Claymore! I-I didn't know what to do!" She thrust something into his hands and then turned and buried her face in Matthew's broad chest.

Claymore looked down at a folded piece of paper. "A note? From Antonía?"

Claire lifted her head long enough to nod but started sobbing. Matthew sighed and handed her a handkerchief. Claymore unfolded the note and frowned over the words, fighting feelings of frustration. Realizing the turmoil her family was experiencing, he graciously read the note aloud.

Dearest Mr. Claymore,

No time for pretty prose. I must embark upon a personal quest, one I must make alone. I hope you will forgive me and wait for me to return. Thank you for my beautiful necklace. And remember to save your kisses just for me.

With deep affection,
Antonía

P.S. Please tell Claire I am sorry about the discarded designer dress. It was a little tight across the bust anyway. Also, not that she would worry, but tell her father that his horse is in good hands.

Although Antonía's letter evoked a bittersweet smile from Claymore, it did little in solving the mystery of her disappearance. Then the last sentence hit home.

"Horse?" Claymore jerked his head up. "The stables!" He pivoted and headed for the door.

Chapter 7

TRUTH AND CONSEQUENCES

Once at the stables, the evidence served only to escalate the man's fears. Outside the stall of Mr. MacMillan's fastest horse lay a discarded dress.

With a sinking heart, he carefully picked up Antonía's empty dress and, pressing it to his cheek, inhaled the faint yet clearly identifiable scent of her. For a single precious moment, Mr. Claymore fantasized that Miss Barclay had never abandoned her dress or . . . him. But, as so often proves the case, the Fates are stingy with time. Accordingly it was not long before the Barclays and the MacMillans burst through the stable doors in one big heap of confused humanity.

Claymore looked directly at Lord Barclay. "My lord, your daughter's letter indicates she left of her own volition, and now it seems she has changed her clothes and"—he pushed open the door of the stall to reveal it was empty—"taken a horse."

"That's her favorite horse in our stables!" Claire said. "She always rides him when she visits."

"So at least we can assume she wasn't abducted," Claymore mused, "but we haven't a clue as to where she has gone." He looked at Claire. "Unless Miss MacMillan could enlighten us?"

"*Moi?*" Claire's big brown eyes widened. "Do you really think, Mr. Claymore, if I knew where Antonía had gone, I would keep it a secret?"

The entire company said in unison, "Yes!"

Ignoring the answer, she said, "I swear upon—upon my favorite blue silk designer gown that I do not know where Antonía has gone."

"Well, we must believe her now," Matthew said, "for I know she loves that dress more than she loves"—he stopped and cleared his throat—"uh, any of her other dresses."

"Very well then," Claymore conceded, "is there anyone else she would confide in?"

Lady Barclay and Claire exchanged looks of sudden revelation. They chirped in perfect soprano harmony, "Minnie!"

All six insisted upon leaving for Barclay Castle, but Claymore knew the last thing he wanted was the burden of the three brothers, not to mention the histrionic Claire riding his coattails.

"Antonía is a woman of courage and impetuosity and, as I have already found, is something of a tease," he said, downplaying the situation and forcing a smile. "No doubt she took it in her head to take a ride and lead me, her newly designated suitor, on a wild chase." He put his hand on his chest. "I am honor-bound to follow." He bowed toward Antonía's mother and father. "With your permissions, of course."

Lady Barclay gave him a sharp look and then nodded. "Yes, of course, why didn't I think of that? Antonía is given to challenging her suitors one way or another." She turned to Claire and her sons. "Go back to the ball, children. Mr. Claymore will find Antonía. Lord Barclay and I will return home, just in case our wayward daughter should happen to show up there."

Claymore was quickly learning that no one disobeyed the matriarch of the Barclay family. Indeed, no one staged a protest of any kind. As soon as they were gone, Claymore turned to Lady Barclay.

"Thank you for going along with my story. Now let us return to Barclay Castle and find out what Minnie knows."

Upon reaching their destination, it took the three no time at all to locate the old nanny because she was sitting in her room surrounded by several bottles of fine Scottish whiskey. The scene was, in and of itself, not unusual, for Minnie was the furthest thing from a temperance advocate. However, on this particular occasion, the shattered bottles scattered around the fireplace clearly indicated something was very much amiss.

After a cursory inspection, Claymore reported that at least three bottles of fine Scottish whiskey had been foredoomed to either the fire or its vicinity.

Lord Barclay approached the old woman and, after a cursory inspection of his own, determined that for the first time in recent memory, Minnie had grossly exceeded her considerable, and impressive, drinking capacity. The old nanny was, plain and simple, plastered.

"Look here, old girl," entreated Lord Barclay, "you must sober up and tell us why Antonía has run off!"

Minnie slobbered and blubbered for a few minutes before she was able to babble anything even halfway intelligible.

"I'm sho sho shorry," she slurred. "I should nether, nether have told my ducky. I should ha' waited. Lady Barclay could ha' helved me with my ducky. My ducky is soo, soo strong-minded, soo impeshuous. I should ha' known better—I knew she'd try something—and from the looksh on your faches I can tell my ducky ish gone. Oh, dear God," she wailed, "my ducky may never come back home. I'm such a shtu, shtupid old woman. I wish the conshumption had conshumed me long ago! But no one here but me undershtands." A coughing fit seized her as Lord Barclay and Claymore exchanged bewildered glances.

"Minnie," Claymore said kneeling beside her, "I am Breck Claymore." He clasped her withered hand in his. "None of this is your fault. No one is blaming you. We just want to know where Miss Barclay may have gone."

The floodgates now opened. With tears running down her face, the old nanny cried, "My ducky went to find her mudder! She went to shee her mudder before it's too late!"

Claymore was puzzled. "But, Minnie, Lady Barclay is right here."

"No, no, Mishter Claymore," she moaned. "Although Lady Barclay raished Antonía, she did *not* give birth to her! My ducky's true mudder—real mudder—blood mudder—is Mary, Queen of Shcots. You know, the poor woman locked up in a grishly English prishon. And of coursh Bashil Throckmorton was the man who orcheshtrated the queen's imprishonment—vile piecshe of shcum that he ish! And he'sh been searching for my ducky shince she was a wee bittie bairn!"

The old woman gripped Claymore's arm with preternatural strength and, staring into his eyes, continued to sob. "Don't you undershtand, Mishter Claymore? You've fallen in love wish a princshess! And she's run off to find her mudder, the queen! The English will kill her or even worsh, they'll deshtroy her life jush like they've deshtroyed her poor mudder's! You mush find my ducky before they do!"

Claymore nodded, feeling stunned. His initial assessment of Antonía's imperial demeanor had apparently been dead-on. Her majestic manner, her regal bearing, and her commanding presence were truths so self-evident that he knew with complete certainty that every word of Minnie's tale was true.

Lord Barclay, however, stood in silence, looking absolutely gobsmacked by the elderly woman's fantastical tale. "Have you been drinking tainted whiskey?" He picked up her pipe from the hearth of the fireplace and sniffed it, then his eyes narrowed in suspicion. "What have you been smoking?"

"Nushing," she replied. "My ducky alwaysh bringsh me my tobaccy and now she'sh gone!"

Lord Barclay shook his head. "None of this can be true! The poor woman is afflicted with any number of maladies that could affect her mind! She's consumptive, she's drunk as a skunk, and evidently in the late stages of senile dementia! She simply cannot be believed!"

"Wait," came a whisper from behind him. Lady Barclay stood staring at Minnie, her face ashen.

"Lady Barclay," bawled the beleaguered nanny. "Schank the Lord, you're here! The Throckmortons have sheen Antonía's birthmark! They know who she ish!"

"Good God, no!" Lady Barclay's words of woe echoed through the room with such abject despair that her husband hastened to her side. She clung to him, crying. "Henry, they'll kill her! Dear God in Heaven, they're going to kill our daughter!"

Henry Barclay put his arm around his wife and led her over to the two chairs near the fireplace. Helping her into one, he took the other, while Claymore stood nearby, his heart stricken for the couple.

"Cassandra, my dearest love," Lord Barclay said, "everything will be all right, but you must tell us the truth."

Lady Cassandra Barclay nodded, and then unfolded the story of their beloved daughter. Cassandra Sinclair and Mary Stuart had been lifelong friends from the time Mary had returned from France, still a young girl but a widow nonetheless. It wasn't long before Mary's duties as Queen of Scotland had kept them from much personal contact, but in spite of life's obstacles, the two friends maintained their close relationship through constant and heartfelt correspondence.

Many years later, when Mary learned that Basil Throckmorton posed a serious threat to both her reign and her newborn child, she turned to her dear friend, now Lady Cassandra Barclay. As both a loyal subject and a faithful friend, Lady Barclay had agreed to help her queen without qualification, without condition, and without question.

And as it happened, on July 14, 1567, after being in labor for many hours, Lady Barclay awoke to discover two swathed babies snuggled beside her—one boy and one girl—the former screaming his lungs out, the latter sleeping peacefully. Miss Minnie Munro was there as well, and introduced herself as a midwife and nanny sent by Queen Mary to assist her in caring for her twins.

"I found out later that a good man, Gus Corbett, loyal to the queen, brought Minnie and the baby here to us."

It was not much later when Lady Barclay discovered the regal birthmark on the baby girl's neck and realized its implications. In spite of the discovery, she had loved her daughter without qualification, without condition, and without question.

When Lady Barclay finished her account, she broke down and sobbed. Lord Barclay kissed the palms of his wife's hands as he consoled her. "There, there, Cassandra, you did exactly the right thing."

"But I should have told you," she said, her voice breaking with the words.

He shook his head. "It wouldn't have made a speck of difference to me either way. Antonía is, and always will be, our treasured daughter. But now, unfortunately, we must assume she's on her way to England, in search of Queen Mary."

Seeking additional facts, Mr. Claymore knelt beside Lady Barclay's chair. "Lady Barclay, I was about to ask Minnie if she knew where Queen Mary is imprisoned, but she appears to have fallen asleep." He glanced over at Minnie, who had unfortunately passed out cold.

Lady Barclay nodded, dabbing at the tears on her face with her kerchief.

"Yes, Mr. Claymore. She resides at an English manor called Chartley Hall. Perhaps Antonía searched my desk and discovered our letters, and consequently the queen's location."

Claymore thanked her and stood. "Lord Barclay," he said in a somber tone, "I must respectfully inform you that my courtship with your daughter is officially over."

Lord Barclay sighed and nodded. "Mr. Claymore, I fully understand and respect your position regarding my daughter. I can well appreciate that few men would dare assume responsibility for her, especially in light of the current state of affairs. My daughter may be the bonniest lass who has ever been born, but God knows, she's a lot of work." Pausing for a deep sigh, he then concluded, "Mr. Claymore, I hereby officially release you from the bonds of courtship—without prejudice—but with deep regret."

Claymore had to smile. "I beg your pardon, my lord, you misunderstand my intent. The courtship is over only because I wish to *marry* your daughter as soon as I can find her."

Lord Barclay stroked his chin and smiled thoughtfully. "Mr. Claymore, if you're man enough to find my daughter, you're man enough to marry her." Then turning to his wife, he asked, "My dear, do you have any objections?"

"None at all," she said and then added with a teary-eyed smile, "but let us pray the marriage lasts a wee bit longer than the courtship."

"Aye," Lord Barclay agreed. "Now you must find Antonía and obtain her consent. But the lass rides at an ungodly pace, and to make matters worse, she borrowed Stewart MacMillan's fastest thoroughbred, so she'll give us a run for our money."

"Sir, I respectfully request that you allow me to pursue Antonía, alone," said Claymore. Though Lord Barclay was far from old, he was stout and opinionated, and sure to slow the journey. Claymore meant to ride like the wind. "I think I can make better time," he added. His meaning was not lost on Lord Barclay.

He nodded. "Very well. I will leave it to you, Mr. Claymore."

Lady Barclay rose from her chair and put her hand on the tall man's arm. "Thank you, Mr. Claymore," she said. "Antonía will undoubtedly head south to the border. Though, admittedly, my daughter does not possess the best sense of direction, she does have an extraordinary memory. On several occasions, Claire and I have taken her shopping at a small boutique near Coldstream Bridge—just a stone's throw from England—so she should be able to remember how to get there by using landmarks."

"How in the world did you manage to get Antonía to go shopping?" asked Lord Barclay.

His wife arched one brow. "Claire and I bribed her by letting her ride Mr. MacMillan's horse alongside our carriage. The same horse she's riding now. Thank God, she chose one of stamina." She blinked. "Oh! I almost forgot—when you reach Chartley Hall, seek out the chapel on the grounds. There you will find the Reverend Goode. Mary has told me much about him in her letters. He will know if Antonía has been there."

Claymore summoned a broad smile. "I will find her," he promised, "and bring her back to both of you, safe and sound."

Good-byes, good lucks, and Godspeeds were expeditiously issued before the determined young man mounted his horse and headed south in the moonlight, intent on keeping his promise.

Watching at the doorway, Lady Barclay turned to her husband and smiled. "That young man certainly knows how to inspire confidence."

It had been a long night, an even longer ride, and Antonía longed to get off her horse because, to be honest, her backside was killing her. Despite the fact that she was an expert horsewoman, no human bottom on God's green earth was designed to withstand that many nonstop hours in a hard saddle. But Providence must have been shining its mercy upon her, because in the near distance, the cerulean waters of Lochleven sparkled in the morning sun.

She dismounted, and although every muscle in her aching body screamed for rest, Antonía refused to succumb to their plea. Instead, she walked her horse the remaining mile to the vast blue loch and stood upon its banks. There wasn't a soul in sight. She took a deep breath and, with a peculiar combination of relief and anticipation, listened to the soft lapping of the water against the shore.

Lochleven was not completely foreign to Antonía. She had heard Minnie speak of her brother-in-law many times and once, as a child, she had even visited the isle with Minnie. Their carriage driver had rowed Minnie and Antonía through the clear, gelid waters to the island. Lochleven Castle had stood in the middle of the land, looking bitterly cold and a wee bit eerie.

The grim exterior, however, existed in stark contrast to the warmth and affability she'd found inside the castle in the guise of Minnie's family. They were servants to a laird who lived elsewhere. Evidently, the laird paid infrequent visits to Lochleven, and when he did, his visits were of a very short duration.

"May I be of service, lass?" A craggy voice with a Scottish burr broke into her thoughts.

Antonía whirled around. A stocky older man with bushy gray hair and kind eyes stood a few feet away, a concerned look on his face. It had been a good many years, but she recognized him and took a tentative step forward.

"Gus? Is it you?"

"Lady Antonía?" He squinted at her for a moment before breaking into a broad smile. "Indeed, 'tis ye, lass! Why, I canna believe it!" He opened his arms and took her into a fierce bear hug that left her breathless. "What a beautiful lass ye've become! And where is Minnie? She dinna send word that she was coming." The old gent held her close as he looked around for his relative.

And while Antonía could prevaricate with the best of them, she simply could not lie to the kind and gentle man half-smothering her. She extricated herself from his bearlike hold and, with a pat on his arm, prepared to tell him the truth.

"Gus," she said slowly, "I came here alone. And . . ." She swallowed hard. "I *know*."

Gus looked puzzled. "Lass, could ye be a wee bit more specific?"

"I know the lies of Lochleven." She took a deep breath and then blurted out the truth. "I know that my biological mother is Mary, Queen of Scots.

Two nights ago, Sir Basil Throckmorton and his son visited Barclay Castle, noticed my birthmark, and now know my true identity." She watched the color drain from the old man's lined, weathered face, but she continued. "Minnie, fearing for my safety, told me as much as she knew, but she swears she doesn't know where my mother is presently imprisoned. That's why I'm here, Gus. I must find my mother."

Gus stared down at her, shaking his shaggy head. "Good lord! The Throckmortons! Have they not wreaked enough havoc on Queen Mary's life? And now, after all these years, they have resurfaced and found her daughter." He dragged one hand through his unkempt hair.

"I must find her," she repeated.

Gus sighed deeply. "And because ye *are* her daughter, I suppose it would do no good to ask ye not to go?"

Antonía shook her head. "None at all."

"Well, then." He stared at the ground for a long minute and then raised his eyes to hers, solemn and regretful. "Yer mother has recently been moved to Chartley Hall, deep in the English countryside, but I beg of ye not to go to her. If the Throckmortons capture ye, they'll throw ye into prison as well. And possibly Queen Elizabeth will consider ye an even greater threat to her throne than your poor mother."

Antonía's throat tightened. She knew his words were true, and if she were honest with Gus—and herself—she was terrified at the thought of facing the Throckmortons again.

"Dear Gus, I understand the risks, but if I don't at least attempt to see my mother, I'll spend the rest of my life regretting it," she said. Refusing to mince words, she added, "We both know she has already outlived her life expectancy with the English. She could be sentenced to death at any moment, and I refuse to stand idly by and await news of her execution."

Gus lifted his gaze to the heavens and then closed his eyes.

"Gus," Antonía asked, unable to keep the amusement from her voice, "are you praying for God to stop me?"

He shook his head. "Nay, lass. I'm praying for bad weather or the arrival of Lord Barclay." He opened his eyes, scoured the sky and then the road, and heaving a big sigh, smiled. "Well, lass, who am I to oppose God's will? But by the looks of ye and your horse, I'd say the both of ye could use some sustenance. We'll feed your horse and let him rest here for a spell while we row over to the castle and feed ye. My granddaughter, Lucy, will be delighted to see ye after all these years."

Seeing right through him, she asked, "Gus, you wouldn't happen to be stalling for time, would you?"

He didn't bother to lie. "Och, of course I am, but ye're not going to get very far if ye don't eat, so you may as well humor me."

After making it across the loch and up to the castle, Gus, Antonía, and his granddaughter Lucy sat in its warm kitchen nattering through a hearty Scottish breakfast. But if truth be told, Antonía was relatively disinterested in chitchat; she was totally focused on achieving her goal. She was going to England and no one was going to stop her, that much she knew. How she was going to get there and how long it would take would most definitely hinge on Gus's spirit of cooperation. Once Lucy went outside to tend to the animals, Antonía turned anxiously to the Scotsman. But before she could even speak, he held up one hand.

"Lass," he said, "for any of the following to make sense, I must give ye some background information on Sir Basil Throckmorton. First and foremost, the man is brilliant. In fact, he's a genius, but a genius gone amuck. Before he wormed himself into the political arena, he was the most renowned physician and alchemist in all of England. His lotions, potions, and herbal remedies have become the stuff of legend in the medical community as well as throughout the general population. With a single wave of his mortar and pestle, the man can cure everything from piles to plague. As a result of his huge brilliance and enormous success, he has accumulated immense wealth and consequently immense power."

"Indeed," Antonía said thoughtfully.

"Aye. But sadly, Sir Basil has mixed as many noxious potions as he has salubrious ones. The man should've been locked up long ago, but after curing Queen Elizabeth of smallpox a few years back, he can pretty much do anything he pleases and the powers-that-be look the other way. In fact, most of the country regards him with a certain degree of awe, along with a certain degree of pure hatred."

"Then I'd say Sir Basil must feel very much at home in the political arena," commented Antonía, whose regard for politicos at court was low indeed.

"Aye, lass," agreed Gus, "and his influence is far-reaching as well as long-lasting. When Queen Mary gave birth to ye here some nineteen years ago, Throckmorton and his villainous cohorts scoured the island looking for ye—a mere infant one day old. Their plan was to take ye from yer mother and use ye as a political pawn to capture the Scottish crown. The queen, who was fully aware that her reign was foredoomed, did everything in her power to protect ye from Throckmorton's treachery. She heard he was coming to kill her newborn child in order to ingratiate himself with Elizabeth."

Antonía shivered. "What a cold-hearted bastard."

"Aye, and much worse," Gus said, "only hours after yer birth, Minnie and I bundled ye up, rowed you across Lochleven, and delivered ye to the Barclays. 'Twas a heartbreaking decision for the queen, but she knew it was the only way to ensure yer safety."

Antonía fell silent for a moment, imagining how hard it must have been for her mother. "And what did she tell Sir Basil when they came looking for me?"

"She lied," he answered gravely. "Yer mother said ye had died at birth. Not surprisingly, he didn't believe her and became so infuriated that he kidnapped yer mother and took her to England, where she's been held captive to this very day."

Her eyes widened at the horrific act of malice. She hadn't seen this one coming either. She felt as if everything in her life was suddenly careening out of control. For the first time since she'd fled Deerfield, she felt fear making inroads.

Gus's eyes softened with sympathy. He reached over to take her hand and clasped it between his two large ones. "Och, lass, I'm sorry ye must learn all of this. Because of Basil Throckmorton ye were torn from yer mother's loving arms the minute ye were born. And I can tell ye, it nearly killed the queen to give up her only daughter. None but the strongest of women could have done what she did."

Antonía's mind was racing even as her heart filled with rage. It was Throckmorton's fault that she had been separated from her real mother, his fault that the queen had been imprisoned. "So Sir Basil stayed in Scotland?" she asked.

"Nay, he went back to his own dark castle in England, known as Wrathbone Manor. 'Tis in fact located near Chartley Hall, where your mother is incarcerated."

"How convenient," responded Antonía, her brain still buzzing a mile a minute. "Gus, I must see my mother. No, more than that, I must *free* her."

Gus stared at her, his eyes widening. "Lass, I understand, but she's guarded every moment of every day. To try and break into Chartley Hall and help yer mother escape is foolhardy at best, suicidal at worst!"

"Gus, I categorically refuse to sit around and twiddle my thumbs while matters go from bad to worse for the woman who brought me into this world. We cannot squander time by dithering and tarrying and being afraid to confront life's challenges! As God is my witness, I shall not allow my mother to wither away in some god-awful despicable English prison!" She paused before imploring, "Now, will you guide me to Chartley Hall, or not?"

"Indeed I will not!"

"Then by God, I'll go alone!" Antonía stood up, trembling with anger. Gus stood, shaking his head.

"Lass, ye know I am quite capable of tying ye up and holding ye here until Lord Barclay comes to fetch ye. I dinna risk life and limb to save ye when ye were a babe to have ye throw it all away now. That wasn't what the queen wanted, and I am loyal to her, always."

The true concern in his eyes as well as the truth of his sacrifice sent a wave of shame over Antonía. She drew in a deep breath and released it slowly, letting her anger go.

"Gus. Dear Gus," she said in a calm voice. "You are a good and loyal man. And yes, you may tie me up and throw me into your cellar until Lord Barclay arrives. But hear me and know this—unless I'm locked in a dungeon for the rest of my days, I will not rest until I meet my objective. And if meeting my objective means knocking down and obliterating every obstacle that stands in my way, then that's what I'll do. Because nothing and no one can keep me away from my mother." She raised her head in determination. "Now, will you help me or not?"

Running a hand through his shock of thick, gray hair, Gus sighed. "There's no stopping ye, is there?"

She shook her head, pressing her lips together in determination.

He gave her a wry smile. "Aye. Ye are just like her. Stubborn and courageous to the core!" With a sigh he shook his head. "I'll have Lucy gather some provisions for our junket south. It's quite apparent ye plan on going one way or another, and I canna let ye go alone. We'll leave today, but first ye must rest a bit."

Antonía threw her arms around the gruff old man and hugged him tightly. "I knew you would give in."

"Careful, lass, or I might change my mind. And I mean it, Antonía, I want ye to rest for a few wee minutes." She opened her mouth to protest and he held up one hand, silencing her. "Please. 'Tis little to ask."

She smiled sheepishly. "Agreed. Thank you, Gus. I'll never forget this."

An hour later, Antonía—feeling refreshed from her wee power nap and fresh clothing borrowed from Lucy—walked with the girl and Gus down to the loch.

After packing the boat with supplies, Gus and Antonía hugged Lucy good-bye, climbed into the small boat, and sculled across the water to the mainland.

As Antonía worked the oars, she experienced a powerful surge of single-minded purpose. Her steely resolve rapidly and resolutely transmuted into an iron-willed decision: She would find her mother . . . or she would die trying.

Chapter 8

THE TREES FOR THE FOREST

Rex Throckmorton lay sprawled across a silken sofa in the huge library of Wrathbone Manor, his muddy boots destroying the fabric, much to his satisfaction. A stone fireplace filled the wall opposite the sofa, bright embers burning in the peat stacked therein. In front of the huge, narrow windows to the right, Basil Throckmorton sat behind a large, elaborately carved desk covered with parchments.

"When are we going back to Barclay Castle?" Rex demanded. "You know how I hate to stay at home. This place is about as stimulating as a mausoleum!"

His father glanced up from his desk. "For once I actually agree with you."

"What do you think they've done with Antonía? Our spy told us she was at the ball, but then she seemed to have vanished into thin air." Rex paused and then put himself in the spy's shoes. "Most likely the bungling idiot got drunk and simply lost track of her."

"Yes, you just can't get good help anymore," Throckmorton replied. "Especially in Scotland."

"I can't believe you let the Barclays kick us out," Rex said, his voice sullen. "I coulda taken out the whole family if you'd only backed me up."

"Indeed," Throckmorton said, shaking his head. His son was a trial, to say the least. He was bullheaded, arrogant, and honestly thought he was going to wed Antonía Barclay. "I thought it best *not* to kill one of the most prominent families in Southern Scotland. Scots find that bad form."

"If you'd let me take Antonía captive like I wanted from the start, she'd be fat with my bastard by now and be forced to marry me."

Throckmorton raised one dark brow, remarking mildly, "Again, since Antonía is the daughter of Mary, Queen of the Scots, I decided it was probably unwise to allow my son to impregnate her against her will."

Rex curled back his top lip. "Queen! Does Antonía know she's the daughter of that scheming whore?"

But the question was left suspended in air because Sir Basil had found the letter he'd been looking for and opened it smoothly with the long, narrow knife he always carried. He read the short missive and glanced over at his lump-headed son.

"According to the maid I planted in the Barclay household to replace the one who usually attends the old nanny, Miss Barclay was informed of her true identity on the evening of the Deerfield ball . . . and then disappeared." He tapped the folded letter against his chin.

"Well, that's just great," Rex said in disgust, rising from the sofa and stomping over to the fireplace. "How are we supposed to find her now?" He kicked at the logs, causing flames to leap up and catch his boot on fire.

As his buffoon of a son danced around the room stamping his foot, trying to put out the fire, Throckmorton sighed. "If you'd just learned your mother was the former Queen of Scots, where would you go?" Sir Basil asked rhetorically. "We shall leave immediately for Chartley Hall and intercept the exquisite Miss Barclay before she reaches her mother. Then, I shall guide her there myself."

Befuddled by any idea even remotely related to subtlety, Rex scowled at his father. "What the hell are you talking about? You're going to *help* her find that Scotch whore?"

Throckmorton glared at his son. Sometimes he really wished he had drowned him as a child. But too late now.

"Rex, you fail to see my true intent," he said, rising from his chair. He walked over to his son, who was now glaring at the fireplace, the fire on his boot extinguished but still smoking. "Amongst your vast constellation of problems is the fact that you lack imagination."

Rex shifted his gaze to his wide belly. "It's not that vast," he said. "And I don't appreciate you always criticizing my manly physique! Nor do I understand why you would *want* Antonía to meet that scheming whore of a mother."

Growing weary of his son's ignorance, Throckmorton replied dismissively, "Let's just say I'm a sucker for mother-daughter reunions."

"Tell me the truth!" Rex demanded.

"Watch your tone of voice," Throckmorton warned, but, sensing his son needed some kernel of truth to fill the huge cavity between his ears, he decided to explain. "Once we have our precious princess in tow, we'll overthrow King James and assume control of the Scottish monarchy. There is, however, the question of how to prove that Antonía is genuinely the child of Mary. Few people are aware of the existence or significance of the Stuart birthmark."

"So how do you plan to do that, dear father?" Rex snickered. "I know! Maybe you could invent a bloodline test or something." He burst out laughing and slapped his belly like a drum.

Throckmorton cocked his head. "No doubt I could do that—not a bad idea, though it's a mystery how you ever thought of it—but it would take too long. I, however, have another way to prove Miss Barclay's pedigree."

Rex closed one eye in thought and then spoke eagerly. "Oh, I know! If we take her to her mother, maybe Mary will recognize her as her daughter!"

Throckmorton slammed his palm against his forehead and fought for control. "It is *said*," he finally went on, "that only the heir to the Scottish throne can hold the Royal Sceptre of the Scots without perishing."

"The what of the what?" Rex asked, scratching his bald head.

Sir Basil frowned. Although his son had always had a problem with lice and his hairless pate was an improvement—suggested by the manor's barber—the shiny orb was a blinding distraction. But Sir Basil moved on.

"Mary is said to be in possession of the Royal Sceptre," Throckmorton said, almost to himself. "Rather like the Scottish version of Excalibur."

"Now you're just talking nonsense," Rex said with a laugh. "Next you'll be saying that fairies and unicorns are real."

"Don't be absurd." The elder Throckmorton went back to his desk and sat down. He stacked up all the papers and parchments on the desk and then lifted a large piece of parchment.

"What's that?" Rex asked.

"A map. I always like to check directions before I set off on a road trip."

"Bloody hell!" Rex retorted. "Only wimps do that. Real men don't ask for directions."

"I'm not asking for them; I'm researching them before we leave."

Rex shrugged. "Still sounds wimpy to me. So when do we go and pick up Antonía?"

"Pick her up?" Throckmorton gave a short laugh. "There'll be a lot more to it than that!"

"Maybe you could lure her by baking a big batch of scones," Rex suggested. "That would certainly attract me!"

Sick of justifying his decisions to a half-wit, Throckmorton exploded. "Look, you idiot, Miss Barclay will come to us neither eagerly nor willingly! Judging from her rather saucy temperament, she'll fight you like a wildcat."

"Don't you mean she'll fight *us*?" sputtered Rex.

"No. I mean you. In spite of the fact that I saved Queen Elizabeth from a near-fatal bout of smallpox, she might misconstrue a visit to Mary as part of a plan to usurp her throne. Which, of course, is my end-run goal. But first things first. And first is the Scottish throne. I'm too well-known to take the chance of being spotted at Chartley. But *you*, my boy, are a different story altogether. No one will recognize you if you're seen."

Viewing his son as a completely dispensable commodity, he went ahead and threw him a bone by adding, "And I intend to ensure your success by giving you a special potion to use on Miss Barclay."

Rex's eyes immediately lit up with a mix of delighted surprise and rapacious excitement. "As much as I like my women full of spit and vigor, it's a lot easier to ravish them when they're unconscious. So you'll taint the scones with poison?"

Fully cognizant of his son's malevolent, albeit stupid, nature, Throckmorton detected the evil glint in his beady little eyes. "There will be no scones. What's more, if you harm or compromise Miss Barclay in any way, I'll bake you a big batch of hemlock biscuits for dinner and shove them down your throat one by one."

"With butter?" Rex asked, his eyes lighting up.

Throckmorton sighed. "What am I thinking? Never mind, Rex. I will send two of my most trusted henchmen to retrieve Miss Barclay."

"That's not fair," whined his son. "Why can't I go after her? And no scones? That's downright mean!"

Sir Basil found himself in a bind. Despite being disgusted by his son's lewd mind, coarse language, and gluttonous appetite, he needed his complicity in several upcoming criminal pursuits. His son was an idiot, but a useful idiot. Unless Rex thought Miss Barclay was going to be the ultimate prize, he would no doubt refuse to be the muscle in the scheme, and henchmen, no matter how loyal, could be bribed in the opposite direction. Thus, after a moment's deliberation, he offered his son a compromise.

"Fine. I'll allow you to accompany the henchmen. However, Miss Barclay is a lady of royal blood and not to be trifled with—therefore, I will order a woman of ill repute for you tonight if you need an outlet for your base desires."

"Fair enough," replied Rex with a vicious smile that revealed yellow, plaque-infested teeth. "But eventually I want Antonía to be the outlet. Or should I say the inlet." He laughed obnoxiously.

What a pig, Basil thought, curling his lip in disdain. He rolled up the map and cast his noisome son a piercing look. "I set the timetable around here, not you. Remember that."

"On one condition," Rex said, his tone cloying. Throckmorton lifted one brow in question. "Just one batch of scones, Fadda dear?"

Throckmorton sighed and then decided that he would indeed bake scones . . . using a highly effective sedating ingredient. He needed some peace and quiet to finish plotting phase two of his plan. Nothing must go wrong, beginning with the abduction of the lovely Miss Barclay. Overthrowing the Scottish monarchy would be impossible without her.

Upon reaching a decisive fork in the road, Gus Corbett slowed his horse and turned to his traveling companion.

"Antonía, lass, we've been riding for six hours or more, and I fear my old bones won't make Chartley Hall tonight. Would ye be willing to camp and get a fresh start in the morning?"

Not in the least tired, and frantic to reach her mother, Antonía glanced up at the sky. It seldom turned completely dark this time of year, and she'd counted on reaching Chartley by nighttime. Still, sympathetic to her friend's plight, she reluctantly agreed.

After watering their horses at a nearby stream and refilling their own water pouches, Gus built a fire. Soon they sat facing each other over the small fire. Eating the supper Lucy had packed for them, Antonía fell silent, restlessness flooding through her veins. The thought of waiting for an hour, much less all night before resuming their ride, seemed too much to bear.

Gus finished a leg of mutton and wiped the back of his sleeve across his face. "'Twas a good meal," he said and then frowned a little, his eyes scanning Antonía's neck. "Where did ye come upon the necklace, lass? 'Tis a beauty."

For a moment, Antonía felt unable to respond to his question. Her lower lip quivered, and to quell the involuntary movement she bit down, hard. She felt vulnerable and utterly defenseless, but had no idea why. The pendant on its fine silver chain lay atop the blouse Lucy had lent her. Gus had insisted she be clothed as a woman, but Antonía had secretly brought along her "riding clothes" pilfered from her brother.

As she lifted the pendant and cradled it in her hand, the image of Mr. Claymore played in her mind. For a fraction of one very uncomfortable minute, she felt so unbearably distraught that she considered rethinking her quest.

But the moment soon passed. With her iron will intact, Antonía ruthlessly crushed her own emotional rebellion. Yes, she missed Mr. Claymore. She longed to have his arms around her, but not yet. She'd find her mother first, no matter the sacrifice.

"A friend made it for me," Antonía finally answered, and unclasped her necklace and handed it to Gus.

"'Tis a replica of a claymore sword!" he said in astonishment, admiring the exceptional craftsmanship. "At first I thought it a Trinity cross of some kind." Examining it more closely, the astute old man's head jerked up without warning and his gray brows moved upward. "Breck Claymore made this for ye."

Now it was Antonía's turn to be astonished. "You've met Mr. Claymore?" It was a small country, indeed.

"Aye, I've made his acquaintance. Mr. Claymore is an extraordinary young man. The laird of Lochleven Castle commissioned a set of claymores for his Perthshire castle. I was sent to purchase and deliver them." Gus handed the necklace back to her. "Your friend is a gifted craftsman, as well as a formidable specimen of a man."

Was it the heat from the fire or was she blushing madly? She said nothing but realized he knew everything, no doubt from her fiery cheeks. She remained silent, awaiting his interrogation.

A sly smile crept across Gus's lips and Antonía braced herself. No doubt he was savoring the fact that he could now tease the young woman who had so mercilessly busted his backside on the fast-clipped journey. He reached into his pack and drew out a flask. After offering her a drink, which she declined, he took a swig and then grinned.

"Apparently Mr. Claymore is the most sought-after bachelor in Perthshire, Edinburgh, Inverness," he said, "indeed, in all of Scotland. Between running his business and fending off lasses, it's a wonder the man had time to make this necklace for ye."

She arched one brow, determined not to let him break her. "Oh really? I had not heard he was a philandering type of man."

"Oh, aye," he said, nodding his head. "Though I would say, since Mr. Claymore spent a fair amount of time and trouble crafting this lovely bit of jewelry for you, he seems to have taken more than a passing fancy for you."

"Thank you," she said, looking daggers at him.

"Aye, and 'tis a fact that a man like Mr. Claymore wouldn't take kindly to the notion of his lass running away from him." His knowing gaze held hers as he smiled. "Especially for the purpose of breaking into an English prison."

Antonía met his gaze unflinchingly. "Perhaps the lass's business is none of Mr. Claymore's."

Ignoring her comment and seeming to revel in his running monologue, he added, "'Tis a fairly safe guess that the formidable Mr. Claymore could easily track down his unruly lady in no time flat. Then, of course, there's no telling what he'd do."

"I'm sure you'd be willing to hazard a guess," Antonía said, rolling her eyes.

He took another drink of whiskey. "Oh aye, aye," he said with a nod. "I'd hazard a guess that Mr. Claymore might just throw her over his knee and spank her—hard." He squinted one eye at her. "And I, for one, would say she would thoroughly deserve it."

Antonía gave Gus an innocent smile. "And I, for one, would say she would thoroughly enjoy it."

Was it the heat from the fire or was the old man blushing madly? Antonía's smile widened, but she decided not to tease poor Gus any further. As he took an especially long drink from his flask, Antonía's smile faded, realizing the truth of Gus's words—well, the part about Mr. Claymore following her at least. If he found her, he would no doubt act like every other male she'd ever encountered and force his decisions upon her, which would no doubt mean thwarting her plans.

And here she was sitting and wasting time, giving him a chance to catch up with her. She sighed. Mostly assuredly, Mr. Claymore was more than smart enough to figure out her plan.

Glancing over at Gus she pretended to yawn. "I think I'll get some sleep," she said. "I assume I'll be breaking my bum before sunrise as usual?"

Gus chuckled. "You have quite the mouth on you, young lady. Aye, we will get an early start." He stood and stretched. "I'll fetch the blankets."

Half an hour later, Antonía lay in silent expectation next to the campfire, the blanket wrapped tightly around her. As Gus began to snore, she released a pent-up breath. After waiting as long as she could bear, she quietly rose, rolled up the blanket, and made her way to the horses. If she hurried, she could reach Coldstream by morning, and Chartley Hall before dusk.

ANTONIA BARCLAY AND HER SCOTTISH CLAYMORE

Breck Claymore reached the village of Coldstream a couple of hours after dawn, tired and hungry, but no less determined to find the woman he loved. With increasing concern he acknowledged that too much time had elapsed and perhaps opportunity along with it. He was more than a little worried that he'd yet to overtake the indomitable Miss Barclay. His greatest fear was that she'd already crossed over the border onto English soil and he'd arrived too late to stop her from storming Chartley Hall.

On this cool and windy day, Claymore paused at a stream outside the village long enough to let his horse rest while he sat and ate bread and cheese hastily prepared by Lady Barclay herself. Though he hadn't known Miss Barclay but a few days, he thought he understood the nature of her strong personality. She was the kind of woman who'd do almost anything to get what she wanted. And while he understood Antonía's impetuous decision to rush to the side of her newly discovered mother, what he could not understand was why she had not shared her plan with him.

He smiled, remembering Lord Barclay's admonition that his daughter was not a woman easily tamed. Perhaps he did have his job cut out for him after all. Ah, well, she was worth it.

After finishing his breakfast, Claymore mounted and rode through the village. He realized that if Miss Barclay had been sighted in town, everyone there would remember. After spotting a pub, he stopped, tied his horse outside, and entered the dreary establishment. The place was dark and dank, with a slight scent of mold, but he ignored the smell and sat down at a rough-hewn table. A few seconds later, a woman with unkempt hair and one eye covered with a black patch approached him.

"Now there's a braw laddie if I e'er saw one," she said in a broad Scottish burr. "What can I get you, dearie?"

"Information," Claymore said, taking her hand. Her one good eye widened as he pressed several coins into her palm. He then went on to describe Miss Barclay.

Blushing and stammering, the woman told him that his beautiful lass had, indeed, passed through Coldstream only two hours before, and it was the talk of the village that one so young and lovely should be traveling alone.

At her words, Claymore jumped up and in a sudden fit of gratefulness, hugged the woman, then turned to find all the two-eyed women in the pub looking aghast, as if wishing they'd been lucky enough to be born with one eye.

He thanked the woman and left the pub. Back on his horse, he considered the road before him. *She's two hours ahead of me and will probably beat me to Chartley Hall*, he thought. *On the other hand, according to her brothers, she could have unwittingly made a wrong turn and ended up in Ireland.*

Claymore smiled at the thought of the able-bodied Antonía swimming the North Sea, a determined look on her face as she headed in exactly the wrong direction. But he had more faith in his Miss Barclay than her brothers did. He'd never met a more intelligent woman, or one braver or more beautiful. He shook his head, aware of his overwhelming depth of feeling for her.

"Mr. Claymore?" a voice said from behind him.

He turned in surprise and saw an older man with a worn face and rumpled clothing sitting astride a tired, panting horse.

"Do I know you?" he asked. The man looked familiar, but he couldn't place him.

"We have met before," the man said. "And if you are the Claymore belonging to Miss Antonía Barclay, then you must be searching for the lass."

"How do you know this?" Claymore looked around, suddenly wary. Could this be one of Throckmorton's men, sent to delay him? But how could they even know he was in pursuit of Antonía? "What is your name, good sir?"

"Gus Corbett of Lochleven."

Claymore relaxed. "Aye, I remember you, and have heard of you as well." He frowned and nudged his horse forward toward the Scot. "What do you know of Antonía? Have you seen her?"

"Aye, she came to me for help to reach her—to reach Chartley Hall, and against my better judgment I agreed. However," he rubbed his grizzled jaw, "Miss Barclay being—well, ye know how she is—apparently grew impatient and left me behind last night as I slept."

"I know the feeling," said Claymore, shaking his head.

"Aye," Gus agreed with a laugh. "She's hard-headed, that one."

"She was seen here two hours ago," Claymore told him. "I'm not exactly sure of the way from here and didn't want to ask the villagers. I'm assuming you could give me directions?"

Gus nodded. "Aye. What's more, I'll guide ye to Chartley. I wouldna want to miss ye giving that wee girl what she has coming to her."

Claymore no longer felt like laughing, though Gus's words brought to mind an altogether humorous picture. If Antonía reached Chartley Hall and was captured by the English, she might be lost to him forever. And that was no laughing matter.

He glanced up at the sun. "Come along then," he said, "let's see if we can outride a wee lass and save her from her own headstrong nature."

Gus shook his head. "Och, laddie, if ye think that's possible, ye dinna know Miss Barclay."

Without another word, Claymore put his heels to his horse and his head to the wind. He knew Miss Barclay indeed, but neither she nor Gus knew what he was capable of when it concerned the woman he loved.

Antonía rode through a fragrant pine forest, hoping it was the one marked on Gus's map, shown to be surrounding Chartley Hall. She felt a little guilty for stealing the map from his saddlebag, and even guiltier for leaving the old man sleeping by the campfire as she took off on her own across the English countryside.

On the other hand, she was probably protecting him from being captured, imprisoned, and drawn and quartered, so when she thought of it like that, her guilt-ridden heart felt vindicated. With guilt swept from her mind, she glanced down at her new outfit. She'd changed into her brother's stolen trousers but had kept Lucy's blouse. She laughed to herself. There was still little doubt that she was the walking image of a fashion faux pas. Claire would be horrified.

Physically and emotionally drained from the long day of traveling, she stopped her horse and took a deep breath. The evocative scent of pine brought the image of Mr. Claymore bubbling to the surface of her weary and troubled mind. For days, she had stubbornly forced him from her thoughts, too afraid that dwelling upon his handsome face would induce her to give up, turn back, and ride home. But she could suppress the thought of him no longer.

As her horse picked its way through the forest, pine needles softening the sound of his tread, Antonía did some serious soul-searching and gradually arrived at the conclusion that there would be no more regrets over the past. She had to be true to herself above all else. But her time for introspection was over.

As she made her way through the forest, Antonía found she was quickly becoming disoriented by the denseness of the conifers casting their branches over her like a great web. After awhile, as much as it killed her to admit it, she was forced to admit *she was lost*. In fact, she was so lost, she could no longer see the trees for the forest, and no longer knew in which direction she was headed.

She dismounted, aware that daylight was quickly fading, especially beneath the thick branches above. All at once, the events of the previous few days caught up with her—the long days in the saddle, the newfound knowledge of her royal heritage, and leaving behind those she loved.

As she stood beside her horse, stroking his comforting mane, Antonía fell victim to her long-held method of dealing with frustration. She cursed, loud and long, and her mind once more reverted to the topic of Mr. Claymore, fully realizing that it was a little early in their relationship to challenge his devotion.

In fact, he might have already revoked his offer to court her. Such a revocation would be completely justified under the circumstances. Railing against both her impetuous stupidity and her stupid impetuosity, and despite being fully aware that her vituperative fit solved nothing, Antonía continued to use it as a welcome emotional release because crying was never an option.

After she was finished, Antonía sank to the ground, feeling utterly depleted. She breathed in deeply several times as she closed her eyes. Finally lifting her head, she felt recharged and prepared to find her way out of the forest.

The question was—which way should she go? She stood, brushed herself off, and then heard the whinny of a horse not more than a stone's throw away. Quickly swinging up on her own mount, she turned him toward the sound—and saw a young man atop a very talkative mare riding toward her. She gasped at his unexpected appearance.

The young man pulled his horse to a stop and bent his head respectfully. "I do beg your pardon, m'lady," he said. "I didn't mean to startle you."

"Where did you come from?" Antonía asked. Oh God, had he heard her unladylike tirade? "How long have you been watching me?"

He smiled and she noted kindness in his eyes. Or perhaps he was just trying to lure her into trusting him with his gentle countenance.

"Only long enough to be able to say that with such an impressive litany of invectives at your disposal, you might find Billingsgate a far better showcase for your talents rather than this dark forest."

Antonía felt her face grow red, no doubt to the color of a rowanberry. She started to apologize but stopped and lifted her chin. She owed no apology to this stranger. "What is your name, sir?"

The young man inclined his head in a polite nod. "My name is Stephen Goode. I am parson of Chartley Hall Chapel. Are you lost? May I inquire as to your name, m'lady?"

As she stared wide-eyed at the charming young reverend, a trio of tentative thoughts crossed her mind. A parson at Chartley Hall? Perhaps being held captive in an English prison was a vastly underrated experience; or perhaps treachery and subterfuge were manifesting themselves in the guise of one very handsome Englishman; or perhaps goodness and virtue were present on the scene and she was looking her guardian angel straight in the eye. *Hmm, it was hard to know.*

"My name is Antonía Barclay," she said, deciding to risk that much. The man's smile disappeared.

"Miss Barclay? Daughter of Lord Henry Barclay?"

"Yes," Antonía said, "and I am not lost. I am just . . . turned around a bit."

"I see," he said. "I'd be happy to escort you to your destination, Miss Barclay, if you would like. Where are you headed?"

"To Chartley Hall. I am—that is—I have an audience with the queen."

His tawny eyebrows shot up. "The queen?" He nodded, and the smile returned. "Do you mean—Mary, Queen of the Scots?"

It was Antonía's turn to be surprised. "Yes. Are you . . . acquainted with her?"

"My dear Miss Barclay, I serve her tea each and every day."

Antonía was circumspect. Could she believe him? Should she share her story with this man? If he were truly a parson, perhaps he could help. But if he wasn't—

"Oh bother," she said with a sigh. "If you are truly a man of the cloth then you will keep what I am about to tell you in strictest confidence. And if you are not, no one will believe you anyway."

"Miss Barclay, I assure you that I am exactly who I claim to be." He gave her an amused smile.

"I'm not sure I believe that smile," she told him, narrowing her eyes. "However, since I am in need of guidance, though not spiritual, I suppose I must trust you." Quickly she told him an abbreviated version of her story. "And now," she concluded, "can you guide me to Chartley Hall? I must meet my mother—unless you think me a madwoman or a charlatan."

The man swung down from his horse and crossed to her side, taking hold of her horse's bridle. Antonía's fingers curled around the small black dagger hidden in the waistband of her trousers. "Miss Barclay, I am delighted to make your acquaintance. Mary speaks of you often."

Antonía blinked down at him. "You call the Queen of Scotland by her first name?"

His lips curved up again. "We are very close friends."

Then it struck her. "Wait! You believe me? You believe I am her daughter?"

"I know that you are. As I said, she speaks of you often. But up until this moment, I did not realize that you knew you were Mary's child." He paused and then said gently, "Miss Barclay, would you like me to take you to your mother?"

In spite of his immediate acceptance of her tale, or perhaps because of it, Antonía hesitated. This was far, far too easy. In fact, it reeked of an ambush. She needed to determine whether he came with a glowing halo and a full set of wings, or spiky horns and hooves.

She shook her head. "I'm sorry, but there are those who would prefer to see me dead. How can I trust you? You may be leading me into a trap."

Reverend Goode gazed up into her eyes and then reached up and covered her hand with his. "I would not lie to you, Miss Barclay. I am a man of God, albeit a Protestant man of God, but a man of God nonetheless, so you can trust me. I would never allow harm to come to Mary's daughter."

"Reverend Goode, if you are intimating that my mother and I share the same faith, then you are incorrect. In point of fact, *you* and I share the same faith. Consequently, if you are telling me an untruth, I shall have no choice other than to convert to Catholicism in religious protest. And should I discover that you're telling me an *elaborate* untruth, I shall be forced to take my protestation one step further by joining the local nunnery."

"Such a protestation would be an unmitigated waste of young womanhood," he said, then moved his hand to his heart. "I swear that I shall never lie to you, Miss Barclay."

Antonía sighed. "If only parsons were required to carry a badge or identification of some sort."

His eyes grew solemn. "As God is our witness, I am who I say I am, and I shall never lead you astray."

After a long moment, Antonía nodded. "Reverend Goode, if you will be so kind then as to lead the way, I shall follow. And if you mean me ill, may God have mercy on your soul."

After the reverend mounted his horse once more, Antonía marveled at the fact that it took only a few short minutes to reach the grounds of Chartley Hall. *It's astounding how short a journey can be when you're following someone familiar with the territory,* she thought. However, when Reverend Goode stopped his horse in front of a conservatively sized house, annexed to a small church, Antonía's suspicions resurfaced.

"My mother lives with you in the parsonage? Apparently you're closer friends than I imagined."

The reverend's gray eyes crinkled with good humor. "Although your mother and I are friends, the queen resides on the top floor of Chartley Hall, which is nearby. Since it's relatively early in the evening, the servants and guards are still moving about Chartley Hall. We should wait until they retire. You'll then have a better chance of visiting your mother unobserved." He gave her a thoughtful look. "I daresay you could do with something to eat and drink, m'lady?"

His explanation sounded plausible, and she was starving. "Very well," she agreed, "but be forewarned that I know how to defend myself."

The corner of his mouth twitched with amusement. "I'll keep that in mind, Miss Barclay."

After helping her dismount, Reverend Goode led her through the deserted sanctuary and into the parsonage. He made certain she was comfortable. He made certain she felt safe. He made certain she drank her tea. As the young clergyman prepared dinner, Antonía observed him with guarded curiosity.

Who was this Englishman? He was so young, certainly no more than five and twenty, and so disarmingly kind, so genuinely solicitous, and so unabashedly adorable. As she watched him dash about the kitchen, she acknowledged that there were few things more endearing in a man than performing domestic tasks well beyond his capabilities.

And the proof was in the pudding, or rather, in the tea, because it was atrocious. Moreover, the bread was horrendous, the soup was ghastly, and the shepherd's pie a nightmare. But his effort to provide hospitality, his wish to serve, and his desire to please proved a thoroughly winning combination. As she valiantly forced down the last bite of his nightmarish pie, Reverend Goode asked if he could do anything more.

She replied with sincerity, "Thank you. You've been immensely kind, Reverend Goode." She then lied with equal sincerity, "And your cooking is superb."

He laughed. "Thank you, Miss Barclay, for your kindness. I am not much of a cook. But please, call me by my Christian name, which is Stephen."

"If you prefer, I shall call you Stephen," replied Antonía. "But you must continue to call me Miss Barclay. I'm a stickler for the social graces."

Reverend Goode nodded, realizing she was kidding. "Yes, indeed, I observed your affinity for etiquette when I first came upon you in the forest, *Miss Barclay*." He couldn't help but blush as he shook his head. "Your expertise in the field of cursing appears to have been richly and assiduously cultivated. Where in God's name did a lady of culture learn to curse so divinely?"

"Guilty as charged, but it's not *entirely* my fault. On second thought, I must change my plea to not guilty by reason of multiple brothers, who are *solely* to blame for my shameful vocabulary. Therefore, you must believe me when I testify to being otherwise innocent and pure."

"I have no doubt of that, Miss Barclay. And now, what can I do for you until you meet with your mother?"

"Tell me about her," she said simply.

The hours passed quickly as Reverend Goode patiently answered Antonía's many questions. Although Queen Mary had spent almost two decades as a prisoner in various places of confinement, she had become neither bitter nor desperate, he told her. As the years of captivity mounted, the queen had graciously accepted her fate by cultivating outlets of happiness within her limited world of habitation. She enjoyed reading, needlework, chess, and corresponding with a number of friends, the most valued being Lady Cassandra Barclay.

According to the parson, the queen anticipated and cherished every letter Lady Barclay wrote regarding her daughter. Adamantly refusing to succumb to mawkish sentimentalism, Mary chose to be grateful that Antonía had been blessed with a wonderful family and often remarked to Reverend Goode that she'd never be able to repay Lady Barclay for the happy life she'd given her daughter. Lady Barclay, in turn, related that she would never be able to repay the queen for the gift of that precious life. Throughout the years, Queen Mary and Lady Barclay had most definitely formed a mutual admiration society.

"So you knew I was telling the truth because of my mother's—Lady Barclay's—letters?" asked Antonía, trying to put the puzzle together.

"Yes, Miss Barclay. I think I knew even before you said your name. For although you don't physically resemble your mother, except for your lofty stature, I know royalty when I see it. We English are attuned to that sort of thing."

"And in spite of you being a Protestant—and a parson to boot—you say that you and my mother have become friends?"

"Your mother and I share many common interests; in particular, the new sport of golf." He broke into a self-deprecating grin. "Actually, it's more on the order of a mania with us."

"The guards release my mother for rounds of golf?" she asked in disbelief.

"Believe it or not, there is a small golf course on the grounds," the reverend said. "Only a few holes, but enough to give Mary some recreation."

"I've heard Queen Elizabeth fancies a bit of golf," Antonía said, musing over the thought. "I wonder—what would happen if Queen Elizabeth ran into my mother on one of your golf outings?"

His smile faded. "Then they would meet for the very first time."

Antonía's amusement ended as well. "The Queen of England throws her own cousin into prison for nineteen years but has yet to meet her? What a sad state of affairs."

"Yes, your mother has been dealt a very unfortunate hand by her own kin."

In open admiration of the man who'd made her mother's bleak life bearable, Antonía said earnestly, "I cannot thank you enough for everything you've done on behalf of my mother. You're a fine and honorable man, Stephen Goode."

He laughed softly. "If treason and bribery are your defining characteristics of a 'fine and honorable man,' then I'm very curious to meet the man who is courting you."

She raised both brows. "So you know about him, too?"

The reverend shrugged with a smile. "No, I didn't know with certainty. It was a presumption only, Miss Barclay."

Antonía returned his smile. "Well, you presumed correctly, Stephen." She paused and then said thoughtfully, "In fact, you and Mr. Claymore are very much alike."

"May Heaven help him then," the young clergyman said, chuckling. "All jests aside, Miss Barclay, I have no doubt that the man you choose to wed will be one of great integrity." He stood and offered his hand to her. "And now, having delayed until it is safe, are you ready to meet your mother, Miss Barclay?"

She nodded, rose from her chair, and tucking her hand inside his offered arm, they left the rectory. As they walked, Reverend Goode explained again that the hall wasn't far away. Though the forest surrounded Chartley Hall, there were beautiful gardens planted within the clearings leading up to the manor. Once outside the entrance to Chartley Hall, Reverend Goode stopped and turned to her.

"I apologize in advance for any acts of duplicity, but if we come upon any servants, I must introduce you as my fiancée in order to avoid suspicion. For you see, Miss Barclay, the servants are acquainted with all of my female relations and I truly cannot think of another explanation for your presence here."

"And what will happen when I disappear tomorrow?" she teased him. "Will you confess to breaking my heart?"

"In a few days' time, I shall simply tell the servants you jilted me for a fine and honorable man." He smiled. "It will make total sense to them. I am, after all, just a lowly servant of God, while you—"

"Aha!" she interrupted. "So I am to be the heartbreaker?"

His smile widened. "As much as I regret the necessity of painting you as the villain in the affair, it may be necessary given the circumstances. However, on a more positive note, I shall no doubt garner a sizable amount of feminine sympathy in return for my performance."

"Well, then I will not leave you empty-handed after all, Reverend Goode."

Oddly enough, the Reverend's ruse was neither needed nor implemented. The guard outside the door asked no questions, only nodded at the two. Once inside, Antonía was once again assailed by the uneasy feeling that, all in all, events were unfolding a wee bit too conveniently. Glancing about the deserted hallways, she broached her concern, but Reverend Goode hastily reassured her.

"The guards are used to my comings and goings," he said as he led her down a corridor. "And as I mentioned, as long as there's no danger of Mary escaping, they are content to look the other way." He stopped in front of a door. "Here we are."

Antonía turned and faced Stephen Goode, too anxious to speak.

He took her hands in his own. "I have not had the opportunity to prepare your mother, Miss Barclay. Your arrival will come as a complete surprise to her."

Choked with emotion, she could only nod her understanding.

The reverend smiled gently. "But your mother is royal through and through, and she has grown accustomed to the unexpected. Once the initial shock is over, she will recover her equilibrium immediately." He gave her hands a reassuring squeeze and then released them.

Antonía's heart pounded with nervous excitement as Reverend Goode knocked softly on the door to the queen's—to her mother's—chamber.

Chapter 9

THE INIMITABLE, INDOMITABLE, AND INDEFATIGABLE MQS

Antonía entered the room, which, lit only by a small fireplace and a few strategically placed candles, appeared shadowy, surreal, and a little bit spooky. Near the window, a statuesque figure arose and, clad in a simple robe, crossed the room to stand before her visitors.

So this is Mary Stuart, Antonía thought. *My mother.* Tall and beautiful, her red hair, faded a bit with the years, flowed down her back in casual disarray. As the queen gazed silently into Antonía's eyes, the girl felt an immediate bond with this regal stranger. After a long, poignant moment, the queen spoke.

"You are, indeed, stunningly beautiful," Mary said. "Of the havoc-wreaking variety." One corner of her mouth moved upward. "I can't help but wonder what havoc it has already wreaked."

Antonía felt her cheeks grow warm and she ducked her head. The queen chucked her under the chin and Antonía lifted her head.

"My dear, darling child," she said, and all at once Antonía found herself embraced by her mother—her real mother—and emotion overcame her as the queen hugged her with all the pent-up feelings of nineteen long, hard years of separation.

She clung to her for several minutes, until at last the queen gently disengaged and held her at arm's length, her gaze sweeping over Antonía. To the young woman's surprise, their eyes met on an equal level.

Mary smiled as if she knew what her daughter was thinking. "Yes, my dear Antonía, you have surely inherited the Guise stature. However, you've also inherited your father's striking good looks." Her voice softened. "You have his crystal-blue eyes and his raven-colored hair."

Antonía gazed into her mother's expressive amber eyes. And then, displaying the same gesture her daughter did when pensive, the queen bit down on her lower lip, shaking her head.

"I—I—can't believe I'm meeting you—that you're my mother," Antonía whispered.

Mary gave her another long look and then kissed her on each cheek before turning to Reverend Goode. "I don't know how you managed it or where you found her, but thank you for bringing her to me."

"It's truly my pleasure," he said. "And I'm certain your daughter will explain the strange concatenation of events that precipitated her visit." He paused and then asked, "Shall I return for Miss Barclay at midnight?"

"Yes, Stephen," replied the queen. "I think it best that my daughter stays at the parsonage tonight. I don't want to risk her safety. That won't be a problem, will it? Or lead you into temptation?"

Antonía wasn't sure she heard her mother correctly until the queen laughed and the reverend turned a bright red, though he laughed as well.

"Your mother teases me because a Protestant priest may marry. She tries to convert me to Catholicism on a daily basis, and I get my share of proselytizing in too, but so far, neither of us has budged from our original position. Still"—he picked up the queen's rosary beads—"prayer is never a mistake." He hesitated slightly. "Until later this evening then, Miss Barclay?"

"Of course," Antonía said, glancing at her mother for confirmation.

The queen smiled. "In the meantime," she nodded at the rosary, "pay special attention to the 'do not lead me into temptation' part."

Reverend Goode took her hand and bowed, smiling. "Your Majesty, you are both a delight and a constant trial." To Antonía's surprise, he placed a kiss on the queen's hand before nodding to her daughter and taking his leave.

As soon as the door closed, the queen guided Antonía to a comfortable settee by the fire, patted her hand reassuringly, and sat down beside her. "I've gleaned from Lady Barclay's letters that you harbor a particular disaffection for mother-daughter tête-à-têtes, and so I feel quite honored by your visit."

"Normally, yes. But this is different. I was so anxious to meet you, Your Majesty," she said, feeling guilty at how quickly she had left behind Lady Barclay, the only mother she had ever known, to meet the queen.

"Now, now, none of this 'Your Majesty' business between you and me," said the queen. "Here at Chartley I'm known as MQS for short, but you may call me anything you wish."

"Very well," Antonía said with a smile. "I gather that my—that Lady Barclay has kept you abreast of all the major developments in my life."

"Antonía," Mary took her by the hand, "please do not hesitate to call Cassandra your mother in my presence, for most assuredly she has been and will remain as such. At this late date, I can serve only as an aunt of sorts, and then only for a brief time more."

"Please don't say that!" Antonía said, unable to control the fierceness in her voice. "I want you to be part of my life for a very long time. And though you are my mother, rest assured that doesn't mean I love my adopted mother any less."

"Splendid," the queen said. "You are a wise woman. Now, to answer your question, yes, Cassandra has kept me informed of your activities. However, she certainly did not inform me of your trip here to Chartley Hall."

Antonía shifted slightly in her seat. "Well, my trip was one of those last-minute types of affairs." She swiftly changed the subject. "In any event, Reverend Goode mentioned that you and Lady Barclay correspond with some frequency."

"When I learned that Cassandra strongly suspected the 'twin' was my child," the queen said, "I asked her to communicate with me throughout your life. Of course she always wrote the letters as if she were simply discussing *her* daughter, and on every level, this was the safest and sagest course of action." The queen's gaze softened. "Cassandra has always been my most loyal and trusted friend."

"As well as an informative one." Antonía felt her cheeks grow hot as she wondered what might have been in the letters. Lady Barclay had certainly disapproved of at least a few of her daughter's escapades. She lifted her chin slightly. "Is there any aspect of my life that has *not* been laid open?"

"Probably not," the queen said with a smile. She leaned toward Antonía and touched her cheek tenderly. "Your good mother's thoughtfulness has been boundless. Words can never do justice to her unsparing generosity, her steadfast friendship, and her loving heart. Her letters showered me with rays of warm sunlight on the coldest and darkest of days."

Mary looked away, as if holding on to an emotion she dared not release. After a moment she glanced back, once again unflustered. "Hearing about you, about the wonderful life you enjoy away from the tumult surrounding me, was always a breath of fresh air, which was sorely needed during unsettling times."

"Some of my childhood exploits probably weren't all that uplifting to read about," Antonía said, smiling.

"Only *childhood* exploits?" The queen laughed. "If it's any consolation, I can't recall any matter your mother related that was exceedingly personal. You are acquainted with Lady Barclay, are you not?" she teased. "Then you know that she is unfailingly proper in all of her actions, especially in her correspondence."

"I'm sorry," Antonía said, reaching for her mother's hand. "I didn't mean to complain. It's evident that the joy you received from reading her letters has buoyed your spirits over the course of this unspeakable and unjust incarceration."

"You speak very clearly and articulately, Antonía," observed the queen. "It's evident that a superb education has buoyed your skills in the language arts."

Antonía made a face. "My brother Will forced me to learn the most tiresome subjects. Wait—" She drew in a sharp breath. "This means my brothers are not really my brothers at all!"

Mary patted her hand. "Of course they are," she said. "Just as surely as Cassandra is your mother and Henry is your father." She hesitated and then asked in earnest, "My darling child, precisely how did you learn that I am your mother?"

Antonía deliberated for a moment. Lying to a perspicacious queen was never a good idea, but she despised ratting on Minnie.

"I don't know how much time we'll have together," urged Mary. "Tell me now and let there be no lies between us. Lives may be at stake."

"Our nanny, Minnie Munro, told me."

Mary narrowed her eyes as if trying to see into her daughter's mind. "Minnie must have had a highly compelling reason to divulge the truth to you, Antonía."

"Sir Basil and his boorish son attended a dinner party at Barclay Castle a few nights ago. I mentioned to Minnie that they noticed my birthmark." Antonía rubbed the nape of her neck. "She was forced to tell me the truth for my own protection."

Mary's eyes flashed with sudden fury.

Antonía drew back, startled, as the queen rose to her feet and began to pace, speaking fiercely.

"Sir Basil Throckmorton is beyond all adjectives evil! As I'm certain you are aware, we have him to thank for my rather extended stay in England. Both he and his son were spawned in the fiery depths of Hell."

"Promise me," the queen continued, a trifle red-faced beneath her red hair, "that you will have no further contact with that horrible man and his son!"

"Happily."

The queen gave her an acknowledging smile but continued her diatribe against Sir Basil. "The man is mad, bad, and treacherous to know. He's a master of using and abusing others in order to foment discord and unrest. So often is brilliance superadded to diabolical ambition."

"I agree wholeheartedly with your estimation of those two," Antonía said, moving to her mother's side and laying one hand upon her arm, hoping to calm her.

Mary drew a deep breath. "Forgive me," she said. "I can usually keep the demons at bay. Now," she went on briskly, "who else knows that the Throckmortons have discovered your true lineage?"

"My guess is that Minnie has informed my parents and brothers, but I cannot be entirely certain of the fact."

Mary cast a shrewd eye upon her daughter. "Because you rode here immediately after Minnie told you about me and didn't bother to inform them."

She smiled tentatively. "Right."

The queen sighed. "God have mercy. You're just like me, impetuous and determined." She shook her head and smiled. "No doubt you rode directly here, nonstop and at breakneck speed."

"Mostly true," she said evasively.

"Antonía," said her mother intently, "I need the entire story."

She inhaled deeply. "I first went to see Gus Corbett at Lochleven. He accompanied me as far as Coldstream, but his riding pace was so excruciatingly slow that I decided to ride on ahead while he was still asleep." She saw a look of mild reproof on the queen's face. She rushed on, "Before we delve into the topic of me ditching poor Gus, I must first ask you about my real father."

Concern flickered in the queen's amber eyes as she sank down upon the small sofa and pulled her daughter down beside her. "Well, I suppose I expected this question would come," she said. "What do you wish to know?"

"There are widely varying accounts regarding the nature of your marriage to my father, the Earl of Bothwell. One theory holds that you married him solely for protection against Sir Basil Throckmorton." Antonía hesitated again, and then forged ahead. "Mother, I'm asking you for the truth about my father."

The queen cast her eyes downward, touched by her daughter's use of her parental title. She then deliberated silently, debating on the proper approach to the question. Her own words came back to her: *Let there be no lies between us.*

"Frankly, my darling," she said, "your father was a difficult man, and I did not love him. But he offered me safety, and I had little choice other than to accept it." She lifted her gaze, and Antonía saw a glimmer of tears in her eyes. "Those were tumultuous times, and to be completely honest, up until this moment, I still don't fully understand everything that happened. It seemed as if one day I was Queen of Scotland and the next I was rotting away in an English prison while my husband was being slowly tortured to death in a Danish one."

Stunned into silence by her mother's candid account of her past, Antonía could summon neither a sympathetic retort nor an insightful condolence to ease the pain so evident in Mary's gaze. Biting her lower lip, she wished she'd never pursued the line of questioning in the first place. Sensing her daughter's discomfiture, Queen Mary did what every sensible woman of Scottish origin does in times of crisis: She called for tea.

"You've had quite a shock, my darling, so I shall stir in a healthy dose of sugar." Picking up a small bell on the table beside her, the queen shook it briskly.

The first servant Antonía had seen since her arrival soon delivered a tray filled with a pot of steaming tea as well as crumpets, scones, and clotted cream. Antonía watched the servant set the tray on the low marble table in front of them; she glanced over at the queen, shocked that she would allow anyone else to see her.

"Don't worry," Mary said after the woman curtseyed and left the room. "My servants traveled with me from my home in Scotland long ago. They have gone with me to each of my incarcerations in England and are loyal only to me."

Breathing a sigh of relief, Antonía watched her mother pour the tea, and realized all at once that their minutes together were dwindling with rapid velocity. Although she had accomplished her goal of meeting her mother, she hadn't mentioned her plan to rescue her. But the timing didn't seem quite right. She decided to wait for the proper opening in the conversation.

After all the tea was drunk, the crumpets eaten, and the clotted cream and scones devoured, both women loosened their corsets and ceintures, respectively, and Mary leaned toward Antonía. "Now, I have something very important to tell you," she said.

"Important? So the rest of this was idle chatter?" Antonía said, smiling.

"Very amusing. Yes, this has all been vastly important, but this is perhaps the most important of all."

Antonía nodded.

"I have something to show you," Mary said, and reaching inside her robe, she drew out a tightly wound scroll. "However, I must make a few markings on one side of the parchment before you examine it." After the necessary drawings were made, the queen handed it to her daughter.

"It's a map," said Antonía in a questioning tone.

"Yes. As you can see, one side of the scroll is a map of Wrathbone Manor in relation to Chartley Hall . . . well, as best as I can recollect." The queen drew herself up sharply and Antonía knew her next words were important. "I just now drew the map for one purpose and one purpose only, Antonía—to help you avoid Wrathbone Manor when you return to Scotland. I don't want you anywhere near that devil's lair. It was only by the grace of God you missed it coming here."

"When did you visit Wrathbone Manor?"

"Sir Basil's estate was my first stop on my path to perpetual imprisonment," she replied and then added with an ironic laugh, "and it's been a succession of English prisons ever since. Though, I must say, Chartley Hall is my current favorite."

"I've heard from reliable sources that Sir Basil was once a renowned physician and alchemist."

"Yes, and as far as I know he still dabbles in formulating chemical compounds for various but mainly nefarious reasons." Mary rolled her eyes in a very familiar manner and Antonía couldn't help but smile. "As much as I deplore admitting it, the man is an absolute genius. Unfortunately, he's also an absolute madman! Throckmorton's basement laboratory is gruesomely well-equipped."

Antonía shivered at the thought of it. Her short encounters with the Throckmortons were enough to last her a lifetime.

"Now, look on the other side."

She turned the scroll over and found something written in what appeared to be hen scratchings. "What is this? Some secret code? Hieroglyphics?"

The queen leaned back against the settee and sighed. "*This*, my dear child, is what I wanted to talk to you about. This side of the scroll provides directions—in ancient Gaelic—to the secret hiding place of the Scottish Royal Sceptre."

"Royal Sceptre? You mean, the one the king carries at state occasions?" Antonía gazed down at the scroll. "I didn't know it was missing."

"I'm not surprised," Mary said. "The Royal Sceptre has been missing for over seventy years. My grandfather—your great-grandfather—King James IV carried it into battle at Flodden Field. As every Scot knows, the English slaughtered the king and his ten thousand men on that fateful day. For the life of me, I'll never understand my grandfather's strategy.

The man had a brilliant military mind and yet he displayed incredibly poor judgment during that battle."

Antonía nodded her head in sympathy. "I suppose even kings are entitled to a bad day every now and then."

Her mother shot her a startled look and then laughed out loud. "You have a remarkable gift for understatement." She reached over and patted Antonía's hand. "In any event, your great-grandfather lost his life, as well as the Royal Sceptre, during the course of that 'bad day.'"

"But how did you obtain the scroll?" asked Antonía, attempting to put the pieces in place.

"It was delivered to me two days ago, with a note explaining its purpose, but its origin remains a mystery. Because of this, I cannot substantiate the document's authenticity, and of course, the timing of the scroll's arrival, so close to your own arrival, raises the issue of its validity."

Antonía frowned. "It sounds highly suspicious to me. But, regardless, what does it say?"

"Unfortunately, I am not proficient in ancient Gaelic. French is more my forte. To be completely honest," she said with a slightly sheepish look, "even if I did possess a proficiency in ancient Gaelic, I'm awful with directions."

Antonía threw her head back and laughed. "Well, that explains which side of the family cursed me with *that* defective trait."

Mary returned the smile, but it quickly faded. "Listen to me well, my dear child—you must find the Royal Sceptre and return it to your half brother, King James."

"Why is it so important? Especially after seventy years?" Antonía asked, and her mother's hand tightened around hers, her amber eyes glowing with passion.

"Some say it's simply a superstition, but since the Royal Sceptre has been missing, Scotland has fallen more and more under English attack. Legend says that the sceptre must always be united with the Royal Crown and the Royal Sword, and only then will the Scottish monarchy flourish." She shook her head. "It's hardly news that since the butchering at Flodden Field, the Stuart monarchy has produced somewhat less than stellar results."

Antonía was perfectly willing to do whatever her mother wanted. She retrieved her hand from the queen and opened the scroll again, pressing it flat on the small marble table to scrutinize it. "And you believe this?"

"I do. And for the sake of Scotland, you must find the sceptre and return it to King James. You—and only you—hold the power to return it to the king."

Antonía's heart sank. If she were tracking down the sceptre, how would she be able to free her mother? Perhaps she could free her mother first, and then find the sceptre. Her mind was careening out of control with quests.

"With all due respect, Mother, why am I the only one?"

"According to legend, if anyone other than a Royal Stuart touches the Royal Sceptre, then great harm will befall them. While I cannot provide scientific evidence to support my claim, I can provide you with irrefutable empirical data."

The queen proceeded to chronicle every horrendous tragedy that had befallen every poor, unfortunate soul who'd touched the Royal Sceptre. Possessing little stamina for grisly details, Antonía soon regretted her skepticism, which had opened the floodgates to the gruesome accounts.

"Mother, please," begged Antonía, "I believe you! And I promise I won't permit anyone to touch the Royal Sceptre other than myself and the king. But how am I supposed to find it if we can't translate the instructions?"

Mary leaned forward and lowered her voice. "Gus, the poor man you deserted back in Coldstream, speaks and reads every form of Gaelic imaginable. He'll be able to determine whether or not the scroll is a fraud, and also decipher it. And if, glory be to God, the scroll proves authentic, you must locate the Royal Sceptre and return it to my son—your brother, the king—as soon as possible.

"Well, then," continued the queen with confidence, "I'm certain Gus will arrive here soon, and after *apologizing*, we can ask him to translate the scroll and determine its authenticity. If it is genuine, then you must wait for your brothers to arrive and then go in search of it."

"My brothers?" she said with a quizzical lilt in her voice. "Enlisting their services will most certainly ensure bungling of the quest, and possibly its failure altogether."

Mary tilted her head and cast an admonishing eye on her daughter. "Your good mother has informed me that Will, Matthew, and Oliver are all steady, solid men who love their sister, and I have no doubt they will come to your aid at once."

Antonía was forced to admit that Mary was right. "True," she said with a sigh.

"I shall not permit you and Gus to leave Chartley Hall unescorted," the queen said forcefully. "I will send word immediately to Barclay Castle informing them of your safe arrival here and include a request for your brothers to travel here and accompany you on your search. I feel certain the sceptre is in England, and as long as you are in this vile land, you will need protection." Mary noticed a look of concern cross her daughter's face. "Fear not, for your brothers are probably on their way here as we speak."

"No, I'm not worried about remaining in England until they arrive," Antonía said, swallowing hard. "Mother, it's possible that someone else may land on your prison doorstep before my brothers and Gus do."

Mary's gaze turned somber. "Basil Throckmorton would not jeopardize his standing with Queen Elizabeth by visiting Chartley Hall, but he'll definitely be lying in wait for you once you leave the vicinity. This is the reason you must stay here until your brothers and Gus arrive."

Antonía shook her head. "No, Mother. The someone else I meant is Breck Claymore."

"Claymore?" reiterated Mary. "Maker of the sword of the same name?"

"Yes," Antonía replied in surprise, and then blurted out, "I'm courting him." She paused, clearly flustered. "I mean he's courting me. Well, I guess we're courting each other."

Mary smiled broadly. "This *is* news! Cassandra and I thought you'd never condescend to court any man."

"You sound just like Claire!"

Mary laughed. "From what I've heard about your best friend, she knows you better than you know yourself. But returning to the topic of Breck Claymore, let's cut to the chase." She arched a ginger brow. "Is he handsome?"

"Oh my God," replied Antonía concisely.

The queen laughed again. "Would you marry him if he asked?"

"Time will tell."

Mary eyed her daughter closely. "But surely Mr. Claymore didn't permit you to ride into the English countryside without protest?"

Antonía stood and walked a few feet away, unable to stay still. "I didn't give him the chance. I left without telling him, but I did write him a quick note. To be quite honest, I thought he'd try to stop me from coming to see you."

"Or perhaps he would have escorted you," the queen suggested, arching a familiar brow.

She shrugged. "True, but unfortunately, I thought of that possibility too late in the game." She noticed her mother's gaze move to the mantle clock.

The queen set her teacup down, all business. "Reverend Goode will return shortly."

"Are you certain we can trust him?"

"He shan't say a word to any living soul about our meeting. Despite being English, *and* Protestant, Stephen is a fine man and will not betray us. I know it's difficult for *you* to believe—being both Scottish and Catholic— but Stephen is a man of honor and integrity." The queen hesitated. "Minnie probably forgot to mention that you were baptized Catholic."

Antonía's jaw dropped. God's teeth! She couldn't believe it! She was Catholic? She was a Roman Catholic?

For the entire nineteen years of her life she had operated under the assumption that she was a product of the Protestant Reformation! And now to find out she had been baptized Catholic? A Roman Catholic! For God's sake, it would've been really nice if someone had told her before today. She felt completely and utterly astounded by the news. She sat down before she fell down.

Observing the look of genuine astonishment on her daughter's face, the queen said softly, "So she didn't tell you." Antonía shook her head. The queen continued, "Minnie is a very wise woman and no doubt supposed it dangerous to inform you or the Barclays. The truth is, you were baptized Catholic mere minutes after you were born. It was horrid enough to send you away when you were only hours into this world, but to do so without God's protection was unthinkable." Her expression softened.

"Turbulent times destroyed our future as mother and child, but I could not allow it to destroy your future in the Church."

Antonía felt seized by a sudden anxiety. Would she have to learn how to genuflect? She could name only four saints from memory, and those were the apostles! How could this have happened? She had become a failure at her faith in a matter of seconds!

The queen cocked her head at her and then laughed. "Fear not, my beloved daughter. God shows up wherever and whenever he's called. It's of no importance that for the last nineteen years of Sundays you walked through a church door different than the one originally intended." She smoothed one hand down her daughter's cheek. "At this stage in your life, Antonía, your religious affiliation is your choice, not mine." She paused and drew a deep breath. "Circling back to the issue of the Royal Sceptre, are you quite certain you wish to undertake the quest?"

"Oh! Yes, I am, Mother," Antonía said. "You can trust me."

Relief flooded over the queen's face. "Thank you, my dear child. I hate to place this burden upon you, but James thinks me a superstitious fool and will do nothing about the matter. And perhaps I am." She shook her head and sighed. "I wish I could do it myself, but though I am given some latitude at Chartley, I am still unable to leave for extended periods."

"I'm glad you brought that up," Antonía said, pouncing on the statement. "I didn't come here with the sole purpose of meeting you, Mother." She leaned forward eagerly. "I intend to bring you back to Scotland with me!" The queen's eyes widened and her mouth quivered. "The security here is negligible at best," Antonía went on. "With Reverend Goode's help we could get you out of here and across the border before the English discovered you missing. Once in Scotland, you can live the rest of your days at Barclay Castle."

The queen shook her head, looking stunned. "Oh, my darling, that is impossible."

Undeterred, Antonía persisted. "But Mother, we'd be honored to have you and you'd be able to visit your son—the king—anytime you wish. Most certainly, he'd protect you from any overbearing Englishman who might seek revenge."

The shock faded from Mary's face and she gave her daughter an adoring look. "I love you for your devotion, my precious daughter, and while your idea is an enchanting one, it is hardly practical. Though I'm certainly no Joan of Arc, I adamantly refuse to sacrifice the lives of others for my freedom. My release from prison would cause violence on both sides of the border. This is where I belong, Antonía. Surely you understand that?"

Antonía shook her head, fighting the emotion welling up inside of her. "No, I don't understand it at all. Mother, I cannot bear the thought of you immured in this musty little room for the rest of your life! I can't bear it!" She threw her arms around her mother's waist and laid her head on her shoulder.

The queen put her arms around her daughter and cradled her for a moment, saying softly, "In my Father's house are many mansions. I can wait."

"What!" Antonía cried, pulling away from her. "You're waiting to die to live? Are you saying that your end is your beginning?"

Mary appeared to mull over her daughter's words for a moment. "I like your statement very much. It has a nice ring to it."

Antonía, however, didn't like the ring at all. "Mother, far be it from me to lecture you on life and religion, but I think your chronology is out of order here. Perhaps your confinement has affected your judgment. But don't worry, once we're back home, everything will begin to make sense to you again."

A gentle smile touched the queen's lips and her voice was full of patience. "No, my dear, my judgment is completely sound. Although the ravages of time have caught up with my body, my brain is still giving senility a run for its money, so please hear me out. If I return to Scotland, my son's enemies will use me as a pawn to spark political turmoil and, ultimately, to usurp his power. My freedom would gravely jeopardize the delicate threads that so tentatively hold Scotland together. I fear any disturbance, such as my liberty, would cut those threads and lead to the downfall of your brother's reign."

"But you don't know that for certain," Antonía said, knowing her mother was right but unwilling to admit it.

The queen shook her head in dismay. "I wish our discussion were purely academic, but it's far from it. My freedom would unquestionably spell certain disaster for Scotland, and I'd never be able to forgive myself for being the cause of it." She reached out and touched her daughter's cheek tenderly. "No, my dear daughter, my conscience would not, and could not, bear such a burden."

"But . . ." Antonía began, and Mary lifted one decisive hand to stop her.

"Please allow me to finish," she said. "Look around you, Antonía. Chartley Hall may not be Holyrood, but it's a far cry from the Bloody Tower. Moreover, I could never in good conscience complain about my treatment, for I am well fed, well clothed, and most definitely well protected. And, let's face it. In this day and age, I fare far, far better than the vast majority of the English population."

"But . . ." Antonía attempted again but was once again thwarted.

"And lastly, and of great importance, my escape would put a very good man in a very bad position. I would never betray Stephen." The queen smiled lovingly at her daughter. "I love you dearly for asking me to return home with you, my darling girl, but I shall never abandon Chartley Hall."

Finally recognizing that her mother's resoluteness on the matter proved an insurmountable obstacle, Antonía surrendered to her mother's wishes. For several wordless minutes, mother and daughter listened to the mantle clock obliterate the present in its relentless pursuit of the future.

"I wish time could stand still for just one moment," Antonía whispered. "Is it asking so much? Is time really so ardently impatient? So frustratingly compulsive?"

Mary hugged her daughter tightly. "It teaches us to value the purity of every single ticking moment."

"But Mother," Antonía said, choking on the word, "when I leave, I may never see you again."

"Aye, my love, that is possible. But perhaps it takes the conscious understanding of both the impatient nature of time, as well as the capricious nature of life, to appreciate the power of the moment. Holding back the obsessive hands of time is an impossible duty, and even royalty falls subject to its rule."

Antonía nodded her understanding.

"My dear one," Mary whispered after a while, "I have a small gift for you." She placed a pewter coin in Antonía's hand. "It's called a blessing token. My mother—your grandmother—gave it to me when I departed France for Scotland many years ago. According to her, the token protects the bearer from any permanent physical harm. It has served me well for many years, and I hope it will be of equal service to you, my beautiful daughter."

Antonía clasped it to her heart, tears threatening. She blinked them back. "Thank you, Mother. I will cherish it always."

The queen gazed into Antonía's eyes and took her hand. "Linger awhile, you are so fair," she said tenderly, and then laughed. "Someone said that to me a long, long time ago—when it was still applicable. Kiss me now, my lovely, for Stephen will be here soon to escort you back to the parsonage."

With her daughter's smooth young hand still resting in hers, the queen fell into a peaceful sleep. Antonía gazed at her mother, memorizing each and every feature of her face, but when the clock struck midnight, Antonía sighed, knowing Reverend Goode would be making his appearance.

But by a quarter past twelve, Stephen Goode still had not arrived. Perhaps he was waiting outside, not wanting to disturb their time together. Carefully slipping her hand from her mother's, she stood up and took the scroll from the small table. What did Reverend Goode know about this, she wondered, for she had no doubt the queen had taken him into her confidence. She tucked the parchment into her ceinture and then looked again at the pewter coin still clutched in her hand.

Antonía was neither superstitious nor very sentimental, but her mother wished her to have it. She gave her mother one last look and walked quietly across the room. After closing the door gently behind her, she crept down the stairs and made her way to the ground floor.

Once outside, Antonía stopped to take in a breath of fresh air, one hand still clasping the blessing token. But within the space of just a few short minutes, "blessing" appeared to be a serious misnomer. *Damn, her mother's token was more like a curse*, she thought. She could smell him before she could see him, but there was no time to react. The stinky, bulky, and extremely strong Rex Throckmorton came up from behind, seized her, and then smothered her face with a damp cloth.

Her last impression was of a bittersweet smell and her suddenly limp body being slung over his hefty shoulders. Her last feeling was one of passionate fury, and her last word was of the four-letter variety. And with that said, the drugged cloth did its work and Antonía felt nothing but black oblivion.

"Gus, we may have to admit we're lost," Claymore said as a cold rain poured down on them. He and Gus had pulled up beneath a tree on the edge of a forest to escape at least some of the deluge. The great tree had widespread limbs to keep them from drowning.

Gus coughed, shivered, and shook his wet head, looking as miserable as Claymore felt. "I dinna understand it," he said. "I've been down this way many a time, but I am fair turned around. Perhaps we should wait until the rain subsides."

"She's already hours ahead of us. We've been wandering around like rats in a maze," remarked Claymore, worried and frustrated. Gus had told him all about Antonía's arrival on Lochleven and the plan to see her mother. "There's no time to waste, Gus. It's entirely possible that Miss Barclay got lost and ended up at Wrathbone Manor."

"Aye, laddie, I understand yer impatience," Gus said hoarsely. "Chartley Hall and Wrathbone Manor are terribly close to each other." He fell into a fit of coughing.

"Are you all right?"

"Aye, aye." Gus nodded. "The rain stirs my old pleurisy, but I'm fine."

Claymore looked out at the driving rain and his impatience turned to resignation. "We will wait," he said, "and pray." He couldn't risk the old fellow getting sicker.

"I'm a Catholic," Gus said. "You want me to go stand on the other side of the forest?"

Claymore smiled. "I am a firm believer in the fact that God hears every man's prayers. Even Catholics'."

Gus chuckled, and the two sat on their horses with heads bowed as they waited out the storm. Gradually the rain lessened and the clouds lightened.

"Well, now," said Claymore, "it seems the Almighty has heard the prayer of both the Protestant and the Catholic."

"Aye, a small miracle," Gus said, and without another word, toppled from the saddle to the ground.

Claymore flung himself off his horse and ran to the older man's side. His face was flushed. The Highlander laid one hand against his brow and knew immediately that his companion had a raging fever.

"Leave me here," Gus said weakly. "Pick me up on the way back."

"If I leave you here, I'll be picking up your corpse on the way back. Let's get you further into the forest and build a fire."

"Leave me . . . ," Gus whispered again.

"And what would I tell Antonía when I find her?" Claymore asked as he lifted the old man in his arms and headed deeper into the forest. "That I left you behind to die? I don't favor being sliced to bits by her invectives."

"But . . ."

"Easy now. After a good night's sleep beside a warm fire, you'll be as good as new in the morning."

With a sinking heart, Claymore moved through the forest, searching for a clearing. Gus was not going to be as good as new anytime soon, and Claymore would have to choose between the old man and the woman he loved.

Chapter 10

CURSING IN SONNETS
AND CLEANING CLOSETS

As Antonía began to emerge from the darkness, she had no idea how much time had passed or if indeed she was still on earth. But despite her bewilderment, she had a strong inkling she was still alive, if only for the fact that she longed to be wrapped in the protective arms of Mr. Claymore. She couldn't be dead if she could think, yearn, and dream of him.

She dragged her way back to consciousness and saw she was resting on a soft bed in a large, dimly lit room. A fire crackled in the fireplace across from the four-poster bed, which was adorned with a gauzy white canopy, and atop her weary body was a white silken comforter. A large painting of two men hanging above the fireplace confirmed her suspicions. There was no denying the portrait from Hell.

A lovely father and son portrait of Sir Basil and Rex Throckmorton.

She was alone, but there was no telling how long solitude would last. Ordering her limbs to move, Antonía tried to rise from the bed, to no avail. Her mind was abuzz with self-recrimination, regret, and despair.

How she could have ever thought abandoning Mr. Claymore was a good idea, she couldn't explain. How she was going to crawl out of this deep, dark hole, she couldn't fathom. *God's nightgown!* What was wrong with her? Why hadn't she simply asked him to come with her? She knew he would move heaven and earth to help her. But, oh no, not she! She'd feared being thwarted, and thus she'd very stupidly struck out on her own.

Afraid she was about to burst into tears, which she refused to do, she instead fell back on her favorite way to manage stress. So, staring up at the ceiling, too weak to move but strong enough to curse like a pirate, she let it rip.

After thoroughly exhausting herself, Antonía eventually fell silent. She was so very sorry for all of it. If only Mr. Claymore were here so she could tell him how truly sorry she was.

All at once, a smooth, refined, familiar masculine voice jarred her from her semiconscious state of contrition.

"Miss Barclay."

She closed her eyes hastily and feigned sleep.

Basil Throckmorton chuckled. "As you've just recited quite an impressive litany of abusive words, I find it hard to believe you are asleep." The smugness of his voice made her want to claw his eyes out. "No doubt your brothers are responsible for your colorful prose."

Antonía felt the firm pressure of a cool palm against her feverish forehead. Her mouth felt as dry as dust, and tasted about as appetizing. But in spite of her drug-blurred brain function and debilitated physical state, she felt a sudden burst of bravado.

"I can curse in colorful sonnets as well, Sir Basil," she said. "No doubt you will be seriously impressed when I recite a fourteen-line verse in iambic pentameter." She opened her eyes and met her enemy's gaze.

Throckmorton laughed. "Welcome to Wrathbone Manor, Miss Barclay. I hope you enjoy your visit. I know I shall thoroughly enjoy every second of your company." He peered down at her and frowned. "Deuced, but I think you're thirsty. Here—" He picked up a goblet from the bedside table and, placing his hand behind her head, gently brought the water to her lips. "Slowly, my dear, we don't want you to become ill."

Nearly gagging on his moot point, Antonía nonetheless forced the water down, because as bad as things were, succumbing to dehydration would make matters that much worse. Her host then apologized for the rather rude means by which she was transported to Wrathbone Manor. She gave him a withering look.

"No need for apologies, Sir Basil, but next time, if it's not too much of an inconvenience, I'd prefer a formal, written invitation. I think it a tincture more civilized than being drugged and dragged to your estate by your missing link of a son."

He smiled broadly. "Miss Barclay, you're like a breath of fresh air."

"Compared to your malodorous son, I suspect that I am," she quipped, and then winced as her head began to pound.

He smiled, less broadly this time. "Although I greatly admire your sharp wit, my son might not—particularly when it's brandished at his expense."

He went on. "Again, Miss Barclay, I deeply regret the manner by which you became our houseguest, but I honestly thought you'd decline a formal written invitation." With an arch of a dark brow and a smirk, he added, "Or even worse, I feared you'd fail to reply at all. Why is it that some people cannot take the time to *répondez si'l vous plaît?*"

"Since you *failed* to issue me an invitation *at all*," she said, "you're asking the wrong person. But in any event, do me a favor. The next time you send your bruiser of a son after me, tell him to leave the pharmacopoeia at home."

"Miss Barclay, if Rex caused you any unnecessary discomfort on your journey to our home, I assure you I did not condone it."

"Right, and every snowflake in an avalanche pleads not guilty."

He chuckled. "I think it's safe to say that neither the drugging nor the dragging damaged your saucy spirit, my dear. However, as a peace offering, I've formulated a liquid compound which will rapidly relieve the wretched headache from which you are currently suffering." Sir Basil placed a loaded tray next to her bedside.

Throckmorton poured liquid of some variety into a small glass and offered the ghastly looking gobbledygook to Antonía.

She took the glass from him and then narrowed her eyes in suspicion. Of course she didn't trust him. Of course he could be offering her poison. However, if the liquid was actually a way to reduce the odious pain in her head, she was almost willing to take a chance. Almost.

"You first," she said.

He smiled. "Trust me, Miss Barclay, this will make you feel better. My formula contains an analgesic derived from the white willow, *Salix alba*, which has been approved by physicians and alchemists the world over. Without plunging into the pharmacology of it all"—and then he plunged into the pharmacology of it all—"a phytohormone called salicylic acid, which is located in the tree's inner bark, has been proven, *by me*, to alleviate pain effectively as well as expeditiously. Since I am the most brilliant physician and alchemist in the world, I know of what I speak, and formulate."

Despite her pounding head, Miss Barclay nearly laughed; but feeling somewhat less than cheery, she found it relatively easy to control her amusement.

"I can't decide which astonishes me more, your sincerity or your modesty, but either way, if you want me to take that formula, you'll have to take it first." As a dozen demons hammered in her head, she hoped fervently he'd take her up on her challenge.

"Challenge accepted!" Throckmorton declared, and took the glass from her. First he examined the liquid, then wrinkled up his nose, and finally downed the noxious-looking liquid. His eyes widened, he clutched his throat and grimaced, and Antonía shrank away in horror as he staggered backward.

Surely he wouldn't—he hadn't—

Sir Basil righted himself and smiled as Antonía exhaled. "My dear Miss Barclay, I do hope I've proven myself to you. Had I intended you dead or in any other similar state of disrepair, your beautiful blue eyes would already be permanently closed or completely vacuous." His voice softened. "I wish only to help you, my dear. Now . . ." He poured a fresh glass of the liquid and held it out to her.

She deliberated for a moment or two. If she wanted to be in any condition to escape, she decided, she must do something about this throbbing headache. With a deep sigh, she accepted the glass, guzzled it all down in one grim gulp, and promptly grimaced at the atrocious aftertaste.

"Good girl!" he said, laughing. "And I do apologize for the rather exotic flavor. Now, in order to prevent the acid from burning a hole in the lining of your stomach—"

She jerked her head toward him. "What?"

"You must eat every bite of this immediately. Porridge provides an excellent buffer for the acid."

Antonía glanced down at the proffered bowl of petrified-looking porridge. "This day just keeps getting better and better." But, wishing to retain the lining of her stomach, she ate it—and, in fact, the porridge tasted every bit as petrified as it looked.

"Chewy," she said, unwilling to let him break her spirit.

"Again, my apologies," he said with a small bow.

Antonía snapped. She pushed the bowl away and turned on him in a fury. "Your laughing apologies hardly reflect the lineaments of sincere remorse! What say you for the umpteenth time, Sir Basil? Yet another specious sorry? Sorry for the drugging! Sorry for the dragging! Sorry for the salicylic acid! Sorry for the porridge! Well, too bad, Sir Basil, because 'sorry' just isn't getting it done! I've had it! You either tell me why I'm here or I swear I'll fling myself out the window!"

Sir Basil gave her a round of applause. "My precious Miss Barclay, I regret to inform you that if you attempt to throw yourself from the window you would incur—at the very most—a broken nose. I had the windows of your room affixed with metal grates just yesterday." Pausing for effect, he then added with a wry grin, "It would seem as if you've missed your window of opportunity . . . so to speak."

"Very funny," she replied. "But for your further information, *no one* tells me what to do. So if I insist upon defenestrating myself, I'll damn well do it. I shall live my life at my own peril!"

"Indeed, Miss Barclay, and you've done such a fabulous job so far."

And at that, Antonía seized the glass and flung it across the room. It shattered against a large vase on a pedestal, unbalancing the object and causing both to crash to the floor. Open-mouthed, she turned to face the man, astonished to see he wasn't angry. He flicked his index finger back and forth as he admonished her.

"Temper, temper, Miss Barclay," he said, removing the tray from her reach.

Emboldened, she demanded, "Why the hell am I here?"

"You're exhibiting strong signs of your Stuart ancestry, but I'll be a good sport and acquiesce to your *request*." Sitting down in the chair beside her bed, he stretched out his long legs while simultaneously leaning back and locking his hands behind his head.

"My dear, you are here because you and I are on the verge of embarking on a joint venture, a merger and acquisition of sorts. But see here, you are in too delicate a condition to talk about this yet," he said soothingly. "Later we shall discuss uprisings, deposing monarchs, and . . ." He smiled, his dark eyes gleaming. "Our impending marriage."

The door opened and slammed against the wall. "Bloody time you woke up, Antonía!" boomed Rex.

He crossed the room and stopped beside her bed, leaning over her to let his gaze rake over her face. His disgusting breath almost made her pass out, and she shrank back into the bed. "I suppose you know by now that you're going to marry me and then we're going to rip the Scottish throne right out from under your milksop of a royal brother."

Antonía's left eyebrow arched upward. "I believe you and your father are both rather confused. I am marrying no one but Mr. Claymore." *So,* she thought, *it would seem that Rex thought he was going to be her groom, when his father had other plans. Interesting.*

Rex glanced over at his father. "Haven't you told her I'm gonna marry her?"

"Evidently, Miss Barclay is quite a loyal young woman," his father said with another smug smile.

Sneering at Antonía, Rex blathered, "You are marrying me. Right?"

She kept mum, hoping he'd drop dead.

"Damn! She won't say a word!"

"It's an exceedingly rare attribute, particularly amongst the female of the species, so you'd be wise to appreciate its value," said Sir Basil, winking in her direction.

"Humph! I think she should begin appreciating me! She only had Scotsmen to consider before." He smacked his blubbery lips. "Wait until she tastes an Englishman."

Antonía could not remain silent a moment longer. "What I appreciate is people who bathe and brush their teeth and do not insult me by their very existence!"

"Children, children," Sir Basil interjected, "play nice." He stood and straightened his jacket before turning to Antonía. "Miss Barclay, I shall return in precisely one hour to escort you on a guided tour of my estate.

The housemaid will be here presently to supply you with fresh clothing and help you dress."

As he headed toward the door, Rex laughed and lifted one lock of her hair, tugging on it. "Oh goody, we have a few minutes to get to know each other better."

Antonía shot Throckmorton an astonished look, but unfortunately he had his back to her. Surely he didn't intend to leave her alone with his bloody awful son!

"Oh, Sir Basil?" she called.

He stopped and looked back at her, and she was struck, not for the first time, by his handsomeness. *How often is physical attractiveness superadded to great villainy,* she mused to herself.

"Yes, Miss Barclay?"

"Didn't you forget something?" she asked.

Throckmorton frowned and patted his pockets. "I don't believe so."

Antonía turned her gaze toward Rex. "I meant your son. Surely you did not mean to leave him behind?"

Sir Basil's dark eyes gleamed with humor. "Come, Rex, let us leave Miss Barclay in peace."

"That would be novel," she said.

"I just got here," Rex grumbled.

"We shall see our guest later. You and I have much to discuss."

Rex grimaced, then his shifty eyes brightened and he moved back to Antonía's side. Leaning down, he whispered in her ear. "Oh, I'll see you later, all right—without my father."

Her heart beat faster, but she refused to let Rex have the last word. "Lucky me."

"Come along, Rex," Throckmorton said, his voice stern. His son backed away from the bed, scowling, and then turned and strode out of the room.

Antonía held her breath until the two were gone, then fell back against her pillow.

She was exhausted from the encounter and wanted only to sleep, but as she already knew, what she wanted didn't matter. A moment later, the key turned in the lock and she tensed until the door opened and the maid entered.

With a sigh, Antonía threw the covers back and swung her feet to the floor. For the larger part of the next hour, the maid helped her prepare for the grand tour of Wrathbone Manor, dressing her in a highly uncomfortable gown, complete with a ridiculous accordion collar.

After dismissing the maid, and beginning to feel stronger, Antonía's mind began to percolate with plans to escape. After several minutes of serious scheming, she decided her best course of action was to pretend that the handsome Englishman was winning her over with his evil charm. She must find a way to inveigle herself into his good graces in order to liberate herself from his control.

Fully aware that she'd be walking a perilously crooked line, she was willing to risk it because, frankly, she didn't have a lot of options. And while she was hopeful that Mr. Claymore would materialize at some point, she had no way of knowing for sure. If only she had told Mr. Claymore, had trusted him with her quest, they would be on their way now, together, to find—

Oh, God's nightgown! Until this moment she had forgotten—her royal mother! Her royal brother! The Royal Sceptre! She felt suddenly faint. The *scroll*! The *coin*! What had happened to them? The last time she remembered having the scroll and her mother's blessing token was when she left Chartley Hall and had tucked them both inside her ceinture.

The first thing to do was search her clothes. But where were they?

Antonía scanned the room for the garments she'd been wearing before Rex had so gallantly dumped her into this beautifully kept hellhole. The room was meticulously clean. No sign of her brother's jacket and trousers or Lucy's blouse and ceinture. However . . .

What appeared to be a closet was situated between the fireplace and a really ugly chair. Recruiting the unreliable aid of her still-shaky limbs, Antonía walked slowly over to the closet and proceeded to rip out every article of clothing contained within its cramped quarters, to no avail.

Undaunted, and in spite of the pounds of clothing she'd been forced to wear, Antonía got on her hands and knees and began searching the dark lower interior of the closet on the off chance the scroll and token had fallen on the floor.

"My dear Miss Barclay, is that you down there?" a now familiar voice asked in astonishment.

Much to her chagrin, she looked up from her awkward position into the face of her elegant host, returned to collect her for the estate tour. Cringing, she attempted to extricate herself with some modicum of grace, but found the stiff farthingale that held out her dress in the appropriate stylish manner was stuck in the doorway. "Yes, indeed, Sir Basil. You've identified me correctly and described my position accurately."

"I hope you're not searching for a secret passageway," he said, laughter in his voice, "because if you are, please understand that as industrious— and entertaining—as your efforts may be, they are completely futile."

Closing her eyes in fury and humiliation, Antonía gave one huge backward thrust and freed herself. She straightened and, still on her knees, looked up at the extremely amused Englishman. She couldn't admit to what she was looking for. He'd either suspect she was trying to escape or would wonder of the importance of her clothing.

"Actually, Sir Basil, I'm positively appalled by the state of your wardrobe and was attempting to reorganize it. The utter clutter makes me shudder."

He shook his head and laughed, then extended his hand to her. Antonía reluctantly took it, letting him help her to her feet.

After looking her up and down, he smiled broadly. "You look perfectly lovely, my dear."

Antonía lifted one eyebrow. If he expected her to thank him, he was mad. Refusing to comment, she simply stood there and met his gaze unflinchingly. Then she remembered her plan—to ingratiate herself with the evil Englishman. She forced a smile to her lips.

"It's a beautiful dress," she said. "Thank you, Sir Basil."

He tilted his head, one finger to his chin. "You're a very rare breed of female, Miss Barclay. I'm pleased that you like the dress. I will have another, grander one for you to wear next week."

Antonía winced. "A grander one?" She glanced down at the sumptuous red brocade gown with its accordion collar that stood out from her neck, giving the appearance of a wagon's wheel. If she fell, she wondered, would she roll down the stairway? Perhaps she should try; it might provide the distraction she needed to get away. "What's happening next week?" she asked.

Throckmorton's mouth twitched slightly. "I intend to introduce you to English society a week from today at a grand ball to be held here."

She stared at him with equal shares of horror and contempt. Forget trying to get on his good side! Sweet Mary and Joseph—not another damn ball! They were proving as prevalent and pernicious as the plague. She saw absolutely no reason to make her presence in England a matter of public concern!

"I will not be attending, Sir Basil," she said. "I'm afraid I will not be sufficiently recovered from my recent abduction."

"Oh, I believe you will be quite well by then, Miss Barclay." He paced around her, looking her up and down like a stableman buying a horse. "Surely you cannot expect me to forgo the opportunity of giving a ball in your honor. It would be such a shame to withhold your extraordinary gifts from my elite circle of friends." He stopped and took one of her hands in his, continuing to coax her with his debonair charm. "Please do not deny me the pleasure of showing you off. I am sorry if you disapprove."

But his coaxing debonair charm backfired because she erupted. "Yet another nugatory apology! You could make a living as a professional apologist! And what do you mean show me off? What am I—another prize stallion?"

"Er, no, my dear. Stallions are male."

"I know that! Then, another prize mare? A pedigreed hound? An award-winning nanny goat?"

Throckmorton remained unflappable. "None of the above, my dear Miss Barclay. You are the most beautiful woman to ever walk God's green earth, and I simply want the chance to introduce you to English society."

"English society be damned!"

"Dear, dear. I am certain if I issued another apology that would only further upset you, Miss Barclay. So I shall refrain." His dark eyes gleamed. "Is it me you hate, or do you simply abhor attending balls?"

Biting her lower lip, she once again remembered her plan and quickly changed her tune, capitulating.

"I beg pardon, Sir Basil," she said with a sigh, trying to look pathetic and winsome. She bowed her head to conceal the anger in her eyes, and then managed to suppress it before glancing up at her captor with the semblance of a straight face. "We both know I'm in a rather poor bargaining position at the moment. Therefore I accept your generous invitation and shall attend your ball."

"Thank you, Miss Barclay," Throckmorton said with a radiant smile. "Though I do not believe a word you've just uttered, I nevertheless find you utterly enchanting. You've made me a happy man by agreeing. Now if you will accompany me on a tour of my estate, you shall make me even happier."

"Far be it from me to take the wind from your sails," she replied breezily. Whereupon Sir Basil anchored his arm around her waist, turned her about, and set course for the lush gardens of Wrathbone Manor.

But after several circuits around the roses, the rhododendrons, the lilies, the peonies, and the lavender, Antonía's legs began to feel as wobbly as a bowl of petrified porridge and she sank against him, clutching his arm. He immediately guided her to a small stone bench where they both sat down.

"I must tell you once again how much I regret allowing Rex to escort you to Wrathbone Manor." He looked down at her, shaking his head. "Why is it that I cannot stop apologizing to you, Miss Barclay?"

But she had very little sympathy for his apparent confusion. Taking a short respite from her original game plan of playing nice, she snapped testily, "I should think it fairly obvious, Sir Basil. You keep apologizing to me because you know your repetition tortures me."

He reacted with a compounded look of mortification and mystification. "Why, whatever do you mean?"

She tilted her head at his feigned ignorance. "Are you aware of the fact that your wonderful son has threatened to share my bed tonight?" She shivered at the thought of being deflowered by that repulsive pig of a man.

Sir Basil looked genuinely shocked. "Miss Barclay, I promise you that my son's idle threat is just that. There is but a single entrance to your chamber by way of a heavily bolted door. I alone hold the key." He reached inside his velvet jacket and took out a long golden ribbon. At the end of it dangled the aforementioned latchkey. "Therefore it's impossible for Rex to gain admittance to your chamber, much less your bed."

"For some mysterious reason your promise fails to inspire confidence," Antonía said. "Unless you are implying that your son is above stealing your key or picking a lock?"

Laughing lightly, he remarked, "My dear, I assure you. I am the only individual with both the exclusive power and the exclusive privilege to visit your room. This key is at all times on my person." He tucked the key away. "And conversely, I am the only one who can allow exit from it as well. So you see, Miss Barclay, your detailed inspection of the closet was truly an exercise in futility . . . although I must say, I greatly appreciated the view." He gave her a mischievous wink along with a lascivious smile.

Oh lovely, Antonía thought, *now I must face seduction by charm instead of seduction by churl.* She gave her host a searing look of reproach, but, determined to inveigle her way out of Wrathbone Manor, she drew in a deep breath and resolved to push forward with her plan.

"If you really wish to learn my reason for crawling about in your closet, I shall tell you."

Throckmorton took her hand in his and lifted it to his lips for a brief moment before nodding. "Do tell, dear Miss Barclay."

Antonía sighed. "I was searching for the clothes I was wearing when your lummox of a son knocked me unconscious and hauled me here." He raised a single quizzical brow, and before he could comment, she hurried on. "During my visit to Chartley Hall, the queen gave me an old coin which I placed in my ceinture for safekeeping. I realize the token means nothing to you, but it's my only remembrance of my mother," she finished, allowing a slight break in her voice at the end.

At the mention of the ex–Queen of Scotland, Throckmorton's black eyes flashed, revealing a glimpse of his truly wicked nature. Antonía leaned away from him. He then cleared his throat and veiled his lapse with instant civility.

"Of course, my dear, your possessions shall be returned to you at once. And though my natural inclination is to issue you an apology for the oversight, I'm resisting the urge because you would undoubtedly flog me to within an inch of my life if I gave you yet another."

"Indeed I would."

Sir Basil gave her a blinding smile. "However, I did do one nice thing for you, Miss Barclay," he said.

"And what would that be, Sir Basil? You gave me a tour of England? Oh, wait—I was unconscious. You gave me new clothing? Oh, wait—you took my own. You gave me food and drink? Oh, wait—only after feeding me drugs that made me weak and ill."

"Yes, all too regrettable. But tell me, Miss Barclay," he said, "did you have any difficulty breaking into Chartley Hall?"

Antonía narrowed her eyes and waited for the other shoe to fall. And, indeed, her suspicions were justified because Sir Basil promptly dropped it.

"I certainly hope you did not meet with any resistance in gaining entrance to Chartley. I gave strict orders for you to be granted instant access to your mother's prison chamber."

Antonía's jaw tightened, and she cast the Englishman a harsh, accusatory look. He had orchestrated the entire break-in. She had realized the rendezvous with her mother had been suspiciously uneventful, but in her desperation to meet the queen, she had chosen to push aside the ease of her entrance to Chartley Hall. And that meant . . .

"Reverend Goode works for *you*?" Antonía exclaimed in horror.

Throckmorton chuckled. "Oh, don't worry. Your parson is as pure as the driven snow. His only desire is to make Mary's incarceration as pleasant as possible. No, I simply bribed the guards—through my informant there—to look the other way when you came to visit. So you see, Miss Barclay, you have me to thank for your uninterrupted visit with your mother."

Antonía's eyes widened as another thought struck her. What if Sir Basil knew about the existence of the scroll and believed in the power of the Royal Sceptre? Even a man of science could be enticed by such a tempting tale. As if reading her mind, his next words sent a wave of panic through her.

"I even allowed the queen to give you the scroll and tell you all about the Royal Sceptre, when I could have had it taken from her by force. But I preferred a more gentlemanly approach." He gave her a slight bow. "I knew you would bring it with you."

"I—I have no idea what you're talking about," she lied.

He turned slightly and leaned closer, his lips almost touching her ear. "I have many spies in Chartley Hall," he whispered. "Do not bother lying to me. Now . . ." He stood and offered her his hand. Antonía took it, her gaze fixed on his as he drew her to her feet. "Let me be frank with you, my dear."

"I thought your first name was Basil," she quipped.

"Droll," he conceded. Looking down at her with a smile, his wicked ambitions and delusions of grandeur were as transparent as a crystal-clear stream. "My plan," he continued, "is to have you lead me to the Royal Sceptre, after which we shall marry and usurp your royal brother's power, and claim the Scottish monarchy."

Antonía remained cool and collected. "Sir Basil, far be it from me to interdict your plan, but I have devised a far superior one, which is that you fry in Hell for all eternity."

"As much as I shall miss your charming company—and your acerbic tongue," he said, "I think you've had quite enough activity for one day. I must insist on taking you back to your room. We want you sufficiently recovered for the ball."

"And what are you going to do in the meantime, my dear sir?" she asked, hoping that he thought she suffered from mood swings rather than malice.

Throckmorton looked at her askance, attempting to diagnose her mercurial temperament. Perhaps it was an aftereffect of the chloroform. Finally, he said, "I have several experiments awaiting my attention in the laboratory. They should keep me duly occupied while you're resting, Miss Barclay."

She had no desire to be locked in her room again, even if the alternative meant being in her captor's company. Besides, a way to escape might suddenly present itself.

"As it so happens," she said, "I have a predilection for medical science. I'd be most interested in visiting your laboratory. Our rest here in the garden has been quite adequate for me, I assure you."

Throckmorton appeared honestly pleased by her pronouncement. "You shock me, my dear. So rarely does the female of the species demonstrate a passion for matters even remotely related to science. However," he cupped her face between his hands and Antonía was forced to stare into his soulless black eyes as he whispered, "you are a rare woman indeed."

His thumbs stroked her cheeks as she stared up at him, breathless. Then abruptly he released her and took a step back, his gaze now mild and benign.

"Yes, Miss Barclay, I'd be delighted to show you my laboratory. But not today, my dear. Your condition proves much too tentative. Tomorrow is the better plan."

He delivered her back to her bedchamber prison, now cloaked in dusky, shadowy twilight, illuminated only by an occasional flicker from the fire. The room exuded a surreal, dreamy aura devoid of worldly interference. As Sir Basil peered down on Antonía, she shivered, feeling ravished simply by the man's incinerating eyes.

"I think I'm more weary than I realized." Antonía backed away from him, and his eyes narrowed to ebony slits, moving in her wake.

"Your lovely sea-blue eyes," he said, following her and standing mere inches away. "The dewy softness of your flawless skin, that irrepressible mouth." He slid his arms around her waist and Antonía's heart began to thud with apprehension. "I will have you, Miss Barclay," he said, "but I will not force you. When the time comes, you will willingly welcome me to your bed, and when you do, I shall at last feel the infinite length of your slender legs beneath me and make glorious love to you all night long."

Throckmorton backed away and, frozen in place, she watched him leave. She stood in the middle of the room and waited for the sound of the bolt to lock into place. She then walked to the window and looked through the interstices of the grates. Her eyes scoured the horizon. The landscape was barren. Not a soul in sight. She sighed in resignation. It was becoming increasingly apparent that she had overchallenged Mr. Claymore's devotion.

So be it. She'd rely on her own wits.

Reverend Goode leaned over the ill man and put his palm to his forehead. The elderly fellow was feverish but alive. After debating his course of action, he was on the verge of standing up when he felt the cold, sharp blade of a sword against his throat. His attacker had approached him from behind and was holding him tightly with one hand while holding his weapon with the other. The voice that spoke to him was deep and hushed.

"Identify yourself."

"My name is Stephen Goode," he said, also in a hushed tone. "I am the parson of Chartley Hall, and I must get this poor man to shelter quickly. He is quite ill." Reverend Goode felt the tight grip around him release as the blade against his neck fell away.

"My sincere apologies, Reverend Goode," said the deep-voiced man. "My name is Breck Claymore."

Stephen Goode turned and faced a tall, strongly built young man. He said, "You must be Miss Barclay's Scottish Claymore."

The young man's handsome face broke out in a smile. "That's one way of looking at it, Reverend."

Chapter 11

SIXTEENTH-CENTURY MEDICINAL BOTANY

As if waking up the prisoner of a pair of lunatics weren't bad enough, she woke up to the doom and gloom of miserable weather. Of course, the vile climate was to be expected. She was in god-awful England after all. Rolling over in the unfamiliar bed, Antonía closed her eyes again, wishing she were anywhere but where she was. For several minutes, she listened to the sound of hard-driving rain lashing the grated windows. She felt absolutely ghastly. Her head still throbbed, her body ached everywhere, and her spirits hovered near rock bottom. But she knew that the new day had to be faced. Pushing back the blankets, she rose carefully and went in search of clothes, determined to be dressed and ready for the guards to escort her to Sir Basil's underworld.

The Englishman's laboratory was aptly located in the macabre depths of Wrathbone Manor, in a former dungeon used during the Dark Ages. Black, bleak, and brooding, it looked like the cave of Hell and stunk like it too. Antonía covered her nose with her sleeve as she paused on the bottom step.

Sir Basil looked up from something he was doing—evil, no doubt—and in spite of the ghoulish atmosphere and rank smell, greeted her in his customary warm and convivial manner.

"Ah, Miss Barclay. Welcome to my laboratory." He dismissed the guards who had escorted her, then gave her a brilliant smile.

Antonía entered the room warily but with wide-eyed fascination as she gazed upon quite possibly every kind of paraphernalia known to the alchemical community.

Smoking flasks, flaming Bunsen burners, spinning centrifuges, teetering test tubes, oozing beakers, Petri dishes, and a multitude of vials blanketed two huge countertops, perhaps six feet wide by twenty feet long. With no outside light available, the room was illuminated by scores of large torches running along the perimeter of its walls made of stone, pitted with holes. Antonía felt as though she were inside a huge honeycomb, but she felt certain that substances far more heinous than honey were being produced within its waffle-stoned borders.

Rapidly scanning the walls for chained skeletons and spider webs, she discovered, much to her relief, that they were agreeably absent. Throckmorton walked over to the stairs, tucked her arm through his, and guided her to a stool in the center of his little house of horrors. Once seated, a fetid, noxious vapor assailed her senses in such a discourteous manner she all but gagged.

"My dear, yet another apology I owe you. I should have—here—" Sir Basil handed her a kerchief and she held it to her nose, surprised to find it scented with lavender. "Certain harmless chemical compounds are more pungent to the human nose than other pleasant-smelling, but far more treacherous, compounds."

Antonía said nothing but recalled her royal mother's warning words, *"The man is mad, bad, and treacherous to know."*

"Once olfactory fatigue manifests, you'll be just fine, my dear."

Little did he know that eau de Rex had already fatigued her olfactory system to a point well beyond the limits of human endurance. However, compared to Rex's horrid odor, the lab smelled positively fragrant, so she waxed philosophic.

"No sacrifice is too great for science," she said with a smile.

He returned her gesture and she wondered how in the world he got his teeth so dazzlingly white. "Where shall we begin, Miss Barclay?"

"Let's start with your area of expertise, Sir Basil," she replied, looking very interested. And rather conveniently, there was no need for Antonía to act interested, because oddly enough, she really did possess a particular penchant for all matters pertaining to medical science.

"Please," he said, "I think by now you can call me Basil, don't you?"

"I prefer to adhere to the social graces, *Sir Basil.*"

"In that case, we'll start our discussion with medicinal botany as it relates to the aging process."

"Geriatrics or gerontology?"

His jaw dropped. "Miss Barclay, already you astound me with your remarkable knowledge of scientific matters. Most people don't know of such terms, much less the distinction between them."

"Don't be overly impressed," she remarked. "I'd gladly read Paracelsus over Chaucer any day of the week."

Throckmorton's eyes creased in amusement. "Actually, I'm using botanicals in conjunction with chemical compounds to create potions that will prevent or postpone the aging process." This time it was Antonía's turn to look surprised. "Does that offend you in some way, my dear?"

"No, not in the least," she said. "I just assumed you would be far more interested in curing smallpox, consumption, typhus, syphilis, scurvy, malaria, dysentery, or some various and sundry form of plague. Naturally, the list of diseases goes on ad infinitum, and I think I'm starting to depress myself." She sighed. "In any event, I'm surprised that one of these many terrible diseases failed to capture your fancy rather than the aging process—though I suspect your 'patients' must be rich and titled aristocrats."

"Miss Barclay, my very intelligent friend," he said, spreading his hands apart, "my passion for antiaging research interests me in and of itself. It has nothing to do with pandering to the rich and titled. And who amongst us can account for our passions? Indulging one's passion is an innate, instinctive method by which one hopes to achieve personal fulfillment. A hold on passion is a hold on happiness. Think of the pathos in traveling through life without passion!"

Antonía nodded in tacit agreement—the man had a point. She thought of her passion for Mr. Claymore, but that made her heart ache so she quickly quashed her emotions.

"Mark my words, my dear," he said. "From small things, big things one day come, and one day, the prevention of fine lines, wrinkles, and sagging, er, parts of the body will be big business. And though admittedly my scientific achievements have already provided me with exorbitant wealth, I've never been governed solely by mercenary motives." He turned, and before she could move, he had pulled her into his arms. "My passion alone motivates me."

Sir Basil's obsidian eyes penetrated so deeply into Antonía's blue ones that it was more than obvious that his passion was *not* confined solely to the laboratory. She immediately pulled away from him.

"Really, sir, you do forget yourself." She walked over to one of the long counters where shining glass bottles and tubes bubbled with a variety of colors and liquids. "I'm still a wee bit confused about your goal. Are you trying to formulate potions to *prevent* aging or prevent the *appearance* of aging?"

"I confess, my initial experiments were related to arresting the aging process; however, after a series of rather disappointing results, I turned my attention to developing treatments to reduce the *signs* of aging, rather than attempting to perpetuate eternal youth."

"Fascinating."

"For example, I developed a cure for botulism a few years ago and recently discovered that same cure can eliminate fine lines and wrinkles when administered in the proper dosage and injected at the proper site."

She looked at the man closely. Despite his obvious foray into middle age, Sir Basil didn't have a single frown line or crow's-foot annexed to his smooth, seamless face. Without thinking she reached her hand to her own face and touched her forehead.

He laughed and she dropped her hand back to her side, blushing. "You have nothing to worry about, Miss Barclay, you're far too young. At the moment, anyway."

She gave him a forced smile and he laughed again. Holding up the second ampoule, the mad scientist extraordinaire presented her with yet another one of his achievements.

"*You* have personal experience with the contents of this potion, my dear."

"Is it your favorite formula for placing unsuspecting women into drug-induced comas?" she asked, an edge to her voice.

"Aha! You speak of an older secret formula—no, it's not that one," he replied, sweeping away her sarcasm. "That one needs work."

"The one you drugged me with needs *work*?" she asked, outraged.

"Forgive me, my dearest darling, I was desperate to have you. But I intend to make amends." Again holding up the ampoule, he explained, "This vial contains salicylic acid derived from willow bark. You'll recall it's the potion that eliminated your splitting headache."

"Right, it's your favorite formula for burning holes in the stomach linings of unsuspecting females."

Ignoring her comment, Throckmorton gave her a roguish wink. "It worked for you, did it not, my dear? Your headache was gone in a flash!"

Antonía shrugged. "I suppose. Well, I guess I should be happy that you didn't try to put leeches on me." She shivered at the thought of the slimy creatures. "Bad porridge as a chaser is preferable to those horrible things. Leeching is one barbaric medical practice that I could personally do without—they're such nasty little beasts." Scrunching up her nose in distaste, she shuddered.

"Spoken like a true lady." He put the vial down and picked up another. This one had bright red liquid inside it. "Now this, this is something quite extraordinary and will replace the potion Rex used on you. I'm calling it 'Rest Assured.' Just a few drops in any drink will cause instantaneous unconsciousness. My new potion is quite helpful if you can't sleep at night and has no short- or long-term side effects. You can rest assured of that, Miss Barclay."

"Thanks, that's comforting, but remind me not to drink anything I'm served for the remainder of my visit." She kept her tone light, but a chill crept over her skin.

Sir Basil laughed, put the vial inside the cabinet, and moved toward an enormous hearth. A colossal cauldron hung over the fire, and the viscous brew inside gurgled. He picked up a large wooden ladle and stirred the contents.

"What is this? A witch's brew?" she asked.

"Indeed, no," he replied firmly. "This formula represents alchemy in its finest, purest form, as it applies only to metals. It's actually an offshoot of a previous experiment whereby my goal was to discover a botanical compound that would cause certain human anatomical features to grow larger."

Antonía's mouth fell open. "I beg your pardon?"

Throckmorton looked at her in faux shock. "My dear Miss Barclay, your imagination is beyond all words amusing!"

She could feel her face growing bright red. "But you—you said—"

"I did indeed. However, my original objective was to discover a treatment for certain *defects* as well as for deformities resulting from trauma. After months of trial and error, I failed to achieve my initial goal. *However*, I discovered the compound has the ability to enlarge metal objects to approximately twenty-five times their original size."

"That's rather brilliant," replied Antonía, sitting up a little straighter. "Please elaborate."

"Two basic steps are required to accomplish the augmentation of metal. First, the metal object must be thoroughly immersed in my formula. Next, the object must come in contact with another metal object while simultaneously being exposed to bright sunlight."

All open ears and genuine interest, Antonía looked over his shoulder as he continued to stir his cauldron. "Must step one and step two occur within a specific time frame?" she asked, casting her eyes into the simmering pot.

"No, Miss Barclay, once the object has been soaked in the augmentation solution it retains the ability to be enlarged indefinitely. Once immersed, the metal's composition and properties become permanently transmuted. The passage of time will not eradicate the augmentation power."

"Suppose I dipped a spoon in the cauldron," she said, "and didn't activate the augmentation by touching the spoon to metal in sunlight for a day? Or a week? Or a year?"

He smiled, looking pleased at her question. "The metal object is subject to augmentation anytime thereafter, with no time constraints. The utility of such a compound—"

A sudden knock on the laboratory door interrupted his lecture on alchemy. Throckmorton sighed and hurried up the dark stairs. As soon as he was out of sight, Antonía removed the miniature claymore sword from around her neck and gave it a furtive, but serious, dunking in the augmentation solution. She then quickly, but painfully—God, it was hot!—tucked her necklace back into its snug little hiding place, just as Sir Basil returned.

"Everything all right?" she asked, trying to sound innocent.

"Yes, of course," he said, appearing somewhat distracted. He crossed to the cabinet and, after taking out his keys, locked it. He then checked his viscous brew and offered Antonía his arm. "It's time for you to return to your room, my dear."

"But we were having such fun," she protested.

"Yes, but I have other business to attend to." He gestured toward the stairs. "After you, my dear."

Antonía was halfway up the stairs when inspiration struck her. The key to her escape lay inside the cabinet, and the key to the cabinet, inside Throckmorton's jacket. Her mind raced, but outwardly she remained calm and composed as she was led back to her chambers. Now that she had a plan, it was only a matter of time before she left this wretched place in the dust.

The September sun's weak attempt to shed morning light upon the English countryside proved sufficiently adequate for Claymore to ride closely behind Reverend Goode through the forest. He held Gus tightly and prayed the old man wouldn't die in his arms. After only thirty minutes, however, the sight of a small building with a cross over the door set some of his fears to rest.

The parson dismounted and signaled Claymore to a small addition to the left of Chartley Chapel. He then opened a door to reveal a room that held a bed, and blessedly, a fireplace blazing in the corner of the room.

"Please put him here on the bed, and let's see if we can get some food and water into him," instructed the reverend.

Claymore nodded gratefully and deposited Gus on the bed's warm blanket.

Pouring water into a glass, the parson asked, "How long has he been ill, Mr. Claymore?"

"Two days, Reverend. He'd been coughing a bit and then fell right out of the saddle. I had no idea he was sick." He gently removed Gus's coat. "You can call me Breck, by the way."

After walking the few short steps to the bed, Reverend Goode set the glass on a table. "And please call me Stephen. It'll save us both a lot of breath."

"That it will, Stephen," agreed Breck. "Let's get his boots off and get him under the blankets."

Once Gus was settled, Stephen felt his forehead and gave a nod. "I think he'll be all right. The fever appears to have broken."

"Thank you," Claymore said in relief. "If you can take care of him, I will pay you whatever you ask."

Stephen shook his head. "Payment is completely unnecessary, Breck."

"Thank you again for your kindness," said Claymore. "As you know, I have another problem to solve."

"The missing Miss Barclay problem."

Claymore nodded. "Right, and I didn't think it safe to discuss on our ride here, out in the open."

"You're a wise man," said the parson, with some embarrassment. "Evidently Throckmorton has either bribed once-loyal servants or planted his people throughout Chartley."

Claymore dragged one hand through his tousled hair. "Please tell me everything you know, Stephen. I'm desperate to find her before the Throckmortons—" He stopped when he noticed the distraught look on the parson's face. "They've got her, don't they?"

"God in Heaven, I'm sorry, Breck, but there's a good chance they do," said Stephen, rubbing the back of his neck.

"Go on, Stephen," urged Breck. "Tell me everything you know so I can find her!"

The parson took a fortifying breath. "Two days ago," he began, "Miss Barclay met her mother and then was to return to the parsonage." He shook his head, looking distraught. "Miss Barclay was to stay here until you, Gus, and her brothers arrived, after which the queen hoped you would help her daughter locate the Royal Sceptre."

"The royal what?"

"Sceptre." He waved one hand. "More on that later. I was waiting for her outside Chartley Hall, but before she came outside, I was attacked. When I awoke, some hours later, she was gone."

Claymore tightened his jaw. "It was most likely that bastard Throck-morton or his degenerate son. I must go—"

"Stay here a moment, please." The man hastily left the room and Claymore paced back and forth in front of the welcome fire until Goode returned a few minutes later with an elderly woman at his side. "This is Anna, my housekeeper. She comes in a few days a week and will look after your friend. We must speak to Mary immediately."

Claymore gave him a questioning look.

Goode gave him back a rueful smile. "Yes, Antonia's mother. Your queen."

Stunned and still slightly disbelieving, Claymore followed the parson out of the room and out of what he now knew was the parsonage. They walked for ten minutes in companionable silence, finally arriving at a huge manor.

As Claymore stared up at the mullioned windows and intricate archi-tecture, Goode went over and spoke to a guard standing by a small side entrance. After a moment, the man nodded and walked around the side of the building, out of sight. The reverend beckoned with one hand and Claymore hurried over, following him inside. Just inside the door was a long staircase. Goode started up, with Claymore close behind.

The stairs opened into a large room. A fireplace blazed with warmth, and a beautiful woman with red hair streaked with gray lay on a long sofa in front of it, clad in a gown of deep emerald green. As the two men entered the room, the woman sat up and Claymore stopped in his tracks, astonished. He knew, without introduction, her identity.

"Mr. Claymore?" she asked. "Come closer, please."

Goode led him over to the beautiful woman and took her hand with surprising familiarity, even as he bowed over it. "May I present Mr. Breck Claymore. I came across him and his friend, Gus, in the forest. Gus has a fever, but I have Anna taking care of him in the parsonage." He kissed her hand and stepped back, gesturing for Claymore to approach.

Still incredulous, Claymore walked toward the woman and sank to one knee, his head bowed. "Your Majesty," he said, hardly able to speak, "I am honored to make your acquaintance."

A soft trill of laughter made him look up to find Mary, Queen of Scots, smiling at him, her hand extended.

"Oh, please, dear boy, let us not stand on ceremony. Come and sit beside me. We have much to talk about."

He obeyed immediately and sat mesmerized as the queen looked intently into his eyes for several long minutes.

"Your eyes are intensely blue and beautiful, Mr. Claymore," she said at last and then dropped her gaze to his body, examining him from stem to stern. "And your physical magnificence unparalleled." *Oh my God, and Jesus, Mary, and Joseph, too,* she thought. "No wonder my daughter fell in love with you, and the fact that you are here in England searching for her speaks for your integrity and devotion to her."

"Thank you, Your Majesty," he replied, still astounded by her elegance. Miss Barclay's beauty was no accident.

"Now." The pleasure faded from her amber eyes and seriousness replaced it. "Tell me, did you find Antonía? Is she well? And what of Gus?"

Claymore shook his head. "Your Majesty, I believe Antonía has been kidnapped. I have been following her ever since she ran away from Barclay Castle in her quest to find you. I promise you that I will find your daughter and make Throckmorton pay for what he has done. As for Gus, he has a fever, but as Reverend Goode said, he will recover."

The queen closed her eyes and gripped his arm as if to keep from falling backward. Claymore moved to put his arm around her for support and glanced up at Goode. The parson hurried over to a table where bottles of wine and glasses rested. He poured a glassful and brought it to the queen. She took a delicate sip and then refused the rest, turning back to her guest.

"Mr. Claymore, if the Throckmortons have taken my daughter, they most likely have fled to their estate, Wrathbone Manor. It's not far from here. It is providential that you have brought Gus with you."

"I know what you are thinking, Mary," Goode said, making the Highlander raise his brows at his familiarity. "But Antonía took the scroll with her."

"I made a copy of the writing," she said.

"Of course you did," the parson said with a smile. The queen returned the gesture. Claymore raised both brows.

"I like to be prepared for any contingency." She gestured toward the connecting room. "Would you mind? It's located in the desk drawer in my study."

"What scroll?" Claymore asked, impatient to be on his way. "Please, Your Majesty, I can delay no longer!"

She nodded. "I understand, but I'm afraid you must, Mr. Claymore. I'll be as brief as possible."

Reverend Goode left the room and in a moment brought a sheet of thick paper to the queen. "Thank you, Stephen." She handed the paper to Claymore. "This should lead you and Antonía to the Royal Sceptre."

Claymore sank back down beside the queen. "What is the Royal Sceptre, Your Majesty?"

"The Royal Sceptre is an ancient artifact upon which Scotland's independence and survival depends," the queen said, a catch in her voice. "Without it, our country will fall to the English. I gave the original scroll to Antonía and asked her to take it to Gus for translation."

"Translation?"

"It's written in an ancient form of Gaelic. Gus can tell us what it says."

Claymore glanced down at the paper. "Gus is delirious with fever." The queen's face fell. "However, I may have some good news for you. Every educated Highlander alive can read ancient Gaelic." He rubbed his jaw. "Well, except for a few Campbells, perhaps."

Her eyes widened. "Thank God, Mr. Claymore. After you find my daughter, it's vital that the two of you locate the Royal Sceptre and that Antonía—and none other—delivers it to her brother, King James." She paused and cautioned him. "Do not touch it yourself, Mr. Claymore. For only a Royal Stuart can handle the Royal Sceptre."

"Your Majesty," Claymore said with unshakeable conviction, "I will not put the search for this—artifact—before locating Miss Barclay. She's my only concern."

"Of course, dear Mr. Claymore," the queen said, touched by the depth of his emotion. "You must save her at once. Sir Basil is a brilliant and engaging man, but he is capable of unspeakable atrocities." She shook her still fiery red head. "With genius so often comes madness—trite but true. However, once Antonía is safe, please do your best to help her find the Royal Sceptre."

"Yes, Your Majesty," he nodded. "I will do my best. But first I intend to search heaven and earth for your daughter. No stone will be left unturned until she's back in my arms where she belongs." His voice softened. "For you see, Your Highness, I plan to marry Miss Barclay. I'm deeply in love with her."

"As she is with you, my dear Mr. Claymore," she said.

His heart seemed to weaken with her words. "Did your daughter tell you that she loved me?"

The queen smiled and rested one hand over his. "Mr. Claymore, when it comes to discussing her feelings, my daughter is far from effusive, but her beautiful blue eyes, so much like your own, clearly expressed her love for you." Cupping his face in her hands, she decreed, affection in her voice, "I hereby bestow my blessing upon your marriage. May God bless you with a long and happy union."

"You are most gracious, Your Majesty."

After kissing Claymore on both cheeks, the regal woman stood, hands on her hips, and gazed down at him, looking altogether like the Queen of Scots.

"Now go and rescue my daughter, take her back to Scotland, and for heaven's sake, Mr. Claymore—*keep her there!*"

He stood and bowed. "Your Highness, once I marry your daughter, she'll spend every moment of her life close to her husband's side, and I intend to stay in Scotland the rest of my days. However—" He hesitated.

"What is it, Mr. Claymore?"

"As much as I would like to claim I'm capable of rescuing Miss Barclay singlehandedly, I've recently learned that Throckmorton has a great many men at his command. Evidently he's building an army, with plans to go against either James or Elizabeth."

"I fear the rumors are true," the queen said solemnly.

Claymore nodded and turned to the parson. "Would you be willing to ride to Barclay Castle and tell Lord Barclay the news? If he can send men to help us, perhaps we can stop Throckmorton once and for all."

Reverend Goode smiled. "I like the way you think. And I would be honored." He glanced at the queen. "As long as Mary can spare me that long."

"Of course, Stephen," she said. "My daughter's safety is more important than anything else! And I mean that, Mr. Claymore. If it is a choice between Antonía and the Royal Sceptre, then the sceptre must be sacrificed."

"Thank you, Your Majesty."

She presented her hand to him and he fell to his knee once again. "God be with you and keep you both safe."

He kissed her hand. "And you as well, Your Majesty."

She bowed her head, and then, with an imperial sweep of the hand, she looked at both men and issued her commands. "Now go, and God bless the both of you."

Her amber eyes gleamed. "We must prepare to turn the tide!"

Chapter 12

MORE AND MORE LIKE LESS AND LESS

Back from her laboratory tour, Antonía shed her gown and donned a silk robe before lying down upon the huge four-poster bed. As she stared at the velvet underside of the wooden canopy above, thoughts of family and home rushed through her mind, and an uncomfortable lump of anxiety formed in the middle of her chest.

The lump was heavy and unyielding. She wondered if the weight would crush her to death. She felt overwhelmed by the terrifying prospect that she would never see her family, friends, homeland, and most notably Mr. Claymore ever again. She still couldn't quite let go of the notion that he would ride to her rescue. Perhaps Mr. Claymore had been delayed for some reason and was somewhere close by, plotting her escape. It was a comforting thought.

At what point had it ever been a good idea to leave Mr. Claymore? God, she was such a fool. She was on the verge of full-blown panic, but she knew it and her knowledge was her power. Understanding all too well the trigger-happy nature of her mind, she realized that her panic sought relief, needed a channel, and required diversion, but she had to act fast. Her panic had gotten a big head start.

Her plan.

Taking a deep breath and releasing it slowly, she thought again about the Rest Assured potion Sir Basil had formulated. If she could get ahold of it, perhaps she could find a way to put it in his tea or wine. If she could keep her disgust of him under control and do a better job of acting as if he were succeeding in seducing her, perhaps she would get the chance. Once he was asleep, she could disguise herself and then use his keys to unlock any door and escape.

Restless, she rose from the bed and crossed the room to the vanity table and picked up the beautifully carved ivory brush provided by her captor. Taking the plush velvet chair in front of the vanity, she began to brush her hair in long, brusque strokes while contemplating her plight.

How would she gain access to his bloody laboratory? Sir Basil had the keys. But if she could filch his keys, she wouldn't need the sleep potion, would she? Yes, she would. There was little chance Sir Basil would let her out of his sight long enough for her to escape if he were conscious. And how would she get his keys unless he was *unconscious*?

Her head whirled with the conundrum, and as frustration flooded through her, with each rough stroke of the brush, she began to curse aloud. Her list of curse-worthy items was fairly long, and for a moment, she stopped to conjure up some variations on the theme. A few minutes later, she resumed ripping away at her tortured hair until her chamber door flew open and a foul odor pervaded the premises. She winced as Rex Throckmorton stood in the doorway sneering at her.

"God Almighty, Antonía, take it easy with the hairbrush! Something tells me you wouldn't look good bald!"

His effect on her was immediate. He infuriated her so much that her mind instantly forgot about her panic and turned its full attention to hating his guts. Now able to breathe freely and brush with a steady hand, she gave him a scathing look via the mirror.

"God Almighty, Rex," she mimicked, "take it easy with your father's kidnapping potion next time. Something tells me I wouldn't look good dead, either."

"Not sure it would make that much difference," he said, "you're so pale." He walked behind her and leered at her in the mirror.

In the reflection, she could see Rex's lascivious gaze drop to the neckline of her robe and realized how the silk curved around her ample assets. "How did you get in here? Your father always locks my door."

"Why? Did you miss me last night? I couldn't get the keys from Fadda like I planned. Hope you didn't cry too hard."

Rex sauntered across the room and dangled the set of keys in front of her. "I picked his pocket."

Refusing to take the bait, she said, "It must've been a nice change from picking your nose."

He leaned down and proceeded to blow his liquor-laden breath into her face. "Has anyone ever told you that you're a real smartass?"

"No," she said. "But on occasion I've been told I'm a real badass."

His rubbery lips curved into a sinister smile. "Glad to hear it! As it happens, I want to feel your perky little ass *real bad.*"

"Too bad for you, I'm busy sitting on it," she muttered, and picking up the brush again, resumed grooming her hair, this time in a calm, measured fashion. She was not going to let him get to her. Now that she knew Sir Basil's nuptial plans, Rex wouldn't dare touch her.

Consequently, she was quite surprised when, without warning, he wrenched her from the chair and pressed her against his bulging belly, his hands seeking out places on her body that they had absolutely no business looking for, much less locating. She stifled a scream, knowing that was exactly what he wanted.

"Just think," he panted, "once we're married, I can see you naked anytime I want and you can see me naked anytime *you* want."

"Over my dead body," she replied, struggling to break free from his lecherous hands and lethal breath.

"Oh, that wouldn't stop me," he sniggered.

After a moment, Antonía realized in alarm that this wasn't one of Rex's slimy little harassments, but a full-fledged attempt to have his way with her. She gritted her teeth, determined to fight him tooth and nail.

However, in spite of her strength of conviction, she was certainly no match for his physical strength, and when she sagged suddenly, Rex picked her up and threw her on the bed. Terrified that her goal of remaining a virgin for Mr. Claymore was about to be subverted forever, she resumed the fight. Rex clamped his meat-hook hands over her thin wrists and held her down.

"That's how I likes 'em," he said, smacking his lips in her face as he rolled against her. "Feisty!" Making a last-ditch effort to avert the inevitable, she prepared to cut loose with a bloodcurdling, banshee-like scream . . . when the door opened, and Basil Throckmorton walked in.

"What the bloody hell?" he demanded, crossing the room in three long strides and pulling his son off the bed. *The man is stronger than he looks if he can move his lug of a son so easily*, thought Antonía.

"I told you that you are not to touch Miss Barclay!"

"Yes," Antonía said, breathless, as she scrambled off the bed and stood near the vanity, trying to put as much distance as possible between herself and the two men. Her voice trembled, but her anger was intact. "In fact, I count almost ten times you've told him such, Sir Basil. If you cannot even control your own son, how, sir, do you expect to be able to control a country?"

Throckmorton's face turned a furious red, and doubling up his fist, he slammed it into Rex's face, knocking him across the room. He strode over to glare down at his son.

"This is your last warning, you stupid lout. If this *ever* happens again, I won't even bother to bury you. How did you get in here?"

"He filched your keys," Antonía said.

"You tattle-telling strumpet!" Rex yelled.

"Hand them over." His father thrust out his hand, and grumbling, Rex handed them to him. Sir Basil tucked them into his pocket and leaned down, speaking distinctly. "Get. Out."

Rex stumbled to his feet, giving his father a vicious sneer as his beady eyes met Antonía's, making her shiver. Throckmorton closed the door behind him. Antonía drew in a deep breath and released it as he crossed the room back to her.

"Are you all right, Miss Barclay?"

"I have made an executive decision," she said, her voice sounding weak to her own ears. She stared down at her hands, forcing the panic to subside.

"Indeed?"

She raised her head and met his amused gaze. "I want to go home. My parents are most certainly a wee bit worried about me by now, so I'd be most appreciative if you'd release me on my own recognizance."

He shook his head as his smile widened. "Ah, my dear Miss Barclay, you will never go anywhere again without me, and since *I* have no immediate plans to return to Scotland, neither do you." He shrugged out of his pale blue brocade jacket and draped it over the end of the bed, then sat down, patting the place beside him. "Come, sit, sweet child. We have much to talk about."

Antonía took her seat once more at the vanity table, facing him. She didn't dare turn her back again on Throckmorton. "I am quite comfortable here, thank you."

He tapped one hand against his thigh. "You *will eventually* grow weary of resisting me, Miss Barclay. However, for the present moment, I wish to discuss business."

Antonía blinked at him. "Business?"

"Yes. Remember I told you that when you were improved physically we would have much to discuss? Well, it's time that you told me where the Royal Sceptre is hidden. I'm well aware of the fact that your mother, the former Queen of Scotland, received and translated the scroll for you."

Having known the issue would surface again at some point, she had an answer prepared. "Yes and no. My mother *received* the scroll, but unfortunately for you, her knowledge of ancient Gaelic is as nonexistent as her navigational skills."

He frowned. "That is indeed unfortunate. I thought all royals of your mother's generation spoke Gaelic."

"Yes and no," she reiterated. "You forget that my mother, in contrast to all Scottish royals preceding her, spent her formative years in France. I believe it goes without saying that her French teachers considered ancient Gaelic nonessential to her education. Actually, my mother's grandfather, King James IV, was the last Scottish ruler to have spoken the language. So it would seem as if you're out of luck—too bad for you."

"On the contrary, Miss Barclay," he said, lying down across her bed and propping himself up on one elbow. "In case you're wondering, I *am* in possession of the scroll. I'm sure if we put our heads together we could find at least one dour, decrepit Scotsman fluent in archaic languages." He patted the bed again.

Gus? Was he talking about Gus? Thank God she had left her friend at the beginning of this cursed journey! Despite her anxiety, she played it tough. "You're out of luck again, Sir Basil, because I'm not putting my head anywhere near yours."

"Come, come now, what happened to your spirit of cooperation?"

Suddenly as sick of playing nice as she was homesick, she spun around and threw the brush at him. Unfortunately, her throw went wide and hit the wall. Antonía rose from her chair and stalked over to the bed to turn furious eyes upon him.

"I *seem* to have misplaced my spirit of cooperation somewhere between Chartley Hall and Wrathbone Manor. Or perhaps it was lost when I was being attacked—again—by your loathsome pig of a son moments ago! I want to go home, and I *shall* go home!"

Throckmorton chuckled, turning Antonía's anger to rage as he crooned in a very annoying sing-song voice, sounding like a certain English singer yet to be born, "You can't always get what you want, Miss Barclay." He pushed to a sitting position and reached for his jacket. "I advise you to view your life from a new perspective, which is the fact that *this is your home now.*"

She looked at him as if to say, "*I think not, you pompous ass.*"

Sir Basil ignored her scalding look and said, "Incidentally, I have something for you." He rummaged in his jacket pocket and then slid off the bed, took her hand, and pressed something flat and round into her palm.

She looked down to see the coin her mother had given her. "Oh!" she said, the word catching in her throat.

He stood silently in front of her for a long moment. Cupping his hand under her chin, he gently tilted her face upward. "God, you're gorgeous." She jerked her chin out of his hands and turned away.

"Come now, my darling Antonía. What can I do to make you happy? Say the word and I will cloak you in velvet and shower you in jewels." He slid his hands up her arms and she shivered. "Despite what you think, I am not a monster. Join me in my crusade, and our lives together will be one fun ball after another! We shall dance and dine every night till dawn!"

Antonía gasped. *One fun ball after another? Dear God, please not that!* Now she knew no matter what, she must escape! The thought of being on display at one English party after another was truly torture! Pulling herself together, she assembled her argument.

"Not a monster? Well, that is debatable. Let me see," she tapped one finger against her chin. "What can you do to make me happy?" She turned around, now in control of herself again. "You could throw your brute of a son into the dungeon. Or better yet, have him flogged." She frowned in feigned concentration, and then brightened. "Wait! I know! Name a really gross disease after him—something with pustules."

Throckmorton smiled. "I'll see what I can isolate," he said. "But first—" He walked over to a large buffet against the wall where a bottle of wine and two glasses sat. Uncorking the bottle with finesse, he deftly poured the red wine into the goblets and held one out to her.

"I don't care for spirits," she said.

"I strongly encourage you, for medicinal purposes, to join me just this once." She gave him a skeptical look. He laughed and replied, "Seriously, my dear, a few sips of red wine will calm your nerves."

"If you leave the room it will calm my nerves."

Sir Basil ignored her remark. "I can provide you with irrefutable scientific evidence proving that red wine contains molecules which stimulate the release of certain enzymes that extend cellular lifespan by alleviating situational stress. This, in turn, prevents age-related disease and perpetuates eternal youth." He paused to flash her a triumphant smile. "In other words, Miss Barclay, if you drink red wine every day of your life, you'll never get sick . . . or old . . . or wrinkly . . . or grumpy."

He waved the wine goblet in front of her.

Folding her arms rigidly across her breasts, she sent him a scalding look she wished would obliterate him once and for all. "You are immensely annoying, Sir Basil."

He laughed. "Although I'm perfectly willing to concede that you are not presently sick or old or wrinkly, you are most definitely grumpy, Miss Barclay."

"I am *not* grumpy!"

"Oh, but I think you are."

"I am not."

"You are."

"I am angry!" She tossed her hair back from her shoulder. "Actually,

Sir Basil, I couldn't care less what you think of me. *And he who cares least controls most.*"

"Oh, I see. So that's your philosophy of life, Miss Barclay?"

"One of them."

"What about the philosophy, *life's short, have fun?*"

She looked daggers at him.

He laughed and said with a raffish wink, "Why don't you have some fun and live a little? Don't worry, Miss Barclay, nobody's watching."

"How do I know the wine isn't laced with your newest concoction?" she demanded.

With a shrug, he took a drink from his glass, and then from hers.

"That's highly unsanitary, Sir Basil," she said. "Now I most assuredly won't drink it."

Annoyingly composed, Throckmorton poured a fresh glass of wine and handed it to her.

"*Fine,*" she said, with that certain female inflection. After finally accepting the wine, she clinked her goblet against his and said, "*Sláinte.*"

Both his brows shot up.

"It means 'good health,'" she explained.

"But in what language, Miss Barclay?"

"Gaelic, naturally," she said, and then took a big swig. It burned very pleasantly going down.

"You speak Gaelic, Miss Barclay?" he asked, setting his own glass down. "I must have misheard you earlier when you stated that Gaelic was a defunct language."

"Actually, Sir Basil, it's one of the few words of Gaelic I know."

He gazed at her steadily. "If I find that you've been holding out on me, Miss Barclay . . ."

Seeing her chance to divert the Englishman from what was no doubt another seduction attempt, Antonía let her temper flare. "Yes, Sir Basil? *If* I've been holding out on you, exactly what will you do to me? Indeed, the question is better stated in the past tense and in the negative—what *haven't* you done to me already? Shall I reiterate the list of offenses which you've perpetrated against me to date?"

Throckmorton opened his mouth to speak, but she was far from finished.

"No, no, on second thought, why should I bother to recite your long list of flagitious crimes? It's abundantly clear that you *never* permit uncomfortable truths to stand in your way! So please finish your statement. If you find I've been holding out on you, what other delights do you have in store for me? What other treats do you have up your sleeve? How many rabbits will you pull out of your little black hat?"

Appearing genuinely surprised by her outburst, he frowned. "Why are you so upset, my dearest Miss Barclay?"

"Perhaps because I don't relish the prospect of being forced to marry you in order to achieve your megalomaniacal goal of overthrowing the Scottish monarchy! And for some unknown reason, tossing my brother off his throne and handing over my country to a vainglorious lunatic and his idiotic son *doesn't quite do it for me.*"

He took her goblet from her and set it on the vanity, moving closer. "So I ask you, my petulant Miss Barclay, what *would quite do it for you*? This?"

The arrogant man took her into his arms, kissing her fully on her parted lips. Swept onto the fast track, Antonia became aware that the dangerous and crooked path she traveled proved increasingly gnarled with perilous hairpin turns.

A frantic knock at the door forced Throckmorton to release her. He cursed all the way to the door, flung it open, and scowled at the man standing there.

"What is it, MacCree?"

"I'm very sorry to interrupt, sir," said the servant, "but there appears to be a pack of rogue sheep trampling the gardens and eating the shrubbery in its entirety."

Throckmorton lifted an incredulous eyebrow. "A pack of rogue sheep? That is so wrong in so many ways I don't even know where to begin." He waved one hand at him. "Why are you bothering me with this? Send some servants out to drive them away."

"We did, sir." The man flushed. "However, they say the sheep are biting them and they refuse to chase them any longer."

His brows collided over furious eyes. "Refuse?" He turned to Antonia. "Forgive me, my dear, but apparently I have some servants to castigate. Drink your wine. I'll return shortly and you'll be in much jollier spirits, no doubt."

Antonía's heart beat more quickly. This could be her chance. If she could sneak out, maybe she could find a way to get into Sir Basil's laboratory and find the sleeping potion.

"Must I wait here?" she implored. "Can't one of your watchdogs follow me and let me take a turn around the manor? I've hardly seen any of the antiquities. And more importantly, I'm going to get really fat if I don't take a little exercise."

Throckmorton laughed. "Very well. MacCree, take Miss Barclay on a tour of the manor but don't take your eyes off her for a moment." The servant bowed. "Don't tire yourself out," he said, his eyes raking over Antonía. "I've planned a late dinner for the two of us. Alone."

As soon as the door closed, Antonía turned to MacCree. "Please wait outside while I dress."

The servant bowed. "As you wish," he said, and left the room.

When she finished dressing, Antonía turned and her eyes fixated on the bed; she was thunderstruck to see that Sir Basil had left his jacket behind. Grabbing it, the telltale jingle of keys in an inner pocket sent a rush of joy through her. They were linked onto a strip of leather, and she tucked the lot of them into a velvet reticule and fastened it to her wrist. She tucked her mother's coin into her corset, and, adding a cloak to her ensemble, she opened the door.

MacCree raised one brow at the sight of the cloak and Antonía pulled it tightly around her.

"I have a chill," she said, shrugging. The servant bowed and led the way. In a state of high exhilaration, she departed to steal the sleeping potion.

Antonía's "tour of the manor" was blessedly uneventful until she gave Mac-Cree the slip by feigning an attack of the vapors. He rushed away to get a glass of brandy, and as soon as the servant was out of sight, she pulled the keys from her corset. Looking back over one shoulder, she hurried down the hallway to the door that led to Throckmorton's dark, dank lair.

Unlocking it, she flew down the stairs, and once inside the dismal room, realized that this was truly her chance to escape! She had no need of the potion, for Throckmorton had fallen victim to one of the classic blunders—underestimating a Stuart! All she had to do was unlock the door leading to the garden, sneak out to the stables, and steal a horse. Her heart lifted. Soon she would be free of this odiferous place and the equally odiferous presence of Sir Basil Throckmorton and his odiferous son!

She headed directly for the outside door and only had to try two keys before finding the one that fit! The tumblers turned and she removed the keys, tucking them back into her corset. Truly, making her escape was proving so easy it was almost anticlimactic. But when a familiar stench filled her nostrils, she knew that, at least in this particular instance, *almost anticlimactic* would have proven quite a bit more conducive to her health than *thrillingly climactic*. She turned as Rex, in a state of drunken glory, stumbled down the stairs and across the room toward her.

God's nightgown! As bumbling and obtuse as he was, Rex had tracked her down again! Antonía lunged for the unlocked door, but in two big strides Rex slammed it shut and pulled her back down the steps with him.

"What d'ya got down the front of your dress?"

In response, Antonía glared at him with all the warm civility of an ice cube; but despite her dire circumstances, she remained incapable of suppressing her sarcasm.

"Frankly, Rex, I'm surprised you have to ask, but if you really don't know then I can tell you this—there are two of them and although neither are what you'd call huge, they're both impressively pert."

"An' I'll see 'em sooner than you think," the drunken man said. "Thanks to me and my *ingenious* detective skills, my father will see you for the sneaky, conniving bitch you are. I'm going to tell him all about your little snooping expedition down here, you nosy Scottish spy."

"Spy? What in the world are you talking about?" Antonía started edging toward the outside door. If she could keep him distracted, maybe she could still make it out of the laboratory.

"You're obviously gathering intelligence for your wimpy wuss of a brother. No doubt King Namby-Pamby of Scotland wants to be King of

England, too! What a joke! Can you imagine King Candy-Ass sitting on the English throne? Can you really picture your weenie puff of a brother running the most powerful country in the world?"

"Indeed, your fair and balanced disclosure of the truth should serve as an example to us all, you stupid clotpole," she said, her anger flaring. "Since King James doesn't even know I'm his sister, and you're the one who kidnapped me and brought me here in the first place, your accusation doesn't make the slightest bit of sense."

"Then why the bloody hell are you in my father's laboratory?" he roared, blocking her way with his massive body.

"I make it a point never to answer questions without legal representation," she said, trying to keep her bravado intact. Rex always made her nervous, but an inebriated Rex made her absolutely terrified. Especially in this dungeon of a room, where no one could hear her scream. "Furthermore, I strongly prefer to write my answers down—I find it easier to organize my thoughts that way."

Rex grabbed her by the arm. "I'll organize your thoughts by bashing your brains in! Now answer me! What the hell are you doing in my father's laboratory?"

Antonía had had it. She was sick of Rex Throckmorton and sick of being afraid of him. Her ire rose, along with her need to release her feelings.

"Why am I here?" She jerked away from him. "I'm here to find the cure for your loathsome personality and your *big fat ass!*"

In a matter of seconds Antonía knew she had gone too far. Rex's face turned bright red as he delivered a backhanded blow so savage that it hurled Antonía backward across the room. As the back of her head slammed against the stone wall, she had the fleeting thought that she'd never see Mr. Claymore again, much less another day.

As she began to feel more and more like less and less, her legs collapsed beneath her, and Antonía slid slowly down the wall, descending into a black, bleak hole of nothingness.

Chapter 13

BETTER LATE THAN A LATE PARTY

B reck Claymore rode all night and arrived at Wrathbone Manor before dawn. After spending half the day disguised as one of Sir Basil's stablemen, he kept his ears open and his mouth shut. By noonday he had learned there were two safe ingresses to the manor without arousing suspicion: through the kitchen door during mealtime, or through Throckmorton's laboratory, whose outside steps led from beneath the manor up to the garden.

Since he had no way of knowing when Throckmorton might be in his laboratory, or if its door was locked, Claymore decided on the kitchen entrance. He spent the rest of the day making preparations. Waiting for the evening meal was almost more than he could bear, but he bided his time until he saw activity in the kitchen.

Making his way warily to the paddock near the stables, he opened the gate and herded the sheep he had driven up from the fields and into Wrathbone Manor's garden. Moments later, a cry rang out for someone to intercept the animals, and the garden was soon filled with men chasing them. Claymore knew he had only a few moments to breach the back entrance to the manor while his woolly minions made mincemeat out of the yard. He saw his chance. Clad in servant's garb, he hurried across the garden and headed for the kitchen door.

As he passed the steps leading down to the laboratory, he heard raised voices and stopped in his tracks. One of them was Antonía's. He paused, listening, but when he heard a crash, he ran down the steps and flung open the door. She lay unconscious on the cold stone floor of Throckmorton's laboratory—alone.

"Miss Barclay . . . ," he whispered, kneeling down beside her.

Peering down on his broken but beautiful Miss Barclay, her surreal stillness and deathly pallor made his heart contract with fear. The right side of her face was bruised and swollen, and her dark hair was saturated with blood. He was desperate to take her in his arms, but at the same time, almost afraid to touch her.

She was so pale, so fragile-looking—like lifeless porcelain—that it was terrifying. Then her chest rose and fell, and relief flooded through him. Thank God, she was alive.

There was no time to evaluate her injury. He had to get her out while he still could. Claymore lifted her in his arms and carried her up the steps leading to the outside. Thankfully, Throckmorton's manor wasn't one with a moat or even a wall. It was more of a starter manor, and thus Claymore was able to rescue Antonía under the cloak of dusk and the noise of rogue sheep.

As he made his way to the horses tied in a grove of trees behind the stables, fury flooded through him. God forgive him, but one thing was for certain—he was going to kill Basil Throckmorton and his fat, ugly son too.

Antonía could feel the strong rhythm of his heart, the soothing touch of his lips against her forehead, and, most definitively of all, she could smell the deliciously piney scent of him—dear God, he smelled so good! Her eyes fluttered open and to her surprise, she was in Mr. Claymore's arms, atop a black stallion.

He was here! He hadn't abandoned her! She wanted to greet him with all the passionate love she felt, but a profound weakness made her feel nearly paralyzed. Still, she gazed at his strong, handsome face and love filled her heart. She lifted her hand, weakly encircling his neck as she whispered, "Cutting it a wee bit close, aren't we, Mr. Claymore?"

"Are you implying I'm late, Miss Barclay?" he murmured softly.

"On the contrary, Mr. Claymore, it was I who was very nearly the late party." She reached up and caressed the crest of his cheek. "But I fear I shall never be able to compensate you fully for your courageous and chivalrous rescue services."

He kissed the end of her nose and gathered her close to him. "My dear Miss Barclay, considering you abandoned me at the ball, you should be grateful I showed up at all." Then his playful smile faded as he brushed her hair back from her face. "You gave me a terrible scare, lass."

She held him as tightly as her fragile state would permit. "Mr. Claymore, I'm so very sorry for everything. I was so foolish. I promise never to treat you so abysmally again. Please forgive me." His eyes were so intense, so startlingly blue, he took her breath away as his words enfolded her.

"My darling Miss Barclay, though you have led me on a wild chase, forcing me to turn over every single stone in England to find you, I'm so relieved to have you in my arms again that I find I must forgive you."

"Thank God," she said and winced as she looked around. "Where are we?"

"Just outside of Wrathbone Manor. We must hurry before they realize you're gone. The rogue sheep have surely been rounded up by now."

"Rogue sheep?" she asked, smiling as she looked up into his eyes. "Ah, you're quite the rogue yourself, my Mr. Claymore."

He leaned his head against hers, his burr broadening. "Please don't ever scare me like that again."

"I promise," she said. "Where are we going?"

"To a little place I found on my way here."

A wave of dizziness swept over Antonía, and she gripped the front of his linen shirt and swayed. His arms tightened around her.

"Hold fast, my love," Mr. Claymore said, "and we'll ride like the wind."

Antonía clung to him as they rode away from Wrathbone Manor and into the wet, dreary English countryside. The warmth of his woolen tartan held her close to him, and for the first time in a very long time, she felt safe.

Once out of range of Wrathbone Manor, Claymore slowed his horse and looked down at Antonía. She was either asleep or unconscious; he wasn't sure which, but she was completely unaware of the grave concern her delicate physical condition evoked in him. She needed time and rest to recover.

On his way to Throckmorton's lair, he'd come across a flour mill and several cottages. Stopping for water at the nearby stream, a young boy had approached him. Luke Wade was his name, and after a few questions, Claymore learned that Wade's small family occupied only one of the cottages. The others were vacant, the unfortunate owners driven out by Sir Basil when they couldn't pay the exorbitant taxes. Claymore had pressed a gold coin into the boy's hand and asked if he'd be willing to make one of the vacant cottages ready for two lodgers for a few nights. The boy willingly agreed.

Now, as Claymore rode up to the cottage, he saw smoke wafting from the chimney and released an anxious breath. Dismounting carefully with Antonía in his arms, he carried her inside, finding one large room warmed by a fireplace.

A bed made of tree limbs, polished to a high sheen, sat against the wall opposite the fire, made up with clean linens. Pulling back the covers, he laid Antonía upon it and kissed her forehead as he covered her with the warm blankets. She didn't respond; and with a worried look, he gently examined her injuries, discovering an ugly bump on the back of her head, a nasty cut on her face, and a deep bruise on her arm.

Worried beyond measure, Claymore found clean, though threadbare, cloths in a cupboard and wet them with water from a pitcher near the fire. Antonía moaned as he cleaned the abrasion on her face and the blood from her hair. As to the latter, he finally gave up, knowing only a bath would cleanse her long, thick hair. Intending only to keep her warm, he climbed in the bed beside her.

Antonía awoke to find the relentless pain in her head had been mitigated to a tolerable level. She looked about her. It was morning. Along with a few flickering flames from the fire, a mellow sunlight pervaded the room. Then the sound of quiet, rhythmic breathing made her roll over and find Mr. Claymore fast asleep.

She smiled and brushed a lock of hair from his face. He had saved her. In spite of running away from him, sending him across the country-side searching for her, and putting him in danger, he had come for her. As she gazed at him, memorizing every handsome, chiseled feature, his long lashes moved and his eyes opened. His beautiful mouth curved into a lazy grin.

"Hello, my lovely," he said, tenderly touching her cheek. "I'm so sorry I was too late to save you from being hurt by that bastard." He propped himself up on one elbow, looking down into her eyes. "Sweet darling, you look like you've been run over by a team of oxen!"

"I don't doubt it," she said, "but there was only one ox and he hit me, rather than ran me over." Mr. Claymore's jaw clenched and Antonía brushed her fingers against the stubble there. Fury turned his blue eyes almost black as he captured her fingers and brought them to his lips.

"As God is my witness, I promise you, I am going to kill Basil Throckmorton."

"Actually . . . ," Antonía hesitated, then rushed on, "Sir Basil wasn't the one who hurt me. It was Rex."

"Then he is the first I'll kill," he said, and then frowned, looking per-plexed. "You say Basil Throckmorton didn't hurt you, my love? The man locked up your mother, kidnapped you, let his son beat the living day-lights out of you, and . . ." His voice trailed off and he looked down at her hand, smoothing her palm with his fingers.

His tenderness touched her deeply. "What is it?" she asked.

"I worry that he may have hurt you in other ways, but you are afraid to tell me." He glanced down at her, and Antonía's breath caught when she saw the passion in his eyes. "I'm going to kill both of them in any case, so please—"

"He didn't," she said, breaking off his plea and cupping his face with one hand. "I promise. I have not been compromised." She gave him a wry smile. "Though if you hadn't come when you did, I daresay that would not be the case."

Mr. Claymore's eyes narrowed. "Perhaps I shall torture them both a wee bit before I kill them."

"Oh, please let me help," she said, clasping her hands together. "I've always wanted to torture an Englishman."

His eyes widened and then he laughed, the tense moment fading, just as she'd hoped it would. "You're an extraordinary woman, sweet Antonía," he said. "How are you feeling?"

"A headache, of course," she said, shrugging and then putting a hand to the back of her head. "Speaking of torture—Throckmorton's worst torture was plying me with a wretched medication for the headache I developed after being knocked unconscious by another noxious potion. It saturated a cloth Rex held over my nose when he grabbed me as I left Chartley Hall."

"A dozen arrows to his heart," Mr. Claymore said calmly. "Wooden stakes pounded into his hands. Shattered glass down his throat."

Antonía laughed and pushed herself to a sitting position. She still felt weak and ached all over, but a need to reassure him outweighed her poor physical condition.

"I'm fine. Just very, very tired. How in the world did you find me?"

"Your mother."

"Um . . ." Antonía bit her lower lip, not sure what to say. Did Mr. Claymore know about her real mother? If not, then would the news that she was the daughter of a queen change his mind about their budding romance?

"Yes, I see now where you get that fiery, regal beauty," he said, a twinkle in his eye. "Not that Lady Barclay isn't lovely as well."

Relief flooded over her. "Then you know."

"Yes, and once I visited Chartley Hall, I understood better why you felt you had to run away from me." He gave her a sober nod. "You do know that you must never do that again, aye?"

Oh dear, he was already giving orders. Antonía pushed down her natural tendency to rebel against authority, reminding herself that Mr. Claymore was not one of her brothers. A mischievous smile formed on her lips. Nor was he her husband—yet.

"You will soon learn that I am a rather headstrong woman, Mr. Claymore. One given to impetuous behavior at times."

"Indeed," he said, arching one brow. "Gus has told me all about your independent streak, and I will tell you exactly what I told him."

She narrowed her eyes. "Which was?"

His voice softened. "That whenever you next feel the desperate need to gallop across the border to meet captive queens and prevent coup d'état, won't you please take me with you?"

Antonía's face lit up. "Damn," she said, one hand to her heart. Mr. Claymore sat up straighter, looking alarmed.

"What is it, Antonía? Are you in pain?"

"No, no," she waved his concern away. "I just realized that the impossible has happened. I have found the perfect man."

He took her hand again and pressed his lips to her fingers before meeting her clear blue gaze. "Aye, and don't you be forgetting it." She laughed as he got out of bed, rearranged his kilt into some semblance of order, and then turned and bowed to her. "Now, Your Highness, are you possibly in the mood for a little porridge?"

Antonía's face fell. "Porridge?"

"I'm afraid that's all that I have to offer; however, I promise that I make a very mean bowl of oatmeal."

How could she say no? She nodded and he went over to the fireplace where she spied a pot, a bowl, and a pitcher of water. Suddenly their conversation caught up with her.

"Gus! You spoke to Gus?"

"Yes, he's the one who led me most of the way here, until—"

"Until what? Where is he?"

"He's with your mother—with the queen. He fell ill with a fever on our way here and we had the luck to stumble upon the Reverend Stephen Goode. He led us to her. She told me how you'd run off to find her and how she told you to wait for me." He shot her a knowing look as he measured out the dry oatmeal.

"And I was going to do exactly that," Antonía said. "And then Rex captured me!"

"Boiling oil," he muttered. "Poured down his gullet."

"Did my mother—did the queen tell you about the scroll and about the Royal Sceptre?" she asked, loving him more every time he came up with another torture for Rex.

"Yes."

"I don't know what to do—I lost the scroll or perhaps Rex found it and gave it to his father. My mother entrusted me with this noble quest and what did I do? I lost the only thing in this world that can lead me to the only thing in this world that can keep Scotland safe!" She threw herself down on her pillow and buried her face in it. "Oh, *merde*! I'm what Claire would call '*une femme incompetente.*'"

Mr. Claymore burst out laughing and she raised her head, indignant.

"Don't laugh! It's true!" She sat up and folded her arms over her chest.

"You are definitely female, but you are *not* incompetent in any language, my darling Miss Barclay."

"Just wait until you get to know me better, my darling Mr. Claymore!" She paused. "I mean that you'll soon discover that I am incompetent, not that I'm not female."

He laughed again but then went silent. He was silent for so long she finally slid him a glance and saw him hanging the iron pot over the fire. He stirred it with a wooden spoon a few times and then crossed to the bed and stood gazing down at her. His eyes were rich with love as he reached downward past his belt for his—toward his—

Antonía turned her head away in pink-cheeked embarrassment. "Mr. Claymore!"

"What? I have something I wanted to show you."

"I daresay you do! And I do want to see, however this is neither the time nor the place for—"

He laid a piece of paper in her lap and she stared down at it, then took a chance and looked over at him. For the first time she noticed under his wide belt was a leather bag hanging just over . . . well . . . just *over*. It had two long leather strips he was presently tying back together.

He hadn't been reaching for—

He'd been reaching for the paper.

Antonía tried to hide her flustered feelings as she picked the paper up and studied it, trying to hide her burning hot cheeks. It was her mother's parchment. The sight of the scroll made her forget her embarrassment and she looked up in astonishment.

"A copy of the scroll! The directions to the Royal Sceptre! How did you find it?"

"The queen gave it to me." He shook his head. "That woman is prepared for anything, it seems."

"Thank God!" Antonía pressed the paper to her chest. "Now we must get Gus to translate it—but we can't—Gus is probably still too ill."

"Lie back, Miss Barclay," Mr. Claymore said. "You're all aflutter. What you need is some porridge, a good draught of milk. After that, I will explain why you need not worry."

Suddenly exhausted and feeling quite a bit less feisty, Antonía sank back into her pillow and prayed she wouldn't fall back asleep, because she really wanted to know what Mr. Claymore had learned about the scroll. But in spite of her prayers, her physical exhaustion prevailed and she fell sound asleep, only to awaken to the smell of something delicious.

Porridge.

It smelled wonderful. How was that possible?

As she ate the lovely creation of oats and milk and honey and butter, Mr. Claymore explained that he, being a Highlander, could of course read ancient Gaelic, as well as prepare gourmet porridge.

"And what did it say?" she asked.

"The Royal Sceptre is supposedly hidden in Ford Castle, which is in partial ruins. It isn't too far from here. Once you have recovered, we can have a look. Would that make you happy?"

She smiled and began to eat her porridge. Before long, she fell back against the pillow again, this time full, content, and completely satisfied with both her meal and his explanation. Her eyes began to grow heavy.

"Antonía," he said, his voice deep and compelling, "if you could wait to fall asleep, I have something important to ask you." Antonía's eyes flew wide open. He had walked around to her side of the bed and drawn up a chair next to her. Sitting down, he took her hand in his.

"In fact, pardon me if I say that for the time being, no more time will be allotted for your affinity for sleeping—for your affinity for English prisons—or for your affinity for getting kidnapped, because as soon as we reach Scottish soil, I want to marry you, my extraordinary Miss Barclay."

"You do? Seriously?"

"Aye. Your father and both of your mothers have granted their unanimous consent to our union. So you see, my darling, you're the only obstacle standing between my objective and me. If you should decide to withhold your consent, then you, and you alone, shall be the cause of my shattered heart."

"Are you saying, Mr. Claymore, that I hold your heart in my hands?"

"My darling Miss Barclay, I'm saying that I am wildly, passionately, and deeply in love with you. In fact, no man on God's green earth could possibly love you more than I do, and when it comes to loving you forever, I'll *never* lose my way." He kissed her hand and looked longingly at her lips. "And though I wouldn't put it past you to torture me mercilessly, would you please end my suffering by answering the following question: Will you marry me, Antonía Barclay?"

Unintentionally torturing him mercilessly, she hesitated. Although he now knew about her royal birth, there was still one thing he didn't know, which could change everything. It all depended on his spiritual philosophy.

"After you hear what I have to say, you might not want to marry me."

"I assure you there is nothing you can say that would make me *not* want to marry you."

She cast him a grateful look, took a deep breath, and blurted it out. "It's recently come to my attention that I'm Catholic. I'm not a practicing Catholic, just a baptized one. However, I knew I'd feel guilty for all eternity if I didn't confess to it before we got married."

A very large smile spread across his face. "That's it? You are a Catholic?" She nodded.

"My dear Miss Barclay, I assure you, your religious affiliation doesn't matter to me one bit."

She blinked. "Well, you're probably the first Scot to ever make that statement. But truly, Breck—if we were to marry, what about our children? You're Protestant and I'm suddenly Catholic! In what faith would we raise our children?"

Mr. Claymore's response was instant but rather unexpected. "We'll seek middle ground and raise our children as practicing Jews."

She stared at him for a moment and then agreed with a laugh. "Fair enough," she said. "They're probably closest to having it right anyway, and they have the most seniority."

He smiled and with his startlingly blue eyes twinkling their magic, brought them back to the real question. "I'm glad to have that issue settled, but I still need an answer. So I ask you again. Miss Barclay, will you marry me?"

She lowered her gaze, her lips parted slightly. Then lacing her fingers in his, Antonía spoke in a hushed voice. "Mr. Claymore, come here to me . . . closer." He obeyed by narrowing the distance between them to a negligible gap, and then she wrapped her arms around his neck, planting a serious kiss upon his seriously attractive mouth.

After a certain amount of time spent lingering in this general manner, she inquired softly, "Does that answer your question, Mr. Claymore?"

"Unequivocally, Miss Barclay. May I encourage you to answer all my questions with equal enthusiasm?"

She gazed at him, her love overwhelming her. "Unequivocally, Mr. Claymore."

With a laugh, he picked her up, took her place in the bed, and held her on his lap. She granted him yet another kiss for his masterful and romantic behavior. After kissing her long and deep, he sighed as he twisted one long lock of her hair around his finger.

"I suppose your newly established royal ancestry means you'll expect the red carpet treatment once we're home."

Antonía looked at him askance and then saw the mischievous glint in his eyes. She raised her chin and held out one hand in a regal manner.

"While I appreciate your encomium regarding my heritage, you can safely roll up the red carpet. In point of fact, genuflection will be the only act of reverence expected." Then fastening eyes with her intended, Antonía swiftly amended her statement. "Excluding Mr. Claymore, of course, from whom other, more gratifying acts of reverence shall not only be expected, but required."

"Reverence?" He raised one brow. "I saw myself more in the role of teacher, not parson. Perhaps I should go and fetch Reverend Goode?" He made to leave the bed, but she played dead weight on top of him.

"So you're saying that you have much to teach me? I am but an apprentice while you are—"

"The master."

Their blue eyes locked and all at once their witty repartee faded away, leaving passion in its wake. Antonía swallowed hard and sank down into her pillow, her heart fluttering with nervous anticipation.

"Well," she said, "as my brother Will can testify, I have always been a most willing pupil."

Mr. Claymore leaned over her, his lips so very close.

"Let's leave your brothers out of this, shall we?"

Chapter 14

BURNING LOVE AND CHARRED HEATHER

C laymore swept back her hair, and after watching in captivated rapture as it cascaded down her back like a dark, silky waterfall, he cleared his throat and spoke, surprised to hear the tremor there.

"Teaching is an art," he said. "However, before we begin, I must make certain all parts to be used in the endeavor are fully operational. To do so, I'll need to make a more detailed inspection at very close range."

He stroked one hand down the side of her face, to her throat, to her bare shoulder. He rather expected her to flinch or draw back, but instead, she reached to link her hands behind his neck and drew him back down to her, until their lips were only inches apart again.

"You're even more masterful than I imagined," she said lightly. "An interrogation *and* an inspection all in one evening. You inspire me immensely with your multitude of talents, Mr. Claymore."

He smiled. "While in most educational settings it would be considered proper to continue to call me Mr. Claymore, I do allow my favorite students to call me by my given name."

Antonía's eyes narrowed. "You understand that I do expect to be your *only* student from now on, dear Breck?"

"Of course," he whispered, and bent his head to begin his instruction at once and in earnest. With every intention of teaching her the finer points of love, as well as its subpoints, Claymore pulled her into his arms and proved he was every bit as passionate about his pupil as he was his professorial duties. As for his pupil's part, Claymore was extremely gratified that she, too, took a highly interactive approach to learning.

Starting at the top and intending to work his way south, he invested a great deal of time and effort investigating every supple curve and dip of his ambrosial Antonía before applying the brakes mid-corset.

Antonía looked at him with question in her eyes and said encouragingly, "If you think I'm going to stop you, Breck, you are quite mad."

He smiled at her highly commendable spirit of cooperation. "And if you think I have any intention of stopping, lovely Antonía, *you* are quite mad." He brought his lips north to hers, kissed her as if his life depended on it, and then paused to take a breath and explain. "Actually, Miss Barclay, during the course of my inspection, I found something nestled neatly in your corset . . . something that has quite left me puzzled.

"Why, Breck, I thought *you* would be able to handle them." He smiled and then plucked her claymore necklace from her breasts and dangled it in front of her.

"You kept it safe, through all of your ordeal."

"Aye," she whispered, and then after caressing the pendant for a moment, she tucked it away again, lifting her eyes to his. "But as much as I adore my miniature claymore, I do believe I'm ready for the life-size version right about now."

He drew back slightly. Did she have any idea, truly, what she was saying? She was so young, so beautiful. How could he be sure she was ready? He refused to compromise her virtue if she preferred to wait until after they were married. But then again, she seemed not only ready, but also willing.

On the other hand, perhaps her innocence prevented full understanding. He didn't want her to experience regrets of any kind. He loved her so much. He wanted her first time to be perfect, because he intended to be her first, her last, her only. No, he needed to proceed with caution. He had to be sure she meant what she'd implied. He therefore advanced with the utmost care.

"My darling, darling Antonía, good girls don't say things like that."

She arched her supple back, leaned into him, and purred contentedly into his ear.

"Good girls don't, Mr. Claymore, but I most certainly do."

At this point, nothing but a battalion of warriors and/or one man's deeply entrenched sense of honor could halt the impending interrogation. And while the former was presently impossible, the latter was very much present on the scene.

"Ah, dear Antonía, I'm getting the very distinct impression you are prepared for my interrogation." He then probed deeper. "But I feel honor-bound to inquire one more time: Are you absolutely positive you're ready to answer my infinite number of questions?"

"Yes, Breck, I'm absolutely positive, but I must insist on answering your infinite number of questions in complete sentences, complete paragraphs, and *completely in calligraphy*."

Totally captivated, he continued, "Now that you've told me your philosophy, what of your schedule?"

"Immediately, if not sooner," she answered. "*Take me now, Mr. Claymore.*"

And in less time than it takes to strike a match, her highly flammable response sparked a firestorm of passion in Claymore. Fully ignited, he swept his beautiful Antonía into his arms and into the fire of his deep, unquenchable love for her. In the full throes of incendiary passion, he was about to quench the fire, when all at once his lovely Antonía stiffened beneath him.

"Mr. Claymore," she said breathlessly, "I mean Breck, far be it from me to interrupt—but I smell smoke."

He had his mouth against her neck and paused from kissing to take a deep, satisfying breath. "Ah, Antonía, the only aroma I smell is the lovely lavender scent of your skin. I just can't . . ." Claymore stopped midsentence when, out of the corner of his eye, he saw the back wall of the cottage was in flames.

Antonía pushed herself to an upright position as Claymore jumped out of bed, threw their clothing to her, and wrapped her in the coverlet from the bed. She clung to him as he picked her up and carried her out the front door. Once they were a good distance away from the cottage, he stopped and fell to his knees in the heather.

Coughing from the smoke, she shivered beside him, pulling the comforter around as they both watched the small house burn. Seeing her plight, Claymore helped her into her clothing and then threw her cloak around her. Once she was clothed, he wrapped his kilt haphazardly around his body and locked her into his arms.

"How did the fire start?" Antonía whispered, staring at the flames licking across the thatched roof.

Claymore shook his head. Could it have been an ember from the fireplace? An overturned candle? All at once the sound of horses approaching made him drop his arm from her shoulders and turn, reaching for the sword at his waist—that wasn't there. Empty-handed he stared up at Rex Throckmorton and half a dozen mounted, armed men.

The Englishman sat astride a huge stallion, casually stuffing a gigantic scone into his big mouth. He was obviously inebriated, swaying from side to side as he finished the first scone and then thrust his hand down into the leather sack to grab another, which he proceeded to mow down, pulverizing it with his hideous yellow teeth.

Six more men sat on horses surrounding Rex. Antonía moved closer to Claymore. He pushed her behind him and, bare-chested, weaponless, faced their foe. Antonía shivered beside him and, glanced up at the thick clouds, one hand on the necklace he'd given her.

"The sun," she whispered, "we need the sun!"

Claymore wanted to know what she was talking about; however, he had no time. He had no sword. He had no backup. He flexed one fist and took a deep breath.

"Well, well, well, who do we have here?" Rex asked, his words garbled by the food in his mouth.

Claymore glared up at him. "The man who is going to kill you," he stated.

Rex laughed, spittle and bits of scone flying out of his mouth. He dragged one sleeve across his face and turned to the men riding beside him. "Well, whatta ya waiting for?" he demanded.

The men swung down from their horses and circled Antonía and Claymore. Claymore wanted to fight them, to save Antonía, but the drawn swords held by the men stopped him. He couldn't take a chance on having her hurt.

"Don't touch her," he warned, pushing her behind him.

"Breck," she whispered, her hand to her throat, her eyes on the overcast sky. Then with swords drawn, the men rushed them, and in a matter of minutes Claymore was on his knees, his arms bound behind him. Two men held Antonía between them.

"'Twill be all right, my love," he said, glaring up at Throckmorton's spawn who was stuffing an English crumpet into his mouth. "Help is on the way."

"Ho, ho! I doubt that!" Rex said gleefully, smacking his lips. "My father's spies report that none of her brothers are searching for her, nor even her father." He narrowed his beady eyes at Claymore, then sneered at Antonía. "However . . . now that I've finished my English crumpet, I'm salivating for a great big bite of Scottish strumpet."

"Over my dead body!" Claymore shouted and stumbled to his feet. Two men rushed to grab him and he struggled against them, to no avail. All six men were built like gladiators. Rex's personal brute squad.

"Well, yeah," Rex said with a laugh that dissolved into a grim smile. "That was always the plan." He swung down off his horse and walked toward Claymore.

"No!" Antonía jerked loose from the men holding her and ran to Claymore, throwing herself over his chest like a cloak.

"Antonía," Claymore said and she lifted her head. He met her terrified blue eyes and stopped fighting. His beautiful, impetuous Miss Barclay was going to get herself hurt. He couldn't let that happen. "It's all right," he whispered. If he were going to die, he would die gazing into her eyes, loving her with all of his soul.

She shook her head. "No!" She spun around. "Please, Rex, take me, but don't kill him. Please," she whispered, "I'm begging you. I'll do anything."

Rex laughed and pulled her away from Claymore. "My goodness, Antonía, I've never seen you grovel in such a delightfully servile manner." He leered down at her. "I like it."

"I swear to you, I mean what I said. I promise I'll do *anything*—*anything* you want—just don't harm Mr. Claymore."

He cocked one brow at her. "Desperate, aren't ya? But even you gotta know your offer don't have a leg to stand on." He took another scone from the bag around his neck and stuffed it in his mouth. "You got nothing to bargain with. You'll do what I want whether he lives or dies."

"You don't understand," she said, lifting her chin. The sight of her trembling lips made Claymore's heart ache. "If you let Mr. Claymore go free, I'll give myself to you—willingly and completely."

"Antonía!" Claymore shouted, his heart pounding. "Don't make any deals with that bastard!" He turned and glared at Rex, his voice now controlled but filled with angry promise. "I'll shake your bones out of your garments," he said. "I'll live to knock your brains out if you touch her!"

"Get ready to die, you piece of Scottish filth." Rex drew his sword.

Antonía fell to her knees and clasped her hands together. "I promise, I'll—I'll gladly—well—I'll *willingly* bed you if you spare him!"

"And then I will kill you, Throckmorton," Claymore said.

She turned around and frowned. "Dear Mr. Claymore, you are not helping," she said, and turned back to Rex. "Willingly," she said again.

Rex laughed long and hard, snorting and sniggering and then fixed Antonía with his beady eyes. "Well, well, well, my little Scottish strumpet, I knew you'd come around sooner or later to admittin' that you wanted me, but honestly?" His lips stretched back over gnarly yellow teeth that had bits of scone stuck between them. "You being willing might take all the fun out of it. Bring the Scotch dirtbag over here to me," he added.

The men dragged Claymore forward, but Antonía held out one hand to stop them. Her captured Scot watched as she lowered her lashes and then flashed them upward again, giving him a look that would bring any man to his knees. The last of the scone fell out of Rex's mouth.

"Are you sure about that, Rex?" she asked softly, walking forward to put one hand on his chest. "Are you quite sure?"

A bit of drool gathered in the corner of Rex's mouth and then he dragged his sleeve across his face and gave her a lascivious sneer. "Tie him up," he said. "I've got other business to attend to!" He grabbed Antonía and began slobbering against her neck.

"Wait! Wait!" she cried.

Rex raised his head, frowning.

She pushed away from him. "I'm not going to copulate with you on the ground like some kind of animal!" she said, sounding outraged.

"I don't wanna copulate. I wanna pluck you like there's no tomorrow!"

Antonía's shoulders went back and her hands braced her hips. "I beg

ANTONIA BARCLAY AND HER SCOTTISH CLAYMORE

your pardon! I am royalty! My mother is Mary, Queen of Scots! I am a princess! The conditions for my willing submission to your—affections— *will* come with four conditions, and *will* be obeyed!"

He blinked at her. "Conditions?"

Claymore's fists relaxed slightly. What was she up to? For the first time in the last few minutes he felt a little more optimistic. Clearly his brilliant and beautiful Antonía had a plan.

"One," she said, "Mr. Claymore will be left here, healthy and unharmed. Two, you will treat me as a lady—with no manhandling. Three, the act will not take place until we reach Wrathbone Manor. And four, you will tell your father about our arrangement as soon as we see him."

"You drive a hard bargain, bitch, but nothing doing," Rex sneered. "You're mine no matter what."

Antonía stepped forward again, cupping one palm to his face and lowering her voice. "The issue is not *what*, Rex, it's *how*." She made an educated guess. "You've never bedded a woman who willingly submitted to you, have you?" She could tell she guessed right. He appeared to be weakening. She purred, "You've never had a woman who *really, really* wanted to do it with you, have you, Rex darling?" He shook his head. She dropped her hand from his jaw. "Now. Are we agreed?"

"Agreed." A big ugly smile split his big ugly face. "Except I'm gonna have to tie Claymore up to a tree or my father will think I didn't do my due diligence." He leered at her. "I can't wait to pluck you like there's no tomorrow."

"And there will be no more talk of plucking," she said firmly, turning away from him. Claymore's gaze met hers, and the hardness mirrored there disappeared. First anguish, and then resignation appeared in her blue eyes, and his heart constricted. Then she lifted her chin, gave him an almost imperceptible nod, and icy-eyed, spun back to Rex.

"Shall we go?" she asked, and headed toward the horses.

Rex ambled over to Claymore and it was all the Scot could do not to headbutt him in the stomach, but now that Antonía had bought him some time, he would control his temper.

"Tie him up to that tree over there, boys," he told his henchmen. "And make sure the ropes is mighty tight." He leaned closer to Claymore and whispered. "I'm gonna pluck her like there's no tomorrow—and then I'm gonna pluck her again." He leaned back and laughed, his big belly shaking as he turned and walked away.

His men grabbed Claymore and tied him to the tree, following the orders to make the ropes as tight as possible. He winced as he watched Rex lift Antonía into the saddle and then swing up behind her.

"Too bad you won't get to help us find the Royal Magic Wand," Rex called back. "My father found out it's at Ford Castle! And we're gonna beat your asses to it!"

He gave heel to his horse, and Claymore watched as Antonía looked back at him once, her blue eyes shining under the overcast sky. Then they galloped away, leaving him behind, but alive.

Feeling like the quintessential boomerang, Antonía was partly frightened, but for the greater part, humiliated to be captured for the second time by Rex and his horde of heinous henchmen, as well as entirely furious that he had left Mr. Claymore bound and gagged! Still, it was better than the alternative.

If only the sky hadn't been so overcast! If only the sun would come out! She hadn't forgotten her secret weapon clasped around her neck—Mr. Claymore's beautiful gift to her, now endued with the power to become a full-fledged sword! If only the English skies would clear. But of course, she would still need a piece of metal to initiate the alchemical change.

After awhile, she noticed they were riding in a northerly direction, toward the Scottish border, but perhaps it was just her directionally defective nature confusing her. As she and her handlers approached the small village of Branxton, however, Antonía knew she had been right. She knew this town, and it was the opposite direction from Wrathbone Manor.

With the ill-tempered English sky frowning down upon them, she realized that if Mr. Claymore managed to break his bonds, he would probably ride straight for Wrathbone Manor to rescue her. Damnation! She bit her lower lip so hard she almost drew blood.

Rex put his big blubbery hand around Antonía's waist and jerked her back against him. "Won't be long now," he said with a sneer. "Soon as I get you where we're going, I'm gonna pluck you—"

"If you say it one more time," she interrupted, "our deal is off!" She glanced back at him, and from the look on his ugly mug, Rex wasn't too happy with her smart remark.

"Look, you icy bitch, I spared your stupid Mr. Claymore even though my father will probably flog me if he finds out. If you don't come through on this deal, I'll track your stupid Scotchman down again and eat his liver for dinner."

"Fine, I'll make good on our bargain, but you agreed to treat me like a lady, and you do not keep telling a lady that you're going to *pluck* her!"

"All right!" he shouted, his spittle striking her on the side of her face. She wiped it off and shuddered, thoroughly repulsed. But her ultimatum seemed to have made some impression on him, because Rex loosened his hold on her waist and kept his voracious appetite under control, leaving her relatively unmolested for the rest of the journey—which ended more quickly than Antonía had hoped.

Within a single revolution of the hour hand, they had reached their destination, and Antonía was astonished to find they had arrived at an ancient castle. Parts of it were crumbling, while others seemed to be livable— perhaps. Sitting motionless, trying to make heads or tails of the unexpected destination, she contemplated the situation with some depth of thought. But unsurprisingly, Rex disapproved of deep contemplation, and so after dismounting, he pulled her abruptly out of the saddle.

Barely managing to land on her feet, Antonía started to remind him of the conditions of their deal, but he seized her by the wrist, jerked her through the castle door, and dragged her down a dim, dank hallway, leaving her breathless.

Sir Basil Throckmorton proceeded to the castle courtyard to confer with his son about all things nefarious. Rex had actually done something right for a change, and Sir Basil's plan was proceeding smoothly. Characteristic of all true megalomaniacs, the Englishman was absolutely confident about absolutely everything in absolutely every situation. He reveled in the fact.

As Sir Basil strode into the courtyard, every henchman stopped mid-task and bowed, proving that he commanded instant respect, as well as a fair amount of bootlicking. Upon locating his slow-witted son leaning against the courtyard wall, eating a scone, he sighed and crossed to confront him.

"Hello, sir," Rex said with his mouth full.

"Good morning. Have the scouts returned with their morning reports?"

"Yeah, her brothers were spotted five miles south of Branxton. I'm pretty sure they want her back."

"Of course they want her back, you idiot," Sir Basil snapped. This added a complication to the plan, but nothing he couldn't handle. "Did you think they'd let us just waltz off with her?"

Rex pondered that for a moment. "Possibly. I figure anybody'd get sick of that icy, pain-in-the-ass bitch after awhile."

Throckmorton turned and stared out over Flodden Field again. "At least I don't have to deal with her Scottish lover anymore." He glanced back at Rex. "You're sure that he's dead."

"As sure as I'm eating a scone," Rex said, obliterating another baked good. "Say, why don't I ride out with a few of our men, kill the rest of them, and be done with it?"

"No," his father said, "let them come to us. Miss Barclay needs to see with her own blue eyes that any rescue attempt is doomed to failure."

"Fine by me. It'll save me the chore of burying their sorry carcasses," Rex said. "If we kill them here, I can just dump their bodies over the border and into their own God-forsaken country. Let the Scotch bury the Scotch! Why pollute our soil with their decay? Why force our maggots to do all the work?" He then blinked in befogged confusion. "You *want* her to witness their killing?"

"Compliance, Rex. The overarching goal is compliance. If Miss Barclay is made to understand that I mean business, she'll have no choice other than to comply with my every order—that is, if she wants her remaining family members to attain their full life expectancy."

"You mean if she doesn't go along with your plans, you'll kill her parents too?"

Throckmorton smiled. "All three of them."

Rex frowned again. "But don't you think that bald-headed trout, Queen What's-Her-Face, will be furious you beat her to the punch by rubbing out her scheming whore of a cousin?"

"On the contrary, Elizabeth will be thrilled. She's forestalled execution only because she doesn't want every Catholic in the country keening over Mary's grave and elevating her to martyrdom status. But in any event, Elizabeth ranks at the bottom of my list of priorities . . . at least for the time being." After a thoughtful pause, he mused, "However, once I oust the King of Scotland, the Queen of England shall surge to the top of my list."

Sir Basil turned and led the way up the stone stairs to the top of the castle wall. Looking out upon Scotland's battlefield of Flodden Field, he let his gaze sweep across the vast countryside before him. "Indeed, it's only a matter of a wee bit of time before I control the whole damn island."

Rex cringed. "God Almighty! Just listen to yourself! You've been spending so much time with her that she's infected you with her irritating Scotch colloquialisms."

Unfazed by his son's abuse, the father said, "The lovely Miss Barclay may infect me with anything she so chooses."

"What do you mean?" Rex asked, giving his father the gimlet eye.

"Nothing at all," he said, brushing aside the question. "Tell me, Rex, have the men found the Scottish Royal Sceptre?"

"Naw, but they're searching the drawing room now. It's the only room they've yet to ransack, so it must be there somewhere—that is, if that stupid stick exists at all."

"Is Miss Barclay comfortable in her room?"

Rex shrugged. "I dunno. Does it matter?"

His father stared at him. Rex stared back.

"Was there something you wanted?" Sir Basil asked with a sigh.

"Yeah, I wanted to know when I could start plucking that little bitch."

Throckmorton turned on him furiously. "Watch your filthy mouth when you speak of her or I'll wash it out with boiling oil!"

"I don't know why you treat her like she's some saint," Rex said with a sneer. "You know she was cavorting in a cottage with Claymore when I found her, and she really seemed to like it. Right before I torched the place, I saw them through the window and it looked like some plucking was about to commence." Rex paused, reconsidered, and then added, "Or at the very least, some serious diddling."

Infuriated at the possibility that Miss Barclay's purity had been tarnished, Sir Basil burst into an uncharacteristic fit of rage. "One more word and I'll surgically remove your tongue!"

"Why do you care so much?" Rex said, his eyes narrowed and filled with suspicion. "I'm the one who should be upset." He shook his head. "How can she want that pasty-faced Scotchman instead of me?"

"Inconceivable."

"Why don't we forget about that damn Scottish Sceptre and clear out of this dump of a castle right now," Rex grumbled. "I don't fancy plucking her in this moldy ruin. I have my standards, you know!"

Throckmorton grimaced but held his temper. "No, we'll leave only when we find the sceptre, and only when we eliminate Miss Barclay's so-called rescuers. We can't have them forever sniffing about like a pack of deranged bloodhounds. They must be eradicated permanently."

Now in total agreement, Rex lent his gung-ho support to the plan. "I'll track them down, butcher them in their sleep, and then personally hand-deliver their hearts to Antonía in a nice little gift-wrapped box." He paused. "I really wish I knew what he was doing to her in that cottage, because she really seemed to be enjoying it."

Sir Basil turned to his son, trying to remain calm. "Rex, I'm warning you for the very last time. One more word on the subject and you'll need to learn sign language in a hurry!"

"Sir, you are in a mood!"

Throckmorton briefly imagined choking the life out of his nitwit of a son. The thought calmed him and he leaned against the castle wall.

"I'm going to give you one simple chore to do, Rex. Do you think you can manage it?"

Rex frowned and massaged the small of his back. "Do I have to lift anything? 'Cause picking up Antonía strained my back. She's heavier than she looks."

His father took a deep breath, hanging on to his temper. "No heavy lifting is required. Simply go and get Miss Barclay and bring her to me in the parlor downstairs. Don't carry her, just escort her," he added.

A smile split his son's face. "Can I have a little fun first?"

He clenched his fists but spoke casually. "I think not. In fact, if you even touch her, I will rip your fingers off and stuff them in your mouth."

Rex frowned. "I'd rather have scones."

"Then do as I say," he ordered. "Bring her to me—without incident—immediately."

"And you'll make some scones?"

Throckmorton counted silently to ten and smiled. "No, but I won't kill you."

"All right," Rex said, then brightened. "Thanks, Fadda."

As his son lumbered away, Sir Basil sighed and wondered, not for the first time, what he'd done to deserve a child like Rex.

As soon as Rex and Antonía and the rest of Throckmorton's men disappeared from sight, Claymore began working on breaking free of his ropes by rubbing them against a rough knot on the wood. It was slow, agonizing work, and took hours to make any headway at all. Finally, just as he realized he was approaching freedom, and the full moon had risen overhead, he heard the sound of horses approaching at a gallop.

Expecting that Rex had sent some of his men back to finish him off, he was astonished to see the three Barclay brothers riding toward him. They reined their horses, dismounted, and ran to Claymore to set him free.

"Claymore!" Oliver Barclay pulled a knife from his belt and cut the ropes while Will handed him water and Matthew pounded him on the back.

"How on God's green earth did you find me?" Claymore asked after taking several swigs of the stream-cold water.

"Luck?" Oliver said with a laugh.

"Deduction," Will offered.

"Providence," Matthew swore.

"I accept all three answers!" Claymore said, clapping the men on the back. "But there is no time for a reunion, lads. Antonía is in grave danger and being held by Throckmorton."

"That wretched bastard!" Oliver swore roundly.

"If Antonía was here she could do you one better," Claymore told the youngest brother.

"No doubt, but remember I taught her!"

"So we're off to Wrathbone Manor?" Matthew asked impatiently.

"No, they're headed for Ford Castle," corrected Claymore. "I'll explain on the way, but there's a minor complication, lads. I have reason to believe that Throckmorton is mustering his own army, and they may lie in wait for us there."

"We heard something about that," said Will.

"Won't be a problem," Matthew added.

"Let's quit wasting time!" Oliver shouted.

"But you don't fully understand," explained Claymore. "Throckmorton may have a couple of hundred men—or more."

"We do understand," Will told him and, smiling, turned and swept one arm behind him, toward what looked like at least a hundred men on horseback riding toward them.

"And more will meet up with us on the way, I'll wager," Matthew said.

"Oh, we brought you a horse." Oliver signaled one of the men riding up.

As the man approached, leading a sturdy black stallion, Claymore recognized the man as Gus.

"Gus!" Claymore called out. "I couldn't be happier to see you, but you should be at home, healing."

Gus gave him a broad smile. "Nay, laddie. I'm exactly where I should be."

In a matter of minutes, Claymore was on the back of his steed, and with Gus and the Barclay brothers alongside, they rode ahead of a multitude of loyal Scotsmen, headed for Ford Castle. Taking a brief glance over his shoulder at the small army, Claymore detected shards of silver glinting in the moonlight. The men carried swords. Not just any swords. Swords five feet long, swords only stout and hearty men could wield.

Claymores.

Chapter 15

HOBSON'S CHOICE OR FUNGIBLE EVILS

Antonía followed Rex down the crumbling hallway. For once he hadn't tried to maul her, and for that she was grateful. Since arriving at the half-ruined castle the night before, she'd gotten little sleep and nothing at all to eat. Now she had to face Basil Throckmorton, and though she hated to admit it, she wasn't feeling up to conversation with her sworn enemy.

There was a door at the end of the hall, and when they reached it, Rex kicked it open and, grabbing her by the arm, flung her inside. She fell to her knees and then looked up to see her alternate nemesis standing with perfect posture in front of a large window, his back to her.

The elegant madman appeared lost in thought as he gazed out the window, and Antonía wondered what deviltry he was plotting now. Rex cleared his throat loudly and Throckmorton turned, his dark eyes flickering over the woman on the floor. After giving her a long, uninhibited stare, he glanced at his son.

"Help Miss Barclay stand, Rex," he ordered, "and quit being an ass."

Grumbling, his son blundered over and lifted Antonía by the armpits, getting in a little squeeze as he did. Antonía whirled around and slapped him in the face. "Why you little—" Rex reached for her, but his father stepped between them.

"Cease!" Sir Basil cast his son an incinerating glare before turning to Antonía. "Are you all right, my dear?" he asked. She stared at him silently. He turned back to Rex. "What did you do to her?"

Rex sneered and blubbered. "I didn't do nothing to her. She's a frigid piece if I ever saw one. Oh, I forgot to tell you something before," he said. "It's important."

"Very well," his father said with a sigh. "What is so important?"

Antonía was suddenly filled with terror, afraid he was going to reveal that Mr. Claymore had been left behind, alive. She had to redirect the conversation. She decided to use big words and high drama.

"Yes, you go right ahead, Rex," Antonía chimed in. "If you'd like a wee word with us, we'd be delighted to listen. In fact, we implore you to indulge your pomposity!"

"Antonía?" Sir Basil furrowed his brow.

"Please, Rex," she said, fluttering her eyelashes and ignoring his father. "Rouse us with your rodomontade! Rivet us with your rhetoric! Mesmerize us with your magniloquence! Astound us with your afflatus! Fascinate us with your fustian! Paralyze us with your peroration! Pummel us with your profundities! Tantalize us with your turgidity!" She stopped briefly to inhale a fortifying breath before resuming, "Let the three of us pledge, here and now, that there shall never be secrets amongst us! Trickery shall be deemed taboo! Deceit prohibited! And chicanery verboten! Because according to your dear old dad, Rex, we're soon to become one big happy family . . . although perhaps not in the manner *you* envisioned."

Rex looked at his father and shook his head. "She's making even less sense than usual."

Sir Basil gazed at her thoughtfully. "Come here, my dear."

Reluctantly, she crossed to his side. Taking her by the hand, he led her closer to the window. "Stand in the light. Let me look at you."

Though fully aware that father and son were fungible evils, Antonía nevertheless felt relatively safer with the father than his plundering thug of a son. But as Sir Basil proceeded to scrutinize every single millimeter of her body, she wasn't so sure.

His black eyes narrowed and he lifted her chin with two fingers, examining her face. "You're more beautiful than ever, if that's possible, but somehow you look different to me, Miss Barclay. I can't quite put a finger on it."

She jerked away from his touch, her temper flaring. "Perhaps it's the bruises I suffered at your son's hands. Or perhaps I look different because

I'm not *unconscious* which, if you recall, is how I spend most of my time when we're together."

"Hmm, I'm definitely not feeling the love. In fact, my acute perception detects quite a bit of turbulence in your vicinity, my dear Miss Barclay. Did you have a rough trip?" He darted a sharp look at Rex.

"Oh, no," she countered, "indeed not, Sir Basil, unless you consider being accosted, assaulted, mauled, and kidnapped *again* as being a *rough trip!*"

"Dear, dear me," he replied in a deceptively mild voice. "Rex, did you accost our Miss Barclay?"

"We made a deal," Rex blurted, wiping one sleeve across his face.

Throckmorton turned at that, his eyes wary. "A deal? What kind of a deal?"

"She promised that if I let Claymore go, she'd do the deed with me," he said, throwing her a lecherous look.

Damn! So much for diverting the conversation! Antonía said, "But remember, Rex, the agreement was that that would only happen once we reached Wrathbone Manor." She shook her head. "It will not be happening here at Ford Castle."

To her surprise, Sir Basil began to turn various shades of crimson. The flush started at the base of his neck, rose over the top of his huge ruffled collar, and flooded into his throat, face, and forehead like something boiling in one of his beakers.

"You left Claymore behind?"

Rex shifted his big feet nervously. "Uh, yeah, but then I sent one of the men back to polish him off."

Throckmorton's eyes narrowed. "You're lying. You've been lying to me since you returned!"

"Well, you know, she was being difficult, as usual, and she, uh, agreed if I let him go she'd, uh, play nice." A sloppy grin stretched across his ugly mug. "You know what I mean, Fadda?"

In two seconds, Throckmorton had crossed to his son, grabbed him by the throat, and thrown him against a wall. Antonía gasped as the man dug his fingers into his son's neck and Rex's face began to turn purplish-red to match his father's, though for a different reason.

"You stupid fool! You imbecile! You are a boil, a plague sore, an embossed carbuncle on my ass!" Throckmorton shouted. He shoved Rex away from him and paced, dragging one hand through his hair before whirling around again.

"Did you touch her?" he demanded.

"No!" Rex squeaked.

"Well," Antonía said, feeling vengeful, "there *was* a little touching. He made me ride in front of him on the horse."

"What bloody difference, at this point, does it make?" Rex said, sounding extremely close to whining. "She's gonna be my wife, isn't she? What does it matter if I get in a little pinch and tickle now and then?"

"Yes," Antonía said, her voice innocent. "What difference does it make?"

Throckmorton glared at her for a long, uncomfortable minute, and then shoved Rex against the wall again, this time knotting his fists into his son's shirt. "She is not going to be your wife, Rex. She is going to be *my* wife!"

Rex's jaw dropped open. "*Your* wife? But that isn't fair. You said I could have her. And that I could be *king*!"

"You can be the prince—the ne'er-do-well, philandering, extravagant gambler," his father suggested. "How about that?"

Rex perked up. "Does philandering mean I get to sail on a boat?"

It was Throckmorton's turn to roll his eyes. "Yes, Rex, that's exactly what it means."

"Agreed!" Rex declared. "But I still get a girl, right?"

"Of course." He stepped back and straightened his own lopsided accordion-like collar. "Perhaps Miss Barclay's friend, Claire."

Antonía's eyes widened. "He will *not* have Claire!"

Rex leered over at her. "Jealous, Antonía? See, sir—she wants me, she really wants me!"

Sir Basil had had it. He smacked his son in the face and, grabbing Rex's shirt, sent him stumbling toward the door.

"You'll have a woman when I say so, and it will not be Miss Barclay!" He shook his fist at him. "Now go and tell the captain of the guards to send four men to that wretched cottage and find Claymore. And if they don't find him—"

"I'll go help them," Rex said, rubbing his reddened face.

"No you won't! You've done enough—more than enough. Now get out!"

Rex glared first at his father and then at Antonía. "Fine," he finally said. "I didn't want her anyway. Talk about a pain in the ass." He stormed out of the room and Throckmorton stared after him for a moment.

"I do apologize—again—Miss Barclay," he said after a long moment. "I promise Rex will no longer bother you."

"I have a sneaking suspicion you'll be taking over that job," she said cautiously.

He straightened his jacket and turned to her as if he hadn't heard her. "Please, sit down. You look as if you might collapse at any moment."

Antonía crossed to two dusty chairs near the fireplace and sank into one of them. She had no intention of letting Sir Basil discover how weak she really felt, but she'd take her rest where she found it.

"Here, let me pour you a cup of tea." He sat down in the chair next to her. A porcelain teapot rested on a small table between the two chairs, and he poured hot tea into a delicate porcelain teacup. She took it gratefully, even though she despised being grateful to him for anything.

He smiled, pouring his own tea, looking more composed by the minute. "Do you know where you are, Miss Barclay?"

"I have no idea," she said. "It looked vaguely familiar from the outside."

"You are now ensconced in *Ford* Castle." He gave her a meaningful look.

Antonía shrugged. "Is that supposed to mean something to me?" she asked.

"I was optimistic that it would. Somewhere in this historic English castle lies the Scottish Royal Sceptre."

Throckmorton raised one brow at Antonía as if he wanted her to clap her hands or cheer. Instead she went cold inside. So, she thought, somehow he had managed to decipher the scroll.

Antonía put her cup down with a bang. "You had the nerve to accuse me of holding out on you, when all this time you knew what the scroll said and where the sceptre was hidden!"

He laughed at her outrage. "There she is, my little Scottish spitfire!" He arched one brow. "Lucky for you, I find your saucy tongue immensely diverting. Rest assured, I would never hold out on you. I still don't speak Gaelic, but your elusive escape forced me to resort to plan B. Let me ask you a question, Miss Barclay. Have you ever noticed that the least likely individuals often possess the most unlikely talents?" he asked.

Antonía tilted her head and narrowed her eyes. "After spending twenty-four hours in the company of your genteel son and his equally genteel henchmen, you'll have to excuse me if I find your guessing games highly irritating."

"Fair enough. I won't play games if you won't. It so happens I found I did have an old Scotch servant in my employ who could read ancient Gaelic, and he translated enough to let me know that the Royal Sceptre was hidden here in Ford Castle, but then"—he scowled—"Rex killed him."

"I'm so surprised," she murmured.

"Anyway," Throckmorton continued, "I now have need again of a translator. Still, it's only a matter of time before I discover the sceptre's exact location. Once it's found, you and I can be married, return to Edinburgh, overthrow your ineffectual brother, and I will take my rightful place on the throne." He picked up a scone from the tray, sniffed it, and put it back.

"Rightful place?" Antonía scoffed. "You can count me out of your little scheme, Sir Basil. For some unknown reason, I'm beginning to feel a wee bit exploited."

"Exploited? Oh my darling, never! You will be my queen. I will drape you in sapphires and rubies and satins and velvets while I right all the wrongs King James has wreaked upon your native land." He beamed at her and Antonía sighed.

"I'm more of a diamonds and leather girl, to tell the truth," she said.

"Tell me," she went on, shaking her head at his insane hubris, "what makes you think you have all the answers? What makes you think you can cure Scotland's ills and determine her destiny?"

"Because I hold an eternal disregard for titles earned without merit," he said. "What makes your brother, King James, so special? What makes him think he can rule Scotland, much less rule it to greatness? What makes a monarch any different from the rest of us?"

"Having been born to the crown?" she suggested.

"Exactly! *Fortuity of birth* is the answer, Miss Barclay," he said. His eyes narrowed. "Why should men of intelligence, insight, and ingenuity truckle to the ridiculous randomness of royal lineage? Why should fortuity of birth subjugate men of superior minds? Does it not make far better sense for brilliant, elite minds to rule?"

"If, indeed, these brilliant, elite minds are not also insane," Antonía remarked disgustedly. She then paused briefly for reflection and added, "And what of *your* entitlement to the style of 'sir,' Sir Basil?"

"Aha!" he exclaimed with triumph. "I knew you'd get around to that eventually." Pointing his index finger upward, he boasted, "My entitlement derives purely from merit and achievement, Miss Barclay. My innumerable contributions to the field of medicine are unparalleled and without equal."

"As well as redundant," she mumbled under her breath.

He continued, "Mark my words, Miss Barclay, the intelligentsia shall one day rise and conquer the world, and I'm here to tell you that the world shall be a far, far better place for it!"

"Spoken like a true revolutionary, Sir Basil," she said, "but why don't we share our warring opinions at a later date? I'm really not in the mood to quibble over silly little notions like the ideology and abuses of absolute power. Frankly, I despise politics, and I am famished and exhausted."

"Forgive me, Miss Barclay, I know you've had an arduous trip." His eyes shone with humor and she thought briefly about poking them out with her teaspoon. "Have a scone. It will strengthen you for what lies ahead." He handed her a plate filled with scones and she took one, devouring it with such gusto she feared she smacked of Rex.

"Excuse me," she said, wiping her mouth. "I was quite hungry."

"Have another, dear Miss Barclay."

She did, but this time she ate it with a higher degree of etiquette. It wasn't until after she finished that his words struck her.

"What did you mean—strengthen me for what lies ahead?"

"I have a surprise for you."

"Lucky me." She sighed. "Okay, out with it."

"Well, since you are going to spend the rest of your life without Mr. Claymore—"

"Far be it from me to crack your crystal ball," Antonía interrupted, "but I *will* spend the rest of my life with Mr. Claymore, in spite of this strange interlude."

"And far be it from me to rain on your parade, Miss Barclay, but I intend to be the *only* man you ever wrap those long legs of yours around. I strongly suggest you expel all thoughts of your family, friends, and ex-fiancé from your mind from now on, because you, my beautiful Miss Barclay, are embarking on a fresh, new voyage of discovery. Consequently, it would be extremely counterproductive for you to pine over your past—in particular, Claymore."

God's nightgown! The man was insufferable. She closed her eyes in sheer wretchedness. Dear God, she missed Breck. She knew she couldn't live without him. She couldn't bear the thought of a future without him. *Damn* the Throckmortons! She'd wrap her long legs around whomever she damn well pleased . . . and there was only one man who qualified for that position.

She opened her eyes and saw a feigned trace of pity in Sir Basil's eyes, and that did more to stiffen her spine than a designer corset! He was up to something . . . something evil. She felt it in her bones and she was not going to capitulate.

"Let me understand, Sir Basil," she said, ready to put him in his place. "Are you proposing marriage?"

He looked a little shocked. "Isn't that what I've been saying all along?"

"Oh, I'm sorry." She gave a little dismissive laugh. "All I heard was a lot of talk about wrapping legs around you and fortuity of birth and truckling to royalty."

He smiled, showing his very white, straight teeth. *Truly*, Antonía thought, *the man was an English anomaly.* "Forgive me, my dear, if I didn't make my position clear. I am most definitely asking you to marry me."

Antonía arched one brow as she rose from the chair and walked over to the fireplace, then turned, her hands clasped loosely together.

"Sir Basil," she articulated slowly, "you mustn't forget the vast disparity in our ages. In relative calendar terms, I was born yesterday while you were born around the time of"—she paused to pinpoint a comprehensively offensive historical date and, after succeeding, thrust it savagely into his ego—"the Battle of Bannockburn."

But much to her dismay, Throckmorton's ego was as tough as a megalith. He smiled at her, clearly eager for more witty words to tumble off her tart tongue.

And tumble off, they did. "I'm still very young . . . barely out of my cradle, really, and surely, you wouldn't debase yourself by robbing cradles." She stopped, acting as if she were giving the matter great consideration. "Although you are a bit of a lunatic, I suspect you do have some degree of respect for my youth as well as for my innocence." She gave him an inquiring look. "That is, if you haven't *forgotten* how young I am. Old age does tend to affect the memory, you know."

The Englishman rose, moved to the fireplace, and then stood beside her. He held his hands out to the flames, as if warming them. She watched him warily. He glanced over at her and smiled. Fully aware of her age, he nonetheless played along.

"Well, my dear, judging from your highly cultivated mind and perfectly developed body, I'd say you're at least five and twenty."

"Aha!" She folded her arms over her chest and lifted her chin. "Not even close! I turned teen and nine only a few weeks ago!"

"Miss Barclay," he said with condescending patience, "while I'm willing to stipulate to the fact that at this particular moment you are rather young, be advised that the dimension of time has a relentless way of marching forward with unforgiving velocity. You're already staring spinsterhood squarely in the face." He then added with a rakish wink, "Admit it, Miss Barclay, wouldn't it be fun to be queen and married to me all at the same time?"

"Better beggar-woman and spinster than queen and married to you!"

"As for your alleged innocence," he continued, "it's possible that a certain intervening event served to change your status." He gave her a questioning look.

She returned his look with a little shrug. "Let's just say some things are best left a riddle, wrapped in a mystery, inside an enigma."

"Perhaps, Miss Barclay," he said, "but in your case, I refuse to allow the question to remain a mystery for much longer. Even I have a breaking point. Verbal foreplay goes only so far, my dear. As much as I revel in your sparkling repartee, I can no longer make love to you with words only."

Her reply was quick and curt. "When it's all said and done, I strongly prefer that everything be said and nothing be done."

Closing the space between them, he countered, "Apparently we're not on the same page, Miss Barclay, because when it's all said and done, I strongly prefer that nothing else be said and everything be done. Consequently your demurrals shall no longer be accepted."

Basil Throckmorton then pulled her into his arms so unexpectedly that she had no time to execute a stiff-arm fend. Holding her so tightly against him that she could barely breathe, much less think, he said, "Take a leaf from my book and turn the page to a new chapter in our story. In fact, let's skip a few chapters and go right to the climax!"

Antonía struggled against him for a moment and then went still and gazed directly into his eyes. He appeared quite amused. She couldn't bear it so struck back. "I think, Sir Basil, it is time to close this book and burn it!"

The amusement faded from his gaze, shifting into haughty anger. "And I think this is one novel that *will* be read, and sooner than later!"

She struggled again, but his arms were like iron and finally she grew still once more. "I will never marry you," she said. "And if you take me against my will, when Mr. Claymore arrives, he will draw and quarter you and then dice you into cube steak."

He released her abruptly and she stumbled backward. The anger was gone, and in its place was his usual savoir faire.

"Darling girl, your happiness is all I desire—well, besides the throne of Scotland—and therefore I will give you a choice. You can marry me, or you can marry Rex." He smiled, triumph in his dark eyes. "Hobson's choice, Miss Barclay?"

"Wrong, Sir Basil," she shot back. "A choice between fungible evils is called a dilemma."

The Englishman stared at her in open admiration. "Good God! With your gift for the arts of language and my gift for the arts of everything else, our children shall be positively brilliant!"

It was all Antonía could do to keep from launching herself on top of the man and bashing his head against the stone floor. As Throckmorton laughed and walked away, she acknowledged that if Mr. Claymore didn't arrive soon she'd be forced to bash her own head against the stone floor.

Chapter 16

OF MACHINATIONS, MACHICOLATIONS,
AND MINDLESS MEN

"Our scouts should be back any minute," Rex reported to his father the next morning, brandishing his crossbow as he spoke. "I figure they'll tell us the bastards are dawdling about in town. The Scotch show a partiality for the pub, but they can't handle their drink."

"Watch that thing," Throckmorton said uneasily. "It's loaded. Did you practice today?"

Rex held his crossbow up and pointed it toward the top of one of the castle's machicolations. "You bet! I can hit a bird in the eye at a hundred yards!"

"Indeed, something to brag about," Sir Basil muttered. It was a miracle his inept son hadn't shot both his own eyes out. "What about the water? Did each and every man drink at least two ladles of water as I instructed?"

"Yes, sir, though I don't know what all the fuss was about. Water isn't exactly what a man wants to drink before he goes into battle. In fact—"

"Haversham!" He cut his son off in midsentence and stepped forward to meet the returning scout. "Well, where are they?" he demanded.

The man seemed disoriented and a little slow. Throckmorton frowned. Perhaps he was just tired. Yes, that was it. He probably hadn't had his water yet. "Wake up, man!" he shouted and slapped him across the face. He blinked and hurried to speak.

"Yes, sir! Approximately one hundred men are two miles north of the castle. The rest are within a mile of us, sir."

He started to walk away, but Sir Basil pulled him back and observed his eyes.

His pupils were large and black, which Throckmorton noted as one of the side effects of the neurotoxin he had recently developed to eradicate his men's power to act according to their own judgment.

"Did you drink your two ladles of water, Haversham?" Throckmorton asked. The man nodded, glowered, and then shook his head.

"The enemy has increased significantly in size," said Throckmorton. "Damn those stupid pipe blowers!" He turned back to Haversham. "I want an exact tally. Take the best scouts and get it done!"

"Yes, sir." Haversham stood staring straight ahead.

Throckmorton whirled around to his son. "Take him to the nearest water bucket and make him drink deeply! Then tell Jenkins to situate the archers and the cannons around the perimeter of the castle walls. Tell them not to fire until the Scots are forty feet from the walls! No entrance is to be left unprotected." He turned and looked out over Flodden Field. "Evidently the Barclays and Claymore have recruited more men than anticipated, but we'll annihilate every last one of them as soon as they cross Flodden ground."

"It'll be just like the good old days," Rex said gleefully. "When will the Scotch ever learn they're just a bunch of veteran losers?"

"*Inveterate*," corrected Throckmorton, wondering why he even bothered. "And remember, Rex, just like the good old days, we take no prisoners. Kill every single one of them. We'll obliterate as many as possible with arrows and cannonade before sending out ground forces with pikes, spears, and crossbows to impale the remainder."

"This battle is shaping up to be one hell of a good time," said his blood-thirsty son.

Objecting on the grounds of semantics, his father replied, "With only a few hundred men, it can hardly be called a battle. It's just another insignificant Scottish skirmish."

"Don't you mean *squirmish*?"

At that moment Sir Basil made a very sincere and silent wish: *May a lightning bolt strike my son dead and save the English language from perpetual torture.* He waited several minutes for his wish to come true, but to no avail. His son remained alive and, to make matters worse, he was spewing more bloated, mangled words of grandiosity. "There are few things finer in life than *scouring* Scotsmen."

Although he was fairly sure Rex meant skewering, he hadn't the strength to correct him. "Take Haversham to the water and give Jenkins my orders! If I find out you've failed me, I'll tie you to a cannonball and blow you to kingdom come! No one is to fire until I give the command, do you understand?"

"Yes indeedy, sir!" Rex said, and pushing the scout ahead of him, tried to get out of sight. But his father grabbed him by the shoulder and spun him around.

"I ask only one thing of you, Rex." And then, clearly and articulately, he yelled into his son's face, "Do your job!"

Sir Basil turned his attention to the resurrected battlefield. He stood on the cusp of issuing the command to commence fire on Flodden Field, but inside he had a very unsettled feeling. Very unsettled indeed, which was very unfamiliar ground for him as well.

Arriving on the verdant pasture of Flodden Field, two hundred Scotsmen awaited orders to skewer their fair share of Englishmen. Not a single soul amongst them was unaware of the chilling Scottish defeat that had occurred on this very ground over seventy years earlier. Ten thousand of Scotland's finest had fallen, including the King of Scotland himself.

Hacked, chopped, sliced, and diced into wee bits and pieces, King James IV had paid an exceptionally dear price for his uncharacteristic display of poor military judgment, as well as his unfortunate choice in weaponry. Slaughtered in a highly dishonorable and barbaric manner, the king's royal remains were strewn across the blood-saturated field with savage delight.

Breck Claymore rode toward the men lining up half a mile from Ford Castle. Hopefully today's battle would unfold in an entirely different way than that of seventy years ago. On this inclement gray afternoon, only a handful of Scots knew that the slain king's great-granddaughter was trapped within the crumbling walls of Ford Castle; but if made privy to her presence, not a single soul amongst them would've flinched at the tragic irony of the situation.

In fact, the knowledge that Scottish royal blood was once again present on Flodden Field would've only made Scottish hearts beat livelier at the prospect of retribution. But then again, any excuse proved sufficient cause to exterminate English pestilence. When Claymore gave the order to stop their advance far short of the fortress, he saw the confused looks on the faces of some of the men. But the Barclay brothers had made it known to all the volunteers that their soon-to-be brother-in-law was in command. And so they followed his orders to the letter.

Anxious minutes dragged by until even Claymore wasn't sure about his strategy, but he knew Throckmorton and he knew Rex, and both of the men were avid fans of instant gratification. If he maintained patience, they would lose theirs. He was soon proven right.

All at once, the enemy unfurled their cannonade in a feckless, reckless demonstration of flagrant incompetence and blatant waste. The huge deadly artillery landed spectacularly, albeit ineffectively, some ninety-one yards from the nearest Scot. Consistently the first to verbalize his thoughts as well as being the only one with vocal cords sufficiently powerful to overcome the cacophony of explosions, Oliver Barclay shouted to Claymore.

"It looks like we may as well cancel the schiltrom formation! What the hell are they doing besides wasting good artillery?"

With the noise now settling down to a dull roar, Claymore replied, "As far as I can see, that's all they're accomplishing. Evidently Throckmorton and his forces have lost their tempers, just as I expected. But in any event, your sister's life is in grave danger. I'm going in after her. Take charge, Oliver, and organize the schiltrom!"

Claymore spun his horse round and rode back through the lines to find Gus. He pulled his horse to a stop when he found him. "Gus, what did the scroll say about the entrances to the castle?"

"Other than the two main entrances, there's an entrance by way of an underground tunnel. According to the scroll, the tunnel begins at the base of a large royal oak tree situated near the south side of the castle."

"Tell Will and Matthew to divert enemy fire away from the castle's south side. I'm going in after her."

"Wait, laddie," Gus said. "Aren't ye forgettin' something?"

Claymore waited anxiously as the old man unwrapped a bundle tied to his saddle and revealed a mighty sword.

"Ye might need this," he said.

"Indeed, I might," Claymore agreed, sliding the sword into the sheath in his saddle. "Thank you, Gus."

"Be on yer way, laddie," Gus said. "'Tis certainly not a time to let the hare sit. Save the lassie!"

Great wafts of thick, relentless smoke crept under Antonía's door and settled comfortably within the confines of her room and uncomfortably within her chest. With burning eyes and a hacking cough, she dragged a wooden chair across the room to the locked window.

After pausing to gather her strength, she picked up the piece of furniture and hurled it—with admirable form, if she did say so herself—against the windows. *Against* and not *through* them, because unfortunately, the glass was too thick to break.

When the cannons had begun booming, she hadn't known what to think, but looking out her small windows, before she tried to break them, she'd witnessed complete chaos below. Scores of mindless men scurried about willy-nilly, discharging artillery in an aimless, haphazard fashion. But to give credit where credit was due, Sir Basil's henchmen had proven immensely successful in accomplishing one task: they had somehow managed to set the whole damn castle on fire.

Realizing she was as good as dead if she didn't get out, Antonía ran to the door and, fully aware that the last fine grains of sand were sifting to the bottom of her hourglass, she began to pound and pound and pound on the locked door as the heavy black smoke all but smothered her, all but sucked the very last drop of vitality from her body.

Antonía stopped pounding. She refused to spend her last earthly moments pounding on a stupid bloody door. The kingdom of Heaven was near. There were some things you just had to accept. But she was determined to leave this mortal coil her way. She'd go out in an honorable and dignified manner. She'd go out on the high road. She'd replay her life, repent her sins, and thank God for every single blessing, for every single second of her life . . . she remembered . . .

Her father putting her on her first horse . . . her mother admonishing him . . . their little daughter was far too young for horseback . . . the lass had to learn sometime . . . she couldn't be coddled forever . . . just look at her sitting up there like a queen on her throne . . . Minnie, in the background, laughing and coughing heartily at the scene, knowing her brothers had secretly taught their little sister to ride months ago . . . Antonía and her mother sitting down at the harp, learning to play . . .

Oliver throwing worms at her so she'd learn to run fast . . . Matthew pushing her in the loch so she'd learn to swim . . . Will imprisoning her in the library so she'd learn to read . . . climbing out the window . . . running to the stables . . . galloping through the woods and jumping the burn . . . arriving at Deerfield to meet her best friend . . .

Claire waiting at the front door . . . tapping her dainty little foot as she scolded, Antonía Margaret Caroline Barclay, one day you're going to break your neck . . . Claire analyzing her every behavior, her every word . . . laughing . . . Claire dreaming of the dress she would wear to the next ball . . . dreaming of her marriage to Matthew . . .

And then, because she really did think she was about to be burnt to a crisp, she let herself think of him . . . *Mr. Claymore . . . She'd loved him from the moment she first looked into his startlingly blue eyes . . . his magnificence ran straight through to his soul . . . her love for him ran just as deep . . . their first kiss . . . waking up in the cottage, safe . . . their preempted union . . .*

Antonía suddenly sat up straight. She didn't feel the flutter of wings, she didn't feel the glow of a halo, and most notably, she didn't feel the familiar sensation of harp strings under her fingertips. St. Peter was *not* calling her home. So what was happening? Of course! Now she understood! Mr. Claymore was on his way! He was running a bit late, but he was coming for her . . . she would see him very soon . . . she would be in his arms again . . .

From that moment onward, she forcefully struck down all thoughts of death and dying. She was alive, and she intended to stay that way! She'd hold onto life until however long it took him to reach her—to hell with the high road and to hell with honor and dignity! She resumed pounding on the stupid bloody door.

Within the mere space of an hour, Throckmorton could not refute the fact that something had gone very, very wrong with his plan for victory. His forces displayed complete ineptitude and utter disobedience, continuously and inexplicably firing valuable ammunition while the enemy stood safely out of range. Sir Basil could make no sense of the pandemonium because, for all intents and purposes, his men should be totally and unfailingly obedient to his every command. The flavorless neurotoxin surreptitiously administered to his men's water should have resulted in their full, albeit fairly mindless, allegiance.

He had tested his toxin by running myriad clinical trials with scientific precision and not once had the toxin failed to produce the desired result. It had, with brutal effectiveness, stripped every man of his free will. As a result, Sir Basil had been able to train an army of mindlessly loyal men who neither asked questions nor formulated critical thoughts regarding his plan to rule the entire isle of fog and greatness. But somehow, some way, something had gone terribly wrong.

And much to his horror, and in spite of his irrefutable brilliance, he suddenly realized he'd committed scientific sacrilege: *He had failed to control his variables!*

Moreover, it took Throckmorton no additional contemplation time to isolate the one and only variable responsible for his failure: *his son's stupidity!*

He took action. Climbing to the apex of the castle's highest machicolation, the disgraced scientist located the stupid variable in a matter of minutes. Amidst the smoke and confusion, he hurled a trio of justified accusations at his son.

"What did you do to compromise the effectiveness of the neurotoxin? Did you make sure every man drank from the special water? Did everyone get two ladles?"

"Of course!" Rex said defensively. "I did just as you said! Sheesh!" He turned to walk away, but his father grabbed him and swung him back around to face him.

"I don't believe you. Either you didn't do what I said or you"—he narrowed his eyes—"or you did something to alter the active ingredient in my formula! Look at the fiasco surrounding us. Even you should be able to understand that the men are no longer following orders. They're annihilating each other! They fired before I gave the command! They've set the castle on fire and the Scots are coming over the wall!"

"I gave them the water!" Rex insisted.

"I specifically formulated my neurotoxin to eliminate their free will for at least a week. They're not due for another dose until next Tuesday—at the very earliest—which brings me back to my original supposition: *You must have done something wrong!*"

But Sir Basil's words fell upon deaf ears, because Rex had turned away again and was now shouting orders at one of the henchmen. Ignoring Rex's command, the henchman continued to discharge ammunition in the general direction of Miss Barclay's penthouse window. Drenched with sweat and bursting with fury, Rex's mean-spirited nature and violent disposition once again coalesced into felonious action. Picking up his crossbow he took aim, fired, and ended the life of the confused, mindless henchman.

"You ridiculous moron!" Throckmorton slammed his son against the castle wall. "You misshapen oaf! Are you convinced yet? If you don't tell me the truth this instant, I'll shoot you myself! *Now what did you do to the water?*" He put his hands around his son's throat, when all at once he remembered. "Wait! What did you say? Just before the battle, something about men not *wanting* to drink water?"

Belligerent to the end, Rex yelled into his father's face. "You always tell me to 'show some initiative,' so I did! I added a little rum to the stuff—to make it taste like grog. The men liked it much better that way! It's the only way I could get them to drink more than one ladle! They didn't like the taste of plain old water!"

Positively made speechless by his son's confession, Sir Basil's black eyes focused on the maelstrom swirling about them—cannons misfiring in all directions, smoke and fire smoldering everywhere, archers casting arrows into oblivion, and his son, his eternally and infernally stupid son, standing before him, his expression one of a spoiled child who has been falsely accused of setting in motion a cataclysmic chain of events.

So often is stupidity superadded to stupidity, Sir Basil thought.

Realizing there was nothing he could do now, the Englishman decided to cut his losses and retrench his plan. Shouting above the chaos, he grabbed Rex and pushed him toward the inside of the castle.

"We're retrieving Miss Barclay and getting out of here before we're blown to bits by our own fusillade."

"But the castle is on fire!" Rex whined in dismay.

Throckmorton pushed him forward. Perhaps if fate proved kind, Rex would run headlong into a Scottish sword and put them both out of their misery.

Dodging in and out of fierce cannonade, as well as an unrelenting incursion of arrows, Claymore rode toward the south side of the castle, but unfortunately, he was greeted by more than one large royal oak tree. Never much of an arborist, much less a tree hugger, Claymore intended to chop down every last tree, if necessary, in order to locate the underground entrance and rescue his darling Miss Barclay.

Pulling his horse to a stop and sliding to the ground, he took the axe he had taken from a dead, staring Englishman and chopped away at the well-established root system of a huge royal oak. But after several vigorous blows—as if by divine intervention—an ear-shattering explosion caused him to reconsider his first choice. Running toward the source of the blast,

Claymore saw the entrance to the underground tunnel had been blown open at the base of a royal oak. The tree had miraculously survived.

Making his way through the tunnel, he arrived in the castle courtyard within a matter of minutes. There he observed the ensuing bedlam and knew his appearance on the scene would thankfully inspire little interest amongst the enemy, who continued to fire upon the Scots with a bizarre inefficiency. Exhausting their ammunition and blowing their own drawers off in the process, it was only a matter of time before they succeeded in their own defeat.

Squandering no more effort in trying to make sense of chaos, he entered the castle through the front door and commenced a room-to-room search of the ruinous, smoke-infested fortress. By God, he'd find Antonía or he would die trying.

Calling her name until his ears ached for the sound of her honey-smooth voice and scouring every crevice until his eyes ached for the sight of her exquisite face, he made his way to the very top floor of the dying castle. Quickly finding the first two rooms deserted, his gaze fell upon the last door, which was closed.

Claymore sprinted the distance to the door; however, when he attempted to open it, he found it locked and bolted with uncompromising conviction. He was in no mood to be thwarted. He gripped his axe and, with an uncompromising conviction of his own, began to chop through the obstacle—all the while urging Miss Barclay to move back, for he had no doubt that she was inside.

Shattering, splintering wood flew in every direction as he struck the door with repeated and furious blows. After skillfully hacking through the very last vestige of the obstinate obstacle, Claymore climbed through the opening to discover the entire chamber enveloped in dense, unyielding smoke. Taking a step forward, he stumbled and fell to his knees. Reaching out for purchase, his hands touched something . . . someone . . .

Antonía. Lying silent and covered in soot and—was she breathing at all?

Claymore gathered his beautiful bouquet of Miss Barclay in his arms and carried her out of the burning deathtrap and into the hallway—not a moment too soon, for as he turned toward the staircase, the chamber ceiling collapsed violently behind them. Realizing the same could happen in the hallway, he ran down the stairs, shielding his precious bouquet from the fires erupting around them until at last he reached the outside door. Kicking it open, he carried her to one of the royal oaks and collapsed beneath it with her body still in his arms.

Now leaning over Antonía, he willed her to life. "Breathe, my darling," he said, cupping her face in his hands. He kissed her sooty lips. "Live!"

Her chest rose once. Then twice. Then her eyes slowly opened and she replayed the scene.

"Cutting it a wee bit close again, aren't we, Mr. Claymore?" she said weakly. "Sheep on the road?"

He sighed in relief and leaned back against the mighty oak, holding her close. "Are you implying I'm late, Miss Barclay?"

"On the contrary, it was I who was again very nearly the late party." Then reaching up and caressing the crest of his cheek, she added, "But I fear I shall never be able to compensate you fully for your courageous and chivalrous actions."

"Never fear, Miss Barclay," he replied, "we will have countless days together for you to compensate me for services rendered." He kissed her forehead gently and gazed down into her smoky blue eyes.

She touched his lips with one finger and saw the exhaustion etched in his face. "You must be so tired. Aren't you tired of holding me, dear Mr. Claymore?"

"My darling, darling Miss Barclay," he said tenderly, "the day I get tired of holding you is the day I die."

"That being the case, I beg you to kiss me. I've missed you so . . . I've ached to be wrapped in your arms. I thought I would die in that room without you. It seems an eternity since your lips last touched mine. Kiss me, Breck, please kiss me."

He lowered his head to hers, and with a gentleness both necessary and vital, touched his lips to hers. Though cannons boomed in the distance, they could not compete with his pounding heart. When she was completely and thoroughly kissed, he pressed his lips against her hair and whispered, "Miss Barclay, I'm a man who always finishes what he starts, but in chronological order. That being the case, I must finish rescuing you before I can start making love to you . . . and unequivocally the latter will require a great deal more time and attention than the former."

The adoration in her eyes was almost his undoing. He had nearly lost her, forever, due to a madman's quest for power. Unthinkable. He stroked her hair back from her face, thanking God he had reached her in time. Carefully sliding her off his lap, he leaned down and kissed her on the end of her nose, and then rose to take stock of their situation.

The cannons had stopped firing, and though smoke still poured from the castle and the courtyard, it seemed the fighting was over, odd as it had been. He frowned, wondering if the brothers and Gus were all right, but he couldn't think of that now. He must keep Antonía safe, above all else.

"What is that?" she asked.

Claymore knelt down beside her. "What is what, my darling?"

"There, where there used to be a wall—you can see into what was a room."

"Bloody hell! The idiots are shooting at their own castle!"

"The fireplace, Breck. What's hanging on the fireplace?" She lifted one hand weakly and pointed. He followed her gesture and saw an ancient coat of arms, carved in stone.

"The coat of arms?"

"I'm not certain," she said thoughtfully, "but there's something peculiar, and yet vaguely familiar, about that coat of arms." She frowned and then shook her head. "Never mind." She looked up at him and her gaze softened. "Can we leave now? Can we go home at last?"

"Yes, my love," he whispered. "We can go home."

"Good, I hate England," she said, smiling.

"Incidentally, I promised your mother that once we returned to Scotland I'd keep you there forever."

"Well, hell," said a terrible, familiar voice, "I think your forever oughta start right now, Claymore—without her!"

Claymore spotted Rex Throckmorton on a rise about fifteen feet away. He lifted his crossbow and pointed it straight at Antonía. All thought ceased. There was only action. He threw himself in front of her, and as the deadly arrow pierced his chest, he heard her scream and thought he had failed. The arrow had missed her, but Rex Throckmorton still remained.

And there was nothing the Scotsman could do about it. He was lying on the ground, blood pooling beneath him.

Antonía kicked and screamed, trying to escape the powerful grasp of Rex, trying to reach her Mr. Claymore, but it was to no avail. Restraining her in a ruthless vise-grip, Rex casually glanced down at the most recent victim of his homicidal instincts as tears of grief poured down his captive's cheeks.

"Help him! Help him!" she cried, her throat raw. "I'll do anything, just don't let him die!"

"Too late, you scheming whore," Rex said with a laugh. He nudged the Scotsman's leg. "Look at that blood. Go ahead, look long and look twice, because it's the last time you'll ever see Claymore." His snide smile widened. "He's a dead man."

She stopped fighting and gazed down at the man she loved. He lay deathly pale and hauntingly motionless upon the courtyard ground, the bloodstain on his linen shirt growing by the second. How could he be so alive one moment and so still the next? It wasn't possible. It didn't make sense. This couldn't be happening. This just couldn't be the last good-bye.

"Let me help him! For God's sake, let me help him!" she screamed, struggling again.

"God's not on the scene right now," Rex cackled. "And quit thrashing around!"

He threw her over his shoulder and Antonía gasped, losing her breath. As he turned and carried her up the hill beside Ford Castle, away from Mr. Claymore, the horrible event kept playing over and over in her mind. Slowly and sadly, the unforgiving truth broke open in Antonía's mind. Mr. Claymore was lost to her. She closed her eyes and fell into a bottomless pit of grief and anguish.

"What have you done to her, you fool?"

The voice of Sir Basil registered, but Antonía couldn't even lift her head to look at him.

"Nothing, I swear!" Rex protested. With a grunt he bent down and deposited her on the ground. She lay back, eyes closed. "But take a look at Claymore over there on the ground. I killed him with a direct hit to the heart!"

"You babbling idiot!" growled his father. "Did you kill him in Miss Barclay's presence?"

"Yeah. *You're* the one who insisted she witness the slaughter!"

"I didn't intend for her to witness *his* slaughter! She could die of shock! Just look at her, she's completely ashen." He took her by the wrist and she did not resist. "I can barely detect a pulse, and her blood pressure is in her boots."

"There's not a thing wrong with her." Rex's voice seemed to come from very far away. "She's just a little wonky from all the smoke. She'll be fine. In fact, she's as healthy as my horse. Just throw a blanket over her."

"You imbecile!" Antonía shook with the force of Throckmorton's shout. "Miss Barclay has a very fragile psyche! Emotionally, she's like a piece of fine crystal! You may well have broken her!"

"I saw those flea-bitten bat-fowling Scottish brothers of hers!" Rex said, disregarding his father's wrath. "I'm gonna murder them to death when I see them again!"

"We need to get out of here and regroup before they see us! Pick her up, you dolt!"

Antonía had no options. Rex carried her away. Away from Mr. Claymore. Away from her brothers. Her eyes closed and, mercifully, she felt nothing . . . nothing at all.

Chapter 17

POTENT POTIONS AND POWER PLAYS

Antonía awakened with a deep, aching pain in the middle of her soul. All of the nothingness she'd suffered in her unconscious state had somehow changed into a scorching grief now that she was conscious. She could feel the grief burning her alive and knew she must alter it into a less toxic emotion before it consumed her. She mentally threw around a few possibilities before ultimately deciding to channel her pain into hate. Yes . . . *hate* would be her *why* to live.

And she would use it to make Rex and Basil Throckmorton pay for what they'd done. No sooner had she experienced this epiphany than one of the fetid objects of her hatred entered the room—a room she didn't recognize, but a man whom she, unfortunately, did recognize. The bastard was positively ubiquitous.

"Surprise, surprise, surprise!" Rex taunted. "How many times have I captured you? I do believe it's one . . . two . . . three times!"

"Frankly, Rex, the only thing that surprises me is the fact you can count that high."

He snorted his response, "And frankly, Antonía, I'm surprised you're still such a smartass now that Claymore's dead."

Claymore was dead. How easily he said the words. How easily he had killed her partner in love. If only the sun would come out, she could transform her necklace into a mighty sword and slay the brute. Bloody English climate!

She clasped her hand to her chest and looked down. Her corset was gone and in its place was a chemise. But more importantly, her necklace was gone, along with the coin her mother had given her. She had kept them both safely tucked inside her bodice.

Noticing the thinness of her chemise, she pulled the covers higher as she tried to determine what could have happened to the keepsakes given to her by Mr. Claymore and her mother, the queen. She looked up to find Rex standing beside her, and as usual, he smelled like a cross between puke and dirty feet.

"You do remember me killing him, don't you?" he prodded, a cruel smile on his ugly face.

She said nothing but forced herself into a sitting position. Swinging her feet to the floor, she sighed. She should feel outrage, shouldn't she? And hate? The all-important emotion. Yet, inexplicably, she felt . . . nothing.

Breck Claymore was gone. Her necklace was gone. Her coin was missing. Her heart was dead. Antonía tried to find the hate, to latch onto it and channel its power, but she discovered she just didn't have the energy for it. She felt enervated and completely apathetic. She looked up at her captor. "If you don't mind, I'd appreciate having my clothes back right about now."

"Why?" he asked, his gaze scouring every square inch of her scantily clad body. "I'm just gonna rip them off you again."

The thought of Rex undressing her—for most assuredly that's what he must've done—should have made her furious and violated. Yet, again, she felt nothing.

"I'm chilled," she told him. "I need my dress and my corset and petticoats. You may leave the room while I dress."

He crossed to a wardrobe and brought the items back to her, tossing them on the bed. Then he sat down in a chair, crossed his arms over his chest, and leered at her.

"I said you may leave the room."

"I'm not going nowhere," he replied, thereby proving not only that he was rude, but also that there really is such a thing as a double negative. After raking lustful eyes over her, he added, "I already got one show last night when I undressed you, but this one will be even better."

She shrugged. It didn't matter. Nothing mattered. She did have a brief second of hope as she checked her corset—no coin, no necklace—and then began the awkward process of getting into her clothing while being ogled by raunchy Rex.

He frowned. "You're getting awfully skinny, Antonía. In fact, you look totally emancipated."

She glanced over at him but decided it wasn't worth the effort.

Rex continued to examine her closely. "Your butt's disappearing."

"These things have a tendency to happen when a person hasn't eaten for a few days," Antonía said. "Of course, you—having never missed a meal in your entire life—would have no way of knowing about that. Perhaps if you eschewed food more than you chewed it, you'd be able to fit through a doorway without turning sideways."

Rex ignored the insult and stuck to his original point. "But on the other hand, you don't have those big old birthing hips like some women do." He paused for reflection. "So you weren't never gonna be no big-butted bitch in the first place," he concluded, thereby proving that not only would Antonía always have a small butt, but also that there really is such a thing as a triple negative.

She shook her head in disbelief while Rex decided to change the subject.

"Sorry to say I can't give you an exact cause of Claymore's death," he boasted, his gaze continuing to roam over her as she struggled with the corset. "My arrow either pierced his gizzard or his liver, but in any case, after we left him there to bleed out"—he leaned forward and grinned at her from the chair—"*he died.*"

He wiggled his eyebrows at her, obviously waiting for a reaction. But if Rex was waiting for an emotional display of anger or despair, he was loitering at the wrong stable, because Antonía was on a slow-moving horse picking its way blindly across the moors.

"What's the difference how he died?" she said, pulling the simple frock over her head and lacing it up the front. "Dead is dead."

Rex's mouth dropped open. "You're not only a stupid bitch, but a heartless one as well! Don't you have any feelings at all?"

"Boo hoo." She lifted one brow. "Happy now?"

Rex jumped to his feet. "God Almighty, what's wrong with you? I thought you loved the man!"

She shrugged and finished tying the laces, smoothing her hands over the crumpled cloth. "Yes, I did, but he's gone. You killed him." Her words were monotone. Her brain was monotone. All of life was monotone without Mr. Claymore.

"You're unbelievable!" Rex shook his head. "I wish I could see how you'd react to the death of someone you hated."

"Be careful what you wish for," she murmured. "Not that it matters, but where are we?"

"My grandmother's house."

"Ah, the Dowager Duchess of Havering."

"The one and only," he confirmed, "but she's in town visiting friends. Well, *acquaintances*. The old bat doesn't have any friends."

What a surprise, she thought. She lay back down on the bed and closed her eyes. Perhaps if she feigned sleep, the noisome lug would bug off. But she wasn't so lucky.

"My father thought you had one foot in the grave last night, so he insisted on stopping here until you recovered. Your clothes were sodden from the rain so we undressed you and then—"

With a sigh she opened her eyes and interrupted him with a weary shake of the head and a languid raise of the hand. "I get the picture, Rex, thanks." She continued with even less vivacity, "Where's your father?"

As if on cue, in walked the subject of her question as well as the other object of her hatred, all in the form of one elegantly handsome megalomaniac. Vibrant and sparkling with good cheer, he smiled at her as he crossed to her bedside.

"My dear, I'm delighted to see you up and about this morning. You developed a fever yesterday evening and I feared the worst, but happily, it broke just after midnight." With a bounce in his step, he walked to her side and placed his hand on her forehead. After a moment he nodded in satisfaction.

"Excellent, Miss Barclay, you remain afebrile." He cupped her chin in his hand, observing her face in a clinical, professional manner. "You're still a little pale, and painfully thin, but with some bright sunshine on you and some good food in you, you'll be restored to full bloom in no time."

"Is there any?" she asked.

"Good food? Oh, yes—"

"No. I meant sunshine."

Throckmorton grinned. "Not yet, but it looks as though the sun is making an effort to burn through the clouds."

"I was just telling her that her clothes got wet last night so we had to—"

"That's quite enough, Rex," interrupted his father. "I'm certain Miss Barclay understands the motive behind *my* actions."

She nodded placidly. "Yes, I understand, but I'd like my necklace and coin returned to me. The latter was in my corset, while the former was around my neck."

Sir Basil reached into his pocket and presented her with her mother's coin but hesitated when it came to relinquishing the necklace. Fully aware of his reluctance, Antonía urged him softly, "What possible threat could my claymore necklace pose?" She extended her hand toward his. "Especially now."

With his molten black eyes appraising her, Throckmorton answered in a slow, measured cadence. "Miss Barclay, I'm willing to make you a deal." Tilting her head slightly to one side, she indicated her willingness to negotiate. "If you eat every bite of your breakfast, then I shall return your necklace to you."

That was fair. She readily gave her assent.

Rex, however, was apparently outraged by his father's decision to bind himself to a verbal contract with Miss Barclay. With his feathers fully ruffled, he crowed, "Sir, I strongly advise you *not* to make deals of any kind with her. To date, she's reneged on every single promise she's ever made. She pretends to agree but in reality, she has absolutely no intention of holding up her end of the bargain. She enjoys lying! She loves lying! In fact, I'd say her lifelong ambition is to craft lying into some weird type of art form!"

But if he intended to ruffle her feathers, he failed miserably because Miss Barclay merely chirped a line written by her favorite playwright.

"'Lord, Lord, how this world is given to lying!'"

"Settle down, Rex," said his father with a chuckle. "We both know Miss Barclay has been blessed with a fecund imagination, so naturally she's predisposed to making a few inconsistent statements now and again. But as fascinating a topic as Miss Barclay's inner workings may be, we must now feed and help her regain her strength." He stopped speaking and frowned. "Strength. Yes, why didn't I think of this before?"

"Think of what before?" Rex asked.

"Never mind," Sir Basil said briskly. "Let's feed this lovely young lady." He gave her a brilliant smile and whisked her downstairs to a dining room full of food. In accordance with her end of the deal, she began to eat a kipper . . . slowly.

"If you don't eat you're going to get even more emancipated," Rex said.

"Rex," said his father, shaking his head in disgust, disdain, and disbelief, "the correct word is *emaciated*."

"Actually," Antonía chimed in, "I'm sedulously working toward Rex's misuse of the word."

"Miss Barclay, you never fail to delight me with your wit." Throckmorton rose from the table. "But please remember that Mr. Claymore was—shall we say—*neutralized*, and therefore all prospects for your emancipation ended with his demise."

"My brothers—"

He cut her off. "As for your ineffectual brothers and their squad of Scottish malcontents, they wouldn't dare travel this far south—not even for you, my beautiful, beloved Miss Barclay."

Sir Basil moved to stand behind her chair, and encircling her graceful neck with his tapered hands, he leaned down and whispered into her ear, "Consequently, my dearest, you are hereby, *officially*, a lost cause to them."

Antonía's lips were trembling, but she refused to give in, refused to let him see her fear. "I see," she said. "May I have my necklace now, Sir Basil?"

He acquiesced to her request, fastening the chain around her neck, and then bringing her to her feet, kissed her resoundingly on the lips. Antonía submitted with little resistance. After he finished, he looked into her eyes and she saw triumph there. A little hate stirred and she fanned the flames, but it flickered out again. The numbness apparently superseded her hate. How disappointing.

"How long are we staying here?" she asked, her voice listless.

"As long as it takes to improve your health, my dear," he replied.

"Then I would like to rest now. May I be excused? I have eaten as commanded."

He frowned. "Is there anything I can do for you, Miss Barclay? Anything at all?"

She gave him a winsome smile. "I hate to ask," she said.

"Please, Miss Barclay," he said, his countenance softening. "What is it you desire?"

She widened her smile and, putting both hands on the narrow table, leaned across until her face was only a few inches away from Sir Basil's. "If you don't mind . . ."

Throckmorton waited. "Yes?"

"What I really want . . ."

His voice grew tender. "Yes?"

"The one thing you can do for me is to . . ."

"Just name it, beautiful Antonía."

She leaned closer until their lips were almost touching, and then spoke distinctly.

"Drop dead."

She straightened and walked away from the table, heading toward the stairs. The sound of Rex laughing at the top of his lungs was strangely comforting.

"Quickly, Stephen, help me remove his shirt," said someone—*a woman?*

Claymore drifted on a tide of pain and confusion. He was floating . . . somewhere. "Antonía," he whispered.

"He's lost a lot of blood," said someone who sounded a great deal like Stephen Goode. But what would Stephen be doing on this ocean with him? He was glad. At least if he died, the parson could say a prayer for his soul.

The waves rocked him again and the pain increased.

"Where did you find him?" the woman asked. She sounded so familiar . . .

"After the battle, he was under one of the royal oaks."

The royal oaks . . . Antonía . . . the arrow . . .

"Antonía!" he cried, struggling now against the ocean that held him.

"Shhh," the woman said—the woman who was not Antonía. "It's Mary, dear Breck, calm down. Your Antonía is all right."

"Your Majesty, Mary," he whispered, "and the angel appeared to Mary . . ."

"His heartbeat is very faint," the woman was saying, and her words came from far away.

The ocean . . . it was so . . . cold . . .

He was sinking beneath the water . . .

"He isn't breathing," the man said.

He released his breath and the water closed over him.

Sometime later, Claymore opened his eyes again. His chest felt tight, painful. Had he been injured? For some reason he had memories of being lost at sea. That made no sense. Had it happened at the ball?

He tried to remember. Shutting his eyes, he saw Antonía waiting for him on the veranda. Beautiful Antonía . . . raven-haired, startlingly blue eyes, she gazed at him . . . she spoke. "Mr. Claymore," she was saying. "Mr. Claymore, I love you."

His eyes flew open. A beautiful woman looked down at him. She was not Antonía. Recognition flickered in his brain. He smiled. "Your Majesty," he said, his voice little more than a croak.

"How are you feeling, Mr. Claymore?"

He started to answer, but instead, the water came down again, suddenly, and carried him away. He heard Mary say, "Oh bother!" before he winked out of existence.

In a state of delirium, he called out Antonía's name, seeking her comfort, but sadly, she flashed through his mind so fleetingly that he had little time to gather her in his arms. All attempts to claim her were met with a crushing pain deep within his chest. Searching for relief, he looked to the sky.

Flocks of angels flew toward him. No, that was not the kind of relief he sought. He would not accept help if it meant surrendering a lifetime with her. Waving them off, he stood his ground. He would stay and fight.

One by one, the angels flew away. The pain gripped him again, but he understood.

Living meant feeling pain. He gratefully accepted the trade-off. Vectoring away from him, the angels disappeared.

When Claymore opened his eyes again, he felt a little better and was able to take in his surroundings. They were unfamiliar—a semi-dark room lit by two or three candles, functional but simple furniture, and . . . a queen.

"Your Majesty," he said, wondering why his voice sounded so weak.

"Ah," she said, "I do think Mr. Claymore has finally returned to the land of the living. I hope you will stay here this time."

He shifted in the bed and groaned at the pain it caused. "Aye, I hope so too. Did I leave for a time, Your Majesty?"

She laughed lightly. "My dear Mr. Claymore, I believe at this point in our relationship you may call me Mary."

He smiled. "Then you must call me Breck. Where am I?"

"At the parsonage near Chartley Hall. We heard news of the battle and I sent Reverend Goode to see what had happened. He found you and brought you here."

"The battle . . . Antonía!" He sat bolt upright and intense pain, as well as a reproachful pair of amber eyes, soon forced him to surrender to the gentle hand pushing him back against the pillows.

"Yes, Antonía is still with the Throckmortons, but do not worry yourself." Her lips curved up, but there was no humor in her eyes. "Antonía will be rescued."

"What happened?" He put his hand to his chest and felt a wide bandage.

"An arrow. Stephen found you outside the castle, alone. After he brought you here, I contacted some of my . . . informants. I received word that Antonía's brothers and Lord Barclay were gathering more men to rescue Antonía."

"I did not know you were skilled in the art of healing, Mary," Claymore said with his hand still resting on the tightly wound wrapping.

She smiled and patted his hand. "There is much you don't know about me, dear Breck. But I had a fair amount of assistance. After Stephen and I removed the arrowhead, we cleaned and bandaged the wound. The arrow lodged quite deeply in your chest, but we were extremely lucky. It missed your heart."

"How long have I been here?"

"Just two days."

"Two days." Two days that Antonía had had to suffer at the hands of Throckmorton and his vile son. "When will I be able to ride?"

"Hmm, a strapping young buck like yourself?" she said, frowning in feigned concentration. "I would think perhaps in three days' time. *If* you do as I say."

"That's too long. I need to free Antonía at once!" Claymore sat up, and the queen once again gently pushed him back down on the bed.

"Not just this minute, you're not," admonished the queen. "If you're a good boy and remain in bed, I'll have Stephen help you sit up and drink some broth. You're not nearly ready to take on any kind of strenuous activity yet."

"But, Antonía." He drew in a ragged breath. "Your Majesty—Mary— she must think I have abandoned her."

A shadow crossed the queen's face. "Unfortunately, I think it more likely that she thinks you dead."

"Dead? Then all the more reason I must leave at once!"

"Listen to me," she said firmly. "You have a fever. You just had an arrow removed from your chest. If you leave your bed prematurely, you risk reopening your wound and hemorrhaging all the way back to Ford Castle." She reached over for something that turned out to be a cool, wet cloth lying on the bedside table. She draped it across his feverish forehead. "And I'm completely certain that my daughter would prefer to welcome home a healthy man, rather than a bloodless cadaver."

Heeding both her admonishing words and equally admonishing brow, he grinned. "Your Majesty, if you don't mind my saying so, you remind me of your daughter."

"In light of the fact that you're in love with Antonía, I consider it a compliment of the highest order. Please understand, however," the queen added softly, "I'm *not* unfeeling toward your plight. I'm willing to make you a deal."

Ah, a deal from the queen. How many men could say they had experienced *this?* "It's highly unlikely I would ever reject a proposal made by my future mother-in-law, *either of them*. What is the deal?"

"If, and only if, you are a very good boy, and if you stay in bed today, we shall evaluate your condition in the morning and see if you are able to ride."

Claymore tightened his jaw. He wanted more than anything to leave immediately, no matter what the risk, but knew the queen was right. He would be no good to Antonía in a bloodless heap beside the road.

She arose from the bed, removed the cloth from his brow, and then put her cool hand in its place. "You must rest now, my dear boy. Reverend Goode and I look forward to the day we can return you, healed and healthy, to my daughter. I must return to my chambers before I am missed. There I will pray for you, for if ever there was a time to unleash the powers of faith, it is now." She kissed him on the forehead, replaced the cloth, and left him to his rest.

Claymore slept fitfully. Fragmented dreams fraught with vivid, troubling images tortured him, and he spent most of the wretched night in this hellish manner. He was cold, then hot, then burning, and then shivering. It seemed never-ending. The delirium seized him, tossing him into the sea over and over again.

From a distant shore, he heard the man talking. The pious man. And the fearless woman. The queen. She was whispering. "Breck, listen to me, you must fight this. Fight it for Antonía!"

Mr. Claymore continued to hear the anxious, worried dialogue.

"It doesn't look good. His fever is too high." There was a long silence and then the woman spoke.

"Then it is decided, Stephen—and no arguments—I am leaving immediately to find Antonía. Take care of poor Mr. Claymore and if the worst should happen—"

"Pray that it does not," the pious man said. "Antonía would suffer greatly."

"Remind him that he must fight," she said. "He must fight to live for Antonía."

"I will tell him hourly," the pious man said, his voice growing fainter. "And I will pray for you, my queen."

Claymore drifted away, but not before he saw the angels dropping from the sky, headed his way again.

"My darling Miss Barclay. *Miss Barclay?*"

Antonía opened her eyes to find Sir Basil staring down at her.

"I do hate to wake you when you are sleeping so soundly, but I have a gift for you." He gave her a white-toothed grin. "In spite of the fact that you asked me to drop dead."

With a sigh, she pushed herself to a sitting position, folded her hands in her lap, and stared back at him silently. It wasn't that she had decided not to speak to the man; it was just that she couldn't seem to make her voice work.

Throckmorton cleared his throat. "Yes, well, the gift is more of a necessity. You see, my dear, we must push on toward Wrathbone Manor by way of Ford Castle. And you, unfortunately, are still too weak to travel."

A tiny spark of resurging grit gave her the power to speak. "Oh," she said, "so the gift is that you are leaving me behind?"

His frown deepened. "No, my dulcet-voiced darling, you are coming with us. Remember, you and me, married, kicking your brother off the throne?" He tapped her under the chin. "Our adventure is just beginning."

"Yes, of course." She stared at him and suddenly felt a surge of triumph. He couldn't hurt her anymore, she realized. For what more could he do? Breck Claymore was dead. And with her epiphany, her fear disappeared. She would bide her time, and then she would kill the both of them. "So what is the gift, Sir Basil?"

His brows darted up. "Indeed. Do I detect a bit of feistiness returning?"

"The gift," she said. "Give it or get out. Or rather, give it *and* get out."

Throckmorton's smile faded. The girl's wild mood swings remained a mystery to him. He continued in a businesslike tone. "Very well then, if you intend to act like that. Here it is." He presented her with a small glass vial, filled with blue liquid.

Antonía sighed. "Another potion? This is your gift to me? No wonder you aren't married."

Unruffled, Sir Basil smiled and shook the elixir. "This is a potion that will give you increased strength and will restore your health and humors completely."

Antonía's heart began to beat rapidly. "Increased strength?" She grabbed the vial from him and held it up. The blue liquid did seem to have a sparkle to it. She lowered the vial. "How do I know you aren't lying to me—again? How do I know this isn't some kind of love potion, formulated to make me a crazed nymphomaniac?"

He blinked thoughtfully. "Why didn't I think of that?" he murmured, then shook his head. "Later, later, Miss Barclay. I thank you for the idea, but in the meantime, this potion is meant to give you the strength necessary for us to leave this place and return to Ford Castle."

She felt the blood drain from her face. "I will not go back there."

"I'm so sorry, my dear girl, but you must. There's still the little matter of the Royal Sceptre. We must locate it as soon as possible."

Antonía clutched the vial, a thousand unruly thoughts running through her mind. If the potion gave her strength, perhaps once at Ford Castle she would be strong enough to kill her two enemies and then go back home to Barclay Castle. Once there, she would take to her bed until she died of grief, but first, she would make the Throckmorton family pay.

She uncapped the vial and put it to her lips. Tilting her head back, she let the cool, rather flavorful liquid glide down her throat, and then handed the vial and cap back to the Englishman.

"When do we leave?" she asked buoyantly.

"Tomorrow at dawn," Sir Basil replied, surprised at her suddenly positive attitude. He resumed with a broad grin, "Dare I hope that you have decided to help me track down the sceptre?"

"Yes, Sir Basil," she said firmly, "you have my full cooperation."

The Englishman gave her a pensive smile. Truly, the girl's drastic mood swings were quite bizarre. He made a mental note to instruct her on ways to alkalize toxic emotions. It would make their life together much easier.

Breakfast the next morning was a hasty and rather silent affair. Sir Basil seemed to be lost in thought, while Rex was lost in a mound of eggs, sausage, and kippers, shoveling them into his mouth as if it were his last meal on the planet.

Antonía mused. She was thankful for the silence, for something extraordinary had happened and she knew she had to play her cards very carefully in the next few minutes.

The night before, an hour or so after taking the blue potion, she'd accidentally dropped her mother's coin and watched with frustration as it rolled under the very wide, very heavy wardrobe in her borrowed room. Dropping to her knees, she had reached one arm under the rock-hard mahogany monstrosity but had been unable to touch the coin. Exasperated, realizing there was no way she could move the heavy piece of furniture, she had nonetheless stood and shoved the side of it with both hands.

It moved three feet.

Incredulous, she'd picked up her coin, tucked it into her corset, and then walked around on the other side of the wardrobe. Placing both hands carefully on the side of it, she barely gave it a push. The wardrobe moved a foot. She pushed it a little harder. Four feet.

Eyes widening, she decided to give it her all. She shoved the wardrobe with all of her might and watched in astonishment as it slid six feet across the room, turned on its side, and slammed into the wall, leaving a crack.

Returning her attention to the breakfast table, she broke the silence.

"So we are going back to Ford Castle this morning?" she asked.

Rex grunted, but Throckmorton looked over at her with interest. "Yes, my dear. How do you feel this morning? Did the potion I gave you help at all?"

"Actually," she said, "though it galls me to admit, I do believe I feel a little more sprightly today. I was wondering if we should bring some more of the potion along, in case I experience a relapse?"

Sir Basil patted his face with his napkin, his dark brows raised in surprise. "An excellent idea, Miss Barclay!" He leaned back in his chair, his hands resting on the arms, looking like a complacent monarch. "Now do you believe in my alchemical abilities, Miss Barclay? Will you trust that I have only your best interests at heart?"

"Well, let's not go *that* far," she said. "I don't think that acquiring the Royal Sceptre is in any way for my benefit."

"On the contrary, my fair princess," he replied. Sir Basil rose and walked around the long table, stopping beside her chair. Unexpectedly, he sank down on one knee and took her hand. "Antonía, you will be queen of Scotland and England. Doesn't that mean anything to you?"

"It might have been a possibility," she said, "if your pig of a son hadn't killed Mr. Claymore." She paused for a sigh and then expatiated. "You see, Sir Basil, if Rex had allowed him to live, I, in exchange for his restraint, would've agreed to live my life in England with you and all your aristocratic cronies without complaint."

"Did she call me a *pig*?" Rex roared as he barreled around the table and stood breathing in and out like a winded bull. His beady little eyes narrowed and he pointed at her. "Just wait," he said, "one of these days—"

"Oh!" Antonía sat up and clapped both hands to her face. "Sir Basil, I completely forgot to tell you something!" She looked down at where he perched on bended knee and smiled. "Your *pig* of a son tried to *kill* me."

Throckmorton came to his feet in one smooth motion and faced his son, who was still snarling at Antonía. "What—did—you—do?" he said, his voice filled with so much disgust and fury that Rex's eyes widened and he took a step back.

"I didn't do anything!" He pointed at Antonía. "She's lying! Again! And for some reason, she seems to feel honor-bound to defend her pack of lies with even more packs of lies!" His father continued to glare at him while Rex stuttered, trying to exonerate himself. "I—I—she—she—" He turned red and finally shouted, "It's her word against mine!"

"Yes," Sir Basil said, looking from his son to Antonía. "What say you, my dear?"

She lifted one shoulder in a shrug. "*I* say, if you believe what *he* says, I have a bridge in London I'd like to sell you."

"Is it a big bridge?" Rex asked eagerly, and then glowered. "I bet you don't even own a bridge."

"Rex," Throckmorton said, "we shall leave in ten minutes. Pack whatever you need for our stay at Ford Castle."

"But it's all burned up."

His father ignored him, and after grumbling for a few minutes, Rex turned and lumbered out of the room.

"Now," Sir Basil said to Antonía, "tell me how my son tried to kill you."

She turned in her chair to face him. "Mr. Claymore died throwing himself in front of me to protect me from Rex's arrow."

Throckmorton looked stunned. He stood silently blinking at her for several seconds, then turned on his heel and stalked out of the room. Antonía sank down in her chair and put her head on the table. *Much too much drama in this family*, she thought. *It was positively exhausting.*

"If your story is true—"

Antonía jerked her head up to see Sir Basil storming back in, his face apoplectic.

He stopped in the middle of the room, shaking his finger at her. "If what you say is true, I will have him drawn and quartered! Now—what say you? Do you have any proof? Any witnesses?"

Antonía stood and walked toward him slowly, stopping just before she passed by. "The only witness . . . is dead." She forced herself to remain composed. "Incidentally, don't forget the strength potion." She strode past him and back to her bedroom.

Fifteen minutes later, to her astonishment, she was clad in her brother's old clothes once again. Sir Basil had had them all along and had left them, clean and folded, on her bed. He said he didn't want her to be uncomfortable on the long ride from the dowager's house to Ford Castle.

It wasn't long before Sir Basil arrived at her bedroom and, to her relief, handed her a dozen vials containing the strength potion. He cautioned her to take only one dose per day. She readily agreed, but as soon as he left the room, she downed three more vials, praying that some terrible side effect wouldn't kill her before she met her objectives.

After putting the remaining vials in her pack, she slung it over her shoulder and hurried to the front steps. There she found Rex and his father engaged in a heated conversation that ended as soon as she arrived.

"Ready to ride?" she asked, looking only at the father.

"Yes, of course," Sir Basil said with a smile and a slight bow. "Feeling better?"

Antonía gave him a steady look for a moment and then replied, "Not yet, but I will, very soon I'm sure."

Outside, three horses awaited them. Naturally, Rex handed her the reins of a horse that appeared as if it had fallen asleep on its feet. She patted the horse, inspected its hooves, and led it away.

"And just where do you think you're going?" shouted Rex.

"My horse has a loose shoe. I'm taking her back to the stables to trade for another." Before either man could object, she led the mare at a fast trot toward the stables.

"Make sure you select a slow horse," she heard Sir Basil say after her. "A nice, slow, hebetudinous horse!"

"What does that mean?" she heard Rex ask. Then moments later she heard, "Ow! Fadda! Stop hitting me!"

Antonía smiled and disappeared into the stables, helped the mare back into her stall, and then quickly looked at the available steeds. There weren't any more stallions, but there was a beautiful black gelding with a white and gray mane.

"Look at you," she said, stroking his nose. "I think we were made for each other."

"Hey, miss, ya don't wanna be ridin' that 'un," a stable boy said from a far corner of the barn. "He's a mean 'un, he is."

"Oh, no," she said, patting the horse's neck lovingly. "He's just misunderstood." Eagerly she opened his stall and led him out, putting all the correct riding accoutrements on him as the boy watched in awe.

Antonía smiled, feeling the strength potion activate in her system. "Women are stronger than most men realize," she said. "Don't forget that, laddie."

She was strong. The vials of potion had worked. In fact, she felt as if she could bench press one of the horses. Instead, she looked around the stables for a weapon. Although killing a human being didn't seem to be something she would normally do, the fact was Rex and Basil Throckmorton just made her feel stabby in general. And now that Rex had killed Mr. Claymore, he had it coming. The man needed killing badly.

She waited for the tears to come, but her eyes remained dry. *Was* she cold-hearted, she suddenly wondered? Frigid and uncaring as Rex had claimed?

No, never uncaring about her beloved Mr. Claymore. Just still in shock. Still numb inside. No doubt the dam would break at some inconvenient, inopportune moment and catch her unawares with desperate, gut-wrenching sobs. She placed her hand over the delicate silver pendant that he had given her. Of course! Mr. Claymore's claymore!

She immediately aborted her search of the stables for a weapon. She already had one. That is, if the sun would cooperate.

Chapter 18

A PUNY LITTLE DIRK
VERSUS A LIFE-SIZE CLAYMORE

Waving good-bye to the stable boy, Antonía led her new horse out of the stables and glanced up at the sky. A curtain of gray still covered most of the sky, but here and there she caught a glimpse of blue. Unfortunately, Rex was standing in her way, his beefy body blocking her view.

"It's about goddamn time you got here!" grunted Rex. "I'm going down to the river to get some water for the horses, and Fadda said he forgot something in the house. I'll be right back, so don't do anything stupid!"

"Not to worry," she responded matter-of-factly, keeping her eyes on the sky. "I've learned to leave all things stupid to your expertise."

He grabbed her by the scruff of the neck and hissed a halitosis-heavy warning into her face. "What you should've learned is that I don't like smartass women!"

And, in a way, Rex was right, because the lesson she should've learned by this point was that her abusive retorts posed a serious risk to her health; but since the cruel twists and turns of fate had so fully deprived her of any prospect for happiness, she suddenly realized she had become absolutely fearless. And strong.

"Release me or I will break your neck," she said, never taking her eyes from his.

Rex started to laugh, but his beady eyes froze on hers, then skittered side to side before he visibly swallowed, hard. Befuddled, he let her go and snarled, "You stupid bitch."

"Rex, I'm beginning to suffer from identity confusion, so what I'd like to know is which sobriquet better applies to me? Am I a smartass woman or a stupid bitch? And you can't say 'both,' because it would be a contradiction in terms—of sorts." She put her hands on her hips and faced him, arms akimbo.

Although answering in rhyme, Rex wasn't very polite about it:

"Your sobriquet of the day

Is anything I goddamn say!"

"Well, that wasn't nice," she said mildly.

"I'm not nice," he grumbled. Then, picking up a water bucket, he seized Antonía by the wrist and dragged her to the edge of the ravine. The river lay below, down a rather steep incline. Releasing his grip, he barked his orders. "Don't move. If you so much as look in the wrong direction, I'll scramble back up the hill and beat you senseless . . . you stupid, smartass bitch!"

He made his way down the ravine to the deep, fast-running river, all the while stealing backward glances at her. Doing as she was told, Antonía stood motionless atop the heath-covered cliff. As she watched his bulky form move clumsily toward the water, she felt the wind pick up without warning.

Wuthering winds swirled around her, wild yet purposeful, and she looked upward, searching the heights of Heaven. The thick, strong bond of gray clouds appeared to be weakening. She continued to search until she spotted her objective—a single sliver of blue pushing through a tiny aperture in the gloom. With one hand on her necklace, she prayed furiously for even a brief flash of sunshine.

But the metal! She had to have a piece of metal to touch to the sword pendant. Turning to go back to the stables, Antonía suddenly stopped and smiled. Reaching inside her bodice, she drew out her mother's lucky coin.

"If there's a God in Heaven," she whispered, and emerging through a barely perceptible fissure in the gray curtain of gloom, a beam of radiant sunshine pierced the clouds, splitting the heavens wide open.

As bright sunlight swept across the hill upon which she stood, Antonía wasted no time in pulling the chain over her head. Lifting the tiny sword in her right hand and the coin in her left, she moved the two closer and closer together. Sunlight sparkled on the surface of the silver sword, and taking a deep breath and saying a fast prayer, she touched the coin to the pendant, and the desired result was most definitely achieved.

Instantaneously, Mr. Claymore's pendant exploded in size—the hilt growing in her hand, the blade extending quickly outward, until Antonía was holding a life-size claymore sword!

A very heavy claymore sword.

"I never thought I'd say this," she murmured, "but thank God for Basil Throckmorton's potions."

Seizing her chance and her claymore, Antonía ran to her horse where it was grazing a few feet away. In spite of the potion, however, she found that just hauling the sword had been harder than she'd imagined. She found her saddle pack on the back of her horse, took out another vial of potion, and drank it down. Ready to mount her horse, she was just about to step into the stirrup when Rex's highly agitated voice made her spin around.

"Like I said before—just where do you think you're going?" he bellowed. Heaving his hefty self up the incline, he stopped at the top and panted like a dog for a moment. "If you get away again, Fadda will kill me! You want that on your head? I haven't never done nothing to you!"

Antonía's eyes widened in disbelief at both his fallacious statement and his abominable grammar. "You've never done nothing to me?" She lifted the sword, feeling the effects of the potion course through her blood. How effortless it was to lift it, to point it directly at such a swine. A swine that badly needed killing.

"I've had it, Rex," she said as she walked toward him, sword held straight ahead—all five feet of it. "I've had it with you and your blowhard father. You've kidnapped me, terrorized me, sexually harassed me, and killed the only man I will ever love." She paused and then added, "I've also had it with you and your God-forsaken country! So I'm going home to Scotland, and nothing and no one can stop me."

"You wanna make a bet?" he sniveled, dropping the water bucket and unsheathing his sword, which compared to the claymore looked like a puny little dirk. She laughed at it.

"Poor Rex. I don't know what you've been told, but size does matter."

He glanced down at his sword and a flush of anger turned his face bright red. "My sword's plenty big. It always gets the job done."

"But does it get the job done well, Rex?" She gripped the handle tighter. "Ah, now that is the question. Does it produce . . . satisfaction? Probably not."

"Shut up, you stupid bitch!" He caressed the hilt of his sword. "My sword is fine. It's just fine!"

"Dear Rex, as I've remarked on a previous occasion, you need killing badly, but in spite of having made up my mind to do it"—she lowered the sword she held, suddenly serious—"I'm not the person for the job. Unless, of course, you force my hand by trying to foil my plans with your toy knife."

"So be it, you stupid bitch. Prepare to be sliced and diced!"

Antonía lifted the sword again, still amazed at how easily she could do it. "Did you miss the enormous sword, you tottering, ill-nurtured lout?" She sighed. She really didn't want to kill Rex. Well, she did kind of want to; after all, he had killed Mr. Claymore. But she knew the act itself would haunt her. Still . . . she didn't want to die. Not yet.

His beady eyes narrowed as the two fighters circled each other, both holding their swords at the ready. "I'm going to kill you," he said, "and then I'm going to pluck you like there's—"

"That's it! I've had it! I can't take that line one more time, Rex! Let's trim the tree with your blood instead."

"I knew it!" he squawked. "You're just like your scheming whore of a mother!" And with those charming words of warm civility, Rex lunged at Antonía with his pathetically diminutive dagger in hand.

Buoyed by the potion coursing through her veins, she found she was able to jump higher, move more quickly. As she moved around Rex, she realized it was similar to dancing, and in a fit of fancy, she executed a single jeté backward, allowing the law of gravity and her foe's innate klutziness to join forces. Landing with an ugly thud upon the ground, Rex nevertheless, and rather surprisingly, leapt back onto his big feet with impressive agility.

Losing, however, was not an option for Miss Barclay. Effortlessly performing a partial pirouette so that her back now faced the river, she lifted the claymore in front of her, point up. "I must admit to feeling a wee bit guilty, so allow me to apologize in advance."

"What the hell are you talking about?" snarled Rex, trying to catch his breath as he lumbered toward her.

"I'm talking about the vast disparity in size between our respective weapons," she answered, baiting him. "Here I am, holding this great big double-fisted sword in my hands, and there you are, holding your puny little dirk in yours."

Infuriated beyond belief, Rex waved his wee weapon back and forth, slicing through air.

"You'd be well advised *not* to advertise your shortcomings," she said. "It hardly seems fair."

With his fury peaking to a head, he took her bait hook, line, and sinker. "You stupid bitch! You're going back to Scotland over my dead body!"

Antonía shrugged. "Have it your way."

Rex charged toward her in an ugly mass of mean-spirited rage, but the final result was not a pretty picture because his innate klutziness—and the law of gravity—joined forces with the water bucket resting innocently at Miss Barclay's feet. As a result, she simply danced out of harm's way, allowing Rex to step into the wooden pail, drop his puny little sword, and tumble headlong down the slippery slope and into the deep, fast-running river below.

Although eager to be on her way, Antonía nonetheless peered over the precipice to satisfy herself that Rex was far too busy thrashing and flailing in the river to interfere with her plans, and he was. Therefore, having resolved the Rex problem, she affixed the giant claymore to her horse, mounted, and headed north to Scotland; but unfortunately *not* before Rex's pitiful cries reached her ears, gained admission to her mind, and consequently clawed at her conscience.

"I can't bloody swim!" he wailed over and over again.

His agonizing appeals were, in fact, doing a very convincing job of proving that he really *couldn't* swim and was, in fact, drowning. For a sweep of the second hand, she vacillated between available courses of action but, ultimately, shook her head in self-disgust. Try as she might, her hatred simply would not submit to her humanity.

Fully aware that what she was about to do was the stupidest thing she would ever do in her lifetime, Antonía dismounted, sighed deeply, and cussed fluently. How she wished and prayed she could derive just a wee bit of sadistic delight from his demise—without the ensuing guilt. But it was impossible. Now she knew she was Catholic.

As she jogged toward the ravine, stripping off her jacket and kicking off her shoes in preparation for water rescue, Antonía was abruptly enveloped from behind.

"And just where do you think you're going?" Basil Throckmorton said, holding her tightly in his arms.

Antonía gasped for air as she answered reproachfully, "Because you neglected your parental duty of teaching your son to swim, I am now forced to rescue him from the river—unless, of course, you'd prefer to do the honors."

Sir Basil lowered her to the ground and she tried to wrench away from him, but his grip was too tight. The potion was wearing off! She fell to her knees, one arm free, and as she huddled against the ground, she took out her emergency vial of potion, pulled the cork out with her teeth, and gulped it down without him noticing.

"Didn't you hear me?" she said. "Your son is drowning! Save him!" She could still hear Rex's panicked cries, but they were growing fainter.

"You're too much, Miss Barclay, you really are!" Sir Basil said with a laugh. "And I just love you to bits for thinking I would, but I have absolutely no intention of rescuing my son."

"So you can't swim either," she posited testily. "You English are unbelievable! You live on an island but you can't be bothered to learn to swim! Then let me go so I can reach him before he drowns."

"No," he said, pulling her to her feet.

She stared at him in horror. "But why not?"

The laughter in his eyes shifted into malice. "So many reasons! Because he tried to kill you! Because he eats like a pig and chews with his mouth open! Because he yammers on endlessly about inane matters! Because he delayed my plans to destroy your brothers and their ineffectual squad of Scottish malcontents!"

"But if we don't help Rex, he'll die." And it was at this precise moment that she realized she could no longer hear his abject cries of terror.

"You've just killed your own son," she whispered.

"Don't take it so hard, my dearest. You're still very young and have a great many things to learn, but in due course and under my tutelage, you shall come to understand that life is all a matter of perspective. Therefore I advise you to view Rex's passing as an act of mercy—on many different levels."

Calling tripe when she heard tripe, she lit into him, her voice tense with anger. "And more importantly, he won't be around to bungle your next power play, right?"

He shrugged. "Well, there is that."

Antonía sagged in his arms, momentarily speechless and positively paralyzed by the black-hearted ruthlessness of the man.

"Miss Barclay?" he asked, lowering her to the ground and kneeling beside her. "Perhaps you need another vial—"

"Don't you intend to retrieve your son's body from the river?" she demanded, stumbling to her feet and backing away from him.

The Englishman rose gracefully from the ground. "Whatever for, my dear?" he asked.

"For a decent Christian burial, that's *whatever for!*"

He tapped one finger against his chin thoughtfully. "No, I think we'll leave him in the river. Fish must eat too, my dearest."

Her eyes widened in sheer horror. The man was unbelievable. But quickly recovering her composure, she remarked, "Your concern for marine life is rather astonishing, Sir Basil. Especially since you have no regard for human life."

"If you're referring to my son's recent departure, it really was for the best," he said, seizing her wrist. "Once again, it's all a matter of perspective, my dearest Miss Barclay. How would it look if my own son was incessantly lusting after my beautiful young wife?"

"It didn't seem to bother you the entire time I was your prisoner and Rex was trying to deflower me morning, noon, and night!" She paused for a breath and resumed. "And I never ever want to marry you! In fact, I despise you with every fiber of my being! If you burst into flames I wouldn't spit on you!" She took a step to her right.

"Temper, temper, Miss Barclay," he chastised playfully, patting her hand. "Now, truly, are you sincerely grieved by Rex's death? I know for a fact that you hated him." He took a step to his left.

"He was your son."

"True," conceded Sir Basil. "But obviously he took after my deceased wife's side of the family, so there really wasn't a whole lot there to love."

Antonía shook her head. "God, you are such a lunatic," she said in a hushed voice.

"Oh, come now, my darling Miss Barclay," Throckmorton said, smirking. "Tell me what you really think."

She shrugged. "Okay." Complying with his request, she shouted, "I think you are one sick son of a bitch!"

But before Sir Basil could respond, a familiar voice chided from the bushes.

"Such language does not befit your royal lineage, my darling daughter!"

Antonía whirled in the direction of the voice and took a step back, stunned. In all her six-foot glory, the former Queen of Scotland stepped into the sunlight, red hair blowing, amber eyes glowing.

"Mother . . . *Mother*, what are you doing here?" asked her astonished daughter, clearly taken aback by the sight of her inimitable, indomitable, and indefatigable royal mother. Thinking quickly, she reached inside her bodice for the last bottle of strength potion at hand. The rest were in the saddle pack on her horse.

"Never mind that now, Antonía darling," the queen said with affection. "What unconscionable act has Basil committed to compel you to employ such unladylike vocabulary?"

Emotionally unable to deliver the devastating news of Mr. Claymore's demise, Antonía shook her head. "This vile man is culpable of so many unconscionable acts it's hard to know where to begin, but working in reverse chronological order—he allowed his son to drown in the river just a few minutes ago."

"I see," the queen said, leveling eyes of pure, unadulterated contempt on her old nemesis. "That being the case, I extend my apologies to you, Antonía, because you're damn right. He is one sick son of a bitch!" She then lowered her voice and continued, "And, Antonía, to answer your original question: Basil, I'm here to kick your ass!"

Throckmorton looked quite taken aback. "Your Majesty," he said, one hand on his chest, "have I done something to offend?"

Mary raised one brow. "Do you mean something such as kidnapping my daughter? Yes, yes you have."

He gave her a dazzling smile. "I haven't seen you for a long time," he said. "What have you been up to?"

"Not much," she replied matter-of-factly. "For some reason or other, the second half of my life hasn't proven quite as action-packed as the first half."

"I'm sorry to hear that, Your Majesty." Another dazzling smile. "But you know you can always count on me for action." He pulled Antonía in front of him and laid his dead son's sword across her neck.

The Englishman laughed heartily, while the queen's countenance darkened.

"You've always been a victim of your own wicked madness, Basil. We haven't seen each other in well over eighteen years, but I can already tell that you're as loony as ever, exploiting and threatening women for your own pathetic purposes!"

"My purposes can hardly be depicted as *pathetic*, Your Majesty. Allow me to enlighten you, my dear queen."

"Could I stop you?"

"No. My purposes can best be described as the mathematics of power: Yours truly plus your gorgeous daughter minus your ineffectual son equals the Scottish throne. And if we take the equation one step further by subtracting your pockmarked cousin Elizabeth, then both problems shall be solved in a single solution."

"Dear God, Basil, I believe you have finally completely lost your mind. Unmitigated evil superadded to hubristic grandiosity equals an abbreviated life." The queen glided gracefully over to the huge claymore protruding from Antonía's horse's saddle and rested her hand on the hilt. "I'm certain you wouldn't wish harm on the most integral part of your equation, so I order you to release Antonía now!"

"Fear not, Your Majesty! I'll be careful to ensure no harm travels my way."

Mary shook her head in disdain. "Don't be obtuse! I was referring to my daughter. Release her so we may engage in a fair fight."

He was incredulous. "Surely you jest, Your Majesty. Are you actually challenging me to a duel? You! A mere woman! And a woman hardly in her prime . . . hardly at the acme of her power. And let's be honest, even at your physical peak, you could barely drive a golf ball half the length of the fairway."

"True," she said, "but I always drove it farther than you."

"That's because you always insisted on hitting the ball from a closer distance! And thanks to your absurd suggestion, Bruntsfield Links is still littered with those ridiculous red ladies' tee boxes."

Mary's eyes burned with fury. "I am finding it harder and harder to restrain my temper, Basil. First you insult my fair sex. Then you insult my age. Worst of all, you insult my golf game. And now you've really gone and done it by insulting my legacy to the sport!" She pulled the claymore from the ground and frowned as the weight of it made it impossible to lift.

Throckmorton smirked at the sight. "You're nothing but a failed monarch who has grossly outlived her significance. No one even remembers you!"

"You bastard!" Antonía cried.

He gave a little wave of one hand. "You know how it is, out of sight, out of mind. But fear not, my dear queen, I predict that one day your favorite cousin will summon the courage to order your execution, thereby granting you the martyrdom status you so fervidly desire. I'm sure I don't have to remind you to wear scarlet on execution day."

Sir Basil's smile widened and he lowered the sword slightly. "I cannot tell you how much I admire your family's loyalty. You chop each other's heads off as nonchalantly as you take your dogs out for a morning walk."

"Chuckle all you want," the queen said, "but I predict your head will roll before mine. You're not the only one with friends in high places."

"Oh, no," he groaned, "here we go again! After all these years, you really haven't changed one iota. You and your God Almighty God! You and your fire-and-brimstone! You and your Papist doctrines! You still insist on putting an eschatological spin on every subject under the sun. But just for the sake of argument, wouldn't your Almighty God throw you into the depths of Hell if—by some incredible stroke of luck—you succeeded in *abbreviating* my lifespan?"

"Far from it, Basil," she said in a smooth, steady voice. "God would doubtlessly grant me a shiny new halo and soft feathery wings for ridding the world of your demonic, blasphemous soul." The queen's gaze shifted lovingly to her daughter. "Moreover, killing to protect one's young is sacred to maternal authority. In fact, it's the one and only exception to the sixth commandment."

"Is that so?" he questioned with a skeptical tilt of the head. "But tell me, Your Majesty, how can you prove your assertion of such an exception? And, even if you were to provide proof, how can you be certain your exception would shield you from the devil's chthonian home?"

"Naturally I cannot prove the validity of my assertion—that is a matter of faith." She then added rather paradoxically, "As for certitude, can we ever be completely certain of any event in life other than death?"

Throckmorton's mouth fell open. "I *beg* your pardon?"

Mary laughed. "Oh, I'm sorry, Basil. How silly of me to omit the *other* certainty while in the company of an Englishman. Death—*and taxes.* Happy now?"

"Jubilant, Your Majesty. But please answer me this, where does forgiveness fit into your theological paradigm? With all your preaching, proselytizing, and pontificating, you must have a homespun homily or parable to spout on the subject of forgiveness." He lowered his lips to Antonía's neck and brushed against her skin. "Ah, my dear, I cannot wait to taste you fully."

The queen's amber eyes flashed red, but the timbre of her voice remained cool.

"Sorry to disappoint, but I will proffer neither a homily nor a parable on the subject. However, I do believe in the adage 'Always forgive your enemies; it will drive them crazy.' Years ago I did, indeed, forgive you, and you, indeed, went crazy—well, *crazier.* But do not mistake my forgiveness at that time for weakness now. A mother can *never, ever* forgive acts of aggression against her children. I am, therefore, putting you on notice for the very last time: *Release my daughter from harm's way and fight me like a man!*"

"Wait!" Antonía cried, still trapped in the Englishman's grasp. "Mother, you've ridden a long way. Is it fair for you to duel without so much as a drink of water?" She paused and then addressed her foe. "Sir Basil, will you allow me to fetch a ladle of water before the two of you battle?"

"But, dear Antonía," Sir Basil said, "how can I trust you to return?"

Antonía went rigid in his arms. "Do you really think I would leave my mother to face you alone?"

He laughed. "If the queen will refrain from trying to beat me to death with a sword she can neither lift nor wield, then yes, you may fetch a ladle from the stables and a pouch of water from my saddle." He gestured toward the black stallion now grazing beside Antonía's horse.

He released her and Antonía ran first to the saddle for the water, and then to the stables. She opened the vial she'd kept hidden and then took the ladle and poured the blue liquid into it. She set the bottle down and added water from the leather pouch.

Slinging the pouch over her shoulder, she headed back to the dueling field.

"Here, Mother, drink up," she said, handing her the ladle.

Her mother took a drink, looking grateful for her daughter's kindness. She made a slight moue at the taste but shrugged and drank the rest.

"Ah!" she said when she finished. "I feel quite refreshed now. Let us begin."

"Oh, but wait," Antonía said. "Sir Basil must have a drink too. It's only fair." Not wanting to get within reach of the man, she tossed the leather pouch to him. He caught it with one hand.

"Thank you, my dear." He tilted his head and smiled. "And you say you don't care."

"Mother, perhaps you would like to get the feel of the sword? It is quite well balanced," Antonía told her. "Let me show you how to grip the hilt."

"Antonía, I know quite well—"

"Listen!" she whispered. Antonía darted a quick look at Throck-morton, but thankfully he was busy guzzling water. She spoke quickly. "Mother, there was a potion in the water you just drank. Sir Basil formu-lated it, and believe it or not, it will give you extraordinary strength. Just stall for another five minutes and it should take effect."

"Antonía, you are quite brilliant, my darling." She raised her voice. "My, this is a marvel of a sword. Have you tried one, Basil?"

"Indeed I have," he said. "And if you could lift it, I would quite fear for my life." He paused, reflected, and then added, "Incidentally, I encourage you to invest immediately in the Claymore family business. The price of the claymore sword is due to increase exponentially!"

"Is that a fact?" Mary said, pretending to examine the sword hilt more closely, while Antonía hovered near. "Why is that, do you suppose?"

"Oh, you don't know? A tragedy really, but a fortuitous one for the Claymore family fortune. For you see, it was only yesterday that my late son killed the even later Mr. Claymore." He cackled wickedly. "Remember, ladies, the first law of economics is scarcity."

A swift, apprehensive glance at her daughter's anguished face was all it took for the queen to verify the fact that Antonía supposed her beloved Mr. Claymore dead. But unsurprisingly, Throckmorton persisted in deriving pleasure in another's misery.

"That's right," he said. "Claymore is as dead as a doornail. I now have your luscious daughter all to myself, and as soon as I kill you, I'll marry her. And together we shall rule England, Scotland, and perhaps we'll expand our territory into Ireland as well!"

The queen suddenly straightened, her eyes widening. Antonía stepped back, holding her breath. Had the potion taken effect?

"Still the megalomaniac, Basil? But enough talk. Let us get down to business."

"Yes." He posed with his sword pointed to the ground, his other arm cocked beside his head. "Let us begin."

To Antonía's dismay, her mother still seemed barely able to lift the sword. Throckmorton laughed and began to dance around her, his smaller sword at the ready.

Standing close to her mother, Antonía stalled for time. "Sir Basil, you still appear slightly parched. Would you like some more water to slake your thirst?"

"My darling Miss Barclay, sorry to disappoint you," he said, laughing, "but you just gave your mother a placebo rather than the strength potion. You can wait around all day, but water tinged with indigo dye shall not make her, or you, any stronger."

Stunned, Antonía replied, "The extra vials you gave me were all fakes?"

"Of course," he replied smugly. "I wasn't so stupid as to provide you with additional active potions." He laughed. "Who do you think you're dealing with? My son?"

"Now that would be impossible, wouldn't it?"

"Thank you for reminding me, Miss Barclay. For a minute there, I forgot he was dead." Throckmorton then smiled and glanced up at the sky. "Thank God for small miracles. Now please, dear, step aside and let me take a stab at your mother."

"No, you sick bastard, I'm not moving one single step."

Shaking his head, Sir Basil sighed. "You know, Miss Barclay, you may be a joy to your mother, but right now you're a real pain in the ass to me. So if that's the way you want it, so be it. But if you get hurt, don't come crying to me." He then resumed moving in a circular pattern around them.

Still standing shoulder to shoulder with her six-foot mother, Antonía kept one eye on Sir Basil as she said under her breath, "We can do this, if we do it together." She gripped the sword's hilt, her hands above her mother's. "Aim for the heart."

"He doesn't have one," whispered the queen. "Go for the jugular. Sweep right to left." She paused and then added, "Remember, my darling, there's no time left for losing!"

At that precise moment, Sir Basil lunged low toward the pair, aiming directly for the queen's heart. But much to his chagrin, he came to realize a wee bit too late in the game that there really is something to be said for the sacredness, and speed, of the mother-daughter bond because—

In a tour de force of twelve cumulative feet of female determination, the queen and her daughter swung the claymore up toward Heaven and then cut downward, slicing into Basil Throckmorton's neck, neatly severing his head from his body.

The result, although extremely gory, nevertheless proved extremely effective. Sir Basil's head rolled right off his shoulders, down the steep ravine, and into the deep, fast-running river below.

Chapter 19

TRIPE TRUMPS TRUTH

Four men galloped across the stark English countryside until the eldest amongst them slowed his horse and came to a halt. The others pulled up as he squinted into the fast-growing darkness.

"Lads, my eyes are not what my ears are. Look to the other side of the river and tell me what you see."

One of the men pointed to the distance. "I see two very tall women."

Another of the men exclaimed in perplexity, "I daresay we're in the market for only *one* very tall woman, Oliver, but . . ."

"Dammit to hell, Gus—there's our sister, I'd ken her backside anywhere! She has that kenspeckle habit of standing akimbo while looking askance! And look what she's wearing! Those are my clothes!"

And with that dubious declarative statement, the four riders descended the embankment, crossed the river, and ascended the opposite side.

As the riders approached the women, Mary was shocked to recognize Gus Corbett.

"My brothers!" Antonía cried and ran to greet them. Gus and the three notorious Barclay brothers dismounted and then hugged their sister. She whirled around and introduced them. "Mother, this is Will, Matthew, and Oliver—and Gus, of course." The four men genuflected in stunned reverence as they paid their respects. Mary was truly touched by their gesture.

"Welcome," Mary said, and then held out her hand to her old friend. "Gus, I'm so glad to see you on your feet and well again."

"Only because of you, my queen," he said, dropping to one knee before her.

The poignant moment was promptly broken by the shortest, blondest of the three brothers—Oliver—offering his opinion on the decapitated corpse. "You two most assuredly got the job done here," he observed, leaning over Basil Throckmorton's body. "What happened?" Antonía quickly told them the tale of Sir Basil's demise and Oliver shook his head. "Where's his nincompoop of a son?"

"Rex and I had a slight altercation, after which he rolled down the hill and drowned in the river." Antonía gestured toward the ravine.

The brothers exchanged concerned glances. Antonía's seemingly casual attitude was apparently worrying the three, but not Mary. She immediately understood that her daughter was camouflaging her pain with a hard-fought façade of calm. Putting a comforting arm around her shoulder, the queen drew Antonía to her side.

"Yer Majesty," Gus said, rising from the ground, "may I presume that ye've escaped from Chartley Hall and plan to return to Scotland with us?"

"No, my dear friend, " she said graciously. "I intend to return to Chartley forthwith. My permanent absence would place a very good man in a very bad position. Moreover, my return to Scotland would seriously compromise my son's reign as well as the stability of our homeland." She paused, silently deliberated, and then turned to her daughter. "Darling, I'd like a word alone with Gus, if you don't mind."

"Of course, Mother."

After walking a short distance, the queen and Gus stopped, coming to rest under the graceful branches of a large greenwood tree. Gus looked expectantly at Mary.

"Dearest Gus," she began, "I am overjoyed to see that you remain fully recovered from your fever. No recurrences, I hope?"

Gus's craggy face split into a lopsided smile. "Thank ye very much for your care and concern, Yer Majesty. I'm fit as a flea! Ye and the parson did a fine job nursing me back to health! After the two of ye cured me and sent me on my way, I ran smack into the Barclay brothers," he gestured behind him to where the trio stood with Antonía, and then added, "and Mr. Claymore, too, but we havena seen hide nor hair of him since—" He stopped as the queen bowed her head and covered her mouth with her hand.

She finally looked up directly into her old friend's cloudy hazel eyes and shook her head. "Rex Throckmorton struck Mr. Claymore with an arrow at very close range. He was protecting Antonía, who was the evil man's target."

"Aye, I ken he would do anything for the lass, Yer Majesty, but is he—?" Gus broke off and stared down at the ground, unable to say the word.

The queen replied quickly, "Mr. Claymore survived the initial blow, but Antonía does not know this and thinks him dead."

Clearly surprised, Gus looked up with another smile. "'Tis wonderful news, Yer Majesty! Then he is alive!"

The queen sighed deeply. "Not necessarily. I left him back at Chartley Hall under the care of Reverend Goode. But Mr. Claymore was a gravely ill man when I departed to find Antonía."

"Aye, I see," said Gus, rubbing his chin. "Then we don't know whether or not he is still alive."

"Precisely, and we cannot give Antonía hope only to snatch it away from her in the event that Mr. Claymore has since perished," said the queen firmly. "When I learn of his fate, I shall send word. Until that time, however, *not a word to anyone on the subject of Mr. Claymore.*"

"Understood, Your Majesty, ye can count on me."

Placing her hand on Gus's shoulder, Mary smiled gratefully. "I always have, and always will, count on you, Augustus Corbett. Furthermore, I will never be able to thank you enough for your undying loyalty to me and my daughter." She paused and took a deep, fortifying breath. "Godspeed to you, my cherished friend, and my very best regards to your Lucy when you return home."

Too emotional to speak, Gus looked down at the ground and nodded his head, then looked up. "God bless ye, my queen, and all of your household."

She smiled and, linking her arm through her friend's, spoke in a louder voice. "Let us rejoin the others. It's time for me to say good-bye."

Antonía turned, looking startled as she took a step toward the queen. "You can't leave now, Mother," she objected. "It's getting late!"

Moving to her daughter's side, the queen took her hand. "Beloved Antonía, I love you dearly and I deeply regret that I must leave you, but leave I must. The summer day is long and I will make it back to Chartley in less than an hour. You needn't worry."

Antonía tried a different tack. "You'll get lost, Mother. You know how we both are with directions."

The queen smiled at her persistence. "Fear not, my lovely child! I left markers along the way, and as you do, I ride like the wind."

"Then we'll go with you!"

"No, my darling," Mary said, softly yet firmly. "I ride fastest alone."

Mary then embraced her second-born and spoke tenderly into her ear, "I love you, sweet child, for all eternity. Your spirit will always be deep in my heart and bound to my soul. Neither of us shall ever be truly alone again." She felt Antonía tremble with emotion. "I know you're in profound pain right now, my dearest Antonía, but Mr. Claymore was a fine and honorable man and he would not wish you to grieve yourself to ruin. Have faith in God, my darling child. He knows what He is doing." Slowly releasing Antonía, she covered her trademark red hair with the hood of her cloak and mounted her horse, which Gus had solemnly led to her side.

Reaching down, she touched her hand tenderly to her daughter's cheek, and after forcing back a threatening tidal wave of tears, she pulled herself together. Sitting tall in the saddle, she then issued a queenly command to the entire group.

"The Royal Sceptre must be recovered before your return to Scotland." The queen saw the brothers exchange another perplexed glance. Nodding to them, she explained, "Antonía and Gus will provide you with all the details." She then turned her horse south and uttered her last words to them. "I beg you not to fail me in this final request. God bless you all." Without further ceremony, Mary, Queen of Scots cantered into the distance and back to prison.

With her brothers and Gus at her side, Antonía watched her mother's regal figure fading from view. But sadly, she experienced only a few minutes of peace before a sharp, burning pain stabbed her in the pit of the stomach. Though sudden, it was hardly unexpected. The hour of crisis had passed, but her *why* to live had died with its passing.

No longer engrossed in the risky business of ridding the world of ninety-two chromosomes of pure unadulterated evil, Antonía felt the cruel recrudescence of despair engulf her in its powerful waters. And once again, she had no earthly idea where she'd find the strength to claw herself out of its black, hopeless depths. Mr. Claymore was gone forever. Now her mother was on her way out of her life as well.

"Antonía!" Will snapped, jostling her out of her trance. "Do you have any suggestions with respect to the remains of Throckmorton's remains?"

Her weary eyes fell upon the beheaded corpse. After lingering a moment, her gaze wandered over to the edge of the ravine. A kettle of vultures circled overhead, looking for dinner.

Her response came slowly, but resolutely.

"The fish have had their fill. Let the vultures have theirs."

Antonía was far from pleased to awaken from a short night's sleep pressed against the cold, hard earth of northern England. Instinctively, she yearned for all things hot: a hot bath, a hot meal, a hot fire. But the one hot thing she yearned for most of all was the only thing she could never again experience: Mr. Claymore.

Unable to tolerate the relentless churning of her grieving mind, Miss Barclay extracted herself from the pile of blankets that her concerned brothers had heaped upon her when she all but collapsed off her horse the night before as they made camp. Stiff, sore, and shivering, she stood and observed her siblings who, oblivious to their surroundings, slept like the dead but snored like the dickens.

In accordance with rules promulgated for old people the world over, Gus had started his day awfully damn early and had just finished building a small fire when he noticed Antonía gazing listlessly down on her slumbering brothers. Immediately going to her aid, the courtly old gent guided her away from the cacophony of vibrating soft palates and toward the warmth of the crackling fire. Once they were seated, he spoke in a gentle, comforting voice that almost brought her to tears.

"My poor lass, I knew ye'd wake up in a very bad way this morning. But it's impossible to bypass grief. Ye have no choice other than to work yer way through it. Letting time pass is the one and only solution."

But she didn't agree with his approach to grief therapy. Her reply was as swift as it was emphatic.

"Then the solution is part of the problem, because I don't want time to pass! The passage of time will only take Mr. Claymore farther and farther away from me, from his memory. Don't you understand, Gus? I don't want to forget him. I don't want my pages to turn without him. I don't want to forget his face, his eyes, his smile, his touch . . ."

"I understand, lass," he said. "But life is not a static condition. At some point, ye must move your life forward. There's no future in the past. Chapters must end so new ones can begin."

"Well, then," she announced, "my new chapter involves joining the first nunnery willing to admit me, because I intend to spend the rest of my life in the confines of a nice, quiet convent far removed from the trifling distractions of daily living, remembering Mr. Claymore."

"Sorry again, lass, but I don't think that's the way yer average nun is supposed to occupy her time," counseled Gus. "I believe the purpose of a nunnery is for religious contemplation rather than mysticizing over dead lovers."

Oliver came striding forward at that moment, proclaiming rather pointedly, "You're joining a convent when Hell freezes over! No sister of mine is living in some crusty old convent. Besides, you don't even qualify. You're not Catholic!"

"You want to make a bet?" snapped Antonía.

"Holy shite!" he cursed sacrilegiously. "When did that happen?"

"On the day we were born."

"What's done can be undone!" expounded Oliver. "We'll have you cured or fixed or exorcised or . . . whatever the word for it is." Pausing momentarily, he then proceeded to trash Christendom from every angle: "And, in any event, I'm pretty damn sure all that Reformation garbage demolished every nunnery in Scotland. Knox and his puritanical pals certainly did a number there. Good luck trying to find a convent still in operation!"

"Actually," said a new voice on the scene, "there's still a batch of convents open for business in the Outer Hebrides. And come to think of it, I heard they've recently franchised into the Inner Hebrides as well."

"Thanks, Will, you're a fount of information," said Oliver dryly. "Now we know where to forward her correspondence."

Matthew, the brother of few, if any, words, arrived next and said nothing, but raised a questioning brow.

Responding to the tacit inquiry, Oliver remarked tactlessly, "Just because Claymore died, Antonía's hell-bent on becoming a nun!"

Matthew looked at his sister with a gentle and sympathetic eye. So often is a reserved temperament superadded to a sensitive soul. He said in as few words as possible: "I'm very sorry about Claymore, Antonía. Gus told us last night after you'd fallen asleep."

She waited for him to say more but he didn't. She finally asked haltingly, "Matthew, did you . . . did you find Mr. Claymore at Ford Castle?"

"No, Antonía, we never found his body. If you wish, we'll search the castle grounds again."

"Yes, Matthew," she said thoughtfully. "We must go back in any event. I'm fairly certain I know where the Royal Sceptre is hidden."

After a full morning's ride, Antonía, her three brothers, and Gus approached the smoldering ruins of Ford Castle to look for the fallen Mr. Claymore. She led her companions into the courtyard, dismounted, and walked toward the fateful spot where she had last seen him. Gus, however, stopped her, placing a wizened hand on her arm and advised, "Lass, let yer brothers handle this one." Gus felt awful about not divulging the fact that Breck Claymore might possibly be alive, but he'd promised his queen that he'd remain silent. And silent he would remain. "Do ye understand?"

Again, she could only nod in agreement. As her brothers spread out to search the charred castle grounds, Gus cleared his throat and spoke again.

"Lady Antonía, last night ye mentioned that ye might know the exact location of the Royal Sceptre."

"I think I do, Gus," she said, trying not to think about what her brothers might find. What would she do if they did find him? She shook her head, fighting off the wave of grief.

"But the scroll, lass? Don't we need to translate the scroll?"

Trying to focus on the matter at hand, she pulled herself together. Maybe if she tried to find the damn sceptre, this wouldn't hurt so much. Taking a deep breath, Antonía cocked her head at her old friend and gave him a grin. "Not if my hunch is right."

Gus laughed lightly. "After all that ancient Gaelic nonsense, ye figured it out using yer own wits."

Antonía waved a dismissive hand. "Thank you for the compliment, Gus, but the scroll narrowed down the possibilities to Ford Castle, which was quite a big help. As for me detecting the exact location in the castle, it may have been a matter of sheer luck."

Gus threaded her arm through his and patted her hand. "Well, Lady Antonía, let's go try yer luck and see if yer hunch is right!"

Climbing over and through the sooty rubble of the courtyard, they entered the castle and proceeded directly to the drawing room, which, aesthetically speaking, wasn't a big improvement over the courtyard. After gingerly stepping over charred, obliterated furniture, Antonía stopped and pointed to the Ford coat of arms hanging above the now defunct fireplace.

Tiptoeing to get a better view, she urged, "Gus, look very closely at the six swords surrounding the shield."

"Aye, lass," replied Gus, squinting his eyes upward, "one appears different from the rest. I'm not certain 'tis a sword at all."

"Precisely," she concurred, pulling the sole surviving chair up to the fireplace mantle and hoisting her long frame on top of it. After carefully removing the pseudo-sword from the coat of arms, she examined it from top to bottom and was fairly convinced that she was holding the Scottish Royal Sceptre. Impressively heavy but simple in design, the sceptre sported the Royal Stuart insignia surrounded by thistles encrusted with amethysts and diamonds. She lowered it to Gus's eye level. It took him less than a minute's visual inspection to make a positive identification.

"No doubt about it, lass," confirmed Gus. "'Tis yer great-grandfather's Royal Sceptre. Before the king fell at Flodden Field, he must've hidden the sceptre by commingling it with the swords in the coat of arms."

"Good. That'll make my mother happy," Antonía said, adding skeptically, "but I still don't believe the legend. How on earth could returning the sceptre to the royal vault assure a successful monarchy? It sounds like tripe to me."

But Gus didn't agree with her on the subject of unverifiable stories handed down by tradition and popularly accepted as historical fact. While she hopped off the chair with her dubious treasure firmly in hand, the wise old man proffered his theory.

"Aye, child, a legend proves a powerful force in its own right. Truth is rarely a prerequisite to a legend's strength or perpetuity. People have always needed to believe in higher yet imperceptible forces, and I don't see that need ever changing. It's a matter of faith."

Antonía held the sceptre closer to him. He took a purposeful step back and advised, "Remember, lass, the legend also holds that only a member of the Royal Stuart family can safely touch the Royal Sceptre. Just in case, let's not tempt fate."

"Right," said Antonía with resignation. "Which means I'm relegated to the distasteful task of returning it to King James."

Furrowing a sandy brow, Gus asked, "Aren't you the least bit curious to meet your new brother?"

"No," she said bluntly. "I already have all the brothers I can manage."

"If ye're truly resolute on the matter, I'll return the sceptre myself," said Gus.

"No, you won't," she countered quickly. "On the off chance that the tripe is true, I'd better do it myself. You're going home to Lochleven as soon as possible. Lucy's waiting for you!"

Gus beamed. "Aye, I knew ye'd do the right thing. Ye are a sweet lass!"

"Augustus Corbett, my friend, I am many things, but *sweet* is definitely *not* one of them."

Gus smiled and said, "I've learned not to argue with ye, but I can always think what I want. Now let's go find yer brothers."

After they joined the threesome in the courtyard, Matthew was the bearer of the bad news. "Antonía, there's no sign of Claymore's body anywhere."

Reacting to the news with admirable quietude, Antonía said nothing.

Oliver, on the other hand, was innately averse to any state even remotely resembling quietude. Accordingly, he filled the empty airwaves with his theory on the mystery of the missing corpse: "It's not outside the realm of possibility that Claymore survived the attack. I daresay he's an extraordinarily large and powerful fellow. It would've taken a mighty blow to put him down permanently."

Will, who was not nearly so sanguine with respect to Mr. Claymore's fate, challenged his brother's theory: "So if he's alive, where is he?"

"No," Antonía said flatly. "He was hit at extremely close range. Not even a man as physically magnificent as Mr. Claymore could've survived that blow." Running her fingers wearily through her blue-black hair, she surmised, "Rex must've disposed of his body after I blacked out. We'll never find him now." And with those sad words of finality, Miss Barclay mounted her horse and, after fastening the Royal Sceptre alongside her claymore, she turned to her brothers and Gus.

"Don't just stand there staring at me. Mount up. We're going home. As you four are my witnesses," she vowed, "I'll never again set foot in this God-forsaken country. Jolly old England, my a—!"

The wind swallowed up her last word, because she was already well beyond the castle gates. She was going home. And nothing and no one was going to stop her.

The tall and tired woman of a certain age rode through the dense pine forest and into the confines of Chartley Hall. She reflected on her day and decided that while she wasn't proud of her deeds, she felt little compunction for them. The sick bastard had left her no choice. His misspent life had been irredeemable, well beyond salvaging. She sighed wearily. Indeed, she was growing too old to thrive on intrigue. She smiled an ironic smile. Funny how everyone wishes to live long but no one wishes to be old. She smiled again. If only it were a truth universally acknowledged that life is better measured in depth, not length.

In deference to her aching bones, the queen dismounted incrementally from her horse, walked stiffly into Chartley Chapel, and placed a signal candle in the windowsill. After crossing herself, she sat down on a hard, unforgiving pew and faced a granite pulpit and a Norman font that had somehow managed to survive the zealous purge of the Reformation. Glancing round the Anglican place of worship, she lamented the dearth of Catholic churches in England, but being a practical sort, she knew God wasn't a nitpicker. He showed up wherever needed. The place was trivial, the people crucial.

Fully aware that it would take well over a month of Sundays to atone for her sins as well as to pray for Mr. Claymore, the queen fell to her knees, whipped out her rosary, and began a hushed recitation of Hail Marys. However, a human voice reached her ears within moments, interrupting her penitence.

"Your Majesty, are you here?"

Jolted from religious contemplation, the red-haired ex-monarch dropped her beads, swiveled about, and replied, "Yes, Stephen, I'm in the front row."

"Thank God!"

"That's the general idea," quipped the queen, who had long ago learned that a sense of humor is essential in surviving 6,752 days, and counting, in captivity. Turning somber, she implored, "Does Mr. Claymore live?"

Stephen Goode smiled broadly, and affecting a Scottish burr, replied, "Aye, Your Majesty, Miss Barclay's Scottish Claymore lives!"

Looking upward, the queen closed her eyes and placed both hands over her heart. "Sweet Mother of Jesus, thank you!"

Helping the queen to her feet, Stephen warned her about their guest's intentions. "He's still weak, but he insists on leaving tonight for Scotland."

Straightening to her full height, the queen's smile dropped to a determined, straight line. "Well, we'll just see about that!"

She followed Reverend Goode cautiously from the sanctuary, sneaking past the guards and into the parsonage. After entering the small bedchamber, they discovered Mr. Claymore strapping on his boots.

"Not so fast, Mr. Claymore!" she decreed.

The man jerked his head up and came to his feet. "Your Majesty, thank God you're safe! And Miss Barclay? Is she safe as well?"

The queen smiled regally. "Yes, dear Mr. Claymore, my daughter is safe and sound."

He sank back down on his bed, obviously relieved. "I've been out of my mind with worry. Thank God, she's safe! But the Throckmortons, did . . . did they hurt her in any way?"

"My dear Mr. Claymore, I assure you my daughter is not only well, but extremely well. As for the Throckmortons, they have been extermi- nated . . . permanently. They are no longer an issue, much less a threat, to my daughter. Antonía is presently in the protective custody of her three brothers and our trusty friend, Gus. As we speak, they're on their way back to Scotland; however, I must again tell you that although my daugh- ter is physically healthy, her heart lies in tatters over your *death*. I could not in good conscience tell her you were alive because you were very much on the brink."

Mr. Claymore's response was immediate and passionate. "I must leave and find her at once!"

But the queen put her foot down. "Absolutely not! Night has fallen. You will leave at first light, and that is only if I believe you are sufficiently strong to make the journey."

She turned away, knowing he had no choice but to comply. Not only had his queen spoken, but also his mother-in-law-to-be.

Chapter 20

A ROYAL MARK MARKS A ROYAL STUART

With the cold blue water of the North Sea to the east and the familiar scent of salt and peat filling the air, Antonía knew she was finally home. Suffering from bone-aching exhaustion and heart-wrenching grief, she failed to notice, much less appreciate, the gentle unfettered beauty of the Scottish lowlands.

For the totality of the journey, she had been lost in thought, and neither Gus nor her brothers dared to interrupt her state of bleak introspection, no doubt fearful she would crumble into wafts of sorrow and blow away in the wind. Accordingly, they maintained a safe distance, while keeping a vigilant eye on her.

The late summer day became increasingly chilly, ridding the countryside of midges while heralding in the brisk, invigorating air of early autumn. Antonía, however, felt neither brisk nor invigorated. In fact, she had so thoroughly thrashed her emotional battery that she felt more dead than alive. And what was worse, she didn't much care. Consequently, she offered little resistance to the inevitable feeling of apathy that settled itself comfortably into the deep black hole in her spirit. At this point, she preferred nothingness over anguish.

Stopping her horse at the fork in the road, she uttered her first words in more than five hours. She was brief and to the point: "Will and I are riding on to Edinburgh to deliver the Royal Sceptre to the king. Tell Mum and Dad we'll be home later."

No one argued with her.

By the time Antonía and Will arrived at the gates of Edinburgh Castle, the sun had long since taken its final bow of the day and there was now only a smattering of stars lighting the Scottish sky. Will, in his capacity as top polyglot to the king, wasted no time in guiding his sister through the rambling hallways of the opulent, yet tastefully decorated, royal palace. Eventually reaching the entrance of an enormous dining hall, they were given the once-over by the king's ancient and irreverent butler, Alistair.

Knowing her dirty clothes and her disheveled appearance should embarrass her, Antonía realized once again she just didn't much care. As they waited to be shown in, Alistair gave her an icy smile.

"So you are the *purported* sister to the king?" Not waiting for a response, the decrepit butler continued. "The king shall not be at all pleased to discover that the blessings of good looks and stature have been bestowed solely upon you, Miss Barclay. As you will soon learn, our ruler comes up rather short in both areas, though admittedly, I could go into great lengths about his markedly agreeable personality."

After exchanging bewildered glances, Antonía and Will followed the sniggering nonagenarian through the vast territory of the dining hall. The room was large enough to seat an army, and probably had. Escorted to the head of the table, they quietly observed the Scottish royal family plowing into their evening supper with eager enthusiasm.

The king, thoroughly enmeshed in dissecting a hefty portion of haggis with a poker-like fork and a saw-like serrated knife, was completely unaware of his arriving guests. Peppering his speech with interesting little gastronomical tidbits, he offered a running commentary on the entrée.

"There's nothing like a hearty dish of sheep's organs mixed with oatmeal and onions to make a man feel like a king!" The monarch then looked down at his plate and boasted with epicurean delight, "But the real trick to the tasty treat of haggis is the culinary art of boiling the organs together in the eviscerated animal's stomach. Cooked properly and accompanied by mashed potatoes and turnips, my exclusive recipe yields a product with a superb nutty texture and an outstanding savory flavor."

"Ahem," Alistair said.

The king looked up, finally spotting his newly employed polyglot, and curtailed his thesis on Scottish haute cuisine.

"Will, my good fellow! Working late, are you? How rude of me! May I offer you a dish of haggis?"

Glancing down at the highly questionable comestible, Will stood open-mouthed for a moment, before making their excuses. "After hearing such an appetizing portrayal, I regret to say that our sister and I have already eaten supper, but we appreciate the generous offer, Your Majesty."

Nodding vigorously, the king resumed scarfing down his food, but unfortunately, his vigorous nodding coincided with swallowing, and consequently, he started to choke. And although the little king was choking fairly violently, his eyes widened in abject horror as his many servants rushed to render aid.

Antonia shuddered as the monarch swiftly summoned his strength and forced the entire lump of haggis down his esophagus in one massive swallow. After a remarkably speedy recovery, he stammered, red-faced, "N-now, wh-where is my s-s-sister? I m-must see her n-now!"

Clearing his throat, the butler bowed to the king and announced, "Sire, please allow me to introduce you to your *purported* sister, Miss Antonia Barclay."

After taking a deep breath, Antonia stepped into the candlelight, straightening to her full statuesque six feet of height. Everyone at the table looked upward, astonishment on their faces.

"You are my s-s-sister?" the king said. "You?"

Without ceremony, Antonia reached into the leather bag she held and took out the Scottish Royal Sceptre. She placed the artifact on the table in front of the king and then gave her half brother a terse nod of the head. "My job here is done. Good-bye, Your Majesty, so nice to meet you."

She curtseyed quickly, gestured to Will, and started walking toward the door with every intention of leaving. But after accomplishing only five long-legged strides in that direction, Antonia was thwarted by a kingly command.

"Not so fast, Miss Barclay," the king said. With a sigh, Antonia turned to face him, hands on her hips, only to see her new sibling staring down at the sceptre.

"Is this what I think it is?" he asked in a hushed voice. He picked up the object she had placed in front of him and rose from his chair.

"I suppose my response must hinge on what you *think* it is, Your Grace. I'm your purported sister, not your purported mind reader, you know."

Outwardly cringing at his sister's answer, Will promptly apologized to the king. Shaking his head, the good-natured little autocrat seemed to take it all in stride.

"No need for amends, Will. If Miss Barclay claims she is my sister and not my mind reader, I tend to believe her. Furthermore, if she were anything less than a Stuart, legend says she'd be incapable of returning the sceptre and reuniting it with the other royal implements in the royal vault." The king paused, his gaze on the object he held in his hand. "Frankly," he said, after drumming his fidgety fingers against his freckled cheek, "I'm not convinced there's any validity to the legend, but it certainly couldn't hurt to have the royal trio back together again."

Antonía responded brusquely. "Actually, sire, whether or not you believe in the legend, or for that matter, in our kinship, is irrelevant to me. The sole purpose of my visit is to fulfill a promise I made to Queen Mary."

Stifling a groan, Will started another profuse apology, but the kindly king waved him to silence and merely smiled up at his purported sister.

"I'm developing a decided kink in my neck, Miss Barclay," he complained pleasantly. "Please let us sit down."

Whereupon the diminutive but convivial king showed his guests into another room, directing them to four gargantuan, overstuffed upholstered chairs. After assuring their comfort in the first two chairs, he lowered his itsy bitsy bum into the fourth.

"This is much cozier, is it not?" Not waiting for an answer, he cleared his kingly throat and brought the meeting to order by putting his cards on the table. "Miss Barclay, I gather that you bear the Stuart birthmark upon the nape of your neck. Since I am obviously not female and therefore *not* bestowed with the familial female mark, I was wondering if I could take a gander at yours."

"And I gather with your gander that you'll be marking my identity rather than admiring my mark."

The king's response proved as rapid as it was peculiar. He popped out of his commodious chair, seized her by the hand, and led her across the room to a large mirrored wall. Too startled to rebel, Miss Barclay went along with the little man. Standing juxtaposed in front of the mirrored wall, the king began reciting a litany of sibling dissimilarities and incongruities.

"Shall we start with the obvious, Miss Barclay? You are tall, I am short. I am fair-haired, you are raven-haired. You have blue eyes, I have amber eyes. My skin is freckled, your skin is flawless. You are extraordinarily beautiful, I am . . . only slightly less so."

Looking pleased with his initial assessment, the king drew in a deep breath of hot air and continued, "Now that I have covered our physical differences, I shall next evince the differences in our dispositions. You are laconic, I am loquacious. I am affable, you are fractious. You are ill-tempered, I am good-tempered. I am agreeable, you are disagreeable. In conclusion, you are drop-dead gorgeous but a wee bit cranky."

He smiled at her reflection in the mirror, blinking his bright amber eyes at her. Against her will, a barely perceptible smile erupted from her stony countenance.

"Thank you for the comparative analysis, Your Grace. You have well established that while *you* have been blessed with all the personality of the family, *I* have been blessed with merely the looks. Is that correct?"

In a measured cadence, the king replied soberly, "That is not the point I intended to establish, Miss Barclay." Folding his scrawny arms across his sparrow chest, he peered upward. "What I *intended* to establish, albeit unsuccessfully, was that you and I are very dissimilar in both appearance and temperament, and consequently no one would ever believe that we were siblings, in the absence of objective proof."

"Oh, I'm sorry," she said, feeling a smidgen guilty about her unintended disparaging remark. "In light of the fact that you've worked so diligently in proving a point which I so sorely missed, my birthmark is yours for the viewing, sire." She turned her back to the king, lifted a profusion of dark silky hair, and allowed him a gander.

"Um, I can't quite . . ."

Hiding a smile, Antonía bent down, liking the man in spite of herself.

The king was obviously delighted. "An extraordinary nevus! Both in formation and design! Look at that perfectly shaped crown of pigmented skin gracing the nape of Miss Barclay's neck! And, of course, the most extraordinary fact of all is that your mark provides irrefutable proof that you are, indeed, my sister!"

The king gave her a devilish grin and proceeded to chip her about her gender. "I've always wanted a sibling, more specifically, a brother, but a sister will do in a pinch."

Having endured years of her brothers' juvenile remarks regarding her big, bold matching X-chromosomes, she was immune to criticism, facetious or otherwise, and rolling her eyes, Antonía made no response, verbal or otherwise.

The king stared at her for a long moment and then smiled apologetically. "I'm sorry, Miss Barclay, I was only joking—truly. Please don't be displeased with me."

Antonía inclined her head. "I'm not offended in the least, Your Majesty, but I must ask you an important question."

Will groaned out loud. "Please, Antonía," he pleaded, "he is the king."

"Fear not, Will," the king said. "I'm most confident I'll be able to withstand Antonía's inquiry in spite of any bluntness annexed to it."

Mirroring her royal brother's informal manner, Antonía warned, "Overconfidence is not a virtue, James."

Flatly taken aback by hearing his Christian name spoken sans title, the king's mouth dropped open. "Dear me," he said, "dear, dear me. So this is what it's like to have a sister! Scolding! Scalding even! I like it!"

Antonía sighed. She had the advantage of having been raised alongside three brothers, and she knew full well the rights, privileges, and tribulations attached to the sibling relationship. Accordingly, she didn't hesitate to hurl a barrage of pent-up hostility his way.

"Why haven't you negotiated the release of our mother?" she demanded.

King James blinked in surprise. "Indeed, my dear sister, you get right to the point!"

"It mitigates the likelihood of the point being missed," she replied.

The king narrowed his eyes in contemplation. "I'm not certain whether your remark was intended as self-deprecation relating to your lack of perspicacity or harsh disparagement relating to my lack of perspicuity."

"Neither, your grace," she replied. "I seek only an honest answer to my question."

"Fair enough," he said, with a slight bow, "I shall honor your question and treat it with the respect it deserves. But first, let's sit back down. My neck is starting to make creaking noises every time I look up at you." The king rubbed his noisy neck, and then, as if no longer able to restrain himself, cried out, "Good heavens, you're tall! Whatever did the Barclays put in your porridge?"

Disallowing digression of any sort, Antonía remained silent and inscrutable.

"Indeed, I gather you're not going to divulge the secret of your height—at least not until after I address your question." Antonía raised a single eyebrow in affirmation.

The king sank back into his chair beside Antonía and presented his defense in a deliberate, somber tone.

"I have not seen our mother since I was an infant. Suffice it to say I don't remember her, much less know her. However, upon my ascension to the throne, my first and only goal was to gain the queen's freedom. In the ensuing years, I negotiated with a succession of English counsels, advisors, diplomats, bureaucrats, and supernumeraries, and each and every one of them granted me assurances and promises, all of which ultimately proved as worthless and disappointing as they were."

Antonía glared at the little man, wondering if he were lying. After all, he was a born politician.

But the king looked straight into her eyes and said with the utmost sincerity, "I swear to you that despite myriad obstacles and myriad obtuse advisors, I never once surrendered my efforts to secure our mother's release." He reached over and placed his hand on hers. "That is, until a few months ago when the queen somehow succeeded in smuggling a letter to me."

"She gets around," commented Antonía. "It's quite impressive."

"You may read the queen's correspondence anytime you wish, but the thrust of her letter entreated me, most vehemently, to curtail all efforts in securing her release. In fact, I believe it fair to say that our mother *begged* me to cease all attempts to free her. She wrote very poignantly regarding her desire not to cause strife and turmoil for the Scottish monarchy and stressed that she considered Chartley Hall her final home, at least in this world."

"You're saying she didn't want to leave prison?" Antonía knew he was telling the truth, because that was exactly what Mary had told her. Still, she wished to hear his full account.

"She emphatically stated that she was not martyring herself in any way and her decision was a conscious, deliberate choice made of her own free will. For weeks I read and reread her letter, struggling to come to terms with it, until eventually, my wise and insightful wife persuaded me to accept and honor my mother's wishes." The king waited a few moments and then leaned anxiously toward his sister. "I believe it's your turn to inform me that I've royally blundered," he said earnestly.

The faintest of smiles passed over Antonía's face. "As much as I'd enjoy delineating the error of your ways, and although I'm quite certain there are many unrelated issues to which blame could easily be affixed to you, I cannot in good faith find fault with your decision regarding our mother. Please permit me to assuage your conscience by assuring you that the sentiments our mother expressed to you in her letters perfectly match the sentiments she expressed to me in conversation."

With her resentment abated and her energy depleted, Antonía dropped her head wearily into her hands, and apologized to the king.

"James, I'm truly sorry for my shabby behavior. I accused you before I met you, I convicted you before I afforded you a word, and I punished you before I understood your position. Indeed, I've exhibited such a blatant disregard for your rights that I might as well have stomped all over the Magna Carta with a pair of muddy riding boots firmly fastened to my feet. You, on the other hand, have treated me with nothing less than open cordiality, unconditional kindness, and unstinting generosity. To be perfectly honest, I feel like an absolute bitc—"

"Whoa there, Antonía," the king interrupted. "You may be culpable of many offenses, but the Queen of England you are not! There is no cause to drag yourself over the coals simply because you've spoken your mind. Frankly, I find your forthright attitude delightfully refreshing. Indeed, we kings are subjected to such constant and obsequious bootlicking—mud notwithstanding—that it's extremely difficult to discern friends from foes."

Antonía bowed her dark head and replied in earnest, "Thank you, Your Majesty, you are very gracious and generous to forgive me." She hesitated slightly before asking, "I have one more question, however." The king smiled and nodded. "Our mother believes that now that the Royal Sceptre is in your possession, Scotland's future will be bright and successful. Do *you*, sire, believe this too?"

King James looked down at the sceptre he held, and then back up at his sister. "Honestly, I do not know, Antonía. However, I do know that I believe in our mother." He held up the sceptre. "Thank you. I know you went through great peril to retrieve this for Scotland, *and me*. I shall not forget it."

Happily convinced that he'd relieved his sister of her self-inflicted guilt, the king was both shocked and horrified when he observed Antonía's entire body begin to rattle and shake in a series of violent tremors. The king's eyes widened in alarm and he turned to Will, gesturing to Antonía with the flutter of both hands.

Will rose quickly and pulled Antonía up and into his arms. "Antonía has had a rough go of it lately, Your Majesty. She discovered her true lineage, she broke into an English prison to visit your mother, she was kidnapped two or three times—I lost count—and then, just a few days ago, Claymore, the man she was to marry, was killed at Ford Castle. She took it hard—but don't worry, she'll recover—it's just a little posttraumatic fallout. She's not adept at crying—she releases emotion after the fact by shaking like a leaf. She's been afflicted with trembling turns since she was a little girl; she'll settle down soon—she's actually quite hearty, quite stout."

But despite Will's explanation, the king looked anything but reassured. Will continued to offer assurances. "Truly, sire, she'll be fine. She gets the collywobbles anytime she's overwrought, overtired, and underfed. It'll pass; it always does. It just takes a little time."

Moments later, and much to the king's astonishment and relief, Antonía's trembling gradually slowed to a slightly less violent level.

"Indeed, I know just the thing to cheer you up, dear sister!" exclaimed the king. "My queen and I shall host a ball in your honor, say . . ." He paused, bobbled his head back and forth, and eventually shook out a date. "Tomorrow night!"

Antonía went completely still while her tiny brother continued his effusion.

"Beautiful young ladies always delight in dressing up in fine frocks and fripperies and dancing the night away! A royal ball in your honor will prove a surefire cure for your troubles, my dear. Social activity always disperses melancholy!" He looked about him with a distracted air and muttered, "The controlled study is floating around here somewhere if you're interested in verifying the validity of my claim." The warm-hearted king then took his sister's hand, patted it gently, and asked, "Don't you feel a tincture better now, my dear? Looking forward to an exciting event always fends off the glums, does it not?"

She took a deep breath and managed a smile. "Yes, you're right, James, and thank you. You're immensely thoughtful." And, displaying only a scintilla of forced pleasure to which the king remained happily innocent, she added, "My family and I shall be honored to attend your ball."

But while her tongue oozed nectar, her mind spun hemlock. Honored as she might be by the king's expression of kindness, Antonía was most decidedly displeased about attending his ball. However, considering she had abused her royal brother so atrociously upon first meeting, Antonía was resolute in her decision to accept his gesture of goodwill, and moreover, she'd do so with good grace.

Although it would be an act on her part, and an excruciatingly painful one at that, Antonía Margaret Caroline Barclay, sister of King James VI of Scotland, resolved to wear the finest designer gown, exude the warmest air of civility, and dance every dance with the gayest of feet.

She groaned inwardly. She couldn't bear to think of the effort it would take to pull it all off.

Later that same evening, Antonía was welcomed back to Barclay Castle.

Lord and Lady Barclay repeatedly assured their daughter that despite her royal blood lines, it would be impossible for them to love her any *more* or any *less*. She was their daughter, had always been their daughter, and would always be their daughter—no matter what her molecular makeup.

But although Lord and Lady Barclay thanked Heaven above for their daughter's safe return, her misadventure had cost them plenty in terms of tribulation and sleepless nights. As a result, they'd asked her to please, please abstain from all forms of reckless behavior for the rest of her life.

Her other family members and friends had a variety of reactions to her news of being the daughter of Queen Mary.

With all due respect to their sister's monarchial ancestry, her brothers expressed their sincere wish that she'd be able to condescend to live amongst them. Their sister informed them that she could certainly do that, if and only if, a certain amount of carefully circumscribed decorum was followed. In other words, her brothers were required to bow and scrape each and every time she entered or exited a room.

Her brothers assured her that as much as they wished to demonstrate the appropriate acts of worship, they were currently suffering from very painful knee ailments caused by chasing their troublesome sister around the countryside, so would she mind very much if, instead of genuflecting, they just cussed each time she entered a room and cheered every time she exited?

Their sister assured them that if this alternate form of reverence was followed, she now possessed the power to order their executions at the slightest provocation. In fact, the quality of her brothers' lives, as well as their very existence, hinged upon her whims and fancies of the moment; and since it was common knowledge that royal blue blood surged through her pedigreed veins, it was protocol for her to practice random acts of cruelty.

Moreover, she was not only expected to practice random acts of cruelty, but to thrive on them as well. Her brothers were therefore on notice, effective immediately, that their fates rested precariously in her hands. She hoped they didn't mind very much. A royal could never have too many holds on capricious fun.

Minnie Munro, despite being tubercular and far, far past her bloom, showed remarkable agility by tackling Antonía as soon as she walked through the door. Having previously learned of her ducky's bad treatment at the hands of Throckmorton and son, Minnie treated the subject as strictly taboo and thus refrained from plying Antonía with questions even remotely related. Instead, the old woman played a happier tune by harping on the superexcellent news that the Throckmortons were, presently and forever, frying in Hell. And since Antonía had returned, Minnie knew she'd be once again rolling in tobacco.

Claire MacMillan, conspicuous in her absence from Antonía's homecoming, was at that very moment returning from Dundee, where her father had been shrewdly investing a considerable chunk of his fortune in the promising industries of the three j's—i.e., jam, jute, and journalism. Although originally intending to stay a fortnight, Mr. MacMillan had immediately concluded his business dealings upon receiving word of Antonía's return. Herding his brood into an exceedingly commodious carriage, he ordered his driver to haul-ass back home, albeit in a much more courteous fashion.

Claire, having been informed of all events regarding her best friend, including the oh-so-exciting king's ball and the oh-so-sad demise of Mr. Claymore, instantly anointed herself healer, therapist, and, of course, stylist to the aggrieved party. With so much work to do, Claire couldn't get back to Barclay Castle fast enough. Was there anyone in the world more driven than a woman on a mission? Indeed, *no.*

After allowing her parents, her brothers, and her best friend to assure themselves that Antonía was indeed back to stay, her emotionally charged first day back home was mercifully coming to a close. The late summer night felt crisp to the touch and lovely to the eye, but unfortunately these admirable climatic traits went virtually unnoticed by the bereaved beauty.

Now alone in her turret bedchamber, her grief resurfaced to fill the emptiness within her, the void left by Claymore's death. For hours she tossed and turned, unable to calm her grieving mind. But she knew that despite her overwhelming sorrow, she needed a good night's sleep for the ball tomorrow night. Thus, after carefully balancing the risks and benefits, Antonía decided it reasonably prudent under the circumstances to swallow her pain. Accordingly, she trotted off to the wine cellar.

Once returned to the solitude of her room, Miss Barclay crawled into a lonely bed and downed the first glass of wine with remarkable ease . . . and the second and third proved equally effortless . . . and then rather suddenly, her perspective changed. No longer did she view the world through a prism of pain . . . *she drifted off to sleep . . .*

She was enveloped in a heaven-sent mist of pine . . . she inhaled deeply . . . indeed, a heaven-scented mist of pine . . . she felt the comforting weight of his body on hers . . . his lips traveling tenderly over the slope of her shoulder . . . across the smooth plain of her throat . . . moving up to her awaiting lips . . . his hands caressing the contour of her breasts . . . slowly making their way downward . . . hugging the gentle curve of her hips . . . she placed a single forefinger upon the perimeter of his perfectly formed ear and traced its outline over and over again . . . until . . . she felt his love lift her up . . . to heights she'd never known . . . he was carrying her higher and higher on silent wings . . . until . . . she became paralyzed with pleasure . . . and then she felt it . . . the shudder of intense ecstasy surging through her body and implanting itself deep within her soul . . . together . . . until . . .

The soothing mist of her altered state slowly but steadily evaporated into the cruel desert of her reality.

Claire MacMillan had arrived with a vengeance.

"Get your skinny ass out of bed, *right now!*"

"Oh, no," she moaned from under a sea of blankets. "It's morning. I must still be alive."

"Although you *are* still alive, it's no longer morning," corrected Claire. "It's three in the afternoon. And you're going to the ball tonight whether you like it or not! So don't even think about avoiding it!"

Surfacing from the depths of bedcoverings, Antonía pushed her hair from her face. "As much as I hate to disappoint you, I have every intention of attending the ball tonight."

Claire spied the empty wine bottles on the bedside table. "You're hungover," she said, narrowing her eyes at Antonía. "Precisely when did you start drinking?"

"It was the work of the moment, but I'm not precisely sure *which* moment," replied Antonía honestly. And then, lowering her voice to barely a whisper, because her head was killing her, she admitted, "A day or two ago, I was seriously considering joining the nunnery, but I now realize I'm better suited for the winery."

"So it would seem," Claire said. Her frown softened and she sat down on the bed beside her friend. "Antonía, I'm so sorry."

Claire's kindness broke the carefully constructed wall around her heart, and Antonía cradled her head in her hands as she poured out her pain to her dearest friend.

"Without Mr. Claymore, the entire world seems depopulated. I miss him so much I can't breathe . . . I can't sleep . . . I can't eat." She paused briefly and then confessed, "But I *can* drink—so I plundered the wine cellar and drank until I fell asleep. Anytime I woke up, I simply quaffed down a wee bit more until I fell back to sleep. Not a pretty picture, I admit, but it seemed the only solution at the time. As for tonight and every night hereafter, I cannot help but think that being dead drunk will help far more than being stone-cold sober." She reached over for an unopened bottle of wine.

Seizing Antonía's arm, Claire removed the bottle from her grasp and set it out of reach. "I cannot tell you how much I regret Mr. Claymore's passing, but paving your footsteps to the grave with a plethora of fine wine will neither resurrect him, nor make him proud of you from above. Excessive drinking only exacerbates heartache. Moreover and more importantly, drinking proves a bad habit and a most unflattering one, particularly in a woman." She stood and pulled back the bedding with great panache, commanding Antonía in no uncertain terms. "Since you are clearly incapable of making prudent decisions, I shall make them for you. Get out of bed, get dressed, and get outside."

For some reason, Claire's authoritative attitude gave Antonía a sense of security. Taking another deep breath, she gave her a grateful smile. "I must hand it to you, Claire. At least you have some semblance of a plan for my future, which is a lot more than I can say for myself." Sitting up, she stumbled out of bed, her legs wobbling as she weaved her way in and out of the closet—with admirable finesse, considering her compromised state. She looked down at the dress she held, wondering how it had gotten there.

Shaking her head at her disheveled friend's gross motor skills, Claire took the dress from her hands and began to help her dress. "We're going to sober you up before your parents discover your ridiculous remedy for insomnia. And for your information, the curative value of walking in the fresh air is remarkably high for excessive drinking."

Once Antonía was properly attired, Claire took her by the arm and guided her out of the room and down the stairs. Feeling a wee bit tetchy, Antonía swung round to file her dissenting opinion, but in doing so, she nearly fell flat on her face on the very last step.

"Good God, you're a mess," Claire said.

"Damn, I forgot about that last step," grumbled the unsteady Antonía. "Is this the bottom step to the landing or the bottom step to the foyer?"

On the brink of responding with another really supportive remark, Claire stopped short when Lord Barclay's stentorian voice thundered through the castle. Addressing his wife, he boomed, "Cassandra, I've just come from the wine cellar and we're missing some of our best wine—two of which I had specifically earmarked for the king's party! Do you know where the hell they've run off to?" He then made a beeline for his wife, who was passing through the foyer.

Claire swiftly revised their exit strategy, turning Antonía around and practically dragging her out the castle's back entrance. After making their escape, the two girls made their way to a small hill overlooking a lily pond.

Antonía stopped and massaged her pounding head. "Let's go back. My head's killing me and the path is getting slippery."

"The more fresh air the better, " Claire said, turning her friend in the direction of the pond. "Keep moving." She then gave Antonía a little push from behind. "You go first."

Antonía grumbled but complied. Struggling to keep her footing, she half-tripped down the path, caught her foot on an exposed tree root, landed on her backside, and slid inelegantly into the pond.

Arriving at water's edge, Claire stared down at her. "The cold water will work wonders on your puffy eyes, Antonía."

Far from turning the world on with her smile, Antonía glowered at her friend in a most unfriendly way.

Undaunted, Claire added, "It'll help with the odor, too. You were smelling a wee bit gamy."

For a moment, Antonía glowered again, but then had a better idea. "Well, in that case," she said, pulling off her clothes and throwing them ashore, "I'd better do the job right."

Claire shrugged, gathering her friend's garments and draping them carefully over some bushes to dry. "Antonía," she hesitated and then

continued in a more serious tone, "Matthew told me most of what happened to you in England, but he was rather vague on how Basil and Rex
Throckmorton met their doom."

Treading water, Antonía replied, "Let's just say my Scottish claymore
and I played a contributory role in both their exits."

"Do you care to be more specific?" said Claire, placing her hands
firmly on her hips.

Antonía pooled a small amount of water into her mouth and sprayed
it out, fountain style. "If you really want to know the gory details, you'll
have to join me."

"This I've got to hear!" Whereupon Claire removed her designer dress,
folded it neatly, and plunged headlong into the lilies.

Breck Claymore rode hard and fast through the border country of Scotland. Ignoring external stimuli, his mind was consumed by a single
thought—the thought of her. Nothing else mattered and nothing else
would ever matter more to him than the thought of her. The fact that she
supposed him dead tore his heart to shreds. Queen Mary and Reverend
Goode protested his departure, claiming he was too weak to travel. But in
the end, Claymore had prevailed, and his caregivers had no choice other
than to bandage his wound tightly and bid farewell.

His thoughts returned to Miss Barclay, and God have mercy on the
man who doubts what he's sure of, because it was with agonizing introspection that he began to entertain serious doubts about Miss Barclay's
love for him. With all that she'd been through, all the time she'd spent
away, all the distance between them, was it possible that her love for
him had diminished or, God forbid, ceased altogether? And this was the
unbearable, tormenting question that plagued him for the remainder of
his journey to Barclay Castle. Without her love, he felt like a dead man
walking . . . well, riding.

However, by the time Claymore pounded upon the castle door, he
had shoved aside all doubts. He meant business. He was once again

determined to prove that not only was he a man who perpetually planned for victory, but he perpetually achieved it.

Accordingly, Claymore, who waited as patiently as a man violently in love could be expected to wait before breaking the damn door down, was just about to do the deed when Minnie Munro opened it, saving it from certain destruction. After expelling a cough that sounded oddly debilitating and vigorous all at the same time, the old lady put her hand to her heart, her eyes brightening as she gazed up at him.

"Aye, if it isn't the late Mr. Breck Claymore! I'm overjoyed to see you! And I happen to know of a young lass who'll be overjoyed to see you as well!" The old nanny spread open her arms and threw herself against him, crying out, "There was a rumor bruited about town declaring you dead!"

Encapsulating the little old lady in his muscular embrace, Claymore chuckled. "Minnie, I'm surprised at you. I didn't take you for the type to listen to malicious gossip."

"Aye, Breck, but I only listen to gossip so as to nip it in the bud. And as for spreading gossip, I prefer to look at it as the dissemination of vital information." She then added tit for tat, "And by the way, I didn't take you for the type to stand about chattering with a doddering old lady while your bonny lass attends a ball in Edinburgh without you!"

Claymore blinked in disbelief. "Miss Barclay is attending a ball?" he asked, feeling a smattering of pain. He was dead, but she was dancing? "Voluntarily?"

Minnie supplied the details with merciful swiftness. "Please don't get the wrong idea, Breck. Antonía's brother, King James, insisted on holding a royal ball in her honor. As you can imagine, our Antonía was *not at all* receptive to his well-meaning overture, but feeling duty-bound to accept the invitation, she feigned enthusiasm."

"But what possible reason could induce Miss Barclay to attend so soon after—" Suddenly embarrassed by the vector of his question, he stopped midsentence.

Minnie, who was no slouch in the workings of the heart department, coughed productively and then finished his thought for him. "So soon after your rumored death?" He nodded reluctantly.

"Aye, Breck. Let me tell you here and now that our Antonía has been an absolute mess since the moment she supposed you dead to this world. She cannot sleep! She cannot eat!" Minnie paused, frowning. "Well . . . she can't sleep without first quaffing down impressive quantities—even by my standards—of her father's fine wine! Then, of course, my poor ducky can't wake up without Claire dragging her out of bed and throwing her into the pond buck naked!"

The old gal then wagged a reproving finger at him and remonstrated, "So don't you think for one second, darlin', that your lass hasn't been grieving for you. Your death has made her thoroughly miserable! These past few days have proven a wretched time for her, as well as for the lot of us who've stood witness to her state of abject wretchedness!"

Claymore felt relief rush over him. Not that he wanted his sweet Antonía to feel pain, but—yes, he admitted it—to know she had grieved his death so wholeheartedly and with such dedication reassured him of her love for him.

"I even overheard my ducky talking about joining a nunnery!" Minnie went on. "Of all the crazy notions!"

Claymore laughed at the thought of that. His Antonía in a nunnery— he stopped laughing. "She hasn't joined one, has she?"

She waved his question away with one hand. "No, no. Her brothers wouldn't allow it. Believe me, Breck, the only reason Antonía agreed to the ball was to make amends with the king. Apparently, she was so bereft over your alleged demise that she became a wee bittie contentious with our wee bittie monarch. So, as you can see, this whole situation is entirely your fault!"

He nodded. "Minnie, I couldn't agree with you more. Every drop of blame should be placed squarely on my shoulders."

"And magnificent shoulders they are, laddie! So, when do you plan to let her know you're still amongst the living?"

"Immediately, if not sooner."

"You certainly do love that lass, don't you?"

With a twinkle in his eye, he answered, "Like you wouldn't believe." He then bowed and offered his arm to the old nanny. "Miss Munro, would you care to accompany me to Edinburgh for the wedding?"

"Wedding is it?" Smiling so widely all her snaggy teeth were exposed, she laid one hand on his arm and squeezed. "As much as I approve of your plan and appreciate your offer, these old bones of mine prove far too rickety to make such a trip in the middle of the day, much less in the middle of the night." She took his hands in hers and commanded him heartily. "Now go and marry your lass. I wish you joy o' her!"

Claymore needed no further urging. With a smile, he leaned down and kissed her on the cheek and headed out the door.

Standing at the doorway, Minnie watched the handsome young man set forth on his mission with exceedingly attractive masculine determination. As he rode into the night, she said wistfully to the clean outdoor air, "I wish I were a wee bit younger, a wee bit less tubercular, and a wee bit less of a chain-smoking alcoholic."

Whereupon the old girl went inside, lit her pipe, and poured herself some whiskey. After inhaling a puff gratefully, downing a shot blissfully, and reconsidering her wish list carefully, she said cheerfully to the smoky indoor air, "Nah."

Chapter 21

COMPLETELY IN CALLIGRAPHY

"Can we go home now, *please?*"

"What are you talking about?" demanded Claire. "We just arrived! And by the way, what happened to your resolve to exude an air of warm civility? And to exchange pleasantries with everyone you meet?"

"My resolve eroded exponentially when I realized the entire population of Edinburgh was invited," said Antonía. "I can barely breathe in here." Glancing over at her friend, she couldn't help but admire her friend's dazzling fashion sense, even if she did feel like she was about to faint.

Claire was gorgeously attired in a size 00 Coco Chanel antecessor, accompanied by an altitudinous pair of size 6 Christian Louboutin forerunners. She laughed unsympathetically and stated in her usual pragmatic fashion, "Oh, Antonía, it's not all the people. It's just your corset. Perhaps I strapped you in a mite too tight, but you'll be fine."

"My God, Claire," scoffed Antonía. "If you don't loosen it, I'm going to faint."

"I'll do no such thing!" snipped Claire, "Just look at the waspish waist I've given you."

"Then I'm taking it completely off," Antonía threatened, turning to leave.

"Honestly, Antonía, you can be so stubborn!" Claire stomped one dainty foot in exasperation. "Follow me."

Claire led the way to the nearest vacant sitting room, closed the door, and promptly loosened the corset's tight stays. "Good heavens, Antonía! Your beauty is truly wasted on you. You should know by now that even natural beauty requires a certain amount of pain and suffering. *Pour être belle il faut souffrir!* " she cried solemnly.

"Still prone to bouts of Francophilia, *chère* Claire?" Antonía remarked, and then inhaled gratefully, but briefly, when an abrupt rap rattled the door.

"Antonía! This is your father speaking. Unless you've swooned onto the floor, I expect you to get yourself out here immediately. The king has requested the honor of your presence *now*. The little fellow is chomping at the bit to present you to his court and all of his guests."

Antonía felt a wave of intense anxiety sweep over her as Claire continued to advise her. "Stop worrying, Antonía. I know you despise being the center of attention, but as we all know, people attend balls for the sole purpose of quaffing down as much of the host's liquor as possible. It's a completely parasitic relationship, so trust me when I tell you that the crapulous crowd will take scant notice of you."

"Thank God for the dregs of high society," she replied dryly.

Claire fixed her with a stern eye. "Listen to me closely. You need *not* be the life of the party. Just aim for quiet dignity."

Unconvinced, Antonía began to think out loud. "I'm thinking liberty. I'm thinking freedom. I'm thinking escape. I'm thinking . . . *back door.*"

Claire folded her arms firmly across her chest. Antonía bit down nervously on her lower lip. Now it was official. Claire had had it.

Scowling her response in such an effective manner as to make words totally unnecessary, Claire's victory came instantaneously. Sighing deeply and resignedly, Antonía accepted her doom.

Thrusting open the door, she proceeded to blast out of it with such alarming speed and determined force that she very nearly obliterated her family in the process.

With irritation, Antonía noted that her entrance into the ballroom produced the usual domino effect of dropping jaws. Starting in the back of the room and rippling forward to the throne, jaws dropped in rapid succession as she did her best to float elegantly through the doorway, weave gracefully through the capacity crowd, and come to a standstill before the king and queen of Scotland, where she sank into a deep curtsey.

All musical instruments quieted, all dancing feet stilled, and all chitter-chatter ceased as the musicians and guests appeared to sense a momentous event in the making. King James hurried down the steps leading to the throne and proffered his hand. Antonía took it and rose to her six vertical feet of pure, unadulterated Scottish beauty. The crowd stared at her in awe and she gave a little mental shrug. *I guess we can't all be beauties.*

Her brother made a valiant stab at disarming the situation. "Indeed, Antonía, you succeeded in selecting a very suitable family for yourself. You resemble the Barclay clan much more than your own blood brother— namely, me!"

It took no longer than a few seconds for a collective audible gasp to rumble through the crowd like a threatening thunderstorm, and Antonía rolled her eyes as gossipmongers, blatherskites, and all such evil kindred spirits took diabolical delight in this decidedly delicious disclosure. Had the king actually confessed to having a sister? If he did, she must be illegitimate!

Several agonizing minutes later, her new brother made it clear that Miss Antonía Barclay was the *legitimate* half sister of the king. The little imperial man then declared that Miss Barclay wished to live her life in relative obscurity, without royal title, without royal privileges, and without royal burdens. The king was equally adamant in declaring that if any of his subjects interfered with his sister's privacy in any manner whatsoever, they could count on setting sail to a whole New World.

With all explanations communicated and all attendant warnings issued, the music resumed and the ball rolled on. Watching her family scatter in various directions, Antonía turned in relief to follow her parents. But relief did not appear to be the order of the moment. Standing in place, she glanced over to one side of the room and saw Matthew locking Claire into a secure, warm embrace. By the look of it, neither of them could keep their hands off the other. *Wedding bells will be ringing for those two any day now,* thought Antonía. She scanned the room for her parents, eager to be safe in their company, but they seemed to have evaporated into the crowd.

Hoping to find Lord and Lady Barclay at the buffet table, she pivoted her head toward the back of the room but was surprised to discover her oldest brother, Will, talking to—of all people—Sophie McGill! Claire's pixie-sized blonde cousin from Aberdeen! Antonía watched with equal shares of horror and astonishment as her brother appeared to be pontificating and Sophie seemed to be enjoying it. Antonía couldn't bear another second of it. She started for the door. Perhaps her parents were touring the palace wine cellar.

But another surprise was in store for Antonía. As she walked purposely across the floor, she stopped abruptly at the sight of her youngest brother, Oliver, whisking away none other than Lucy Corbett onto the dance floor. Antonía couldn't believe it! How in heaven's name had Gus's granddaughter gotten here? But she had little opportunity to speculate on the mystery.

With love and romance blooming everywhere except in her garden, Antonía's spinster status reared up and stabbed her hard in the heart. With Mr. Claymore dead, she faced life alone, without a partner. She felt her grief resurfacing. But she couldn't fall apart at the ball—with everyone watching her! Antonía bolted for the door. The king, however, had other plans.

Catching her wrist, he tucked it neatly under his arm and guided Antonía outside onto the palace's mezzanine balcony. But the king's timing, and topic of conversation, could not have been worse. He said, "Please allow me to extend my deepest sympathies regarding Mr. Claymore's passing. I am very sorry for your loss, my dear sister, and if I can do anything to alleviate your distress, I shall gladly do so. You have only to ask, Antonía."

Antonía had not shed one single solitary tear since Mr. Claymore's demise, but now it was inevitable. She'd predicted that her breakdown would happen at the most inconvenient, inopportune time possible, and she was right. Slowly but steadily, she felt her tears, the sorrowful manifestation of a tragic loss and a future lost, tumble down her face.

Her royal brother looked absolutely beside himself with distress. He seized her forearm with one hand while frantically flagging down his butler with the other. Alistair continued his approach in his usual measured manner.

"Sire, I bring you news," Alistair said, and then paused, lifting one brow.

"Yes, yes, what is it, man?" the king demanded.

"Your sister's purported husband has arrived."

Looking thoroughly flustered by the announcement, James spun back toward his sister. "Antonía, you're married? I did not know that!"

"Nor did I," said Antonía, her tears slowing from a torrent to a trickle at the newsflash.

"My dear sister, you've been under considerable strain of late. It's completely understandable if your marital status merely slipped your mind."

Antonía shook her head emphatically. "No, of course I'm not married. That's one little detail I would not be likely to forget. I may bend under strain, but I never break."

The king sought to reassure her. "Fear not, Antonía! If you should find your husband to be the least bit disagreeable, I shall promptly have him thrown over the balcony and into the moat!"

"Thank you, James, that's a comfort," she said. "Well, I suppose I should see who this imposter is, shouldn't I?" Turning to the aged butler, she lifted her own questioning brow. "Alistair, would you please take me to my purported husband?"

"Certainly, Miss Barclay, it would be my pleasure," he replied, offering his arm.

Navigating their way through the congested ballroom, Alistair cleared his throat and, to her shock, showed signs of being almost human. "Miss Barclay, please allow me to apologize for referring to you as the king's *purported* sister. I have known your mother, Queen Mary, from the time she was a young woman, and there is no question in my mind: You *are* her daughter. You and your dear mother share many of the same qualities and mannerisms. In fact, the similarities are quite extraordinary."

She looked keenly into his eyes. "And, of course, the similarity of our birthmarks provides irrefutable proof of my authenticity."

"Aye," answered Alistair with a rare broad grin. "And I commented to the king that *your* reputation—rather than his—would suffer from your newly established kinship."

Antonía smiled and remarked, "I'm sure your comment was well received."

He frowned thoughtfully as he continued to lead her through the throng. "You see, Miss Barclay, I have known your brother all of his days, and I've considered it my lifelong duty to treat him as normally as possible in order to imbue him with a sense of humility. By God, I was not going to allow his inherently humble nature to become sullied by his own celebrity!" He paused and remarked with a sigh, "So seldom is humility superadded to the kingly profession."

Antonía stopped walking and placed her hand on the old man's arm, bringing him to a stop as well. "Without your stabilizing influence, Alistair, I fear our king may have turned into a terrible little tyrant, rather than the intelligent, charitable monarch he proves himself to be."

Alistair smiled warmly and, without a trace of his trademark irreverence, replied, "And you, my dear Miss Barclay, have already proven an excellent influence on our little king. Between the two of us, just imagine what we can accomplish." She smiled in agreement.

The nonagenarian and the statuesque beauty resumed their progression through the heavily peopled ballroom, until Antonía stopped with an audible gasp. A man stood a few yards away, and he was looking straight at her.

Without warning, she was overcome by a vertiginous blend of joy and disbelief. She didn't understand . . . she didn't see how it was possible . . . she couldn't reconcile what she saw with what she knew . . . with what she *thought* she knew . . . until she came to the wretched and inescapable conclusion that there could be only one explanation: *She had gone completely mad!*

It had finally happened. Her inexorable grief had overchallenged her psyche. Her weeping soul had swept away her mind in a torrent of sorrow. Her nerves had shattered into tiny microscopic shards and were now lying in a heap of anguish upon the palace floor!

As Antonía moved to stand before the ghostly apparition, she could've sworn she heard her father exclaim rather indignantly, "Why didn't someone tell me he was alive? It would've saved me several bottles of imported fine wine!"

Then her mother's soothing voice replied, "No one told you, darling, because no one supposed him alive. This is a miraculous revelation to us all!"

As warm maternal sentiments have a tendency to do when emotions run high, Lady Barclay's words triggered a recrudescence of her daughter's crying jag. Consequently, as relief washed over Antonía and ecstasy flooded through her, teardrops once again slid down her cheeks. She was beginning to believe her eyes, and they were telling her with unequivocal certitude that Mr. Claymore was very much alive.

And it was in the crucible of that moment when she felt her world, slowly but surely, turn right-side up. Now fully restored to a normal upright position, Antonía silently thanked God for the return of her Mr. Claymore who, though sometimes late, *always* got the job done.

As she stared at her partner in love, she heard her brother Oliver implore his majesty.

"Why is she crying, sire? Dare I say this is the happy part?"

The king squandered no time in placing his wee little self in between Antonía and the physically magnificent newcomer and offered his assurances to Oliver.

"No need to worry, young fellow. Our sister was already on a roll long before setting eyes upon our new guest." Peering upward, the king queried, "The late Mr. Claymore, I presume?"

"Yes, sire," replied the Scotsman. He turned to Antonía and added, with a gentle smile, "but I do hope I'm in time."

With a faint grin, the king bowed slightly and removed himself from between the two.

Antonía looked up into the tall Highlander's eyes, and the burning blue blaze of his eyes pervaded her soul with such profound passion and intense potency that she damn near fainted on the palace floor.

"Mr. Claymore," she said, on the whisper of a sigh, just as he lowered his lips to hers.

But her royal brother laughed so loudly and unexpectedly that it caused Antonía to pivot her head away from Mr. Claymore, and she experienced only a soft brushing of his kiss. The little monarch then seized her hand, turned her toward the crowd, and called for goblets of wine to toast the couple.

After every guest in the great hall had received their goblet of wine, the king raised his goblet and made an eloquent toast, first to Mr. Claymore—expounding upon his bravery and courage in the face of English treachery, and then to his sister—praising her for her fortitude and strength against the evil Throckmortons.

Breck Claymore bowed in appreciation, while Antonía continued to hold fast to his arm, as if she feared he might die on her again if she let go.

"And now," the little monarch continued, "perhaps you would be so kind as to announce your intentions toward my sister?" He squinted the long way up at Claymore.

"My intentions, Your Majesty," Claymore said, "remain true and steadfast—to marry Miss Barclay." He grinned and made an elaborate bow toward the king. "With your permission, sire, of course." He glanced over at Lord and Lady Barclay. "I've already received parental and, I hope, fraternal consent?" He moved his gaze to the three brothers and they lifted their goblets to him in solidarity at last. His gaze drifted down to the woman at his side and she smiled up at him, opened her beautiful lips to speak, and—

"Marry my sister?" interrupted the king. "Indeed, sir, I do believe that first you have a lot of explaining to do before I even permit you to glance in Miss Barclay's vicinity!"

Claymore had little choice other than to tear his eyes away from his beloved Antonía and redirect them farther down toward his future royal brother-in-law, who, at this juncture, was in a state of full rant.

"Mr. Claymore," said the king in a stern tone, "do you realize that your ostensible death has driven my sister to indulge in the immoralities of drinking in excess, sleeping in excess, and swimming naked in excess? And to top it off, she's threatening to join any nunnery willing to overlook all of her excesses!"

Claymore glanced back at Antonía and saw her blue eyes widen. He smiled and turned back to the impatient little king who was presently tapping his tiny foot in agitated perturbation.

"Yes, sire," Claymore said at last, "I have heard accounts of your sister's excesses and I love her excessively for each and every one of them. In fact,

I am deeply, desperately, and inconsolably in love with Miss Barclay, and I would sooner stop breathing than live my life without her."

At which point, each and every person in the room—of the female persuasion—sighed contentedly at the Highlander's proclamation of true love. The king, however, once more demanded further explanation.

"Indeed, sir, that is the question, is it not? How is it that you still breathe? Why are you not dead? Reports of your survival have been not only grossly underestimated but completely nonexistent! By all accounts, you should be unequivocally dead, Mr. Claymore. So I ask you, sir, by what strange concatenation of events do you remain amongst the living?"

"An English parson found me, and with your mother's invaluable aid, they restored me to health."

"My mother?" said the king in disbelief. "Mary, former Queen of Scots?"

"Yes, sire," confirmed Claymore, now gazing into Antonía's eyes. "Not only did the queen save my life, but she also bestowed her blessing upon our marriage."

"Indeed," said the king thoughtfully and then arched a royal brow at Antonía. "Dear sister, what say you to Mr. Claymore's proposal?"

Antonía had a peculiar look in her eye, as if she were about to make a mad dash for the door. *Had he been wrong?* Claymore wondered, feeling panic rush through him. Did she not love him as deeply as he loved her?

At that moment, the current and percipient queen of Scotland took pity on Antonía's obvious state of torment and whispered into her ear, "Don't make it complicated, my dear. Simply tell the man you love him."

Whereupon Antonía smiled, turned to Claymore, and stated with faultless elocution, "I love you, Mr. Claymore."

He started to speak, but she interrupted as she started to explain herself in excruciating detail. She was, after all, Antonía Barclay, and was not known for her breviloquence.

"I have always loved you, I will always love you, and I will never stop showing you how much I love you. In fact, Mr. Claymore, I really must insist upon proving my love for you by answering your infinite number of questions in complete sentences, complete paragraphs, and *completely in calligraphy*." She paused and, lifting a hand, tenderly caressed the crest of his cheek. "In further point of fact, you can plan on page after sensuous page of passionate prose . . . and immediately, if not sooner."

Antonía's steamy sentiments were far from lost on Claymore. He took her in his arms, gazing down at her with all the love he felt for her. "And you, my darling, darling Miss Barclay, can plan on me loving you with everything that I've got. In fact, you can plan on a lifetime of loyal devotion, unwavering adoration, and unbridled lovemaking."

He paused, and gently cupping her beautiful face in his hands, he concluded, "In further point of fact, you can plan on being completely wrapped inside my love . . . and immediately, if not sooner."

"Ho! Ho! Hold on a minute!" cried the king, once again wedging his exiguous form in between the towering lovers. "This is Scotland, *not* England. We are the Stuarts, *not* the Tudors. *There shall be absolutely NO acts of calligraphy performed outside the sanctity of marriage.*"

Undaunted by her brother's warning, and no longer able to quell the overpowering force of acute physical desire, Claymore pulled Antonía into his powerful arms and greeted her with all the enthusiasm—within the realm of public decency—of a man violently in love.

As was anticipated, Claymore's romantic overtures caused the king to erupt into a spastic display of autocratic hyperactivity. Gesticulating wildly to the queen, the king exclaimed, "Holy Moses! Where is Alistair? I need him to locate a clergyman at once!"

"Your grace," said Alistair, approaching the king, "not only did your mother bless Miss Barclay's and Mr. Claymore's union, she has sent Reverend Stephen Goode from Chartley Hall to officiate the ceremony."

The king stood silent for a moment. Finally, he said in awe, "I am positively gobsmacked by my mother's foresight!" The small monarch then turned and addressed the young cleric standing beside Alistair. "Are you willing to perform the ceremony *immediately*, Reverend?"

"Your grace, I would be honored," said Stephen Goode, bowing.

"Thank God," Claymore said. "And thank you, Reverend. And Your Majesty," he hastily added.

King James nodded and smiled warmly. "Splendid! And *I* thank you, Reverend, for understanding my predicament." The king paused thoughtfully and then went on, "Reverend, we have a Bible project underway that could use the attention of a pious polymath such as yourself. If you'd be willing to lend your scholarly imprimatur to my new version of the Good Book, I'll gladly set you up as chairman of your own committee."

And then working himself up into an excited dither, the small Scottish monarch subsequently released the first official curse word he'd ever used in his entire life by trumpeting, "In fact, with you in the mix, we'll create a *GODDAMN* masterpiece!"

The queen, astonished by her husband's inopportune and impious utterance, took swift action and employed her sharp elbow to thwart the king's ramblings as well as his further use of coarse language.

Promptly responding to his wife's pointed gesture, the king massaged his rib cage as he nodded his gratitude to the reverend. He then turned toward his subjects and, with a flick of a deleterious recessive sixth finger, announced, "But presently, let us bear witness to the blessed and joyous union of my sister, Antonía Barclay, and Mr. Claymore!"

As the ball—turned wedding—turned reception—wore into the wee, wee hours of the morning, the newlyweds thanked one and all before attempting their much-desired escape from the palace. But the king, being the prototype for all future control freaks the world over, made the unilateral decision that Mr. and Mrs. Claymore would spend their wedding night within the confines of his palace.

The king's man, Alistair, had done them the great service of engaging King James in an earnest conversation with Reverend Goode over his translation of the Bible, and so Mr. and Mrs. Claymore were at last able to slip away from the madding crowd.

As Mr. Claymore carried Mrs. Claymore to their room, she remarked that the early morning sun had just risen above the softly rolling hills of Southern Scotland. Mr. Claymore replied that it was the first and, unequivocally, the *last* glimpse of sunlight his darling bride would see for the rest of the day, and he sincerely hoped she didn't mind too much.

In response, Mrs. Claymore delighted her new husband by assuring him that it would make her day to spend her day making passionate love to him. In fact, she continued to delight Mr. Claymore by informing him that she'd be more than willing to spend the greater share of their lives together in such an agreeable and befitting manner . . . and she further informed him that she believed it her womanly duty to ensure that each and every time felt like the very first time . . . and indeed, that very first time was mercifully close at hand because, at long last, they would finally be allowed to finish the moment.

Once the door to the bedroom closed behind them, nothing else mattered but the deep love they felt for each other. They had fallen in love, suffered hardship in their courtship, and yet their suffering served only to vivify their blessings. Having weathered the storm together, they were now stronger and better off for it.

Accordingly, Mr. Claymore, being gratefully aware of the richness of their bounty, steered their marital partnership skillfully out of a wide berth and set sail for smooth, open waters. But even the calmest sea casts off a few mild ripples and consequently causes even the best-made ship to rock gently in its wake.

And, naturally, the female amongst them was the first to detect the motion. Thus Mrs. Claymore experienced a brief wave of anxiety when her husband, after deftly removing every last layer of her clothing, promptly removed every last layer of his own, and stood before her in all his manly glory. *She gasped at the sight of his . . .*

Heavily bandaged chest.

She listed slightly.

He steadied her in his powerful arms and, in a husky voice, assured her, "Don't fret, my darling, darling Antonía. It's what all the tough guys are wearing this season."

His playful words and masterful actions instantly quelled her worry. She now understood that her husband was feeling no pain. Fully restored to health and fully ignited by his great desire for his bride, he broke into a firestorm of passion. In less time than it takes to strike a match, he swept her gently off her feet, settled her tenderly into bed, and proceeded to adorn her with his loving kisses.

And, as two pair of blue eyes melted into a sea of one, Mr. Claymore's infinite number of questions were answered by Mrs. Claymore who, true to her word, responded in complete sentences, complete paragraphs, and *completely in calligraphy*.

In fact, over the course of the Claymores' extraordinarily long and extraordinarily happy marriage, Mr. Claymore faithfully told Mrs. Claymore that he thoroughly enjoyed every sensuous page of her passionate prose. Consequently, he highly encouraged her to indulge her craft as often as she desired, and because she had been blessed with an unlimited imagination . . .

Antonía Barclay Claymore wrote an infinite number of sequels to their story of pure, unadulterated love, thereby proving that not only could romance survive marriage, but also, with seasoned grace, it could flourish.

Fait accompli.

AUTHOR'S Q&A

Q: *When did you first know you wanted to write this book and how did that knowledge become apparent to you? Have you written other books, published or unpublished?*

A: My intrepid aunt, Alice Carter Steinbach, who is mentioned in the dedication, was a gifted writer and author. Many years ago, she introduced me to the sly wit and lively mind of Jane Austen and, most importantly, Jane's brilliance in crafting her characters' flaws and foibles. Her plots were all basically the same, but Jane's character development was pure genius. She burrowed into her characters' minds, analyzed their every thought and action, and then proceeded to jump from one character's mind to the next and then back again. After immediately becoming a "Janeite," the first seeds of writing a book germinated in my mind, but it took a considerable amount of time for the process to reach fruition. Although I have written other books, as well as some seriously boring legal opinions, *Antonia Barclay and Her Scottish Claymore* is my first and only publication to date. However, if signs point in the right direction, *Antonia Barclay Claymore and Her English Foil* will be coming down the pike promptly.

Q: *What practices do you follow when you write? Do you have a special room or place where you like to write? If so, could you describe it?*

A: Writing this book seemed to be a four-step process: conceiving, scaffolding, vivifying, and finishing. Conceiving was the creation of the idea for the story, scaffolding was the mapping out of the story's plot, vivifying was the description of the story's world and the animation of its characters (making them come to life), and finishing was the Herculean task of pushing myself to finish the story. In general, once I conjured up the idea for the story, I would map out the plot in my mind in the morning and put it to paper in the afternoon or evening, attempting to get at least the bare bones written down to keep the book pushing ahead in my mind. On days when I had more time to devote to the project, I would bop back and forth between vivifying what was already written and scaffolding the next series of events. As for my writing location, this may sound peculiar and a bit louche, but I often wrote in my bathroom, because it's the only room in the house that afforded me privacy. An added and unanticipated bonus to the bathroom locale was that writing in front of a mirror helped with writing action scenes as well as describing characters' movements and gestures, which was a constant challenge for me. The battle scene was my least favorite to write.

Q: *What led you to the specific plot, setting, and characters of* Antonía Barclay and Her Scottish Claymore? *What research did you do in terms of the history of Queen Mary and the times?*
A: British author Lady Antonia Fraser is the easy and only answer to both questions. Lady Antonia's enthralling biography, *Mary Queen of Scots*, has been a longtime favorite of mine and it is the overarching inspiration for the story. And I also confess to borrowing Lady Antonia's first and middle names for my heroine Antonía Margaret Caroline Barclay. One small point of departure, however, may be the pronunciation of "Antonía." I'm not certain how Lady Antonia pronounces her first name, but Antonía Barclay's name is pronounced "AntoNEEa." Secondly, while the setting is where it was, and Mary Stuart is who she was, the remaining characters were created and operated solely according to my instructions as puppeteer. The plot and themes, however, were a different story. I did some serious heavy lifting from Jane Austen and some lighter, fluffier lifting from Thomas Hardy, particularly toward the end when the storybook comes to a close.

Q: *When did you first envision the character of Antonía? When and how did you know you wanted Antonía to be Mary's daughter?*
A: After reading all I could find on Mary Queen of Scots and finding no more, I was forced to trot off to the archives of my own imagination. And

there I found Antonía Barclay, Mary's should've-been daughter, waiting for me and waiting to come to life. Her character more or less spontaneously combusted in my brain. Naturally, Antonía had to resemble Mary in some ways, and this is the reason for Antonía's lofty stature, independent spirit, and aptitude for riding. However, for plot purposes, Antonía could not be a dead ringer in terms of appearance, and thus Antonía did not inherit her mother's trademark red hair and amber eyes. So it's not necessarily that I wanted Antonía to be Mary's daughter, but rather I desperately wanted Mary to have a daughter, to have had a daughter. And at this juncture, you can probably tell that I have to remind myself that Antonía is not an authentic historical figure, merely a figment of my imagination, but imagining will always make her real to me. And, of course, there's always the off chance that history got it wrong, that Mary really did have a daughter, and Antonía really did exist.

Q: *Did you model Antonía's beauty and intelligence after someone you know? What do you want your audience to learn from her?*
A: Antonía's beauty is not modeled after anyone in particular, but she certainly has the physical traits of a present-day supermodel with her super long legs and her super small butt. However, the attribute that sets Antonía apart from the stereotypical supermodel of any era is the thinking power of her big bold brain. She possesses an agile and cultivated intellect that, together with her strong personality, gives her the ability to match wits with evil genius Sir Basil while effortlessly, and often humorously, outmatching wits with his dimwitted nitwit of a son, Rex. But in spite of her beauty and intelligence, Antonía is far from perfect, especially in the context of her sixteenth-century time frame. Tenacity, perseverance, and self-reliance are probably not personality traits that were desired, instilled, or encouraged in the sixteenth-century young woman. But Antonía doesn't care one whit what others think of her or what is expected of someone of her gender and social class. She trusts herself and is secure in herself. No swooning, kowtowing, or boohooing for her. Antonía is a tough critical thinker who is often contrary to the point of being a pain in the neck, but that's who she is and if the entire world knows it so much the better; suffering fools gladly and squandering time

were not her deals. She makes no apologies for being herself, and when she sets goals she sticks to them, despite the obstacles and her own limitations. But having spouted all that platitudinous wisdom, I hope readers simply enjoy escaping to another time and place.

Q: *Can you please comment on the character of Claire MacMillan and her relationship with Antonía?*
A: With her small efficient hands and no-nonsense attitude, Claire Mac-Millan wrote herself into the story with little assistance from me. She knows everything about her best friend Antonía, every quality, every flaw, every attribute, and every foible. Therefore, when the situation necessitates, Claire doesn't hesitate to kick Antonía's butt in line. Since neither young woman has a sister, their close relationship serves as both a friendship and a sistership. They know they can shove each other around all day long, but by dinnertime all will be forgiven and forgotten. An unbreakable trust and obvious comfort level exist between the two best friends that cannot be plundered by a frantic world or any individual, including any of their respective family members. They are each other's refuge and hiding place from life's demands and worries. Using present-day psychobabble, Claire and Antonía are one another's support systems.

Q: *Which character was the most challenging to create and why?*
A: Breck Claymore was unequivocally the most challenging character for me to create, because he is a man of quiet dignity and by definition he couldn't do a whole lot of talking. His calm solidity, stoic determination, and integrity had to be conveyed through action, not words; thus his dialogue could be neither lengthy nor abundant. The novel is Antonía's story from beginning to end, and I tried to insinuate Mr. Claymore into it without eclipsing her light while also maintaining his strength of character. He had to possess both alpha and beta male characteristics in order to attract Antonía's attention initially and then as their relationship develops, he draws on these same characteristics to cope with her strong-willed and high-spirited nature. As a result, I made Mr. Claymore a self-made man with a job, a fortune, and a set of seriously broad shoulders. But despite Mr. Claymore's fine qualities and his magnificent male

musculature, he had roamed the Scottish countryside for nearly three decades without finding a woman worth marrying. Until, of course, he crosses paths with Miss Barclay. I'm not certain if I achieved my objective here, but I attempted to cultivate a new breed of man: The Alpheta Male. A man sufficiently secure and confident in his masculinity to view a woman as an equal partner in all respects, a man willing to relinquish both calling the shots and claiming the top position as a matter of course.

Q: *What was it like for you to create this long-ago and make-believe world and live in it?*

A: Creating a chick-lit period piece about the adventures of a sixteenth-century royal supermodel was like stealing Penelope Pitstop's pink racecar and having my way with it. Zooming through the wacky back roads of my imagination, I savored every hairpin turn, every open straightaway, and all the messy dirt life kicked up behind me. However, as a result of my thrill-seeking lead foot, I had to be careful not to become too power-crazed and turn Antonía Barclay into Superwoman. It's a make-believe world, but the characters, most notably Antonía, had to be made believable. Otherwise it would be impossible for readers to care about her and empathize with her problems as the plot unfolds. No one likes a little Miss Perfect! Which brings me to the subject of men. Since as a general rule men like facts and information while women prefer emotion and detail, I do not expect a guy to read or understand this book. It's pretty much a girls-only joyride, but if the occasional dude happens to hop aboard, please know that we respect you for coming along for the ride.

Q: *The characters of Sir Basil and Rex must have some interesting stories related to their conception. How did they come about in your head? Was it especially fun to write their fates?*

A: Sir Basil Throckmorton is an egocentric genius with a hyperthymic personality disorder. He is highly energetic, relentlessly productive, and absurdly upbeat. Despite any and all obstacles thrown in his path, his bouncing good cheer cannot be squelched. It may be temporarily stymied, but it's never permanently eliminated. As we see throughout the story, Sir Basil's chronic cheeriness irritates Antonía to no end. Sir Basil is hardwired to be happy and there's nothing she, or anyone else, can do about it, except for, possibly, his mean-spirited and obtuse son, Rex Throckmorton. As mentally dull as his father is brilliantly sharp, Rex provides the only potential stumbling block to his father's persistently optimistic outlook. Time and time again, Sir Basil ponders the conundrum of how this dunce and thug of a human being came to be his offspring. However, Sir Basil appears to overcome even this high hurdle by turning his son into his personal "useful idiot." In other words, Sir Basil does all the thinking while Rex does all the dirty work. On the one hand, it was gratifying to write the exit scenes for these two bad guys, both of whom needed killing badly, but on the other hand, it was hard to say goodbye to Sir Basil's extraordinary brain and Rex's extraordinary brain cavity. P.S. Of all the characters' dialogue, Rex's was the easiest to write, because I didn't have to worry about grammar, word choice, or niceness. Unfortunately, this doesn't say much for my character.

Q: *The chapter title, "A Munro, a Corbett, and a Graham" is an interesting one. Can you share why you chose those particular names?*
A: For several years I've subscribed to a magazine called *Scottish Life*. This delightful publication offers well-written and informative feature stories on Scottish towns, castles, beaches, museums, history, art, music, hotels, gardens, festivals, wildlife, and pretty much every other subject relating to Scotland and the Scot. However, my favorite sections are called "Ben & Glens & Heroes" and "Notebook," which provide short, concise, current-event articles regarding local Scottish happenings, and they are often very humorous, unwittingly or not, I'm never quite certain given the unique flavor of the British sense of humor. Returning to the question at hand, I first learned of the Munros, the Corbetts, and the Grahams from stories written in these sections about a subset of mountain climbers called "Munro baggers," whose objective is to climb as many of the Munros as possible. The Munros, named after Sir Hugh Munro, are mountains in Scotland over 3,000 feet; the Corbetts are peaks between 2,500 and 3,000 feet; and the Grahams are between 2,000 and 2,499 feet. There are additional classification criteria other than height as well as other classifications, such as Donalds and Murdos, but the technicalities

are much better left in the capable hands of the Scottish Mountaineering Club. In any event, I decided to pay tribute to these hearty and fearsome Scottish mountaineers by using the surnames Munro, Corbett, and Graham and giving them their own chapter in the book.

Q: *The plot of the book is delightful and your technique of including so many interesting and unusual words provides a very clever backdrop for the action. What is the origin of your obvious love of the English language?*

A: The English language is so accepting, flexible, and diverse. It's a delicious witches' brew of words from other languages along with lots of other great stuff like palindromes, homonyms, onomatopoeias, and an infinite list of rule-breaking exceptions! In particular, I have always adored the printed word. Accurate pronunciation, however, is not my strong suit, and I'm often, and justly, accused of mangling "big" words in my speech. My defense against this allegation is that at least I'm trying to use different and little-used words instead of relying on the same old safe and tired lexicon. It may sound odd, but sometimes I feel sorry for ignored or forgotten words, so I feel obligated to haul them down from the attic and walk them around the block for some fresh air.

READER'S GUIDE

1. What was your impression of the opening paragraphs of the book? How did they make you feel? Were you immediately on Antonía's side and drawn into the action, or did you have a different reaction?

2. Discuss the author's remarkable ability to allow the reader to live seamlessly and simultaneously in two worlds: the world of Scotland and England in the 1500s and the world of today. What particular instances of this cross-world experience did you find most entertaining?

3. Discuss a character or characters with whom you identified and why. What is it about that person that you found compelling or interesting? Discuss your favorite character, good or evil.

4. What did you learn about British and Scottish history that you didn't know before? Did you enjoy receiving a history lesson about the life of Mary Queen of Scots in such an entertaining way?

5. Discuss Antonía's character. What are the qualities you admire most about her and why?

6. Discuss the sources of Antonía's fearlessness. What makes her want to be like Minnie?

7. Discuss the emotions expressed by the characters in the book that seem exactly like emotions that would be expressed today. An

example might be when Claire says, "Stop worrying, Antonía. I know you despise being the center of attention but, as we all know, people attend balls for the sole purpose of quaffing down as much of the host's liquor as possible." Discuss other conversations that make you feel right at home in Antonía's world.

8. Along the same lines, discuss the concoctions formulated by Sir Basil Throckmorton that attend to present-day ills or concerns. Also discuss the experience of having his concoctions connect to the present but also being part of his world in the past.

9. How did Antonía's relationship with each of her mothers differ? Was one relationship stronger or weaker than the other? Or just different because of circumstances? Did nature versus nurture play a role?

10. Discuss the description of Antonía's relationships with her brothers and how you felt about her siblings.

11. Which character made you laugh the most and why?

12. How many subtle references to historical figures, authors, movies, and TV shows can you find?

ABOUT THE AUTHOR

J ane Carter Barrett is a graduate of Duke University and lives in Austin, Texas. Mary, Queen of Scots and Jane Austen have been lifelong subjects of fascination for her. *Antonia Barclay and Her Scottish Claymore* is her debut novel. Better now than never.